## BY SUSAN ELIA MacNEAL

*Mother Daughter Traitor Spy*

### THE MAGGIE HOPE SERIES

*Mr. Churchill's Secretary*
*Princess Elizabeth's Spy*
*His Majesty's Hope*
*The Prime Minister's Secret Agent*
*Mrs. Roosevelt's Confidante*
*The Queen's Accomplice*
*The Paris Spy*
*The Prisoner in the Castle*
*The King's Justice*
*The Hollywood Spy*

# Princess Elizabeth's Spy

*A Maggie Hope Mystery*

## SUSAN ELIA MacNEAL

BANTAM BOOKS

NEW YORK

2023 Bantam Books Mass Market Edition

Copyright © 2012 by Susan Elia MacNeal
Excerpt from *His Majesty's Hope* by Susan Elia MacNeal
copyright © 2013 by Susan Elia MacNeal

Published in the United States by Bantam Books,
an imprint of Random House, a division of
Penguin Random House LLC, New York.

BANTAM BOOKS is a registered trademark and the B colophon
is a trademark of Penguin Random House LLC.

Originally published in trade paperback in the United States by
Bantam Books, an imprint of Random House, a division of
Penguin Random House LLC, in 2012.

ISBN 978-0-593-60054-2
Ebook ISBN 978-0-553-90757-5

Cover design: Victoria Allen
Cover illustration: Mick Wiggins

Printed in the United States of America

randomhousebooks.com

2 4 6 8 9 7 5 3 1

Bantam Books mass market edition: June 2023

*To Judith Merkle Riley, 1942–2010,*
*mentor, friend, and the real Maggie Hope.*
*Thank you.*

"Be a governess! Better be a slave at once!"
—Charlotte Brontë,
*Shirley*


Cryptogram: Message written in a cipher or in some other cryptic form which requires a key (qv) for its meaning to be discovered.

—*A Lexicon of Cryptography*
("Most Secret," Bletchley Park)

PRINCESS ELIZABETH'S SPY

# Prologue

The midday summer sun in Lisbon was dazzling and harsh. But while nearly everyone else was inside taking a siesta, the Duke of Windsor, formerly King Edward VIII of England, kept up his British habits, even on the continent.

He and his wife, Wallis Simpson, the woman for whom he'd abdicated the throne and now known as the Duchess of Windsor, sat outside at the Bar-Café Europa, which catered to tourists and British expats. The town square was nearly empty, except for a young American couple walking arm in arm and a few pigeons strutting and pecking for crumbs in the dust.

Wallis, slender and elegant, wore a scarlet Schiaparelli suit, a bejeweled flamingo brooch, and dark glasses. She sipped a Campari and soda, the ice cubes clinking against one another in her tall glass. Next to her, the Duke, slight and fair-haired, toyed with a tumbler of blood-orange juice and read *The Times* of London. He was only forty-six, but the strain from the abdication, and subsequent banishment from royal life, made him look older.

A shadow passed over his page. The Duke looked up in annoyance, then smiled broadly when he saw who it was—Walther Schellenberg, Heinrich Himmler's personal aide and a deputy leader of the Reich Main Security Office.

"Schel! Good to see you—sit down," the Duke said.

"Thank you, Your Highness," Schellenberg replied in accented English, sitting down on the delicate wire chair. The Duke and Duchess had befriended Schellenberg on their tours to Germany before the war, visiting with Prince Philip of Hesse and Adolf Hitler.

"Hello, Walther," Wallis said.

Schellenberg removed his Nazi visor hat, with its skull and crossbones, to reveal thick brown hair parted in the center and glistening with a copious amount of Brylcreem. "Good afternoon, Your Highness. May I say you look particularly beautiful today?" he said to Wallis, a smile softening his angular features.

"Thank you, Schel," she replied, warming to his use of *Your Highness,* which Hitler had also used when they'd visited him at the Berghof, his chalet in the Bavarian Alps. Technically, neither Hitler nor Schellenberg needed to address her that way, as she'd never been awarded HRH status by the current king, a snub indeed. His wife, Queen Elizabeth, referred to Wallis only as "that woman."

As she offered her hand to Schellenberg to be kissed, the scent of L'heure Bleue mixed with Mitsouko—a heady mix of carnations and oakmoss, Wallis's signature scent—wafted around her in the heat.

"They threw a rock at our window last night, Schel."

The Duke frowned. "Shattered the glass. Could have killed us."

"I know, sir. Terrible, just terrible." And he did know—Schellenberg himself had arranged the rock-throwing incident in order to frighten the Windsors, leaving false clues to make it look as though British Intelligence were to blame. If the Windsors were scared enough they'd come around to the Nazis' point of view, he was certain of it.

"It's terrible," Wallis said, smoothing her glossy black hair, cut down the middle with a narrow white part. "They hate us. The British just hate us now."

"Now, now, dear," Edward said, reaching over to take her hand. "It's not the British people. It's Churchill and his thugs. And my brother and that wife of his. Silly old Bertie as King George VI, indeed. It's as if I'd never been King!"

"You can't abdicate and eat it too, dear," Wallis said with a tight smile.

Schellenberg cleared his throat. "I've heard from the Führer."

"Oh, how lovely!" Wallis exclaimed, extracting a cigarette from a gold case and fitting it in a long ivory holder. The Duke pulled out his lighter and lit it for her; she smiled up at him as she drew her first inhale.

"He gave me a number," Schellenberg said, knowing quite well the two were having money problems since the abdication. He took a small folded piece of paper from his pocket, put it on the table, and pushed it toward the Duke. If fear alone couldn't persuade them, perhaps money could.

The Duke of Windsor waited, simply looking at the note for a few heartbeats, then reached for it. Slowly, he picked it up and opened it. He read the number and then handed the slip over to Wallis. She examined it, arching one perfectly plucked and penciled eyebrow, then handed it back.

"Quite a bit of money, Schel," the Duke said, pushing the paper away.

"But it's not just about the money, sir," Schellenberg said, placing the paper in one of the ceramic ashtrays and then lighting it, letting it burn away to ash. "Germany has taken Austria, the Sudetenland, and Poland. We've taken the Low Countries and France. When Germany invades England—and it's just a matter of time before London falls—your people will need you." He looked to Wallis. "Both of you. You know it's only a matter of time now. We're establishing air supremacy, and as soon as we take out the Royal Air Force, we'll invade. Your younger brother, the present King, has aligned himself with Winston Churchill and his gangsters. He won't be permitted to stay on the throne, of course."

"Of course," Wallis murmured. She had no love for either the King or Queen, who had never acknowledged her and, in her opinion, had taken every opportunity to humiliate her. Why her husband couldn't have simply stayed on the throne when he'd married her, she would never understand—or forgive.

"And his daughter, Elizabeth, raised with the same propaganda her father espouses, can't reign either, so . . . And then we'll need you—*both* of you," Schellenberg stressed, "to urge the British to accept German occupation. With you as King, and the Duchess as Queen, of course."

"It's not about me, Schel," the Duke said. "We need

to end the war now before thousands are killed and maimed in order to save the faces of a few corrupt politicians. Believe me, with continued heavy bombing, Britain will soon be desperate for peace. The people will panic and turn against Churchill and Eden—and the current King, too, of course. Which presents the perfect opportunity to bring me back as sovereign." The Duke sighed. "Of course, I can't officially support any of this, you know."

"What other options do you have?" Schellenberg asked.

There was a long silence. The Windsors knew they were running out of opportunities.

"Bermuda," Wallis said finally, rolling her eyes and tapping ashes into a ceramic ashtray crudely painted with a bullfighter holding up a red cape. "Churchill and the present royals want to banish us to that godforsaken little territory. Conveniently out of their way."

"Then don't go," Schellenberg urged. "You have the Führer, and the British people, counting on you to step up. To be their King and Queen."

The Duke and Duchess locked eyes. "What do you say, dear?" he asked her.

The Duchess took a moment for a long exhale, blowing out a thin stream of blue smoke. It had been a long few years for her. First there was her affair with him, when he'd been the Prince of Wales. The unexpected death of his father, King George V, had been both shocking and painful for both of them. Their relationship nearly collapsed when Edward had taken the throne, crushed by the disapproval of the rest of the royal family.

They'd thought, perhaps foolishly, that once the

family got to know her better, they'd accept her. But no. The royal family, in particular the newly crowned George VI and Queen Elizabeth, had made it overwhelmingly clear Edward would never be able to marry her, a two-time American divorcée and a close personal friend of Joachim von Ribbentrop's, Foreign Minister of Germany, and still stay on the throne.

Edward had chosen her and abdicated—but it had nearly killed him. And it broke her heart to see him made to choose. Their love had survived, but only just. Even in the bright sunshine of Portugal, they had their good days and bad.

"We're going to enjoy ourselves at the villa of our good friend, Ricardo do Espírito Santo Silva, for now," she replied, finally. "If—and only if—Germany invades . . ." She shrugged her narrow shoulders.

"—you can count on us to do the right thing," the Duke finished. "For the British people, of course."

The three of them nodded.

"Excellent," said Schellenberg, rising. "That's what we hoped you'd say. *Heil Hitler!*"

# Chapter One

Bletchley was a small, seemingly inconsequential railway town about fifty miles northwest of London. However, since 1938, the town was also the home of what was officially known as the Government Code and Cipher School. But those in the know referred to it as Station X. Or War Station. Or just the initials B.P., for Bletchley Park.

The Bletchley estate, the former manse of Sir Herbert and Lady Fanny Leon, was a red-brick Victorian monstrosity in a faux-Tudor style. Now, under government control, it bustled with men and women in uniform, as well as civilians—mostly men in baggy wrinkled trousers and herringbone tweed jackets with leather elbow patches. The house's formerly lush lawns were flattened and worn from all the foot and bicycle traffic. The gardens had been trampled to make room for hastily assembled huts and office buildings.

Although it was a secret to most who worked there, the real business of Bletchley was breaking Nazi military code. The cryptographers at Bletchley Park had a reconstructed Enigma machine used by the Germans (a gift from the Poles), a code key used in the Norway campaign, and two keys used by the Nazi air force. Though they received a huge volume of decrypts, they still couldn't be used for practical purposes. Under the leadership of Alan Turing, Peter Twinn, and John Jeffreys, they were still waiting and working, hoping for a miracle.

The Nazis thought their codes were unbreakable, and they had good reason to believe so. When a German commander typed in a message, the machine sent electrical impulses through a series of rotating wheels, contacts, and wires to produce the enciphered letters, which lit up on a panel above the keyboard. By typing the resulting code into his own machine, the recipient saw the deciphered message light up letter by letter. The rotors and wires of the machine could be configured in an almost infinite number of ways. The odds against anyone breaking Enigma were a staggering 150 million million million to one.

Benjamin Batey, a graduate of Trinity College at Cambridge with a Ph.D. in logical mathematics, worked in Hut 8 trying to break Nazi naval decrypts. Batey had been toiling away for eight months in the drafty hut. It stank of damp, lime, and coal tar.

His office was one room of a dozen, divided by flimsy partitions made of plywood. The noise from the other workstations drifted about—low conversations, thudding footsteps, a shrill telephone ring, the steady clicks of the Type-X machines in the decoding room.

The harsh fluorescent overhead light cast long shadows across the concrete floor as Batey and his office-mate, both youngish men in rumpled corduroy trousers and heavy wool sweaters, worked at mismatched battered wooden desks piled with sheaves of papers. Thick manila folders with TOP SECRET stamped in heavy red ink across them were heaped haphazardly on the floor, dirty tea mugs were lined up on the window's ledge, and steam hissed from the paint-chipped radiator. Blackout curtains hid the view.

Usually a prodigious worker, Batey couldn't wait to leave. He had a date.

"So, is she an imaginary girl? Or a real one?" asked James Abbot, his officemate. Abbot was young, but his face was pale and drawn, and he had dark purple shadows under his eyes. They all looked like that at Bletchley. Sleep was considered an unnecessary extravagance.

Batey was not amused. "I don't kiss and tell, old thing," he said, shrugging into a wool coat and wrapping a striped school scarf around his neck.

"I say," said Abbot, putting his worn capped-toe oxfords up on the desk and leaning back, "at least comb your hair. Or what's left of it."

It was true. Batey might have been only in his late twenties, with a face that still had the plushness of youth, but already his dark hair was receding. It could have been genetics, or the prodigious stress Batey was under as a boffin, as the cryptographers were called at Bletchley. Generally, he was too sleep-deprived and distracted to give his appearance much thought, but it hadn't gone without noticing that in the confines of B.P., the boffins were at the top of the pecking order, as far as the women there were concerned.

It was the first time Batey had been viewed by the fairer sex in such a positive light, and, suddenly, he was in demand. And so, while at first he believed it was absolute insanity that someone like Victoria Keeley, who turned heads at Bletchley with her tall, slim figure, pale skin, and dark hair, would be interested in someone like him, he'd slowly grown to accept and even appreciate it.

There was a knock at the door. Abbot's eyebrows rose.

Batey cracked the door open, but it was too late, Abbot had already caught sight of who it was. "Victoria Keeley, Queen of the Teleprincesses—what brings you to our humble abode?" Abbot said, leaning back even farther in his desk chair.

Victoria had a profile as sharp as Katharine Hepburn's and an aura of offhand glamour that came from being a recent debutante who spoke flawless French and rode and played tennis superbly. "Only a tele*countess*, Mr. Abbot," she replied with her best cocktail party smile. "Despite my family's august lineage, I can't quite aspire to royalty."

"Ah, all you lovely girls are princesses to me," he quipped, grinning at her.

"That's funny, I've heard you say we're all the same in the dark." She batted her eyelashes as Abbot gasped and nearly fell over in his chair. "The walls are thin, Mr. Abbot," she admonished, as he tried to right himself.

She turned to Batey. "Are you ready?" She already had her gray overcoat on and was finishing pinning on her black velvet hat. Batey caught a whiff of the pungent, oily scent of the teletypewriters she worked with all day. It clung to her dress and hair, as alluring to him—on her, at least—as Shalimar or Chanel No. 5.

"Yes," he said, putting on his felt hat and pulling on leather gloves.

"So, where are you two going?" Abbot asked. He

picked up a sheaf of tea-stained papers and rose to his feet. "Mind taking these out for me?"

"Concert," Batey said, as he accepted the papers. "Bach. Fugues. Bletchley Park String Quartet."

"Well, have fun, you two," Abbot said. "*Someone* has to stay here and mind the shop."

In the narrow hallway, Victoria pulled Benjamin close. "I thought this day would never end," she said, nuzzling his neck.

"Not here." He still needed to dispose of the papers in his hand. There was a room with a shredder, and then all the tiny scraps of paper were put into a large bin marked CONFIDENTIAL WASTE.

She was tall in her heels, and her lips reached his ear easily. "We don't even have to go to the concert," she whispered. "I don't even know how I'd be able to sit through it, knowing . . ."

Her tongue swirled in his ear and Benjamin groaned.

"Let's go," he said in a low, anxious voice.

On their way out they saw Christopher Boothby, who worked in the main office, doing administrative work. The two men were wearing the same navy, red, and yellow striped Trinity College scarf. As they passed, Boothby gave the couple a wink and a smile.

Afterward, in Victoria's tiny bedroom in the drafty cottage she shared with one of the other teleprincesses, Benjamin fell asleep.

As he snored lightly, Victoria slipped out of the warm bed and wrapped herself in her chenille robe. Going to his coat, she rummaged through the pockets, taking the papers he was supposed to have shredded and dropping them into a drawer.

Then she crawled back under the covers and gave him a gentle nudge, then a harder one.

"What?" he mumbled.

"Darling, I'm so dreadfully sorry. But my roommate is such a little priss—and if she catches you here she'll tell the landlady . . . who won't approve at all."

"Sorry?" Benjamin echoed, rubbing his eyes. "Right. Yes, of course," he said, standing up and pulling on his plaid boxers.

"Thanks ever so much," she said, "for understanding. Well, and *that,* too."

"Oh, thank *you.*" He stepped into his trousers, his features boyish when he smiled. "You know, I really do want to take you out. A concert, the pictures, a nice dinner—or at least as nice as you can get these days. Please, let me take you somewhere."

"You're a sweet boy, Benjamin Batey," she said with a sigh, getting up and kissing the back of his neck as he finished buttoning his shirt. "A very, very sweet boy."

She helped him with his coat, scarf, and hat, and then sent him on his way. The door clicked closed and she waited as the sound of his footsteps receded.

Then she picked up the black Bakelite receiver and dialed. "Yes," she whispered into the telephone, "I have something you'll want to see. I'm leaving for London now. Should be there in a few hours, give or take. Yes, of *course* I'll use an alias."

Then, "I love you too, darling."

———

Claridge's in London was a large red-brick hotel located in fashionable Mayfair, still elegant despite the removal of all of its lavish wrought-iron railings, which had been taken down to be melted for munitions. After her long train trip in the blackout, Victoria was grateful to check in, under an assumed name, and retire to a warm, damask-swathed room, worlds away from the shabby indignities of Bletchley.

After placing the decrypts carefully on the bed, she went into the marble bathroom and drew a bath, noticing that Claridge's had "forgotten" the five-inch watermark for hot water rationing. She turned on the tap and out poured a scalding stream, to which she added a liberal handful of sandalwood-scented Hammam Bouquet bath salts. She sighed as she undressed, then slipped her long and elegant limbs into the bath, reclining against the slanted back of the tub. Benjamin was just such an easy target. He was lovely, really. It wasn't his fault, the poor dear. . . .

The front door clicked open, then closed quietly. With the water still running, Victoria didn't hear it. Then there was a loud thud. "Darling, is that you?" she called, lifting her head.

There was a silence, then the bathroom door creaked open.

"Darling?" Victoria called, sitting up in the tub.

The shot went directly between her eyes. She slumped back into the bath, bright red blood streaming down her face and into the water, turning the froth pink and then crimson. As her pale slim body slipped down under the bubbles, her mouth fell open into a perfect O of surprise.

# Chapter Two

Maggie Hope had fallen yet again and was covered in cold, wet mud. She pushed back a soaked lock of red hair that had fallen in her eyes, leaving a trail of dirt across her forehead. To add insult to injury, it began to rain, large, cold drops falling faster and faster. Still, it didn't matter. She and the other eleven women would all be done when they'd finished the obstacle course and not before. "Get up, Hope!" Harold Burns, the training leader, bellowed to Maggie from the sidelines.

Burns was a wiry man in his early fifties, a veteran of the Great War. His light hair was thinning, and the brown splotches on his face were testament to a life lived outdoors. He wore corduroy trousers, a heavy cabled sweater, and Wellington boots, and carried a clipboard. He had a perpetually perplexed expression on his face, as if to say, *How the hell did I get here of all places? Training all of these . . . women.*

Maggie tried to stand, then slipped and fell yet again.

He glowered. "I said, get *up*! Keep going!"

When Maggie had been Prime Minister Winston

Churchill's secretary, she'd never thought of herself as potential spy material. And yet now she was living somewhere in Scotland, in a dilapidated Edwardian manor house the government had taken over for training purposes, known unofficially as Camp Spook. She slept on a hard thin cot in a bedroom with peeling wallpaper that she shared with two other girls.

She and her fellow MI-5 trainees did daily exercises in a roped-off area of the garden. There, in their coveralls and plimsolls, they did push-ups, sit-ups, and rope climbing. Today they were split into two teams, competing to finish an obstacle course, which included wriggling through an oil drum, crawling through the mud under netting, crossing a man-made pond with only a few planks and a rope, navigating through a "minefield," and climbing up an old factory ventilation shaft.

As Maggie tried to right herself once more in the slippery black mud, Burns was shouting, his face turning red from the exertion. "Come on, keep going! The Nazis are after you! What are you waiting for? Move! Move! *Move!*"

With grim determination, Maggie struggled to her feet and ran onward through the mud, toward the next obstacle, a ten-foot chain-link fence they were supposed to scale and then drop from. With a running start, she jumped up onto the fence, then began clawing her way up to the top, blinking away raindrops. Her teammates who'd already finished the course were on the sidelines.

"Come on, Maggie!" the girls chorused. "You can do it!"

Her hands were clumsy from the cold and her breath burned in her lungs, but she made it to the top, swung her legs over, then jumped down to the ground.

Something popped and started to pinch in her right knee, but she ran on to the next challenge, picking up one of her fallen mates in a fireman's carry. The girl, a tiny thing named Molly Stickler, lay on her back in the mud, waiting. "Don't drop me again, Hope," she warned. "Not like you did last time."

Maggie ignored Molly and reviewed the task at hand. As she'd practiced, she rolled Molly over onto her abdomen and straddled her. She extended her hands under the girl's chest and locked them together. She lifted Molly to her knees as she moved backward.

"Careful!" Molly complained.

"You're 'the casualty,'" Maggie muttered. "Casualties aren't supposed to talk."

Maggie continued to move backward, straightening Molly's legs and locking her knees, then walking forward, bringing the limp girl to a standing position. Gently, gently, every muscle burning, Maggie maneuvered the girl's body into the proper position.

"The Nazis are coming, Hope!" Burns yelled from the sidelines. "They'd have *shot* you both by now!"

Undeterred, Maggie followed protocol. Rising to her feet, she carried the girl over her shoulders toward the finish line, hair dripping, covered in mud, oblivious to the agony in her knee.

But just before she reached the end, her foot slipped in the mud. She skidded like an ice skater, and then toppled backward, taking Molly down with her.

"Ooof," Molly gasped as they hit the ground. "Ow! Goddamn it, Maggie, that *hurt*."

"Under ten minutes today, Hope. Better." Burns looked at his stopwatch. "Slightly."

Maggie gave him a pinched smile as she got up, then

offered her hand to help Molly. His "slightly" was a small victory, considering her legs felt like rubber and her injured knee throbbed. Then she limped over to the rest of the group, to cheer on the next girl, who was just starting the course.

"No," Burns called over to Maggie, through the rain. "Get cleaned up and dressed, Hope. And meet me in the dining room."

Was this it? Was she going to be thrown out of the program?

The dining room had a lingering sense of the house's former grandeur. The faded and water-stained wallpaper had squares of bright perfection, where large paintings must have once hung, four-sided ghosts of the manor's past opulence. Still, a cheerful fire crackled and popped in the grate and the brass was polished. Mr. Burns was already seated at the table when Maggie came in, washed and combed and dressed in clean, dry trousers, a white blouse, and a cabled wool cardigan.

The wireless was on. Maggie could hear the fourteen-year-old Princess Elizabeth addressing in bell-like tones the children who'd left London for the relative safety of the British countryside: *"Before I finish, I can truthfully say to you all that we children at home are full of cheerfulness and courage. We are trying to do all we can to help our gallant sailors, soldiers, and airmen, and we are trying, too, to bear our own share of the danger and sadness of war. . . ."*

Mrs. Forester, an older woman with a tight gray bun and wide hips, both chaperone and housekeeper, peeked through the door. Maggie knew from several conversations over cups of tea that she was grateful to have the job—a widow, both her sons were in the Royal Navy, floating somewhere in the North Sea. She found that cooking and cleaning for the girls of Camp Spook kept her mind occupied and tired her out enough during the day so she could manage at least a few hours of sleep at night. "Will you be wantin' any tea, Mr. Burns?" she said, her plump face folding into a smile as she walked into the dining room and turned off the wireless with a loud click.

"No, thank you, Mrs. Forester," Mr. Burns replied. In front of him was Maggie's file, a thick folder labeled MARGARET HOPE.

"Very well," she said and left.

Burns looked at Maggie, then gestured to a straight-backed chair. "Please sit down, Miss Hope," he said.

Maggie did.

He cracked his knuckles. "Mr. Frain, head of MI-Five, sent you to me, with the highest recommendations," he began. "He let me know a bit of your role in taking down the Prime Minister's assassination plot and preventing the bombing of Saint Paul's."

Maggie permitted herself the slightest—just the slightest—feeling of pride.

"Frain also tells me you have excellent instincts when it comes to code breaking. Also that your French and German are flawless."

The slight feeling grew just a bit brighter.

"During your time here, you've applied yourself and worked hard."

*I passed!* Maggie thought with a glow of pride. *So where am I going? Dropped behind enemy lines in*

*France? Undercover in Germany?* Her pulse quickened with excitement.

"However," Burns said.

*However?*

"However?"

"Your background in academics and then as secretary to the Prime Minister hasn't been conducive to the, er, physical aspects of spy work. We have certain standards for our candidates, and, Miss Hope, I'm afraid you have not attained them."

*What?* Despite the warmth of the fire, Maggie felt cold. She'd worked hard. She'd learned how to shoot Sten and Bren guns and hit targets. She'd learned to transmit Morse code, jump out of a plane, and kill with various implements—a pen, a dinner knife, her bare hands. She'd been (with Mrs. Forester supervising, of course) tied to a chair, blindfolded, and interrogated for hours and hours by "Gestapo" officers with no rest, food, or water.

In the mental aspects of the training, Maggie had excelled; in the endurance aspects, she'd failed. The most egregious was a twenty-five-mile cross-country trek all the candidates had to do in the cold and rain. Only a few miles into the course she'd tripped on a tree root, fallen, and knocked herself unconscious. After coming to, she'd limped almost a quarter of a mile before Burns and his men picked her up. The doctor at Camp Spook diagnosed her with a sprained ankle and hypothermia.

"I cannot, in good conscience, recommend undercover work in Europe. I'm not convinced you're physically up to it."

*There has to be some mistake.* "Mr. Burns, I can assure you—"

"My mind is made up, Miss Hope. I've spoken to Mr. Frain, and he's asked that you return to London. He'll inform you of your new position when you arrive."

"New position?" Maggie was bewildered.

"Probably reading through mail for possible codes, that sort of thing. Desk work." Burns struggled to let her down gently. "But it's all important work, Miss Hope. There are no small jobs. After all—"

Maggie bit her lip to hide her disappointment. After everything she'd been through, she was, once again, going to end up behind a typewriter, fighting with no more than the stack of papers in her inbox? No, no, no—she was not.

"—there's a war on," Maggie finished for him. "But you can't afford to waste me behind a desk. I speak perfect French and German. I'm smart, smarter than you, most likely, and I—"

"I'm sorry, Miss Hope," Burns said. "But when you're over there, there's not a lot we can do to keep you safe. And if something happens—and Lord knows it will—we need to know you can take care of yourself. I'm not convinced you're up to it. And so I can't, in good conscience, recommend you."

"But, Mr. Burns—"

"I have a daughter your age, Miss Hope. I wouldn't even consider dropping her behind enemy lines at all, let alone if I thought she might not survive."

Maggie saw he was sincere, if narrow-minded. "Thank you, Mr. Burns," she said, relenting, at least for the moment. She might have lost the battle, but she wasn't ready to concede the war. "However, I must tell you I *will* take this up with Mr. Frain." Surely Peter Frain, head of MI-5, who personally recruited her, would see the folly of Burns's decision and set things straight.

"Of course, Miss Hope. Good luck to you."

Mr. Burns watched her as she left, a pale and serious-looking girl with reddish hair, pretty when she smiled. He'd come to admire her grit, even if her performance hadn't been up to par, and wished he had better news for her. Although the news he had would most likely keep her alive. Very few of the British spies dropped in France or Germany survived more than three months, if that. And no women had been dropped yet.

"Oh, well," he muttered as he packed up her file. "Frain will find *something* for her."

Abwehr was the German counterpart to MI-5 and MI-6, located at 76/78 Tirpitzufer, Berlin, in an imposing neo-classical building topped with huge black-and-red Nazi flags, snapping smartly in a cold wind under a brilliant blue sky. The Nazi spy organization had three main branches: die Zentrale, or the Central Division; Abwehr I, II, and III, which dealt with foreign intelligence collection, sabotage, and counterintelligence, respectively; and the Foreign Branch, or Amtsgruppe Ausland, responsible for the evaluation of captured documents. The Foreign Branch was run under the direction of Luca von Plettenberg.

Claus Becker answered to von Plettenberg and was in charge of information received from Britain, specifically. He was a short man, round, in his early forties, with an agreeable face and an infectious smile. A native Berliner, he'd worked as a grocery store clerk before joining the Nazi party in 1925, after reading Hitler's *Mein Kampf.*

He'd worked his way up through the SS before transferring to Abwehr in 1938. He was a bachelor, living in a spacious apartment in Mitte, and had a sweet-tempered miniature greyhound named Wolfgang, who went everywhere with him on a thin black leather leash. People at the Foreign Branch knew to be affectionate to Wolfgang if they wanted to keep their jobs.

Becker was sitting behind his desk in his office, facing two junior agents. Torsten Ritter and Franz Krause were both young, short, and swimming in their too-big gray uniforms—nothing like the robust blond men from the propaganda posters boasting Aryan supremacy. Still, they were smart, they were blue-eyed, and they were Nazis. The office was large, as was Becker's mahogany claw-foot desk, over which hung a large official portrait of Hitler by Heinrich Knirr. The two junior agents sat on low black leather chairs, facing Becker.

"Come, Wolfie!" Becker called to his small greyhound, who ran to him, tail wagging, and licked his hands. "Sit!" he commanded. The slender gray dog went to his vermilion velvet pillow under Becker's desk and settled down with nary a whimper.

Becker turned his attention to the junior agents. "And?"

Ritter began, "We have word our agent in Bletchley has managed to obtain an actual decrypt from their so-called Enigma machine."

Becker gave a hearty chuckle, warm and rich. "I'll believe it when I see it."

"Sir," Krause said, "we received a short radio dispatch from London, telling us our contacts are working out their escape, with the decrypt, as we speak. They've asked us to have the money ready."

Becker made a steeple with his hands, still smiling. "Ah, yes—the *money*." He leaned back in his chair. "You know, I have the utmost respect for your operation, I really do. But to suggest that England has broken our codes . . . a joke, surely."

Ritter spoke up. "But they say there's a whole group of British code breakers working on it. And they've done it. And they have a stolen decrypt to prove it."

"If the British have broken it," Becker objected, "why haven't they shown their hand? Why haven't they evacuated their cities when they know that air attacks are coming?"

Krause shrugged. "We're not sure how fast they can break each message, sir."

"If they can break them at all." Claus looked up at the ceiling. "Which I sincerely doubt."

"But the code *can* be broken, yes?" Krause insisted.

Becker sighed. "The Enigma machine has a hundred and fifty million million *million* ways of producing its cipher, according to how you set its three rotors and how you connect its plugs. It is, in a word, impossible to break."

Ritter and Krause sat very still.

"However," Becker said, "I will permit you to continue to work on what, I believe, is a wild-goose chase, if only so I will own your souls when it comes to nothing. By the way, there's a huge air attack coming up soon, payback for the bombing of Berlin. If the British can decrypt our messages, surely they'll evacuate the city in question. Then we'll know if, indeed, they've broken it."

Becker opened his desk drawer and took out a dried pig's ear, passing it down to the dog, who began gnawing on it. "Good boy," he said to Wolfie, rubbing the velvety fur on his back. "Oh, that's my good, good darling boy!"

He looked back to the two agents. "In regard to more important matters, everything is in place for Operation Edelweiss. We have our two operatives ready to go. When Commandant Hess gives the word, the plan will commence. It won't be long now."

He rose to his feet, gave a delighted smile, and clapped his plump hands together. "That will be all." Then he raised his right arm. "Heil Hitler!"

Wrapped in a magnificent green silk robe embroidered with red-and-gold dragons, Prime Minister Winston Churchill was lying in his bed at the Annexe to No. 10, working at his Box, which held all of his most important documents. His cheeks were flushed with anger. One memo, from Lieutenant Colonel Stewart Menzies of MI-6, on the topic of the Duke and Duchess of Windsor, and their many conversations with Walther Schellenberg in Lisbon, had him in a foul temper.

"Where's Tinsley?" he bellowed to his butler, David Inces.

Inces was used to his employer's temper. "Sir, she's—"

Mrs. Tinsley, his head typist, appeared in the doorway. "Right here, Prime Minister," she said, bringing in her portable noiseless typewriter and setting up at the desk. Inces left.

"Letter to the Duke of Windsor!" the P.M. barked.

Mrs. Tinsley waited, fingers poised over the keys.

He began dictating. " 'Sir, may I venture upon a word

of serious counsel. Many sharp and unfriendly ears will be pricked up to catch any suggestion that your Royal Highness takes a view about the war, or about the Germans, or about Hitlerism, which is different from that adopted by the British nation and Parliament. Even while you have been staying at Lisbon, conversations have been reported by telegraph through various channels, which might have been used to your Royal Highness's disadvantage.

"I thought your Royal Highness would not mind these words of caution from your faithful and devoted servant, et cetera, et cetera. Got that, Mrs. Tinsley? Yes? Excellent. Get the letter dispatched as quickly as possible. Go!"

He picked up the telephone receiver on his bedside table. "Nelson at S.O.E.—*now!*" S.O.E. was short for Special Operations Executive—Churchill's special team of black ops, who were able to do things even MI-6 couldn't. Or wouldn't.

There was a pause, then a man's voice came on the line: "Yes, Prime Minister?"

"Get the Duke of Windsor and Wallis Simpson out of Portugal *immediately*. Kidnap them in the middle of the night if you need to, just get them out!"


In the garden of Buckingham Palace, under a cold late-afternoon mother-of-pearl sky that threatened rain, the hedges of the gardens were covered in spiderwebs dotted with beads of dew. There, Queen Elizabeth stood, holding a gun.

"That's right, darling," King George VI called to her

as the chill wind picked up. "Just bend your knees the slightest bit. Brace yourself for the recoil. Then squeeze."

She did, and the gun fired with a loud *bang* that caused a murder of crows in a nearby oak tree to shriek and take flight. The bullet hit its intended target forty paces away—a wooden cut-out shaped like a man. On its face was a photograph of Hitler.

"Jolly good!" the King exclaimed. "You got him right in the n-n-n-naughty bits."

The Queen, in a Wedgwood-blue coat and hat that matched her eyes perfectly, smiled. "Good," she said. "That's where I was aiming."

When Scottish aristocrat Elizabeth Bowes-Lyon had married Albert, Duke of York, the second son of King George V and Queen Mary, she'd never expected to become Queen, let alone a wartime one. But when Edward, the firstborn son, had abdicated the throne to wed Wallis Simpson, Albert had become King George VI— and Elizabeth had become his queen consort. When the Blitz began, she reached out to her people, touring the decimated East End, offering comfort and support to the grieving and homeless. For her steely inspiration, Adolf Hitler had called her "the most dangerous woman in all of Europe."

The palace's black-clad butler walked up to the King and Queen and bowed. "Your Majesties," he said, then gestured to the bald, stout, pink-faced man in a dark pin-striped double-breasted suit behind him. "The Prime Minister."

"Welcome, Winston!" the King said, as Winston Churchill bowed.

"Thank you, Your Majesty," he answered in his gruff smoke- and whiskey-laced tones.

The Queen smiled as the P.M. bowed and kissed her offered hand. "Your Majesty," he said.

"Care to take a shot, Mr. Churchill?"

"I would love to, ma'am. Alas, I'm afraid I'm fighting Mr. Hitler on a far less literal plane."

"We're learning how to defend ourselves." The King indicated the target. "Getting better."

"Good," Churchill said. "We've made it through the Battle of Britain, but, just between us, invasion's still a distinct possibility. Glad you and the Queen decided to stay in England, though. Keeps up morale."

"Halifax wanted us in C-C-C-Canada—do you remember? And the girls, too."

A corner of the P.M.'s mouth twitched. He and Lord Halifax, a supporter of Neville Chamberlain's appeasement policies, didn't agree on much. "Didn't surprise me at all, sir."

"Well, living at Windsor Castle's been wonderful for them," the Queen said. "All that fresh country air. And it's easy enough for us to see them on the weekends. They've transformed one of the dungeons into a bomb shelter, can you believe?"

Churchill cleared his throat. "Your Majesties, we've heard some radio chatter indicating the Germans are going forward with the plot we discussed recently."

The King took the gun from the Queen. "Nazis want to replace me with Edward, do they? The Duke of Windsor can stage his abdic-c-c-ation, in reverse?" His fingers squeezed the trigger and the bullet exploded into what would have been Hitler's kidneys.

"A little higher, dear," the Queen said.

"Have that *w-w-w-woman* wear a crown?" The King's

tones indicated the contempt he still felt for Simpson, the American divorcée for whom his brother abandoned the throne. "She had an affair with Ribbentrop!"

Joachim von Ribbentrop had been appointed ambassador to Britain with orders to negotiate the Anglo-German alliance. Wallis Simpson had been a regular guest at Ribbentrop's social gatherings at the German embassy in London; it was rumored that the two were having an ongoing affair. It was also rumored that Ribbentrop might have used Wallis Simpson's access to the then King Edward VIII to funnel important information about the British to the German government.

"Von *Brickendrop*," the Queen said, using Ribbentrop's London nickname, inspired by his cloddish manners and tactless behavior, "sent her seventeen carnations every day she was in London. Seventeen, allegedly for the number of times they made love!"

"The Nazis hold Mrs. Simpson in high regard, yes," the P.M. said. "She was always one of their biggest supporters, from the beginning. But what we've heard is that the Germans not only want to assassinate you, sir, but kidnap the Princess Elizabeth as well—since she's first in line to the throne. At fourteen, she's old enough to rule."

The King blanched. "Lilibet . . . "

"On top of all the Coldstream Guards we have in place at Windsor, what else do you suggest, Prime Minister?" the Queen asked.

"Actually, I had an idea. . . . There's a young woman from MI-Five," the P.M. said. "She used to work for me, actually. She's smart, circumspect, an eye for the unusual and out-of-place—and able to put two and two together.

I'd like to have her at Windsor to keep an eye on things, from the inside."

The Queen looked at the King. She nodded. He smiled at her and took her hand.

"Of c-c-course," the King said. "What is her name?"

## Chapter Three

Maggie's one consolation after her poor performance at Camp Spook was that she could finally return to London. When David Greene, her friend and one of Winston Churchill's private secretaries, pulled up to the servants' entrance of the great house in his old Citroën, she slid in and gave him a huge bear hug.

"Maggie, love," David managed, "you're crushing me."

"Sorry," she said, settling into the worn leather seat. "But I've missed you."

"Missed you, too, Mags," David replied as the car pulled away with a few splutters and pops. "Number Ten isn't the same without you." There was an awkward silence as they both thought of who else was missing.

"And I've missed Number Ten," Maggie said, evading the unspoken question. "How is everyone—Mr. Churchill, of course, and Mrs. Tinsley, Miss Stewart, Mr. Snodgrass, Nelson . . . And how are *you*? How's it working out with that nice fellow from the Treasury? Freddie, was it? Freddie Wright?"

"Oh, Maggie," David said as he shifted into second gear, "keep up, darling. Freddie is so *very* last month. There was also Francis, then Timothy—let's see—then Rupert, Felix, Robert, Hamish. . . ."

"Oh, my!" Maggie said, laughing. David, like her Aunt Edith back in Boston, was "like that." While he could be himself with Maggie, it wasn't something he was able to share with many others in London, especially at No. 10.

"So how was it?" he asked. "I'm dying to know. I realize you can't tell me much, but anything you can share—"

"Oh, David," Maggie said, words tumbling over each other, "is there any way I can come back to work for Mr. Churchill?"

David swerved to avoid a large white sheep standing in the middle of the road, *baa*-ing to his woolly fellows still in the high grass. "Bad, huh? Well, the Old Man has a new girl now, a Marion something-or-other. . . ."

"I see," Maggie said, trying not to let the hurt she felt show.

"Was it really *that* horrible?"

Maggie gave a delicate snort. "Worse. I may be a decent mathematician, but I'm terrible at anything physical. It was a living nightmare. Nonstop gym class."

David, who was fair and slight and wore thick glasses with wire frames, nodded, understanding. "First off, you're a *brilliant* mathematician. And second, people like you and me, well, we aren't cut out for all that robust outdoorsy life anyway—thank goodness I found fencing. So, what now?"

"Good question." Maggie shrugged. "Tomorrow I

meet with Peter Frain. We'll see what happens and go from there. Surely there *must* be something I can do."

As they approached London, in the gray dimming light, Maggie could see smoke rising from the city, its acrid stink unmistakable. The skyline had changed as well; there were gaps where tall buildings had once proudly stood, like the smile of an aging prizefighter. London, as well as Bristol, Cardiff, Southampton, Liverpool, and Manchester, had been under attack from the Luftwaffe since the summer, in what Churchill had called the Battle of Britain. London had been bombed nearly every night since September.

Maggie was silent, both sickened and awed by the destruction that had happened since she'd left.

Across one building's brick side was chalked, *"There will always be an England!"* Some of the letters had been blasted away, but it was still legible.

"Bloody Nazis," Maggie said, taking it all in—the death, destruction, and defiance—as they drove closer and closer to the city.

David gave a grim smile. "Bloody Nazis."

Back at David's flat in Knightsbridge, Maggie was surprised. She expected girlish voices filling the air, but instead there was only gloom and thick silence.

"Where is everyone?" she called, her voice echoing as she put her suitcase down.

After the horrific events of last summer, Maggie and her flatmates Sarah, Charlotte (better known as Chuck), and the twins, Annabelle and Clarabelle, had moved in with David, who had a ridiculously large flat—originally a pied-à-terre his father had bought for business trips to London. David had taken it over after graduating from Oxford and beginning a job as private secretary to then M.P. Winston Churchill.

"Well, Sarah, as you know, is on tour."

"Oh, of course, she's dancing the Lilac Fairy in *Sleeping Beauty*. I'd forgotten."

"Yes, Freddie Ashton still loves her." The Sadler's Wells Ballet was traveling across England, both to build morale nationwide and also because the bombing in London had become so horrific that it was difficult, if not downright dangerous, to continue to give nightly performances.

"The twins left their production of *Rebecca* and joined the Land Girls. They're off farming somewhere in Scotland. And Chuck's either working overnight shifts at hospital or off to Leeds to prepare for the wedding. I think she's there now, actually." Chuck was engaged to be married to Nigel, an RAF pilot and one of David's best friends.

"So, for the moment, it's just you and me?" Maggie said, unpinning her hat.

"More or less." David looked at the grandfather clock. "Jumping Jupiter! I've got to run—needed back at the office, don't you know."

David turned to leave, then called back to Maggie, now shrouded in darkness, "You'll be all right, then? There's some tea in the cupboard and a bottle of decent Scotch. The Anderson's still in the back garden—just in case. And don't forget the blackout curtains, yes?"

"Thanks, David," she said, with more enthusiasm than she felt. "Say hello to everyone at Number Ten for me. See you when you get back."

When David left, Maggie took off her coat and hung

it in the closet. David's flat looked the same as it had when she'd left—Paul Follot art deco velvet sofas in deep blues, wood-paneled walls, polished herringbone floors punctuated with Chinese geometric-patterned rugs in golds and crimsons. The walls had originally been hung with oil paintings, landscapes and portraits by Duncan Grant and Roger Fry. Now they'd been rolled up and sent to David's parents' home in the country for safekeeping. Only the frames were left, now displaying comics and photos torn from *Tatler, Britannia,* and *Tales of Wonder.*

She picked up her suitcase and walked down the long hall to the bedroom she'd had for only a few days before she'd left for Arisaig in western Scotland, footsteps echoing. She put the case down and sat on the bed. The air in the room was stale and cold from being closed up for so long.

"Things have changed," she whispered to herself in the murky darkness. "Of course they have—they always do."

*And how illogical of me to think otherwise.*

Affected by the quiet, she went back to the parlor and went through a cabinet with David's record collection, selecting a Vera Lynn album. She slid the hard black disk from its paper sheath and fitted it on the turntable. She turned the phonograph on, then carefully placed the needle in the groove. After a few crackles and pops, the music poured forth and, through the shadows, Lynn sang out:

"*We'll meet again*
*Don't know where*
*Don't know when*

*But I know we'll meet again*
*Some sunny day. . . ."*


They came in the night.

But this time it was real, not one of Alistair Tooke's nightmares. He was in his bed in one of the narrow houses of the Great Park Village when he heard the knock. He looked over at his wife. Marta was also awake and clutching the sheet, drawing it up to her chin protectively.

"Probably just some sort of frost—and they're worried about the roses," he whispered in what he hoped was a reassuring way. Alistair Tooke was the Head Royal Gardener at Windsor Castle and had worked there for more than twenty years, almost as long as he'd been married to Marta.

"Of course, dear," Marta replied, her German accent barely noticeable after so many years, but he noted she'd slipped out of bed and had started to get dressed.

From below, the knocking had turned into insistent banging. Alistair wrapped his flannel dressing gown around himself and made his way down the narrow, steep staircase.

"All right, all right!" he called as he made his way to the door. When he opened it, he was blinded by the bright flashlights shining in his face.

One man, older, with bushy gray eyebrows and thick lips, stepped forward with an air of importance. He was wearing the uniform of the British Home Guard. "We've come for Marta Kunst!" he bellowed. "Where is she?"

"My wife is Marta Tooke. We've been married for over thirty years."

The man pushed past Tooke, into the hallway, and the rest, a group of four, followed. "Marta *Kunst* Tooke is charged with being an Enemy Alien under the Defense Act, B Registration."

Alistair felt a prickle of fear run down his spine, but he wasn't going to give the man the satisfaction of knowing it. "Yes, yes—we know that," he said, running his hands through his thick white hair. "But her papers are all in order. And we work for the Royal Family!"

He could hear Marta making her way down the creaky narrow staircase. "I'm taking care of it," he called to her. Still, she came, fully dressed in a heavy wool skirt and cabled cardigan.

"Marta Kunst," the man said to the tiny older woman, "you have relatives in Germany. You've sent them chess moves, which our censors suspect to be code. You'll be sent to a British prison camp until the authorities get to the bottom of it."

"What?" Marta put a blue-veined hand to her throat. "I write to my Cousin Albie—we play chess! It's perfectly innocent!"

"We'll see about that," the man said. He gestured to his comrades. "Take her." Without preamble, they clamped a pair of handcuffs on her and began to lead her out of the house.

"Marta!" Alistair called in anguish.

"It's all right," his wife said, trying to reassure him. "I'll be back before you know it."

They hustled her out the door and into the waiting van.

"I'll do everything I can!" Alistair called after her. "I'll go to the King!"

———

The London police identified the woman who checked into Claridge's under a false name and was shot in the bathtub as Victoria Keeley, missing from Bletchley Park. An autopsy had revealed that from the angle of the gunshot wound, suicide was an impossibility.

As soon as the word *Bletchley* was introduced, MI-5 took over the case.

Peter Frain, head of MI-5, immediately called in Edmund Hope, his Bletchley undercover operative. Edmund was a former London School of Economics professor, until he'd been in a car accident that killed his young wife and severely injured him. He'd been recruited as a spy and been at Bletchley since its inception, posing as a brilliant but mentally unstable code breaker. But his real job was working for MI-5, tracking a suspected traitor in their midst, one that could ruin everything everyone at Bletchley was trying so hard to achieve. Victoria Keeley's death could possibly be linked to the spy.

The two men met late at night in a small conference room in Bletchley's main building, the former manor house. It was the first time the two had seen each other since the events of the summer, where, among other things, Maggie discovered her presumed-to-be-dead father alive and well—and working for MI-5 at Bletchley Park. But Edmund and Frain had known each other for years and enjoyed an easy camaraderie.

"Victoria Keeley worked as a teleprinter," Edmund explained. "She wouldn't have access to the decrypts themselves. Bletchley's extremely careful not to let anyone know anything they don't need to—each hut knows very little about the other parts of the operation. However, Miss Keeley was beautiful," he said. "She had a lot of beaux. Specifically, some of the code breakers."

"Anyone in particular?"

Edmund shrugged. "Lately a young code breaker named Benjamin Batey—I saw them together a few times. He would have had access to that sort of decrypt too. Miss Keeley may have gotten her hands on it somehow and passed it on to someone."

"There was no decrypt found in the room. Worst-case scenario is that whoever killed her took the decrypt as well." Frain stood up. "Well, then," he said. "Let's bring young Mr. Batey in for a chat, shall we?"

"One more thing," Edmund told him. "I hear you're going to have Maggie working with an agent named Hugh Thompson."

"Yes, Thompson's good," Frain replied. "Young but promising. I think they'll make an excellent team."

"Considering his family history, do you think that's wise?"

"They'll never find out," Frain said. "Never. I promise you, Edmund." He held up his hand. "I give you my word."

# Chapter Four

The next morning, Maggie picked her way through the rubble outside David's flat to get to the Sloane Square Tube station, her Rayne pumps crunching on shards of broken glass. A sullen sun tried to shine through an overcast sky. The cold air rang with the wails of sirens from emergency vehicles and stank of smoke, ash, and petrol. Fires still smoldered here and there. A charwoman poured a bucket of dirty water over a dark bloodstain on the pavement, as a body, wrapped in a white bedsheet, was being loaded into a rusty Black Maria.

Maggie saw that an entire town house had been flattened the night before. As she passed, she noticed a woman in a Jaeger suit, hat, and gloves stumble and nearly fall over as she took in the wreckage. "This—was—my house," she said to one of the volunteer firefighters still hosing down the charred remains.

"Get her a seat," one fireman in a tin helmet called to another. They found a chair that must have been blown out of the window from the force of the explosion. It was silk, singed and covered in soot but still functional. The woman sat down and crossed her ankles primly in the middle of the street. "I went to the country—that's where my children are—I was only gone one night. . . ."

The fireman motioned to the ARP warden. "Mug o' tea for the lady here? She's had a bit of a shock." Then he went back to hosing down a smoldering fire.

Maggie gritted her teeth and walked on. Some of the bombed-out shops had put up signs: *"Back as soon as we beat Hitler," "Keep Smiling,"* and, at a street fruit seller's cart, *"Hitler's Bombs Can't Beat Us—Our Oranges Came Through Musso's Lake."* On the remains of a wall and floor that had the appearance of a gallows was a rope with a noose tied in it and a sign: *"Reserved for Hitler."*

Inside the Tube station, Maggie walked down the stopped escalator steps, careful not to disturb those people who were still sleeping, slumped against the wall with only thin wool blankets for warmth. Since they'd lost their homes, a vast number of people had taken shelter down in the Tube stations. They slept on the steps or in makeshift bunks against the walls on subway platforms. The air was rank with the smell of unwashed bodies and human excrement from the covered buckets lining one wall.

A group of old women in dirt-stained clothes were huddled around a coal brazier, making what Maggie guessed was a pot of tea. She made her way through the sea of humanity and finally caught her train.

She was headed to the offices of the Imperial Security Intelligence Service, which everyone called MI-5. Headquartered in a sandbagged building at 58 Saint James Street, MI-5's mission was national security.

After showing her ID to one of the guards in the lobby, she was permitted access. The building was massive and her steps echoed along the well-polished hallways. "I'm here to see Mr. Frain, please," Maggie said to the receptionist, an older woman with thick glasses named Mrs. Pipps.

She hung up her gas mask and coat on the hooks by the door and removed her gloves and placed them in her handbag. Then, straightening her hat, she sat down to wait.

Peter Frain, a spy during the Great War and a former professor of Egyptology at Cambridge after that, became head of MI-5 when Winston Churchill had become Prime Minister in May 1940. Maggie had met him over the summer, after she'd discovered hidden Nazi code pointing to three specific attacks, including the assassination of the Prime Minister. When Frain had seen her in action, plus learned of her fluency in both French and German, he'd asked Maggie to leave her job as secretary for the P.M. and come work for him at MI-5, which she'd done, intrigued by the possibility of working undercover. She'd had high hopes of being dropped behind enemy lines on a clandestine mission.

And despite her wretched showing in the physical tasks at Camp Spook, she was still determined to do it.

Finally, she was ushered into the room to find Peter Frain behind a large oak desk, a reproduction of Goya's *Lord Nelson* hanging on the wall behind him, next to an official photograph of King George VI.

Frain had the same black, slick-backed hair and cold gray eyes Maggie remembered, and, despite the privations of wartime, yet another impeccably tailored suit. In front of him was a manila folder, thick with papers.

Maggie could see her name on a label and then, over it, the heavy red-inked stamp, TOP SECRET.

"Ah, Maggie," Frain said, rising to his feet. They shook hands. "Please, take a seat." They'd been on a first-name basis since their exploits of the summer. Still, the informality sounded a bit out of place in the austere offices of MI-5.

Maggie had the distinct and uncomfortable sensation of being called to the dean's office. Still, she refused to let that show. "Good morning, Peter. A pleasure to see you again," she said, sitting in the chair opposite his desk.

"And under more agreeable circumstances than last time," Frain replied, his wintry features momentarily warmed by a smile.

"Indeed."

"I've had a chance to look over your file." He folded his long, tapered fingers. "You scored well on the Intelligence test. In fact, your answer to the first question on the maths section could be the basis of an article for a mathematics journal, if we had the time for such things. Perhaps after the war."

Maggie's stomach lurched a bit. "Perhaps."

"However . . ."

*Oh, here it comes.*

"In regard to your physical skills—"

"Peter, I can assure you—"

"Not a bit of it, young lady," Frain interrupted. "The job I have in mind for you won't have any wall scaling or puddle jumping, I promise you."

Maggie cocked an eyebrow. "Really?"

A job? Was he talking about a *real* spy job, or a desk job in some subbasement, reading the personal letters and private communications of senior officials and officers and flagging anything that looked suspicious? Was he, perhaps, talking about working at Bletchley? After all, her newly found father was there, acting the role of a mad cryptographer while ferreting out a spy. . . .

"As you undoubtedly know, the Royal Family has decided not to send the Princesses to Canada or Australia for safety's sake but to keep them here, in England."

"At an 'undisclosed location in the country,'" Maggie said, having read newspaper reports of the Princesses' whereabouts.

"Yes." Frain nodded. "And since you've signed the Official Secrets Act, I can tell you the young Princesses have been sequestered in Windsor Castle. It's close enough to London that the King and Queen can work at Buckingham Palace during the week but then return to Windsor to be with their daughters on the weekends. Windsor's not on any particular bombing path, so attacks there have been infrequent. And there's ample shelter in the castle's dungeons."

*Who would have thought the dungeons of Windsor would be found useful once again?* "Yes," Maggie repeated, growing impatient. *What does this have to do with me?*

Frain picked up the heavy green telephone receiver. "Mrs. Pipps, please have Mr. Thompson come to my office."

He turned back to Maggie. "Mr. Thompson will be your handler while you're at Windsor. Your cover story is to tutor the Princess Elizabeth in maths. Of course, the King and Queen know why you're *really* there, but as far as anyone else in the castle knows, you're just a tutor. You'll report to the Princesses' governess," he said, turning through pages until he found the name. "A Miss Marion Crawford."

*A tutor? To a child? Was the man serious?* "Surely you're joking, Peter," she said, struggling to make sense of what he was telling her.

"No, Maggie. There's a strong probability Princess Elizabeth may be in danger. She's second in line to the throne, after all. We need someone at Windsor to keep an eye on things."

"You want me to be her—her *babysitter?*" Maggie was shocked and not a little disappointed.

"I wouldn't have chosen that specific word. *Nanny* is more commonly used here. Or the more archaic *governess.*"

"There must be a platoon of guards in place at Windsor to protect the princess. I'm much too important an asset to waste taking care of a child, Peter, and you know it." *To go from being a typist to being a nanny? What's wrong with these men in charge?*

"I'm quite familiar with your talents, Maggie, and I would never waste them. Why don't you think of yourself more as a . . . a sponge."

"A *sponge?*"

"Soak up any and all information. Observe everything you can at the castle—and then report anything and everything through Mr. Thompson back to me."

"An undercover 'sponge,'" Maggie snapped. "Just fantastic."

The door opened and a figure appeared. "Ah, there you are," Frain said. "Maggie, meet Hugh Thompson, your handler. Mr. Thompson, Miss Hope." Hugh was about her age, in his mid-twenties, with a high forehead, hazel eyes, and fine lines hinting at a life of unremitting anxiety. He was astute, motivated, and efficient, different from many other men of his age and class, who tended to take more for granted. When war had broken out, he'd begun to work at the office around the clock, stopping only rarely for a pint with friends or to practice his beloved cello. His efficiency flat in Bloomsbury was unfurnished, except for a bed and a bookshelf and a pile of newspapers. His one indulgence was attending the occasional Chelsea Blues game.

"I've heard a lot about you, Miss Hope," he said.

"And what, exactly, have you heard?"

"Mr. Thompson's one of the agents who helped track Michael Murphy and his plan for bombing Saint Paul's Cathedral this past summer."

"Glad you got him, Miss Hope," Hugh said.

It seemed a lifetime ago. "Thank you, Mr. Thompson, for your part in it," Frain explained.

But there was no time for pleasantries. Now she needed to make her stand, to draw a line in the sand. It was time.

Maggie rose to her feet and addressed both men. "Mr. Frain, Mr. Thompson," she said. "I'm through allowing myself to be confined to so-called 'women's work.' I'm also through with patronizing men giving me half-truths and withholding information. That will end here and now.

"I will consider—*consider*—going to Windsor Castle to be your 'sponge.' But only if you tell me everything—and I mean *everything*—you know. I'm not going into another situation blind. Not only is it unsafe, but I can't do my best work."

Frain cleared his throat. "I can't do that."

"Well," Maggie pronounced, "then I can't go to

Windsor." Her heart was beating wildly, but she was determined not to let them know. She walked briskly to the door. "Cheers!" she called back over her shoulder.

Frain and Thompson exchanged a look.

"All right, all right, Miss Hope!" Frain called after her. Maggie paused, her hand on the knob. "You're right. You do deserve more information."

"Thank you," Maggie said, sitting down once again. *Score one for the ex-typist!*

"As you know," Frain said, "although we've made it through the summer and fall attacks, we're still getting pounded by German aircraft. Their plan, of course, is to invade and conquer England. First by taking out the RAF. And then invading the coasts, moving inward, finally reaching London and establishing their supremacy.

"In the countries they've already invaded, such as the Netherlands and France, the Nazis have made a point of working within already existing structures. So, Churchill would be assassinated—if he could even be taken alive— and it's probable someone like Lord Halifax would be put in charge of the country. He'd reassure people, you know, 'I know this Hitler and he's really not such a bad chap—let's all keep it together for the sake of Britain and cooperate with the Nazis.' Et cetera."

Hugh cut in: "A familiar figure like the Duke of Windsor, who only abdicated a few years ago, after all, might help people rally together under Nazi rule. The Duke's been a longtime admirer of the Nazis—he and Mrs. Simpson have made numerous trips to Germany, meeting with high-ranking officials and even Hitler himself. Last time he was there, Goebbels allegedly said it was a shame the Duke wasn't King anymore. Because, of course, if the Duke were still on the throne as Edward VIII, it would be so much easier for the Nazis' invasion—they'd already have their own king in place."

"King George VI has no such alliances?" Maggie asked.

"No, he and the Queen don't," Frain answered. "Which is why the Nazis need the Duke of Windsor. He and the Duchess are in Bermuda now—sent off recently on Churchill's orders. But our intelligence tells us that when they were in Portugal they'd been approached by Walther Schellenberg, Heinrich Himmler's aide. Schellenberg offered them fifty million Reichsmarks to return to the throne."

"I see," Maggie said, processing what he was telling her.

"So, the King's life is in danger. But if they killed him, many people would want Elizabeth to rule—not the Duke of Windsor. And so she's in danger too. Serious danger. The most likely scenario is kidnapping. I doubt they would try to assassinate her outright—not that they'd blink, of course, but then the tide of public opinion might turn against them if they killed a young girl."

"What specifically do you know about threats to the princess?" Maggie asked.

"There's an intelligence officer in Germany known as Hess," Frain said. "Chatter we've picked up suggests Commandant Hess has been receiving radio transmissions sent from Windsor. We don't have the whole story, I'm afraid. But as I've said, we'd like someone to keep an eye on things. It's possible the person making radio transmissions to Hess is in the royal family's inner circle—one of the nursemaids, perhaps. An underbutler. The governess."

"I see," Maggie said. *Well, that's different, then.* "I'd be honored to go to Windsor—and do everything I can."

"Brilliant!" Hugh exclaimed. "Er, right," he corrected himself, off Frain's disapproving glance.

"You'll work at Windsor during the week," Frain continued, as though he'd never doubted her commitment. "On Sunday afternoons, you'll walk into the town of Windsor. You will meet with Mr. Thompson, to report on how things are going. I don't want anything written coming in and out of the castle. If you need to reach Miss Hope, Mr. Thompson, you may ring her using the code that something she's ordered from a shop has arrived and she needs to pick it up. Maggie, that call will be your cue to meet with Mr. Thompson. Is that understood?"

"Yes, sir," Mr. Thompson and Maggie both answered.

"When do I leave?" Maggie said.

"Friday," Frain replied. "I'll arrange for Mr. Greene to drive you. I doubt he'd mind."

*He'll be thrilled to be thought of as a chauffeur.* "How long will I be there?"

"It is . . . unclear," Frain said.

*Windsor Castle. Of all places.*

"That will be all, Mr. Thompson," Frain said. "I'll send Miss Hope down to your office shortly."

"Yes, sir." Mr. Thompson gave Maggie a quick smile and then left.

When the heavy oak door had clicked shut again, Frain turned to Maggie, a softer look on his face. "And, Maggie, I'm sorry to hear about John."

"Thank you," she managed, as her heart lurched. Then she raised her chin. "Will that be all, then?"

"Yes," Frain said. "Mr. Thompson's office is three floors down."

Maggie made her way down to the smoke-filled windowless offices crammed with battered wooden desks, dented beige filing cabinets, and worn green carpeting that the junior MI-5 agents called home.

Mr. Thompson caught sight of her in the hallway and waved. "This way," he said, ushering her into the small office he shared with fellow agent Mark Standish. He moved a pile of papers from a wooden chair to the floor. "Please sit down."

"Hello," Maggie said to Standish.

"Pleasure to meet you, Miss Hope," he replied, blinking and looking up from his paperwork. Like Hugh, he was dedicated to his work. Unlike Hugh, he was married to his childhood sweetheart, with a two-year-old girl and another baby on the way.

Hugh took the seat behind his desk. "Miss Hope, ah, Maggie," he said, "there's a bookshop in the town of Windsor, Boswell's Books—the proprietor is a retired agent, Mr. Archibald Higgins. There's a room in the back. We'll meet there the second Sunday afternoon you're at the castle. Afterward, we'll work out a system where we can indicate meeting times and various places that won't seem suspicious."

"Yes," Maggie said. There was a long silence. In the silence, she took in his desk, piled high with papers and folders. Perched at the edge, nearly pushed over, was a framed photograph of a young blond woman in a spring dress, laughing at the camera. *His wife?* She rose to her feet.

Hugh sprang to his as well, almost knocking over a pile of folders and running his hands through his wild crop of hair.

"I look forward to working with you, Hugh," she said, extending her hand.

"Me too!" Hugh blurted as they shook. "I mean, I look forward to working with you, also." Maggie gave him a pained smile.

When the sound of her footsteps receded, he sat down at his desk and began sorting through papers madly.

When the click of her heels could no longer be heard, Mark spoke. "So, you're the handler for Maggie Hope."

Hugh reached for several more folders from his inbox. "Yes, thank you, Sherlock. Now I know why you're such a brilliant agent. Those ace skills of deduction."

Mark grinned. "Lucky bastard. She's a looker, she is."

Hugh opened the top folder and began making notes. "Really? I hadn't noticed."

Maggie was pulling on her gloves in the building's lobby when she caught sight of a familiar figure, tall and thin, with receding mouse-brown hair streaked with gray. "Dad?" He didn't notice her. "Edmund?"

Edmund Hope spun on his heel. "Margaret!" he said, shocked. "What are you doing here?"

"Meeting with Mr. Frain," she replied. "You?"

"Just . . . meetings."

Maggie and her father hadn't seen each other since their awkward reunion a few months earlier. And since Edmund Hope was undercover as a mad cryptographer at Bletchley, there wasn't much opportunity for social interaction.

"How—how are you?" Maggie asked. "How have you been?"

He looked down at her in the way he used to sort out a maths problem or squint at a crossword puzzle. "Uh, fine . . . fine. And, er, you?"

"Persevering." She paused, searching for something to say, then added, "John's missing. His plane was shot down over Berlin."

"I heard."

*You did?* Maggie thought. *And you didn't even call me?*

There was another awkward pause. "Well, I should go," Edmund said.

"Wait—"

There was a tense silence.

"Dad," Maggie said, trying to keep her tone light. "Could we have tea? Lunch maybe? I'd still like to talk with you about my mother."

He looked at her strangely. "I'm afraid I must return to Bletchley, Margaret."

"Well, I could meet you next time you're in town. When is that?"

Edmund still looked distracted. Panicked, even. "Dinner. Two weeks from Thursday. That would be fine."

"Let's meet at six at a place called Bell's Tavern in Slough."

"Fine," Edmund said. Then, "I need to go, must hurry back. . . ."

Maggie watched him leave. *Who is this man, really? This father I'd believed was dead all my life—until last summer.* She shook her head. *Well, dinner together will be the start to finding out.*

## Chapter Five

David had picked up ingredients for dinner. "Poor Man's Stroganoff, I'm afraid," he said in the kitchen in his flat.

"I'm impressed you're cooking at all," Maggie replied. "Sounds delicious, especially after what passed for food in Scotland. What can I do to help?"

"Set the table, if you don't mind. You remember where everything is, yes? This shouldn't take too long."

David puttered in the kitchen, opening a tin of tomatoes and adding them to the small amount of ground beef he was frying. "Mmmmm . . ." he said, taking a deep appreciative sniff as the tomatoes sizzled in the hot frying pan.

Maggie, taking out silverware and napkins from the drawers, looked him over. David was a young man, slim and handsome, with fair hair and round, silver-rimmed glasses. It hadn't been that long since she'd last seen him, but he'd seemed to have filled out and become less boyish, more mature.

"There are candles too, and a bottle of decent Bordeaux in one of the cupboards if you can find it," he said. "Black-market special."

As Maggie finished setting the table, David brought in the two plates.

"Smells wonderful," Maggie said, sitting down and putting a linen napkin in her lap.

"Not bad," David admitted, pouring the wine and then sitting down.

"Cheers," she said, and they clinked glasses.

David watched her cut a tomato with her fork in her left hand and knife in her right, then put down the knife at the right-hand edge of the plate and switch the fork from left hand to right. "You still eat like an American," he said, rolling his eyes in mock horror. "I was hoping maybe they'd drill that out of you at spy camp."

"I *can* eat the way you do, the British way," she retorted, "but I choose not to. Why I'd want to hang on to my knife the way you all do is beyond me. You look positively medieval."

"I think in medieval times they used their hands," David mused. "And these days it might be smart to hang on to one's knife. But at any rate, you're looking good, Mags. Maybe you didn't love Camp Spook, but the fresh air and sunshine have been good for you. You're not as pale. Or as skinny."

"Thank you," Maggie said dryly. David was like the brother she never knew she'd always wanted. "Looks like I'll be getting more fresh air and sunshine in the future."

"Really? Where's Frain sending you?"

"Windsor Castle. I'm going to be tutoring the Princess Elizabeth in maths, of all things."

"Merciful Minerva, you're going to be a *governess*? I thought—"

"Me too." Maggie shrugged. "But apparently there's chatter about some sort of threat to the Royal Family, including the Princess Elizabeth, who's next in line to the throne." She laughed. "Besides, I know I'm a good tutor. After all, I taught those two boys next door maths for more than a year before I came to work at Number Ten."

"Oh, right," David said, remembering. "Cheeky boys."

"Well, they had a lot of energy. Surely the Princesses will be more decorous."

David snorted. "Don't know about that," he said, reaching for his wine. "You grew up in America, after all—exactly what do you know about British aristocracy?"

"Not much beyond the historical, I'm afraid," Maggie said.

"All right, impromptu quiz—what do you say when you meet the King and Queen?"

Maggie gave David a wry look. Frain had forgotten about royal etiquette lessons. "Hello?"

David smacked himself on the head. "Oh, my dear Eliza Doolittle—we have a long night ahead of us."


After an evening of curtsies, and when to speak, and when to use "Your Majesty," and when to use "Your Highness," and how to back out of a room without tripping, Maggie and David collapsed on one of the angular deco sofas in a fit of giggles.

"So you're off on Friday, then?" David asked, after they'd quieted somewhat.

"Yes," Maggie said. "Frain suggested you drive me."

"Oh, he did, did he?" He smirked. "Fine, as long as MI-Five gives me petrol rations."

There was a comfortable silence, then David ventured, "Are you going back to the house?"

"No, I haven't been back. I don't want to go back." She smoothed her skirt. "I've rented it out to several of Chuck's fellow nurses. Apparently, the old pile is still standing."

"I understand. But it might be good for you to go back. Get rid of some old ghosts, perhaps?"

"Too much—too much happened there last summer. I have no wish to go down memory lane."

"I'm not sure denying everything that happened is helping, though, Mags."

"I'm not ready," Maggie snapped. Then, more gently, "And how are *you* doing with all this?"

"Well, you know the Old Man promoted me, yes?" Prime Minister Winston Churchill had named David as head private secretary—his right-hand man.

"Yes, congratulations. You deserve it."

"It's serious stuff, Mags. As the Old Man says," David said, pulling in his chin and affecting his best Churchillian tones: " 'The price of greatness is responsibility.' " Maggie had to laugh, remembering all of Mr. Churchill's mannerisms and verbal tics.

"Look at this." David pulled a small silk drawstring pouch from his pocket.

"What is it?"

"One of the 'perks' of my position." He opened it and deposited its contents on the table. It was a single oval capsule. "Cyanide tablet. The brown is rubber casing," he explained, "to protect it. If I need to use it, I'll have to crush it between my teeth."

"Good heavens!" she exclaimed. "Put it away."

"I try not to think about it." David grinned as he put it back in the pouch and deposited it in his pocket. "It's been good at Number Ten, Maggie. Only . . . ?"

"Yes?"

"It's not the same. With you away, of course." David paused. "And—without John."

"Yes."

"I still can't believe he's gone."

"He's *not* gone. His plane was shot down. That's all we know. Everything else is speculation and conjecture."

"Maggie, if there were anything to know, any hope to hold out, I think the office would know. The Old Man's pretty torn up over it too. John was practically a son to him, after all."

Maggie swallowed. "I refuse to give up hope."

"Good for you, Mags—good for you. It is your name, after all."

Maggie had a sudden memory of her first day working with the P.M. He'd called her Miss Holmes by mistake, and when she'd corrected him, he'd said, "Yes, yes—Margaret Hope," and then, "We need some hope in this office." Maggie was convinced it was one of the reasons he'd accepted her and let her stay on, at least in the early days.

"Besides—it's just like Schrödinger's cat, after all."

"Cat?" David said, roused slightly.

"Schrödinger's cat," Maggie insisted. "Surely you must have discussed it in physics class? Erwin Schrödinger's illustration of the principle of quantum theory of superposition."

David groaned. "Oh, Maggie. I've been out of university for far too long. This war's killing all my brain cells."

"Look, Schrödinger proposed that you place a—theoretical, of course—cat into a steel chamber, along with a vial of hydrocyanic acid and a very small amount of a radioactive substance. If even a single atom of the substance decays during the test period, a relay mechanism will trip a hammer, which will, in turn, break the vial and kill poor Mr. Puss.

"Now, an observer won't know whether the vial has been broken, the hydrocyanic acid released, and the cat killed. And since we cannot know, the cat is simultaneously dead *and* alive—according to quantum law, at least—in a superposition of states. It's only when we break open the box and learn the condition of said cat that the superposition's lost, and the cat becomes either dead or alive."

"So John's dead? *And* alive?" David said. "And, this being the real, not theoretical, world, he may never come back and we very well might not ever discover a body. What I'm trying to say is—we may never know, really."

The words *dead* and *body* hung in the air. Maggie realized the pain David must be feeling. He and John had been best friends at Oxford and had gone to work for Churchill together. They'd defended him when all of England thought him crazy with his Nazi warnings and worked together through the first of the Blitz. They were brothers in all but blood.

"And that's why I refuse to give up hope," Maggie said simply. "Because until we know, it's both."

"I'll tell you this, wherever John is, he's *not* overly thrilled to be compared to a cat."

"Oh, David!" Maggie exclaimed, tossing a sofa cushion at him.

"Whatever helps, darling. But you are," he said, patting her head, "a very strange girl."

When David had gone to bed, Maggie stayed up with her untouched snifter of cognac. She riffled through the newspaper. *"Suicide at Claridge's?"* screamed one of the headlines.

*Why can't David get a respectable paper and not these tawdry tabloids,* she thought with a twinge of irritation. Maggie scanned the article: Apparently some poor girl had killed herself in the bathtub.

But without the tasks of the day to distract her, her thoughts, as they always seemed to do, went to that fateful phone call she'd received earlier that autumn. It had started with a note left on the cot in the room at Camp Spook that she'd shared with two other women. With excellent penmanship, Mrs. Forrester had written, *"Flight Lieutenant Nigel Ludlow rang at 11:30 a.m. He asked you to return call."*

The world had stopped for a moment as Maggie considered the meaning of this. Nigel was in the RAF too—he had joined even earlier, while John was still working with Mr. Churchill. He'd never called Maggie before, but it could be about anything, really. Something to do with Chuck? The wedding?

As Maggie ran downstairs to use the black telephone in the parlor, she tried to ignore the fact that her hands were cold and trembling. She picked up the receiver and dialed the numbers.

She reached the pilots' mess. "Flight Lieutenant Ludlow?" On the line there was a crackle of static and the sound of men's voices in conversation and the clatter of dishes and cutlery. "Of course. Just a moment."

There was a loud *bang* as he must have thumped the receiver down. Interminable minutes as Maggie waited, waited for Nigel to tell her everything was all right. They'd laugh about what a nervous Nellie she'd been and she'd make him promise not to tell John. . . .

"Maggie?" She heard Nigel's voice boom over the wires. Was he somber? Distracted? Jolly? She couldn't tell.

"Hello, Nigel." She fought to keep her voice steady. "You rang?"

"Yes, yes, I did. Are you sitting down?" He spoke to her as if she were a small child. Maggie slumped into the chair next to the telephone table, feeling suddenly faint.

"Tell me," she said.

"John asked me to call you, you know—in case of anything—"

Maggie's nerves were stretched to the breaking point. *Just tell me!* "Yes?"

"Well, a bit of bad news. His Spit went down somewhere near Berlin. The plane's gone. It's possible, of course, he managed to jump, but I'm afraid we haven't heard anything in over a week. . . ."

*The plane's gone?* She pictured John hitting the ground in his Spitfire, a ball of flames.

"You, you think he could have jumped?" she managed.

"Well, it is possible." A long pause, which made

Maggie think Nigel didn't pin much hope on it. "Anything's possible." Then, "Maggie? Are you still there?"

"Did you, did you—" Her voice broke. "Call his parents?"

"His commanding officer did." Then, "Maggie, I'm so sorry—if there's anything I can do—" But the receiver had slipped from her fingers and hit the floor with a dull thud. Maggie drew up her feet and laid her head on her knees as the tears finally came.

She didn't know how long she'd sat there, crying, when Mrs. Forester found her. "Are you all right, dear?" she inquired from the doorway.

Maggie looked up, her face tearstained, hot, and red, and made an attempt to wipe at her nose with her hand. She tried to speak and nothing came out but more silent sobs.

"There, now," Mrs. Forester said, sitting beside her and replacing the phone's receiver. She procured a starched linen handkerchief from the depths of her bosom. "Here you go," she said, handing it to Maggie.

"Thank you," Maggie managed, wiping at her eyes and nose.

Mrs. Forester sat next to her, a plump and comforting presence, not saying a word.

Maggie took a rattling breath. "I think—I think he might be dead," she said finally.

"Who, dear?"

"John, John Sterling."

"Air force?"

"Yes. His plane crashed. In Germany."

"Yes."

"I don't know. He might have jumped before the crash. No one knows. . . ."

"Then that, my dear, is what you have to hold on to. That your young man's alive and he'll send word. Maybe not today. Or tomorrow. But that he *will*."

Mrs. Forester stared through the window, a distant look on her face. "It's what I did. When I got the phone call about my Bernie."

Maggie wiped again and looked up.

"My husband. The Great War. He was a pilot. Plane went down over France. He was missing too."

"And—did he come home?"

There was a pause as the question hung in the air. "No, dear," Mrs. Forester said. "But I felt it was my sacred duty to hold on to hope for as long as possible.

"Now, I want you to go and wash your face with cold water. And then come to the kitchen and I'll make us both a nice cup of tea. You've got a long journey ahead of you and you won't be any good to anyone if you don't keep your strength up."

When Maggie made no effort to move, Mrs. Forester stood up and grasped Maggie's hand, pulling the young woman to her feet. "One foot in front of the other, dear. That's how all journeys start. Go upstairs. Go."

As Maggie, zombie-like, made her way up the stairs, she heard Mrs. Forester mutter to herself, "And *this* is why we didn't want this damned war."

Maggie heard the front door open and footsteps in the hall. "David?" she called, suddenly wary.

"Just me," she heard.

Maggie sprang to her feet. "Chuck!" For those low gruff tones could belong only to Charlotte McCaffrey, known to all as Chuck. She ran to the tall, broad-shouldered woman and gave her a big hug.

"Maggie!" Chuck's strong features were rendered something close to beautiful with her smile. "Wasn't expecting you tonight! But I'm glad to see you." She slipped off her low-heeled oxfords and sank into the sofa, sprawling in her inimitable Chuck-like way. Maggie studied her, for she hadn't seen her since the end of the summer. Same chestnut hair, same thick, dark eyelashes, same sturdy build. It was good to see her.

"Long shift?" Maggie asked. Chuck was a nurse at Great Ormond Street Hospital for Children.

She stretched and yawned. "Endless."

"David and I already ate, but there are leftovers, if you're hungry. Can I warm something up for you?"

"Thanks, but I already ate at the hospital. Though what passes for food there just might get us admitted as patients. So, I know you can't tell me much. . . ." Chuck began.

"Anything, really."

"And that's fine. I just need to know one thing."

"Yes?"

"Can you get away right after the new year? Come to Leeds?" Leeds was Chuck's hometown.

Maggie considered. "I don't know where I'll be yet. . . ." Then she caught the unmistakable look of joy and excitement in her friend's eyes. "What's happening in Leeds?" she asked, her smile growing, for she knew the answer.

"The wedding! Nigel and I finally set a date!"

"That's wonderful, Chuck," Maggie said, taking her friend's hand. "I'm truly, truly happy for you and Nigel.

And you know I'll move heaven and earth to be there."
Maggie tried her best to focus on Chuck and Nigel's
happiness, and not on thoughts of John.

"Oh, am I being terribly rude? You know me—I'm
such a tactless oaf. I didn't even ask you about John."

"Nothing new," Maggie said, fighting back sudden
tears.

"They'll find him." Chuck patted Maggie's hand.

"Of course." Maggie rubbed a fist over her eyes.
"Now, let's talk wedding."

Chuck groaned. "You know I loathe all that girly-girl
frippery. Not that there's any to be had, with the rationing. I thought I'd just make over one of my dresses."

"But there are readings to choose, flowers, saving
sugar rations for wedding cake. . . ."

Chuck looked serious. "Maggie, would you be my
bridesmaid?"

"Of course!" she said, thrilled.

"I want you and Sarah to be there with me, at the
altar. We've already been through so much together. . . ."

"Of course I'll be your bridesmaid, Chuck. I'm honored." *This is when I would have asked Chuck to be* my
*bridesmaid, if only . . .*

"If it's too hard, you know, with John . . . missing . . ."

"Chuck," Maggie said, looking her straight in the
eyes. "I'm so happy for you and Nigel—you two are perfect for each other and deserve your happily ever after.
I'd be delighted to be part of the wedding party."

Pleased, Chuck sat up. "What did you say you and
David made? Now that you mention it, I'm absolutely
*starving.*"

———

It had taken Alistair Tooke several impassioned letters, dozens of pleading phone calls, and a serious threat to let Windsor's gardens go to seed, but finally he was able to obtain a late-evening interview with the King.

He approached King George VI cautiously, hat in hand. He had spoken to the King before, of course. But it was always outside, in the fresh air, and the topic was the health of the Windsors' many varieties of roses or the productivity of the victory gardens. This was different.

The King's study was a large room, with high-vaulted ceilings and tall windows. The monarch himself was at a large carved rosewood desk.

"Yes, Tooke?" the King said, looking up from his paperwork, his face long and careworn, his eyes clear and blue. The walls were upholstered in red watered silk, although the heavy gold frames that had once displayed paintings by artists such as Rembrandt, Rubens, Canaletto, and Gainsborough were empty, the canvases in indefinite storage. But floor-to-ceiling bookcases filled with leather-tooled volumes still graced the walls, alternating with long tapestries. The windows behind him were blinded, covered in impenetrable blackout curtains.

Alistair gave a nervous bow. "Your Majesty," he said, taking a few steps forward on the soft Persian carpet. Suddenly realizing how dirty the thick soles of his shoes were, he stopped.

The King blinked. "Well?"

"It's—it's about my wife, sir. Marta? Marta Tooke? She teaches piano to some of the young 'uns? Well, they came for her." He took a step closer as the words tumbled out of his mouth. "They just came in the middle of the night and took her away. In handcuffs, sir."

The King scratched his head. "Who? Who came in the night?" Then, "Ah, yes, Marta *K-k-k-kunst* Tooke. She's your wife, is she? Something to do with sending letters to Germany?"

Tooke felt a hot wave of rage crash through him. He took a ragged breath and continued. "My wife is innocent, sir," he insisted, hands wringing his hat. "She's a good woman, a fine woman. . . ."

"Of course, of course, Tooke," the King said reassuringly. "We just need to follow p-p-protocol here. The whole thing will be sorted in a few days, and then she'll come back here, safe and sound, none the worse for w-w-w-wear." With a deep sigh, the King surveyed the mountains of paper on his desk, then rose. "Duty calls, I'm afraid, Tooke."

Alistair Tooke suddenly realized something very, very important. "Sir, Lady Lily is German. She's German too. Before the war, she used to come by our flat. She and Marta would drink German coffee and speak German together."

"What?" said the King, distracted, rounding the desk with a manila folder in his hand. "Oh, right, right. Lady Lily." He walked to the door.

Alistair turned to follow and pressed further. "Lady Lily isn't in an internment camp, after all. Sir," he added.

The king had already passed Alistair and had entered the hall. "Lady Lily's p-p-position here is quite relevant," he said.

It had been a long night and a long day, and Alistair Tooke was not his usual self. "A Lady-in-Waiting, sir? *Relevant?*"

"Yes, Tooke," the King snapped. "Lily Howell is a family friend. And she's needed here at the castle. I'm sorry about your w-w-w-wife, but it *will* sort itself out." And then he was on his way, down the oak-paneled corridor.

"Bleeding buggered buggering bastard," Tooke muttered under his breath, standing on the carpet, feeling abandoned and betrayed. "What if someone *you* loved were taken away?" He clenched his fists and deliberately ground his muddy boots into the carpet, leaving black stains.

## Chapter Six

Maggie knew about Windsor Castle.

She knew it dated back to the time of William the Conqueror. She knew it was where King Henry VIII awaited the news of Anne Boleyn's execution, where Queen Elizabeth I celebrated her first Christmas, where Charles I's severed head was laid to rest, where George III went mad, and where the young Queen Victoria and Prince Albert had spent their honeymoon.

And Maggie had seen pictures of Windsor Castle, of course. When she was growing up in Wellesley, Massachusetts, long before she came to London, her Aunt Edith had a biscuit tin with a picture of the castle with the Royal Standard waving proudly from its Great Tower behind official portraits of King George V and his wife, Queen Mary—the current King's parents.

But nothing had prepared her for the reality of the sheer mass and scale of the castle, dark and shadowy in the gathering lavender twilight. It was tremendous. For just a moment, the heavy clouds parted and a beam of sunlight pierced through, illuminating the gray stone crenellated walls, battlements, turrets, parapets, and towers. The mullioned windows lit up with liquid gold.

It was the stuff of fairy tales, if you could overlook the heavy antiaircraft guns on the various roofs, along with Coldstream Guards in their tall bearskin hats on patrol. There was, after all, an evil sorcerer and his minions to guard against.

David went through the security checkpoints and drove Maggie up Windsor's High Street, past the high stone walls of the castle's Lower Ward. She couldn't help but feel somewhat tiny and insignificant. "Just an old pile of rocks, Mags," he said, sensing her apprehension.

"Of course," she said. "And I have a job to do. Two, really."

David took a left at the bronze statue of Queen Victoria and pulled up to the Henry VIII Gate, with its towers, arched windows, and carvings on the portcullis of the fleur-de-lis and the combined roses of Lancaster and York.

Maggie was overcome with the weight of the castle. Not the immense physical weight but its burden of history, violence, and power.

"See those holes?" David said to Maggie.

"Yes," she said.

"Used for pouring boiling oil on unwelcome visitors."

That, finally, got Maggie to smile. "I'll keep it in mind."

David drove past the Henry VIII Gate, through the Lower Ward and parade ground. They passed the changing of the guards, in their long gray coats and white sashes, with drums and fifes. Tires crunching on gravel, they drove past the Round Tower and the Middle Ward, through the Norman Gate. Under the unblinking eyes of stone grotesques and gargoyles, David pulled up the car and stopped at an unassuming double doorway of oak and glass: the tradesmen's and servants' entrance. They were greeted by a tall and slim older man in an elegant black morning coat and starched white collar. He had a beak-like nose, hooded eyes, and bushy silver eyebrows.

"Welcome to Windsor Castle," he said solemnly, as he opened the car door. "You must be Miss Hope. We've been expecting you. I am Ainslie, the Royal Butler." As the Royal Butler, Ainslie oversaw the castle's male staff, which included footmen, underbutlers, pages, coal porters, fender smiths, a clock winder, and the so-called Vermin Man.

"Thank you, Mr. Ainslie," Maggie said, taking his proffered white-gloved hand and getting out of the car.

"Just Ainslie, Miss."

*Oh, right*—Maggie remembered David's lessons on addressing household staff. "Of course, Ainslie," she said.

Ainslie went to the car's trunk and took out her valise and a worn blue-leather hatbox full of photographs and ephemera. "Thank you," she said.

"Yes, Miss."

Maggie turned. "Thanks, David. For the ride, for everything—"

"My pleasure, my dear," he replied, as he slid back into the driver's seat. "Remember, KBO."

That was *not* how the chivalrous Mr. Churchill had

introduced the initials to her when she'd been one of his typists, and he'd admonished her to "Keep plodding on." "David, I'm touched. Have I graduated from 'plodding' to 'buggering'?"

He gave her a puckish look over the rims of his round glasses. "You've earned the right, Maggie."

She spluttered laughter. "*Non illegitimi carborundum* then, David."

"I've told you I was always terrible at Latin."

"It means 'Don't let the bastards wear you down.'"

He grinned at her. "I shan't," he answered. And with a quick toot of the horn, he drove off over the cobblestoned pavement, making his way back to the Long Walk.

As two footmen appeared and picked up her bags, Ainslie blinked. "Miss Hope, please follow me."

They entered the castle through the servants' entrance, passing through the porter's room. Inside, as they walked the endless Gothic corridors, the air was chill, damp, and gloomy, with thick violet shadows. The dim wartime bulbs made the corridor look almost gaslit. Pictures had been removed and ornate gilt frames stood empty, like blind eyes, lining the hall in long perspectives. There were a seemingly infinite number of malachite pedestals minus their marble busts of royals and dignitaries. The high, ornate, gilded ceilings, like fondant on a society wedding cake, were besmirched with water stains.

The paneling was dark, almost black in the dim light. The air smelled of ancient stone, antique furniture, and wood polish—beeswax and turpentine. It smelled of majesty.

Here and there, doors were open and Maggie could peer into some of the rooms. There were holes in the ceiling, tangled wires dangling down like tree roots, where grand crystal chandeliers must have once hung. Cupboards and cabinets were turned to tapestry-covered walls. The high ceilings, high enough to induce vertigo, were adorned with scrolls, flourishes, and gilt. What furniture was left was covered with sheets, to protect it from dust.

As Maggie and Ainslie walked on, their footsteps echoing off the thick walls in the long, icy corridors, Maggie saw a large black spider skitter behind a heavy tattered velvet drape. They passed other rooms with shadowy figures of what had to be servants, ARP Wardens and volunteer firemen, blacking out the mullioned windows, the square panes of glass pierced by the last weak rays of the setting sun. Although no one knew the Princesses were staying at Windsor Castle, it was on the flight path from German air bases to London and was, of course, recognizable from the air.

One older man, missing a few teeth, passed Maggie and Ainslie. He touched a hand to his metal helmet and said, "By the time we get all the blackout curtains closed, Miss, it's morning again." His voice echoed in the vast corridor, his breath visible in the frigid air.

Maggie smiled in return, but Ainslie shot him a stern glance and the man returned to his curtains.

"Their Majesties are at Buckingham Palace at the moment," he said. "But I'll take you to meet their Royal Highnesses in the Lancaster Tower. Then to your rooms, in the Victoria Tower."

———

After a long walk through the cold and dim corridors, it was a relief finally to reach the Princesses' nursery, an oasis of warmth and color and light in the Lancaster Tower. It was decorated in warm shades of rose and fawn, with colorful watercolors and oil paintings that must have been done by the Princesses themselves. The room was filled with toys and books, neatly stacked in bookcases and cupboards, a wooden rocking horse in one corner. The air was warmed by burning birch logs in the massive stone fireplace, guarded by an ornate burnished fender. In front of the fire, on needlepoint pillows, lounged four black-and-sable corgis with snowy white bellies. The sound of the dogs' gentle snoring was punctuated by the snap of the flames in the fireplace.

Two girls, one older, one younger, both with glistening brown curls and gentian blue eyes, sat on the sofa facing the fire. They were dressed alike, in white blouses, navy wool cardigans, and green plaid skirts. Both were knitting.

The older girl gave a sigh. "I do wish socks didn't have heels," she said in a high dulcet voice, struggling with her needles. "Knitting is not my favorite."

"If it doesn't have fur and fart, you don't like it," the younger girl quipped.

"That's not true, I—"

"Oh, yes—bonus points if it eats hay."

Ainslie cleared his throat. "Your Highnesses, this is Miss Margaret Hope. Miss Hope, this is Her Royal Highness the Princess Elizabeth and Her Royal Highness the Princess Margaret."

Maggie bobbed in an awkward curtsy.

"Good evening, Miss Hope," Princess Elizabeth said, looking up from her knitting. "I hope you had a pleasant journey from London."

"Well, hello there!" Margaret said, jumping to her feet, obviously intrigued by the new person. "Who are you?"

Maggie was about to reply, when Elizabeth answered, "She's the new governess, Margaret—to teach me maths. Crawfie told me."

"Do *I* get to learn maths?" Margaret wanted to know.

"No, these are maths for me," Elizabeth told her sister with just a touch of superiority. "I am fourteen, after all. While you are only eight."

Margaret glared and stamped a small foot. "Not *fair,* Lilibet. You always get to do *everything* first!"

"That's because I'm older."

Margaret stuck out her tongue at Lilibet, then turned back to Maggie and gave her a piercing look. "Well, we can't call you Margaret—because that's *my* name. We'll have to call you Hopie. After all, we call Miss Crawford Crawfie and Mrs. Clara Knight is Alah."

*Hopie? Oh, no. No, indeed.* "How about just plain Maggie?" Maggie suggested conspiratorially. "Besides, only my Aunt Edith, who lives far, far away in the United States, calls me Margaret anyway."

Princess Margaret considered. "All right." She circled Maggie, looking her up and down, taking in everything from her rolled hair to her resoled pumps. "Your hair's red, but it's more of an auburn, so that makes it prettier. Not like Sir Humphrey, whose hair is, unfortunately, the color of carrots. Of course, it's fine if *carrots* are carrot-colored—but *not* the tops of people's heads.

I'm glad you're so young and pretty. Are you really from America? You *do* talk funny. Do you know any movie stars? Shirley Temple?"

"Margaret!" Princess Elizabeth admonished. "That's enough now. Don't overwhelm poor Miss Hope."

"You're not Queen yet, Lilibet!" Princess Margaret snapped.

Princess Elizabeth rolled her eyes. Obviously it wasn't the first time she'd heard that. "You don't need to be a queen to be polite."

Ainslie gestured to the woman seated across the room. "Mrs. Knight, this is Miss Hope, the Princess Elizabeth's new maths tutor. Miss Hope, this is Mrs. Knight, the Princesses' nanny, known as Alah." Alah was an older woman with black hair, handsome features, and a no-nonsense expression. "Alah was originally nanny to the Queen."

"How do you do," Maggie said.

"How do you do," Alah responded with a Hertfordshire accent. She went over to young Margaret and smoothed her curls protectively. Margaret looked up at her with an expression of absolute adoration.

*Ah,* Maggie realized, *she's territorial. Of course. It must be difficult to have someone new come in.*

"Alah is responsible for the Princesses' out-of-school life—their health, their baths, their clothes. To help her, she has an undermaid and a nursemaid. You shall meet them later. You'll also meet Crawfie, Miss Marion Crawford, the girls' governess," Ainslie explained. "She's responsible for them from nine until six. You'll discuss Princess Elizabeth's academic schedule with her."

"Of course," Maggie said, raising her chin just the

slightest bit. "I look forward to it." She looked at Alah. Maggie could sense the love that the woman had for her young charges. *There may be a threat at Windsor,* Maggie thought, *but I doubt it comes from Alah. But who knows about the rest of the staff?*

After the perfunctory goodbyes, there was more walking through maze-like icy stone corridors. "I feel there must be a Minotaur lying in wait somewhere," Maggie joked, disconcerted by the silence.

Ainslie did not respond.

Finally, he announced, "The Victoria Tower, Miss." They began to climb a circular staircase. The stone of the steps was worn smooth in the center. A few of them were crumbled at the edges. Ainslie and Maggie climbed. And climbed. And climbed.

Maggie was a bit out of breath when they reached the top. "Here are your rooms," the butler said, opening the heavy wooden door for her. She felt a prickle of girlish excitement. *I'm going to live in a tower in a castle!*

She took a few steps inside; Ainslie followed, turning on a few lamps with silk fringed shades. The sitting room was small, with kelly-green walls dotted with a few oil landscapes and a small chintz-covered sofa and small table pulled in front of a stone fireplace. A fire, set and lit by one of the castle's fender smiths, popped and cracked merrily behind the iron grate, although it didn't seem to be throwing much heat. Maggie shivered.

Ainslie opened a door to the bedroom; the canopied bed was piled high with large pillows encased in white linen with handmade lace, topped by a crimson duvet. "There's a radiator in here, Miss. In case you get cold."

*In case?* Maggie thought but refrained from saying anything.

"The toilet and bath are"—Ainslie paused delicately, indicating a steep and narrow staircase—"on the roof."

"On the roof?" Maggie repeated, dumbstruck.

"Castles weren't originally built with indoor plumbing, Miss Hope."

"It's enclosed?"

"Of *course,*" Ainslie replied, looking shocked.

"Well, how refreshing," Maggie managed.

He pointed to a bell, wired near the main door. "In the event of an air raid, you will be warned by watchers stationed on the Round Tower, and then the Wardens will ring the bell. After dinner, I shall show you the way to the shelter. It's in the dungeon." As he walked to the door, he added, "You'll be expected to join the rest of the staff at eight sharp for dinner in the Octagon Room."

He cleared his throat. "We dress."

It didn't take Maggie long to unpack her suitcase. *Better than the dock in the War Rooms anyway,* she decided, although she wasn't thrilled by the idea of nights in a dungeon. *It must be quite safe from raids, at least. And it can't be any worse than an Anderson shelter.*

She glanced at the tiny gold watch on her wrist. *Seven o'clock. How did it get to be so late? And Ainslie's "We dress." What does it mean, exactly?* She was annoyed yet again that Frain was in such a rush to get her installed that he hadn't found time to get her properly briefed. *"You're a bright girl, you'll manage,"* indeed. Maggie was glad he thought so highly of her, but it didn't help her figure out what to wear for dinner.

She'd brought all she had, but it wasn't that much. Skirts and blouses, mostly. Some sweaters. A few pairs of flannel trousers. Several wool dresses. Oxfords, plimsolls, and fur-lined boots. One sky-blue gown tipped in black velvet. Back in London, she'd had flatmates to borrow from.

But she couldn't think of that now. She pulled out one of her dresses, dark green wool with a lace collar and silver buttons. It would have to do. She brushed and rerolled her hair, dabbed on some lipstick, and changed clothes. When she opened her door to the corridor, she felt a palpable chill. *I'll just wear my coat, then.*

It was only after she descended the tower stairs that she realized she had absolutely no idea where the Octagon Room was.

Maggie walked for what felt like miles through long, dimly lit, icy corridors filled with spidery shadows. Her feet, in her thin-soled pumps, were freezing from the rough, cold stones—all the carpets must have been rolled up and put into storage for safekeeping—and she pulled her coat tighter around her, wishing she had taken her hat and scarf as well.

After twists and turns through the stone passageways, Maggie saw at the end of yet another long, cold hallway what looked to be a spectral figure. It was hard to tell: The few lightbulbs were the wartime-issue ones with low wattage, and all the blackout curtains covered the windows.

She squinted. Surely it was a person. It couldn't be a ghost—*oh no. Highly illogical—as well as quite improbable. Aunt Edith would be appalled at such Gothic flights of fancy.* Despite herself, she began a mental inventory of all the people who might possibly be ghosts—*Henry VIII, of course. And poor Anne Boleyn. Jane Seymour, too. Queen Elizabeth I. Charles I, maybe? King George III . . . Oh, stop it,* she told herself firmly. *This is no way to start your first night.*

"Hello?" she called, her voice echoing down the hallway.

The figure turned and stared at Maggie approaching in the dim light, the taps from her leather soles echoing in the frigid air.

It was a man, she realized. Tall, very thin, wearing an RAF-issued shearling jacket. He was standing, hands clasped behind his back, staring at an empty gilt picture frame. Without looking up, he began speaking. "There used to be a Rembrandt here," he said. "At least, that's what I remember. Damned war's changed everything. . . ."

As Maggie walked closer, he turned. In the dim flickering light, she could see he was young, around her age, with close-cropped golden curls, dressed in brown corduroy trousers and a wool sweater with twisted cables and honeycomb under the shearling jacket. His face appeared handsome. And yet, as Maggie approached and he turned from the shadow of the wall, she could see that one side had been horribly disfigured, transformed by angry red scar tissue and rectangular white skin grafts. His left eyelid had been reconstructed, and some gauze and tape were visible on his neck. As much as she tried not to stare, for a long second she couldn't help it.

His face broke into a crooked smile. "I don't bite, although it may look as though I might. Souvenir from Åndalsnes, I'm afraid."

Maggie nodded. "I'm sorry."

"Don't be."

"I'm a bit lost, actually. . . ."

"It isn't hard to lose your way here."

"I'm Maggie," she said, holding out her hand. "Maggie Hope. I'm going to be teaching Princess Elizabeth maths. How do you do?"

He enveloped her small hand with his scarred one. "Well, hello, Maggie, Maggie Hope. It's a pleasure to meet you. You're cold," he observed.

"I didn't realize it was going to be quite so drafty."

"Samuel Pepys declared Windsor to be 'the most romantique castle that is in the world.'" He shrugged. "Must have visited in the summer."

"I'm trying to find the Octagon Room and I'm lost. I've just arrived, you see. I really feel as though I should have been issued a map, or a guidebook, at least."

"Street signs at the juncture of the corridors?"

Maggie smiled. "Exactly."

"Well, I happen to know the way to said Octagon Room." He offered her his arm. "May I escort you?"

"I'd be delighted." Maggie took the proffered arm. "By the way, you never told me your name."

"Gregory. Gregory Strathcliffe . . . *Le Fantôme*," he added to himself as they walked.

"You're much, much too substantial to be a phantom," Maggie said, squeezing his arm. *Le Fantôme de l'Opéra* was one of her favorite books.

"Then *La bête. La belle et la bête.*"

"I'm only beastly in the morning," Maggie quipped.

He raised one eyebrow. "I can see we're going to get along, Maggie Hope."

———

Endless corridors, staircases, and sudden turns later, they were at the double doors to the Octagon Room, in the Brunswick Tower.

As they stood in the outside doorway, Maggie could hear the meal was already in progress. "What's the worst they can do—cut off my head?"

"Oh, we haven't done that here for, well, at least a few hundred years," Gregory answered gravely.

Maggie grasped the rose-and-dragon brass door-knob and opened the ornately carved wooden door.

It was a dark cavern of a room, with a high vaulted Gothic ceiling and the dim light from tapered candles glinting off the silver table service. Seated around the long, linen-covered table were Ainslie, Alah, and at least twenty other people with pale faces—the men in white ties and black dinner jackets, the ladies in long gowns— in the middle of their soup course. A black marble fire-place roared orange at one end of the room, which was, in fact, octagon-shaped.

One of the men, short and slender, with an Edwardian center part and a bulbous red nose, dabbed his lips with a linen napkin, then rose to his feet. "Miss Hope, I presume?" he boomed in a port-wine voice.

"Yes," she said, taking a step inside. "Sir."

The other staff members paused in their conversations to listen, and a tense silence fell over the room.

"You. Are. Late!" he intoned.

"Well, I'm here now," Maggie said.

"I am Baron Clive Wigram, Governor of the castle. Meaning the Keeper—the Keeper of Time, among other things. We are all, always, on time. We"—he took in

Maggie's simple frock and coat—"*dress* for dinner. Do you understand, young lady?"

It had been a long day. Maggie was cold and hungry. And she wasn't in the mood to deal with a pompous idiot. "I *am* dressed, Lord Clive. And I should think you wouldn't be so quick to point out my supposed fashion faux pas. Wasn't it Queen Victoria herself, here at Windsor Castle, who drank from her fingerbowl, when one of her dinner guests did by mistake? Obviously, *she* understood the difference between good manners and slavish adherence to etiquette."

"Well, Miss Hope, I—I . . ." Lord Clive spluttered. At the table, there was soft whispering. One of the footmen standing near the wall, a tall young man in a powdered wig, gave her a discreet wink. From behind her, Maggie heard a snort, and then Gregory stepped into the room.

Lord Clive colored slightly. "Oh! Lord Gregory!" he said, in a much more cordial tone. "I didn't see you there."

Gregory gave a brilliant smile, which pulled at his scar tissue, causing it to turn white. "If you don't mind, Lord Clive, I think I'll take Miss Hope for a bite in town."

"Why, Lord Gregory," Maggie said, playing along with him, "that sounds just lovely. Since I'm already late. And not *dressed* for dinner."

"Oh," said Lord Clive, "oh, I didn't mean . . ."

"No, of course you didn't," Maggie said. "Thank you so much, Your Lordship. Ladies, gentlemen—*bon appétit*." And with that, Maggie took Gregory's arm and walked out of the room with him.

"My hero!" she exclaimed, after the heavy door

clicked closed. "Although now I'm hungry enough to gnaw on a table leg."

"I'll tell you what," Gregory said. "Let's get some real food and a pint—and then I'll draw up a map of the old pile for you." When he smiled, his scars were less noticeable. "Come on, then."

## Chapter Seven

They walked through the middle and lower wards, out the Henry VIII Gate and down the cobblestone walk to narrow and picturesque Market Street. It was another side of Windsor—as much as the castle belonged to the Royals and their community, the town was full of a different history: Shakespeare's *The Merry Wives of Windsor,* the house where "pretty, witty" Nell Gwyn trysted with King Charles II, Christopher Wren's Guildhall, the Crooked House.

At the Carpenters Arms, Maggie refused to let Gregory take her coat. "I don't think I'll *ever* be warm again," she told him, trying to make herself heard over the cacophony of the crowd, as they walked over the worn red-flowered carpeting through the smoky warmth and past the throng at the long dark wooden bar, where a bartender in a white apron pulled on one of the taps. Next to him was a sign proclaiming *"No Guinness. No Sausages. No problems."*

"It's a good walk from the Upper Ward of the castle, true," Gregory said. "Still, better than dinner with that crew. More snobbish than the Royals themselves, if you ask me." He found them a rickety wooden table near a fireplace outlined with ceramic tile painted with red and pink roses.

Maggie sat down and watched as Gregory removed his overcoat. A young waitress with a blond bun made her way toward them in the dim golden glow from the brass sconces with Victorian etched-glass globes. "What would you like?" she asked over the noise of the crowd and a recording of the Andrews Sisters singing "Begin the Beguine."

Maggie had already glanced at the menu. "Cider, please. And the shepherd's pie."

"Two. But I'll have an ale." The waitress stared in horror at Gregory's face for a moment before composing her features. She gave a nervous smile and walked away.

"You know, Clive's not really so bad," Gregory said, turning back to Maggie. "Distinguished military career, then private secretary to the Sovereign. Retired just a few years ago to Windsor and only recently been named Governor. He tries to run things with military precision—a bit obsessive about time, but I think he quite misses ordering a bunch of sailors about."

"Of course." Maggie was ready to be magnanimous, now that her toes were beginning to warm up. "And what about you? What brings you to Windsor?"

Something closed in Gregory's face. "I'm here as equerry—an assistant of sorts—to the King. Was a pilot before that, if you couldn't tell by the jacket. Got a bit singed early on in Norway. Not just my face, either. Scars go down my left side."

"I'm so sorry," Maggie said. *What if it had been*

*John?* she thought. *What if it is John, burned and somewhere in France or Germany?*

"The equerry position goes to some poor wounded soldier every six months or so," Gregory said, arranging and rearranging the table's salt and pepper shakers, bottle of vinegar, and HP Sauce. "We get to live in the castle, do a few things for His Majesty, heal up a bit. Not a bad situation, by any means." His face darkened, eyes looking to the middle distance, seeing things only in his memory. Then he shook his head, as if to clear his nightmares. "All things considered. I'll have to go back to military duty after the new year. I'm not looking forward to it."

The waitress brought their drinks and pies.

"Oh, heaven," Maggie said, eyeing the steaming plate of vegetables and some kind of meat covered with a browned crust of mashed potatoes.

"Careful, it's hot," Gregory warned, as he took a sip of his beer. "And probably made with actual shepherd."

"At this point, I don't care," she declared, sticking her fork into the mashed-potato crust. "I'm starving."

After she'd eaten a bit, and Gregory had pushed his food around on his plate, he said, "So you're teaching the little Princesses maths, then?"

Of course she couldn't tell him MI-5 had placed her there. "Yes," she said, through a bite.

"Excellent idea! Crawfie's a good Scottish lass, but she's not that well educated, really. Of course, Lilibet's taking a few classes at Eton, my alma mater, but if she's going to be Queen someday . . ."

"Exactly," Maggie agreed, taking a sip of cider. "So, not just pure maths but statistics, economics, even physics, architecture, engineering—"

"And how do *you* know all that?" Gregory asked, surprised. He'd finished his ale and set down the empty glass. "No offense, of course."

"Long story." Maggie laughed. "I majored in mathematics at Wellesley College, back in the States. I was going to go on to do a Ph.D. at M.I.T. when my British grandmother passed. So I came to London in thirty-eight to sell her house, and, well, never left."

"Well, good for you, then," he said. "I studied classics when I was at university—could hardly get past algebra, let alone calculus. How'd you get the position with the Royal Family?"

Maggie had practiced her cover story. "I worked as a typist at Number Ten Downing Street for a while, but I wasn't that fast. Or accurate, if you must know. When word came the King and Queen were looking for a maths tutor, I was recommended. Seemed like a good fit."

"Hmmm. Downing Street, you say? Did you know Churchill?"

*Oh, if he only knew . . .* "Not really." Maggie shrugged. "Just in passing. I was pretty low in the pecking order."

Gregory motioned to the waitress to bring another drink, and she nodded her assent.

Maggie noticed his still-full plate. "Aren't you hungry?"

"I had a late lunch." Then he smiled. "Of course you must have a beau pining for you."

Maggie stopped, fork hovering in midair.

"Oh, I'm sorry," he said. "I just assumed, pretty girl like you . . ." The waitress brought his drink and he took a gulp.

"John Sterling. He's in the Royal Air Force too," Maggie told him. "His plane crashed. He is, as they say, 'missing.' But I refuse to believe he's—" The word *dead* hung in the air between them.

"Then don't," Gregory said, his eyes serious. He was about to say more, when the door to the restaurant opened and there was a loud burst of feminine laughter. "Oh, no," he groaned.

"What?" Maggie said, looking around.

"A gaggle of Ladies-in-Waiting," he whispered. "I hope you brought cotton for your ears."

The gaggle in question was three well-dressed and attractive young women. Without preamble, they descended on Maggie and Gregory, who rose to his feet.

"London was absolutely *mad,*" complained the slender blonde in lilac and black, kissing Gregory on the cheek and taking his seat, while he turned to procure more from another table. She had the profile of a cameo. "Lily," she said to Maggie by way of an introduction, sticking out her hand. "How do you do?"

Maggie shook the extended hand. "Pleasure to meet you."

"Barking mad," amended a ripe raven-haired beauty with glossy scarlet lips and nails.

"That's Louisa," Lily said, pointing.

"Hello, there," said Louisa, already scanning the crowd for the waitress.

"We were bombed out of our hotel," the short, plump one with pink cheeks said. "Claridge's! Bombed! Can you believe? It truly *is* the end of civilization!" Then, to Maggie, "I'm Polly—and you are?" She arched a plucked eyebrow.

"Maggie," she replied. "Maggie Hope. The Princess's new maths tutor."

"A *governess*?" Louisa rolled her eyes.

"Yes," said Maggie.

"I loathed my governesses," she said. "Used to torture them mercilessly."

"What a lovely dress you have on," said Polly. "Glad to see you've taken 'make do and mend' to heart."

*Did she* really *just say that?* Maggie thought. *She did! What a—*

"Play nicely, ladies," Gregory warned. "Claws in."

Maggie realized she was working, and needed to get to know these women. She took a deep breath, then remembered the newspaper article she'd seen at David's apartment. "Claridge's? I heard there was a suicide there over the weekend, a young girl?"

"Ugh," said Lily, pushing back a blond wave, blanching. "There were police officers everywhere. We went to London for some semblance of civility, and what did we find? Air raids, bombing, suicide . . ."

"And not enough clothing rations to buy anything decent." Louisa sighed, looking down at her black cashmere cardigan edged in sable. She looked like the wicked queen from *Snow White* with her white skin, black bobbed hair, and blood-red lipstick. Her eyes were rimmed with kohl.

"So, you're teaching the Princesses?" Polly asked. She affected the same look as Louisa, but her plump face didn't have the same angles and planes, her bob was dyed an unflattering black, and the waxy red lipstick she chose only accentuated the sallow color of her skin.

"Oh, the *Princesses*!" Louisa laughed, leaning over to read the menu and exposing impressive cleavage.

"Strange little creatures, aren't they? For years everyone whispered there was something wrong with Margaret, but it turned out Alah just wouldn't let her out of the pram."

"Lilibet's all right," Lily said. "But all she talks about are dogs and horses. Horses and dogs. All the livelong day—"

"Well, I think Margaret's awfully clever," Polly cut in. "Maybe a bit spoiled, to be sure. But she does liven the place up. Oh, here we are—you!" she snapped to the waitress. "Yes you, girl. I'll have a shandy and the soup," she said to the waitress. "I wish they'd get some decent help in this place—appalling is what it is." As the other two young women ordered, Maggie caught Gregory's eye. He was smiling in a bemused way.

"How do you know Gregory?" Lily asked, leaning back in her chair. She looked tired now, shadows under her eyes.

"We met today," Maggie answered. "I was lost—and he was kind enough to help."

"I'm sure," Louisa said, with a sideways glance at Gregory.

"Oh, when I first got here I was late for everything," Polly said. "Where do they have you?"

"Victoria Tower," Maggie said.

The girls all gave one another quick sideways glances and laughed. It was not a nice laugh.

"What?"

"We're there too," Lily explained. "Fair maidens in a tower."

"Ha!" Louisa snorted.

"You'll need to know how to avoid Mrs. Lewis, the ARP Witch. I mean, ahem, *Warden,*" Polly said.

"And how to sneak in and out without getting caught," Lily added.

Polly gave Maggie a cool look. "You'll have to come by and meet Louisa's snake."

*What?*

"His name is Irving," Louisa told Maggie. "Delightful creature. And I had a rat named Feinstein, but he got away. Lewis still doesn't know about Irving, though."

*Two can play at this game,* Maggie thought. "I love snakes," she said. "And I'd love to meet Irving. He sounds charming." *More charming than his owner, most likely.*

Lily looked over as Maggie took a large spoonful of her shepherd's pie. "Ugh, how can you eat it?"

"It's rather tasty, really," Maggie said.

There were beads of perspiration at Lily's hairline. Then she seemed to gag the slightest bit. "Excuse me, please," she said, rising from her seat.

*Is she ill?* Maggie wondered. When the other girls continued to chatter away with Gregory, she excused herself as well.

In the ladies' loo, Lily was already retching into one of the toilets. Maggie waited until she was done, then wet a towel with cold water and handed it to her when she emerged.

"Thanks," Lily murmured, wiping her face. She went to the sink and stuck her head under the faucet, rinsing her mouth out.

"Are you all right?" Maggie asked, concerned. "Maybe you caught something in London?"

"Oh, I caught something, all right," Lily said. "But it was about three months ago."

For a moment, Maggie didn't understand. "Oh?" Then she did. "*Oh.*"

"The actual reason I was in London," Lily said, looking into the mirror and smoothing back her golden hair. "I was late, so I went to a doctor. He confirmed what I suspected."

Maggie noticed there were no rings on any of Lily's slender fingers.

Lily suddenly turned and met Maggie's eyes. "Don't tell anyone?" the blonde said, suddenly sounding vulnerable. "The other girls—they wouldn't understand."

"Of course not," Maggie promised.

"Thanks ever so much," Lily said breathlessly. Then, taking a deep breath, she opened the door. "After you."

# Chapter Eight

Maggie had gone to sleep with the drone of Messer-schmitts and Heinkels in her ears, on their way to London to drop their deadly cargo—it was no wonder the next morning she woke with a start and clutched the hand-embroidered linen sheets, her heart racing with fear and her body damp with perspiration. She'd been having a nightmare, something about men parachuting from fiery airplanes, Lilibet being taken away in a black van, the Queen weeping in despair, running through endless stone corridors. . . .

Through the door to the bedroom, Maggie could see a young girl with creamy skin and dark eyelashes put down a tray on the table in front of the embers of the dying fire in the sitting room. She was wearing a black dress with a starched white apron, cuffs, and collar. A maid's uniform.

Maggie panicked, heart in her throat, at the appearance of the intruder. *I suppose I could take her,* she thought, *if I had to,* thinking of the moves she'd learned at Camp Spook.

"Good morning, *Mademoiselle*," the young woman said.

"Er, hello," Maggie said, after she caught her breath, heart still thudding in her chest. *Good heavens, Ainslie might have warned me.* She shrugged into the robe she'd left at the foot of the bed the night before and put on slippers, blinking as the girl pulled back the blackout curtains from the lancet windows and let in pearly gray light. "Who are you?"

From her position in bed, Maggie could see, through leaded glass squares, the vast expanse of grayish-brown land that surrounded the castle and the shadows of ancient trees in the distance.

"Don't mind me, *Mademoiselle*. My name is Audrey Moreau," she said in a thick Parisian accent. "But you are supposed to call me Audrey. Ainslie said I should tell you that, because you are American and probably do not know these things."

*Thank you ever so much, Ainslie.* "Audrey's a beautiful name." Maggie wrapped her robe around her, walking to the sitting room, and perching on the sofa. "And I'm British, despite my accent." She'd never been woken up with a tea tray, and took a bite of toast as her tea steeped. "Thank you very much, Audrey. Have you been at Windsor for long?"

"About eight months ago, *Mademoiselle*. I was able to get out of Paris before France fell, *Merci Dieu!* I'm cousin to Cook's husband—that's how I was able to secure this position."

"*Merci Dieu*, indeed," Maggie said.

"Because of rationing, one egg—a real one, not the powdered sort—will be served to each castle resident only on Sundays," Audrey told her. "By order of the

King. He, and the Queen, and the Princesses, all adhere
to the same rules."

"Really," Maggie said, thinking of the vast quantities
of rationed food Mr. Churchill would put away on a
daily, let alone weekly, basis. Still, no one on his staff
begrudged him his extra meat and eggs and cream.

"Chance of rain today, *Mademoiselle*," Audrey
warned as she finished the last of the curtains. "Oh, and
before I forget, Miss Crawford would like to see you in
the Princesses' nursery at nine. It's Saturday, I know, but
she insisted."

Maggie's eyes went to the small clock on the mantel.
"That's in half an hour! Oh, dear!"

Audrey left. As she dressed, Maggie turned on the
wireless for the news. The BBC was issuing reports
about Coventry, which had been demolished. "*The German Luftwaffe has bombed Coventry in a massive raid
which lasted more than ten hours and left much of the
city devastated.*

"*Relays of enemy aircraft dropped bombs indiscrim-
inately. One of the many buildings hit included the
fourteenth-century cathedral, which was all but destroyed. Initial reports suggest the number of casualties
is about one thousand. Intensive antiaircraft fire kept
the raiders at a great height, from which accurate bombing was impossible.*

"*According to one report, some five hundred enemy
aircraft took part in the raid. Wave upon wave of bombers scattered their lethal payloads over the city. The
night sky, already lit by a brilliant moon, was further
illuminated by flares and incendiary bombs.*

"*The German High Command has issued a communiqué describing the attack on Coventry as a reprisal for*

*the British attack on Munich—the birthplace of the*
*Nazi party. The German Official News Agency de-*
*scribed the raid on Coventry as 'the most severe in the*
*whole history of the war.'*

*"Home Secretary Herbert Morrison was on the*
*scene within hours of the all-clear. He met the mayor*
*and other local officials and afterward paid tribute to*
*the work of the National Service units of the city, who*
*had 'stood up to their duty magnificently.' "*

*Horrible,* Maggie thought. *Horrible, terrible, awful,*
*tragic . . . And yet, we're supposed to keep buggering on.*

On time but out of breath, Maggie made it back to the
nursery—thanks to the maps Gregory had drawn out
for her and with glances out windows to orient herself.

Miss Crawford was already there on the long
damask-covered sofa. She was a young woman with a
largish nose, thin lips, and dark-brown hair set in neat
rolls. "Please sit down, Miss Hope," she said with a
Scottish lilt, indicating a pink brocade chair. She did not
look pleased.

"Did you hear about Coventry, Miss Crawford?"
Maggie asked, still struggling to breathe from the long
walk and trying to come to terms with the magnitude of
the attack.

"Yes, Miss Hope," Miss Crawford replied. "However, I've made it my policy that the war stops outside
the nursery door. I'd appreciate it if you'd adhere to it.
And please call me Crawfie—everyone does."

"Of course."

Maggie looked down at the schedule on the table.

| Monday | Tuesday | Wednesday | Thursday | Friday | Saturday |
|--------|---------|-----------|----------|--------|----------|
| 9.30 Bible | Arithmetic | Arithmetic | Arithmetic | Arithmetic | 9.30–11.00 Riding |
| 10.00 History | History | Geography | History | History | |
| 10.30 Grammar | Grammar | Literature | Poetry | Writing and Composition | |
| 11.00–12.00 Break for elevenses and games in the Garden. | | | | | 11.00–12.20 Revew of week's work |
| 12.00–1.00 One half-hour silent reading and one half-hour reading aloud. | | | | | |
| 1.15 Dancing Class or educational visit with Queen Mary | Singing | Drawing More walks and out to tea | Music | Riding | 1.15 Lunch in garden with King and Queen |

"The Princesses are riding right now?" Maggie asked, feeling a sudden stab of fear over their safety. "Who's with them?"

"The Princesses have been riding for years, Miss Hope. They are quite accomplished horsewomen."

"Of course," Maggie said, but she wondered if this was perhaps a lapse in judgment.

"They're usually accompanied by one or more of the Queen's Ladies-in-Waiting," Crawfie added. "And there are Coldstream Guards patrolling, of course."

*All right, then.*

"And you should know the Princess Elizabeth takes

her history lessons privately with the Headmaster of Eton," Crawfie added.

"Yes," Maggie replied, trying to tread delicately. "I've heard Eton is close to Windsor Castle."

"You know," Crawfie said in a burst of rapid-fire words, eyes flashing, "you might think I'm just a simple, uneducated Scottish girl, but I am quite qualified to teach the Princesses, let me assure you. I was going to get my degree in child psychology, you realize. But then, you see, the King and Queen wanted someone young to be here for the children. Someone to go on long walks and have lots of energy. So . . ."

"Of course. Child psychology, really? How fascinating—you must tell me all about it. Jean Piaget and *The Moral Judgment of the Child*, yes?"

"Honestly, I don't even know why the Princess Elizabeth needs additional work in maths." She sniffed. "It's not as though she'll ever have to do her own household books."

*Well, I'm not* really *here to teach maths,* Maggie thought impatiently. *But, still—why shouldn't all women, let alone one who might be the future Queen, learn maths?*

"But, Crawfie—maths *are* important. The study of mathematics develops the imagination. It trains the mind to think clearly and logically. Elegantly, even. It challenges our thinking. It forces us to make the complex simple. The Queen-to-be will most certainly need to understand economics, statistics, all the maths related to the military. Yes, and perhaps she doesn't have to do her own household books—but she might very well want to keep an eye on them."

Maggie stopped to breathe. She'd forgotten how passionately she believed in the importance of mathematics, and how she'd missed it. "In short, it's *exactly* what the future Queen of Britain needs to study."

"Well," Crawfie managed. "I never thought of it quite like that."

They heard footsteps and voices from the hall. Princess Margaret cried, "Lilibet, Lilibet—wait for me!"

The Princess Elizabeth burst through the door. "Crawfie! The most horrible thing's happened! Lady Lily's *dead*!"

Crawfie blanched. She looked over at Maggie, then back to the Princesses, still in their riding habits and tall boots. "Girls, this is no time for games," she said sternly.

"No, Crawfie, no!" Lilibet's words tumbled out. "We were out riding and I said I wanted to gallop. I went ahead, and then, and then . . ."

Crawfie held out her hands to the girl, who was visibly shaken. "Come, now," she said in gentle tones, wrapping her in her arms.

Since Crawfie was occupied, Margaret went to Maggie. "I was with Michael, the groom. On my pony. I didn't see anything." She sounded just the slightest bit disappointed. Still, Maggie took one chubby, sticky hand in hers and pulled Margaret in, to give her a hug. Margaret wrapped her arms around Maggie and let herself be hugged, then climbed next to her, putting her arms around her and snuggling close. Maggie could smell her—a combination of fresh air and sweet apples.

"She'd fallen off her horse," Lilibet continued in her clear bell-like tones. "And she was very, very still. And so I dismounted, to see what was wrong with her. And then I realized—" She struggled to continue.

"Yes?" Maggie said softly.

"She—" Tears filled the Princess's deep blue eyes. "She was missing her head."

As Crawfie called for Alah and the two women bustled about with cool cloths and tea trays for the Princesses, Maggie excused herself.

Taking another look at the maps in her pocket, she went back to Victoria Tower for her coat and hat, then left the castle, its high walls encrusted with moss and lichen, and wrapped in gauzy spiderwebs.

She made her way in the damp chill toward the castle's stables. And she wasn't the only one. There were Coldstream Guards patrolling outside, while inside the main stable, the King and Queen were being briefed by Lord Clive. Maggie was used to seeing official photographs of King George VI and, of course, photographs of both him and his wife, Queen Elizabeth, in the newspapers, but it was another thing to see them in person. She was surprised by how much smaller they seemed than she imagined, the King with fair slicked-back hair and a tweed suit, the Queen with her old-fashioned bangs, periwinkle-blue wool coat, and a jeweled brooch in the shape of a corgi.

Maggie slipped inside the wooden stable door and listened.

"Apparently, Lady Lily had taken the lead and was riding ahead of the Princess Elizabeth," Lord Clive was saying. "The path goes through a wooded area. The police officers have told us they found a piano wire, strung up across the bridle path, affixed to two large trees. I'm sorry to say, your Majesties, that Lady Lily was beheaded—by this wire."

"There, now, dear," the King said to the Queen.

"Would Your Majesty like to sit down?" Lord Clive asked.

"No, thank you, your Lordship," the Queen replied resolutely. "I'm fine. Please continue."

"Well, ma'am, I'm afraid that's all we know for sure. The police are at the scene now. Of course they'll do an autopsy."

"Yes," the Queen said, her gentle face grave. "We must call Lily's parents immediately."

"Are you sure, dear?" the King said.

"Of course," she replied, raising her chin and squaring her slight shoulders. "I'll do it right away. And please send the detective in charge to see me when he's finished, Lord Clive." The King and Queen turned and left to return to the castle.

Maggie turned to leave and stepped on a creaky board.

"Miss Hope," Lord Clive said, catching sight of her, his eyes narrowing with suspicion. "What are *you* doing here?"

"I—I heard the commotion and thought I'd see what was going on," Maggie answered.

"Nothing that concerns you," Lord Clive said as he approached her. "Although it is curious—you're here only one night and already someone is dead."

"It's terrible, sir. I met Lady Lily last night. She seems—seemed—like a lovely girl."

Lord Clive was not won over. "I'm keeping an eye on you, Miss Hope."

"Of course, Your Lordship."

*And I'll be keeping an eye on you too.*

At the crime scene, the corpse was already wrapped and two men were transferring it to a battered Black Maria. A stocky older man in a camel-hair overcoat and gray felt hat with a notebook seemed to be finishing up as Maggie made her way over to him.

"Hello," he said in neutral tones, his breath cloudy in the cold air. His eyes were bright and penetrating, his jowls heavy, his mustache streaked with gray. "My name's Detective Wilson." Detective Chief Superintendent Wilson of the Windsor police department had served his country in World War I, and then rose through the ranks of the police force to his current position. A widower, with a son serving in the Royal Navy, Wilson originally tried to become involved with the war effort but had ultimately decided that staying on in Windsor wasn't necessarily a bad idea. For the war had certainly not brought any respite from transgressions. If anything, the stresses of war had intensified the number and viciousness of local crimes.

"Maggie Hope, sir. Pleased to meet you—although under horrible circumstances."

"Yes," he said, his eyes going to the body, which had been safely stowed in the vehicle. The car spluttered as it warmed up, then the engine turned over.

"Did you know"—he consulted his notes—"Lily Howell? You look about her age."

"I met her yesterday, sir. I understand she was one of the Queen's Ladies-in-Waiting."

"Yesterday?" the detective queried.

"I arrived yesterday from London," Maggie told him. "Last night I had dinner at the Carpenters Arms with Gregory Strathcliffe. While we were there, Lily and two other Ladies-in-Waiting—Louisa and Polly—joined us. We all walked back to the castle together."

"Really?" Detective Wilson said, scribbling on his notepad. "About what time was that?"

"It was around midnight. I remember because I was worried about oversleeping without an alarm clock."

"And what do you do at the Castle, Miss Hope?"

"I'm tutoring the Princess Elizabeth in mathematics."

"I see. And when was the last time you saw Lily Howell?"

"We're all—that is, we were all—staying in Victoria Tower." Maggie looked back at the hulking structure, where age-blackened chimneys emitted thin threads of smoke into the cold air. "She and the other girls have rooms on the lower floors. I'm up on the top, so I said good night to the three of them just after midnight, then continued upstairs." She rubbed her gloved hands together, to warm them. Overhead, a peregrine falcon with a black head and a black-and-white tufted breast glided by, then dipped down and settled on a nearby tree, folding his large wings. His laughing cries were borne away by the cold wind.

"Did anything . . . happen . . . that you recall?"

"No, sir. It was a pleasant evening." *No need to mention the morning sickness. At least, not until I've run it past Frain.*

Detective Wilson tipped his hat. "Thank you, Miss Hope," he said as he walked back to the road and to his waiting car. He opened the door and got into the driver's seat. "I'll be in touch." He started the engine.

"Yes, sir," Maggie said. She held up one hand as he drove off toward the castle.

Anything related to the crime had been removed. Still, as Maggie walked to a group of bare trees by the side of the path, she could see where the wire had been attached to the tree and rubbed through the bark. *Oh, Lily . . .*

*Well, the facts are these,* she thought, taming her racing mind with logic. *Lily Howell is dead. She was decapitated by a wire tied to two trees, stretched over a bridle path. But was she the intended victim?* Maggie remembered Crawfie's schedule of the Princesses' activities. Both girls were supposed to be riding today.

The falcon looked down at Maggie with keen black eyes. He made a high-pitched *"key-key-key-key!"* cry, which floated up into the cold air and hung there. Then he flew off.

*Frain said the Germans were planning on kidnapping Princess Elizabeth, not assassinating her. But he could be wrong. Had someone intended to kill the Princess? Had Lily Howell just been in the wrong place at the wrong time?*

# Chapter Nine

As Maggie approached the castle, her ears were assaulted by the barking of a pack of corgis. Back at No. 10, she'd liked having Mr. and Mrs. Churchill's pets around, even if some of the other staff members complained. But compared to the corgis, Rufus and Nelson and the rest of the Churchill menagerie were downright civilized.

These dogs, with their big pointed ears, large, sleek bodies, and tiny legs, swarmed around her, yapping, jumping, and pulling at the hem of her coat. With all the teeth and fur and noise, Maggie didn't even see Princess Elizabeth walking behind them.

"Dookie!" the Princess called, her sweet childish voice ringing out. "*Dookie!* And the rest of you! Leave poor Maggie alone!"

Poor Maggie had a sudden urge to turn and run, but instead knelt down, putting out a hand for the dogs to sniff. "There, now," she said in gentle tones. "It's all right. See? I'm perfectly friendly."

Without warning, one of the corgis bit her hand, teeth sinking into the tender flesh.

"Ow!" Maggie cried. "Ow, ow, ow!" she said, shaking her hand, wishing she could say so much more.

"Dookie!" the Princess admonished. "Bad dog! Very bad dog!"

She ran over to Maggie, with the grave air of one who was used to looking after canine injuries. "Let me see."

Maggie gingerly took off her glove and stuck out her hand. The dog's fangs had torn through the leather and lining but hadn't broken the skin. Still, her hand bore the imprint of red, angry tooth marks.

"Oh, it's not so bad, really," the Princess said, inspecting it.

Maggie gritted her teeth. *Easy for you to say.*

"You should have seen Lord Livingston!" the Princess said. "Dookie bit him and there was just blood everywhere. They can't help it," she continued earnestly. "None of them can. It's how they're bred. They're hunters, after all. It's just their nature to bite."

"Really," Maggie managed. "And his name is Dookie?"

"His full and formal name is really Rozavel Golden Eagle. But yes, he's called Dookie, because he was supposed to go to my father, who was the Duke of York at the time. That's what the breeders called him when he was born, and the name just stuck."

"I see," Maggie said through tight lips.

"You aren't going to tell Crawfie, are you? Or Alah? Or Mummy and Daddy?"

Maggie saw an opening to win the girl's trust. "No,

I won't. I promise. You're right—Dookie's only doing what's in his nature."

"Oh, thank you." The Princess brightened. "I can fetch you an ice bag, if you'd like."

"That's all right. But I wouldn't mind an escort back to Victoria Tower. The castle's rather confusing." She smiled. "I might have to start dropping bread crumbs. Although then I'd probably be fined by the ARP Warden."

"You would," the Princess said. "But I must *insist* that first I take you to the kitchen, so Cook can give you some ice for your hand."

Maggie smiled at the young girl's motherly tones, especially after the morning she'd already been through. *Score one for the British stiff upper lip,* she thought. "Of course, Your Highness. Thank you." Then, "By the way, should you be wandering around by yourself, especially after what happened to Lady Lily?"

Lilibet had the grace to blush. "I am in the habit of sneaking out a lot," she confided. "It gets so dull inside, with all the knitting."

"I know, but you probably should be with someone." Maggie made a mental note to talk to Alah about it.

"Yes, Maggie." As they strolled, Maggie looked at the Princess in profile. She was fourteen, but she seemed younger. Her neck looked so slim and vulnerable. How close had she come to dying today?

"I met with Crawfie this morning," Maggie began. "She showed me your schedule. You and your sister are very busy girls."

"Oh, and you don't know the half of it. They make us knit too. For the soldiers, of course. I'm terrible at it, especially socks. Can't turn a heel. I pity the men who get my socks, they're all so lumpy and bumpy."

"Usually you ride on Saturday mornings, yes?"

"Oh, yes, every Saturday. I love to ride. Margaret's still a little scared, but I love to gallop."

"But you ride with someone else? One of the Ladies-in-Waiting?"

"Oh, you mean because of what happened to Lady Lily?" The Princess's face clouded. "It's terrible, isn't it?" For a moment, she looked to be on the verge of tears, then shook her head and squared her shoulders. Maggie could see the queen she would someday be.

"Yes, I'm so sorry," Maggie said.

"Lily and I often rode together. She wanted to compete in the Olympics, except they won't let women ride yet. Her specialty was dressage, but she just loved to gallop. . . ." The Princess's throat closed and her voice became husky.

"There's to be a memorial service Saturday. At Saint George's Chapel. You *will* come, won't you?" the Princess said earnestly, tears filling her clear blue eyes. "Lady Lily was so very lovely."

Maggie looked up at the castle's many windows, glinting like blind eyes in the reflected sun. Who might be behind one of those windows, perhaps wishing harm to a sweet little girl? Or a Lady-in-Waiting? *I'm going to find out,* Maggie vowed. *And I'll do everything I can to keep this girl safe.*

She smiled and reached down to take the Princess's small, soft hand. "Of course. Of course I'll be there."

———

The warm, cavernous kitchen had high clerestory windows that vaulted like a culinary cathedral. Hanging burnished copper pots of all shapes and sizes lined the walls. The floor of black and white tiles was covered in coconut matting, and the air was filled with sounds of knives chopping through heavy root vegetables and the toasty malt aroma of baking bread. A small army of staff in white hats and aprons was coming and going with trays laden with china and silver.

Cook, a tall, thin woman with gray-streaked blond hair tucked under her starched white cap, hands rough and scarred from years of kitchen work, bobbed a curtsy at the Princess. She took one look at Maggie's hand and procured an ice pack. "You've fared better than some, Miss," she said, shaking her head—for Maggie's was not the first corgi bite she'd witnessed in her fifteen years at the castle. Maggie and Lilibet sat down at an enormous scarred wooden table.

"It's true," Lilibet said. "Some people bleed so much, we have to fetch a doctor to stitch them up."

*Fantastic,* Maggie thought. *It's not bad enough the Germans are bombing us nightly, Ladies-in-Waiting are being beheaded, and the Royal Family is in danger— I need to fend off rabid corgis too?*

The wireless was on, broadcasting BBC news. "Have you heard about Coventry, Miss?" Cook asked.

"Yes, I'm afraid so," Maggie admitted. "It's terrible."

"Germans hit it last night but good. They're sayin' there were more than a thousand dead. Terrible damage to the factories there."

The Princess's face was somber. "It's horrible, Cook."

"It is, Your Highness."

"I'm going to write to the families of every single person who died," Lilibet said.

"That's a lot of letters," Maggie said.

"I know," Lilibet retorted. "But what good is it being a Princess, if I can't help people? I can't make it better, but I can let them know their loss hasn't gone unnoticed or unmarked."

Maggie was impressed by the young girl's compassion and understanding of her position.

Cook's hard face turned tender as she looked at the Princess. "Maybe you'd both be wantin' a cup of tea, then?"

Maggie had learned during her tenure in England just how restorative tea could be. "Thank you." She glanced down at the slender Princess. "I think we both could use one."

"And maybe a bit of Brown Windsor Soup too? Miss Hope, it's the favorite of His Majesty."

Lilibet made a surreptitious gagging face. Apparently, Brown Windsor Soup was not the Princess's favorite dish.

"Cook, I'd be honored," said Maggie.

"Don't eat the soup," Lilibet whispered, when Cook's back was turned.

"I think I must now," Maggie whispered back.

"Well," the Princess said, looking like a regular fourteen-year-old girl again, "don't say I didn't warn you."

Detective Wilson and his deputy were using the servants' dining room to question the castle's staff about the murder. About fifty people or so were lined up in the corridor, each waiting his or her turn. "And who are you, Miss?" Wilson's assistant said to Maggie as she walked by, on her way to Victoria Tower.

From the table inside the room, Detective Wilson looked up from his conversation with Audrey Moreau. "It's all right, Jim," he said. "That's Maggie Hope, Princess Elizabeth's maths tutor. I've already spoken with her."

From the other end of the long corridor, Maggie heard loud yelling, incongruous in the castle, and turned to see who it was. "That's Sam Berners, Miss Hope," said the man waiting in line for his turn to be questioned. He was trim, with silvery gold receding hair, a pink scalp, and a kind smile. "By the way, I am Sir Owen Morshead, the castle's librarian. I must compliment you on the way you handled Sir Clive last night."

"Oh," said Maggie. "Yes, well—"

"If you ever find yourself in need of anything for the Princess from the library, please do let me know."

"Thank you, Sir Owen, that's very kind of you."

The loud voice became even louder and was now spouting profanity. "Get yer hands off me—I tell ya I ain't seen nothin'!"

"Master of the Mews," Sir Owen said. Then, off Maggie's confused look, "The Royal Falconer. He keeps to himself, mostly. Bit of an eccentric."

Maggie saw a large bearded man with rough, unkempt hair being dragged into the hallway by two Coldstream Guards. His clothes were covered in bird excrement, and his right arm and hand were encased in a protective leather gauntlet. "I don' know nothin'!" he was protesting loudly in a thick Scottish accent. "I din' see anythin'!"

"Everyone must talk to the Detective, Sam," one of the footmen waiting to be questioned said. "Even you." Maggie recognized him as the one who'd winked at her, her first night at the castle.

"Don' have nothin' to say," Berners grumbled, taking his place in line, under the watchful eye of the Coldstream Guards.

"He's positively medieval," Sir Owen whispered to Maggie. "Probably a quarter raptor himself. But he's part of the castle, as much as the Long Walk or the stones of the Great Tower."

"Where are the birds kept?" Maggie asked, curious.

"Oh, there's some sort of structure up on the roof," Sir Owen answered. "Sam has a room in the castle, but he prefers to sleep with the birds—as if you couldn't tell. He and the largest falcon, Merlin, are inseparable."

Maggie shook her head. *A decapitated Lady-in-Waiting, rabid corgis, and a man who lives with birds?* "I thought living in a castle would be interesting, Sir Owen," she said, "but nothing—absolutely nothing— prepared me for this."


It wasn't difficult to find Lady Lily's room. The police had left the door ajar.

With another look to make sure she was alone, Maggie let herself in. Lady Lily's sitting room was much like her own. However, since Lily had been at Windsor Castle longer, she'd amassed more possessions. Down powder puffs, half-empty bottles of nail varnish, and tubes of Elizabeth Arden lipstick covered the dressing table. A half-empty bottle of Tabu. A crystal vase of dying red roses, black now, thorny stems decaying in greenish water.

Maggie started in the bathroom. In the medicine chest she found aspirin, antacid, tooth powder, and a worn-down toothbrush. Odor-o-no, a boar-bristle hairbrush, and tweezers. A tin of bluebell-scented powder. Some still-damp lace brassieres and silk panties hung over a line strung across the tub, along with garter belts and several pairs of stockings.

She removed the top of the toilet tank and looked inside. Nothing. She went through the small clothes hamper. Nothing. And nothing on top of the medicine cabinet, either.

In the bedroom, she lifted the mattress as best she could and looked underneath. Nothing. Nothing relevant in the drawers of the bureau or the nightstand, either. *Of course,* she thought, *Detective Wilson and his men have probably already been over everything already.*

The closet was crammed with clothes for every occasion, including garment bags stuffed with gowns of nearly every hue imaginable and a number of furs. A search of her many satin shoes turned up nothing either.

Maggie went back into the sitting room. She stopped by the bookcase, which was empty. She squinted at it. The dust indicated books had been there for a time and had recently been removed. *Now, that's odd,* she thought. *Why would someone take Lily's books?*

She mused for a moment, then realized she'd already met the very person who might be able to help her.


"Hello, Sir Owen!" Maggie said as she entered the King's Library, a suite of rooms on the north side of the Upper Ward, adjacent to the State Apartments. Sir

Owen, who'd returned from the questioning, was sitting at a carved mahogany desk in the first room, which had on it a few silver-framed photographs and a low vase of yellow roses.

It was a beautiful chamber, with high molded ceilings, intricately inlaid floors made from precious woods, and two stories' worth of gold-tooled leather books. There was a long wooden table in the center of the room, polished to a mirror-like sheen, and tufted burgundy leather chairs. *What a wonderful place to study,* Maggie decided. *Too bad my days of scholarship are on hold, at least for now.*

Sir Owen looked up from a volume in front of him, the thin skin around his eyes crinkling when he smiled. "Miss Hope, how lovely to see you again—this time in the library. Is there, perhaps, a mathematical tome you need to find? For the Princess's course of study?" He rose from the desk chair. "Most of the castle's collection is in storage, I'm afraid, for safekeeping. I'm quite proud to say we have a small but quite important group of illuminated manuscripts, including the *Sobieski Book of Hours.* There's also a fine group of incunabula dating from the period before fifteen hundred, including the *Mainz Psalter,* the second book ever to be printed with movable metal type. But of course they're not accessible now."

*Oh, I would love to have the opportunity to see those books. If only.* "Actually, Sir Owen, I was interested in finding out if you had any knowledge of what happened to Lady Lily's books. They're missing from her bookshelf."

Sir Owen gave her a quizzical look.

"Louisa and Polly wanted them," she improvised quickly. "To remember her by."

"Yes, of course," he said, forehead furrowing. "Well, the kind of books Lady Lily read, romances and such, aren't really the sort we shelve here. However," he said confidentially, "the Housekeeper, Mrs. Beesley, is a great aficionado of love stories, mysteries, and the like—and she has a lending bookcase in her parlor for the staff to use. Perhaps they've found their way to her?"

"Oh, thank you, Sir Owen," Maggie said. "Thank you very much."

After another trip through icy winding corridors, Maggie found herself at the door of the housekeeper's parlor. She rapped at the door. "Come in!" called a high-pitched, thready voice.

Maggie opened the door and there was Mrs. Beesley, sitting at a plain wooden desk in a small, narrow room. She was younger than Maggie had expected, with brown hair in rolls, narrow shoulders, thin lips, and a serious expression in her eyes. "Yes? May I help you?" she said.

"Hello, I'm Maggie Hope, the Princess's maths tutor," she began. "You must be Mrs. Beesley."

"Yes, please come in," Mrs. Beesley said.

*In for a penny, in for a pound,* Maggie thought, stepping inside. "Well, I was talking to Louisa and Polly," she began. "The Ladies-in-Waiting."

"Oh, it's hard to hear those names without thinking of our poor Lady Lily."

"Yes," Maggie said. "And that's what brings me here, actually. You see, Louisa and Polly wanted a few of

Lily's books, to remember her by. There were some in her room apparently, and now they're gone—"

Mrs. Beesley's eyes narrowed. "Now, if you're accusing me—or my staff—of pinching those books . . ." Her fingers worked at the handkerchief's hem.

"No, no, of course not," Maggie assured her. "No one's accusing anyone of anything. I was just hoping to find out where they'd been taken, is all. No offense meant."

"None taken," Mrs. Beesley said stiffly, hands still now.

"Sir Owen said you're a great reader," Maggie said, "and that you have a sort of lending library? Is it possible the books might have gotten in there?"

"It's possible, I suppose," Mrs. Beesley said. "The bookcase Sir Owen's referring to is in the hallway. You're welcome to take a look. Or borrow a book, if you're so inclined, of course."

"Thank you, Mrs. Beesley."

The bookcase was a tall one, filled with penny dreadfuls and dime novels in lurid colors, along with a few romances, Gothic horror stories, and a few copies of the King James Bible. Sure enough, there was a wooden crate next to the case, filled with romance novels. Maggie bent over to rummage through them, taking out a few books, flipping the pages. Nothing. She went through book after book with Lily's personal bookplates, trying to be charitable about the girl's choices in novels. Pulp romance mostly, terrible stuff, but here and there was a novel Maggie recognized. But in terms of clues, there was nothing. No letters, no notes, no scribbles in the margins.

*Well, what were you expecting, exactly?* Maggie thought. *The name of the baby's father in calligraphy? The murderer's identity written on a bookplate?* She pulled out Gaston Leroux's *Le Fantôme de l'Opéra* and flipped through it. Nothing.

She sighed. It was the only decent book in the bunch. She looked upward, saying, "Would you mind terribly, Lily?"

The corridor didn't answer; neither did any ghosts. "Thank you." And she tucked the book under her arm as she walked away.

Back in her room, Maggie kicked off her shoes and curled up on the sofa in front of the radiator with *Le Fantôme de l'Opéra*. As she opened it to the first page, she noticed the endpaper on the book's inside cover didn't lie smoothly.

*What on earth—*

Heart beating faster now, Maggie ran her fingers over the paper. There was definitely something in there.

With a hatpin from the stand on her dresser, she made a neat slit in the endpaper, then pulled out a folded piece of paper. Maggie read it. She read it again. A third time, for good measure.

She sat perfectly still, overcome with shock. It was a decrypt of a German cipher: "U-boat commander Hempelmann, in grid square 4498, had sunk one tanker. . . ."

*Oh, Lily, Lily, Lily,* Maggie thought. *Where did you*

*get this? Who gave it to you?* And then, with the shock of realization, *And what were you going to do with it?*

She checked the date: It was a recent decrypt, dated November 17, 1940. The Friday the Ladies-in-Waiting had all gone to London for the weekend.

The day the woman at Claridge's had been murdered.

*Oh, Lily—what were you involved with?*

*And what happened to you, as a result?*

# Chapter Ten

The memorial service for Lady Lily Georgina Howell at Windsor Castle's St. George's Chapel was well attended by somber-looking castle residents, all dressed in black from head to toe. In the pews, Maggie saw recognizable faces mixed with the unfamiliar. Alah and Crawfie. Sir Owen, Lord Clive, and Mrs. Beesley, and Mr. Berners, who'd cleaned up fairly well. Ainslie, Audrey, and the winking footman. Louisa and Polly, who caught her eye and then began whispering behind their hands. Maggie was sure they were saying nothing good. There was Gregory, across the aisle from the two girls; he gave her a quick nod.

Maggie turned back to observe the architecture. St. George's showed the same concern for bombing that the rest of the castle did. The stained-glass windows and quatrefoils were taped and boarded, and much of the statuary had been removed for safekeeping. However, nothing could diminish the beauty of the vertical lines of the Late Gothic soaring stone arches and the fan-vaulted ceiling, built in the English Perpendicular style, or the black-and-white chessboard marble floors in the Quire. The icy air inside the chapel's thick stone walls smelled of piety and pomp.

As the priest's voice rang out as he began his homily, Maggie first thought of her flatmate, who'd died during the summer—twice. And then of John. *Will we ever be able to find a body? Have enough closure for a memorial service?* Then she shook her head. *No, he's alive. Alive. I'm sure of it.* She stood in prayer with the other congregants.

As the choristers in their ruby robes and white collars sang the last bars of Vivaldi's "Cum Sancto Spiritu," the great organ thundered out the magnificent closing notes and the final *Amen* echoed against the vaulted ceiling. The congregation rose as the Royal Family left their pew and began to walk down the aisle. Then the rest of the people began to follow, row by row. Outside, large and low gray clouds darkened the hazy white sky. The chapel's bells chimed relentlessly as the stern wind caused overcoats and dresses to billow.

"Wonderful music, the Vivaldi *Gloria*." Gregory fell into step beside her, wearing a raincoat and a Trinity College scarf. His limp was more pronounced than it had been the previous night, and one hand held his hat against the wind. " 'Cum Sancto Spiritu' is joyful and yet somehow defiant, with that wonderful section of syncopation. I think Lily would have approved. I'd like it played at my own funeral, someday." He laughed, a small and bitter laugh. "Someday, a very, very long time from now." Maggie noticed his pallor and how much the scars pulled on his face.

"Were you very close to Lily?" she asked as they walked together on one of the gravel paths of the Lower

Ward, heading to the Henry VIII Gate. Overhead, geese flew by with their long necks outstretched, honking mournfully.

"We grew up together," he replied. "Although I went off to Eton and then to Cambridge. We met up again here, at the castle."

"It must have been nice to see a familiar face."

"It was." They walked in silence for a while, as Maggie debated what she could ask without tipping her hand.

"I'm afraid I need to get back to the Equerry's office, even on a Saturday," Gregory said, finally, lifting his hat. "A somber morning, to be sure. But better for having seen you."

Maggie smiled. Further questions could wait. "I agree. And I have a most pressing errand in town." She displayed her corgi-bitten glove. "In this cold, it would be foolish not to pick up another pair. I only hope I have enough clothing rations."

Arms crossed over her chest in the face of the frigid wind, Maggie walked out the Henry VIII Gate and down the cobblestone drive. She passed the blackened, bronzed statue of Queen Victoria, plump and proud with her orb and scepter, and turned onto High Street. It was early Sunday afternoon, and she and Hugh Thompson were supposed to meet at Boswell's Books around three. *Very well*, Maggie thought. *Might as well pick up a new pair of gloves while I'm at it.*

The town of Windsor in daylight was charming, with narrow stone streets and bright, tidy shop fronts. The architecture was quirky and whimsical, with buildings nestled close to one another, sporting an assortment of small ivy-covered turrets, Corinthian columns, cupolas, high round windows, sloped slate-tiled roofs, and windowboxes of fading flowers. Unlike London, it was still unscathed by bombing. Maggie heard the occasional car engine and the clip-clop of horses' hooves on cobblestones in the distance. The air was fresh and sweet compared to London's, but when the wind blew a certain way, there was the unmistakable smell of horse dung.

Maggie bought, with her allotted rations, a new pair of leather gloves at W. J. Daniel, then picked up a copy of *The Times* at a newsstand and went into a narrow café for a cup of fragrant tea. After finishing a number of articles on the bombing of Coventry, she looked at her small watch and realized it was nearly three. She braced herself against the cold and went back onto Peascod Street, then saw a bookshop. BOSWELL'S BOOKS, the sign read. As she opened the door, a tiny silver bell jingled.

Inside, it was warm and cozy. Books lined the walls from floor to ceiling, and there were tall sliding wooden ladders for reaching the top shelves. The shop was long and went on, with a long aisle down the center, bisected by rows and rows of bookshelves. A worn blue Persian rug lay on the floor and, in a patch of weak sunlight, a fat ginger cat groomed himself.

Maggie smiled at the bent older man with tiny silver spectacles behind the register. The retired MI-5 agent? Archibald Higgins? "Boswell, I presume?" she asked, gesturing to the cat.

"The one and only," he replied. "Cheeky devil. May I help you find anything, Miss?"

"No, thank you," Maggie answered. "Just browsing."

"As you wish," he said. "Back room's nice and quiet if you want to catch up on your reading."

"Thank you." Maggie walked from the front of the store to the back room, perusing titles, looking for any sign of Hugh. In the stacks, she found a section of mathematics books and journals, including Princeton University's *Annals of Mathematics*. Maggie pushed aside a wave of bitterness. Once upon a time, she'd wanted, more than anything, to do her postgraduate work at Princeton—with people like James Christopherander, Albert Einstein, Luther Eisenhart, John von Neumann, and Alonzo Church. Not to mention Alan Turing, who'd been at Princeton but returned to England in '38 when war was declared. However, they didn't admit women. And M.I.T. wasn't exactly second tier.

Maggie pulled out a copy of Turing's *Systems of Logic Based on Ordinals*, found the back room, settled into a worn leather armchair, and began to read. Eventually, she became aware of a figure in the aisle behind her.

Maggie looked up. It was Hugh, dressed in a heavy wool overcoat, Anthony Eden hat in hand. He looked down at her book. "Turing!" He whistled through his teeth. "A little light reading?"

Maggie smiled. "I find computability theory fascinating."

Hugh leaned against the bookcase. "So, how goes it?" he asked in low tones. "Are you, er, I mean, is everything—that is—all right?"

"It's been . . . interesting," she answered. "You heard about what happened?"

"Yes." He nodded. "We also know you were one of the last people to see the victim alive."

"I met Lily at the Carpenters Arms. She was just coming back from her weekend in London, at Claridge's. There was a possible suicide there, over the same weekend."

Hugh looked at her, startled. "How the . . . ?" Then, "Yes, there was a suicide at Claridge's that weekend."

"Well," Maggie pressed, "don't you think it's significant? What if it *wasn't* a suicide? What if the woman saw something? Or knew something? And what if Lily's death wasn't a suicide? There could be a connection."

"Well, see what you can find out. Start with the victim's friends. Become friends with them. Find out what they have to say."

"Can we find out what the autopsy report says?"

"Of course. I'll let you know as soon as we receive it."

"There's something else," Maggie said.

"Yes?"

"You'll find out from the autopsy report, but you should know now. Lily was pregnant."

Hugh scratched his head and stared. "How the devil do you know *that*?"

"She told me. After she threw up in the ladies' loo."

"Right, then."

"She said she was about three months along. I didn't mention it when I was questioned by Detective Wilson. But I would like to tell him."

"Of course."

"And," Maggie said, reaching into her pocket, "I found this." She pulled out the decrypt she'd found in Lady Lily's room.

Hugh took the paper and looked it over. His eyes widened. "Wizard!" he exclaimed. "But how did she get this?"

"I don't know how she got it, but it was hidden in her copy of *Le Fantôme de l'Opéra*."

"Thanks for this, Maggie," he said, tucking the decrypt safely into his suit pocket.

"I thought at first Lily's death was an accident and that Lilibet, er, the Princess, was the intended victim," Maggie said. "But now . . . I don't think so."

Hugh looked at her. "You may be right."

"But if Lily was murdered, who's a suspect? Someone who knew she'd stolen a decrypt? Or someone who knew she was pregnant? The baby's father, maybe someone married and/or high-ranking who wouldn't want to be named as the father? And what, if anything, is the connection between Lily's stay at Claridge's and the supposed suicide?"

He sighed. "I don't know. But we need to find out." He ran both hands through his disordered hair. "There's a murderer at Windsor Castle and you're making progress finding him."

"Or her," Maggie said, thinking of Louisa and Polly.

"Or her. Or them, for that matter. Which means you need to be even more careful. And there's still the matter of the Princess's safety, as well."

"I haven't forgotten," Maggie said. "I'm always careful. And I'm not frightened."

"You should be." Hugh reached into his pocket and procured a piece of paper and a pen. He scribbled a number on the paper. "My direct line. Memorize it, then get rid of it," he said, hazel eyes serious. "If you ever find you need anything . . . ?"

Maggie took it, unexpectedly touched.

After a few moments, she heard the shop's bell jingle, indicating Hugh had left.


Back at MI-5, Hugh went directly to Frain's office. "I thought you'd sent Miss Hope on a bit of a wild-goose chase, sir, I really did. But already she's found out more than the police have."

Frain didn't look up from his papers. "Really? And what did she find out?"

"She knew Lily Howell was in London, at the same hotel and at the same time that woman committed suicide—if that's indeed what happened. She knows it might indeed be a murder. She knows Lily Howell was three months pregnant. And," Hugh pulled out the piece of paper Maggie had given him, "she gave us this—" Hugh handed over the cryptograph.

Frain read it, eyes inscrutable. "Thank you," he allowed. "That will be all."

"Yes, sir."


Hugh left Frain's floor, walking down to the small subterranean office he shared with Mark Standish.

"I'm going to the funeral," he announced to Mark, as he got his coat and hat. Mark was looking at photographs of potential IRA mailbox bombers with a loupe magnifier, without much luck.

"I'll meet you there," Mark said, without looking away from the photographs. The service was for a fellow MI-5 officer, Andrew Wells, who'd died in the line of duty, killed by a Nazi spy's stiletto in St. James's Park after Wells recognized her. MI-5 covered up the murder, saying it was an accident. The spy was still at large in London.

Mark gestured to the photograph on Hugh's desk. "Are you meeting up later with Caroline?"

"Of course," Hugh snapped as he shrugged into his overcoat.

"I'm just checking, old thing. Just checking."

The funeral was being held at St. Martin-in-the-Fields. Hugh climbed the stone steps and pulled open the imposing doors. The interior was cavernous and dim in the fading daylight, lit by brass chandeliers and large beeswax candles in tall sconces. Somber music poured from the organ as Hugh walked down the aisle, his footsteps heavy on the marble tiles. He made his way to a hard wooden pew in the front of the church and took a seat, a world away from the bustle of Trafalgar Square outside.

As he sat, people began to file in, taking their seats or exchanging greetings. It was a small service; they all sat near the altar. A small boy and his mother slipped into the pew in front of him. The boy, who was about six or so, with soft golden curls, began to fidget. He was dressed in black, as was his mother, who was dabbing at her eyes with a cambric handkerchief.

Everyone stood as the pallbearers brought in the large black casket, with the Union Jack draped over it and a wreath of crimson poppies. Andrew Wells's casket.

They all sat down again as the silver-haired priest began his homily. "We brought nothing into this world, and it is certain we can carry nothing out. The Lord gave, and the Lord hath taken away—blessed be the name of the Lord."

The boy began to kick the leg of his pew, his worn oxfords making a loud banging that reverberated through the church.

"Shhh, love—don't do that," she said, placing her hand on the boy's leg.

The boy twisted in his seat and stared back at Hugh. "That's my daddy, you know," he said, pointing at the coffin.

Hugh looked up at the coffin, then back at the little boy. "Then you must be Ian Wells," Hugh whispered back. "I knew your father. He was a hero."

Without warning, the boy was out of his seat and lunging at Hugh, burying his face in his shoulder and wrapping his thin arms around his neck, hugging him tightly, and sobbing.

Hugh held him; the boy's hair smelled warm and sweet. "My father died in the line of duty, too," he whispered, patting the boy's back. He could feel sharp shoulder blades through the boy's jacket. "It was a long time ago. I was about your age, actually."

The boy looked up at Hugh with wide hazel eyes, damp plump hands still on his shoulders. "Do you still miss him?"

"Every day," Hugh answered. "It gets better—it does—but it never quite goes away."

In the Amtsgruppe Ausland offices of Abwehr in Berlin, junior agents Torsten Ritter and Franz Krause were sitting in black leather chairs in a large empty conference room, radio on the long table in front of them, waiting. Outside, the sky was cerulean, with just a few high feathery cirrus clouds. Krause was tapping his fingers nervously.

"Do you *really* need to do that?" Ritter asked.

Krause stopped. "Sorry."

"By the way, my mother said to tell your mother hello," Ritter said.

Krause grimaced. "I try not to talk to my mother."

"Well, I'll tell mine that she says hello back. It'll make her happy."

They stopped speaking when the radio began to emit a series of short beeps. It was a radio message from their British contact, code-named Wōdanaz. The contact in Windsor tapped out code, slow and deliberate—his "fist," or typing style, as individual as a fingerprint. Ritter scribbled it down, then, as per protocol, asked the operator to repeat the message. He checked it against what he'd written, then acknowledged the contact and signed off.

Ritter consulted the Morse code book to decipher the message.

"It says they smuggled out the decrypt from Bletchley," Ritter read as he translated.

"Excellent!" Krause said. "We just secured our retirement—gold, girls, an endless supply of beer . . ."

"Wait. I'm not done." He clicked his tongue against his teeth. "This isn't good. Frijjō is dead. And the decrypt is missing."

*"Scheisse!"* Krause pounded his table with his fist. "Fucking Becker's going to have our heads."

"Becker?" Ritter said. "He doesn't even believe the

British can break Enigma. This will just confirm what he already suspects."

Krause laughed, a bitter laugh. "You *should* be scared of him. Don't let his affection for little Wolfie charm you."

"I'll tell you who I *am* scared of."

"Yeah, who's that?"

"Commandant Hess."

Krause's smirk faded, as the name, and its significance, reverberated. "We're not working on that operation, though."

"Still, Operation Edelweiss had better go off without a hitch—because I've heard about what happens when Commandant Hess gets angry. Makes Becker look like a pussycat."

## Chapter Eleven

At the castle, Maggie was getting dressed for dinner. Although she would rather have stayed in her rooms to read the Turing, which she'd purchased at the bookshop, she resigned herself to getting through the meal.

She pulled out the gown she'd brought, held it up and looked at it. It was an angelic blue chiffon, with black satin edging and black roses on one shoulder. The last time she'd worn it, she'd been with John. He'd asked her to marry him, and she, angry that he'd joined the RAF, had turned him down. Looking at the dress, Maggie thought bitterly, *I was a fool. And I still am.* She closed her eyes, and her shoulders sagged. *And I hope to God I'll get a chance to make it up to him.* She put it on, along with fur-lined boots and her coat.

Maggie, already suspicious of the two other girls in Victoria Tower, went to find them. She had no personal interest in befriending them, but they were Lily's best friends and could possibly have some information, and so . . .

She went down a flight of stairs and knocked at the

door. There was no answer. She knocked again. "What?" she heard as the door cracked open. It was Polly.

"What do you want?" the girl snapped.

"Why hello, Polly," Maggie replied, masking her annoyance. "Is this your door? I thought we could all walk to dinner together."

"It's Louisa's, actually," Polly said, cigarette in hand, opening the door a little wider. Inside, Maggie could see rooms similar to hers. Louisa, though, had done some decorating. Maroon scarves covered her lamps, making a reddish glow. Her walls were papered with prints of Italian Futurist painters popular with Fascists: Giacomo Balla, Umberto Boccioni, and a few others Maggie didn't recognize. The air was thick with smoke from pungent clove cigarettes, and Lale Andersen's "Lili Marleen" was playing on the phonograph.

Louisa was in the bathroom, applying her eyeliner. "Who's there?" she called.

"Hello, Louisa, it's Maggie."

"Who?"

"Maggie Hope. We met at the Carpenters Arms with Gregory." A pause. "And Lily."

Louisa emerged from the bathroom in a long red dress with a black jet lavaliere, the kind of necklace Victorians would have worn in mourning. "Ah," she said. "The governess. Shouldn't you be walking with Crawfie?"

"And how lovely to see you tonight, too," Maggie said.

Polly grimaced apologetically. "She probably came to see your snake."

Louisa smiled, a cold smile. "Would you like to meet Irving?" she said.

"Uh, of course," Maggie replied.

Louisa walked over to her dresser, where there was a covered glass container. She reached inside. "He's a ball python," she said, picking up a long, muscular snake. Maggie figured he was about four feet long and about five inches around, black and covered with silvery chartreuse blotches. "Here!" she said, tossing him at Maggie.

Instinctively, Maggie held out her hands and caught the snake. He was cold but dry, not at all slimy, and began to curl around her arms. Maggie saw his black shiny eyes and his forked tongue heading toward her neck.

"They like heat," Louisa said.

Maggie stood perfectly still, unwilling to flinch. "Hello, Irving," she said in a steady voice. "It's a pleasure to meet you." As he tried to wrap himself around her, she extricated herself, handling him carefully. "I think he likes me."

Polly and Louisa looked almost disappointed at Maggie's dégagé reaction.

Maggie deposited Irving back into his container and replaced the lid. She went to Louisa's loo and washed her hands, calling cheerfully through the door, "Shall we go to dinner now?"


They made it to the Octagon Room just in time.

"Miss Hope, you'll be seated here." Lord Clive gestured to an empty chair to the right, in the middle of the long table covered in starched white linens. Maggie noted, with satisfaction, that his tone was much warmer now. Louisa and Polly were seated at the other end of the table. She noticed the friendly footman and gave him a smile, which he returned before arranging his face back into the neutral mask of a royal servant.

"Thank you, Lord Clive," Maggie replied. She went to take her seat.

Dinner was made in the castle's kitchen out of wartime rations supplemented with winter vegetables from the considerable Victory Gardens. According to the menu, handwritten in French, tonight's repast was mock goose—layers of potatoes and apples baked with cheese—with pickled onions, and beetroot pudding for dessert. Maggie sat between Sir Owen, the King's librarian, and Mr. Alistair Tooke, the Head Royal Gardener. From across the table, Gregory raised his wineglass and gave her a grin.

Maggie took a bite of mock goose, then turned to her white-haired dining companion. "Delicious, don't you think?"

He looked past her, not meeting her eyes, as though he didn't understand her words. "Quite," he said finally, in a quiet voice.

"I'm Maggie Hope, by the way. Princess Elizabeth's new maths tutor?"

"Tooke" was the response. His eyes seemed unfocused.

"Are you feeling all right, Mr. Tooke?"

He seemed not to hear her.

Sir Owen, seated on Maggie's other side, turned to her. "Your accent tells me you're an American," he observed as the next course was being served.

"British, actually," Maggie answered, "but I was raised in the United States, near Boston."

"Do you have any idea of when the Yanks are going to join us in this endeavor?"

"Soon, I hope."

"Well, they *are* taking their time about it, aren't they?"

During the time Maggie had been in England, she'd heard quite a bit on the subject. "Indeed," she said tartly.

"Well, you know the Yanks," said another older man across the table with a monocle and handlebar mustache. "Late to every war."

Maggie bit her lip, retorting with choice words—in her head.

Later, as the dinner dishes were taken away, Lord Clive rose. "Ladies and gentlemen," he said, his voice carrying throughout the expansive space. "We have, as a community, suffered a terrible loss this last weekend. I was pleased to see so many of you at Lady Lily's memorial service. Please be assured we will be doing everything we can to cooperate with the authorities and bring the person responsible to justice."

There was a collective murmur. Sir Owen called out, "Hear, hear!"

Maggie looked at Louisa and Polly, seated on either side of Gregory, who shot each other a look before turning their attention back to Lord Clive.

"However," the Lord continued, "life does go on. And I'm pleased to inform you that the Prime Minister, his wife, and select members of his staff will be joining us to sleep and dine for Christmas. They will enjoy three days and nights of Windsor Castle's hospitality."

There was another low murmur from the table, a more excited one this time.

Lord Clive cleared his throat again. "Of course, we

wish to show the Prime Minister and his staff exactly how gracious our hospitality at the castle is. I'm calling on all of you to put your best foot forward." He looked around the table. "That is all."

Sir Owen rose and helped pull out Maggie's chair. "Miss Hope, we've been told *you* come to us from the Prime Minister's office."

"Yes, Sir Owen," she said, as they waited to file out.

"You worked for Churchill, did you?"

"Yes, sir."

Louisa called over, "Is he as pickled as people say?"

"Excuse me?" Maggie said.

"Sorry, I'll speak 'American,'" Louisa said. "I mean *drunk*. Is Churchill a drunk? That's what *we* hear, at any rate."

"No," Maggie said, getting angry. *How dare she?* "I've never seen him drink to excess. In fact, one of his favorite quotes is, 'I have taken more out of alcohol than alcohol has taken out of me.'"

Louisa gave a cat-like smirk. "I, for one, wanted to see Lord Halifax as Prime Minister."

"Then you must enjoy goose-stepping. Lord Halifax would have surrendered by now," Maggie snapped, color rising in her face. "Where Churchill never will." She saw Gregory bite his lip to stop himself from laughing.

"Miss Hope! Lady Louisa!" Lord Clive admonished. "May I remind you that not only are we at Windsor Castle, but the Nazis are the enemies? Enough!"

The company was excused. Mr. Tooke left without saying a word to anyone, eyes downcast. "You mustn't mind Lady Louisa," Sir Owen told Maggie as they walked out together into the chilly corridor. "She's very . . . colorful."

"I see," Maggie said.

"And you mustn't mind Mr. Tooke either. Hasn't been himself lately."

"Oh, I'm sorry to hear that. Has he been ill?"

"His wife passed recently."

"Oh, I'm sorry."

"She was German, you see. Lived here for years, though. She was only recently sent to some sort of— camp. Apparently, the strain was too much for her. She died of a heart attack. Poor bloke just found out this past week."

"That's terrible." Maggie was aware of the camps, of course. The Prime Minister had given the go-ahead for their creation. He might be the Prime Minister, and he might be a great man, but it didn't mean Maggie agreed with everything he did.

"Poor thing's in shock." Sir Owen shook his head, then turned to go. "Lovely to see you again, Miss Hope. Cheers."

"Cheers," she replied, her mind full of internment camps.

Gregory was at her side. "Well, you definitely spiced up dinner!" Then he turned serious. "It was a rather stressful meal—considering what happened over the weekend."

*One regular dining companion missing.* "Of course," Maggie said.

"Lady Lily was a particularly sparkling presence at meals. She'll be missed for a long time to come."

"I only met her the once, but she was charming. Was she . . . engaged?"

Gregory frowned. "Not that I know of, at least. Why do you ask?"

Maggie wasn't about to tell him she knew Lily had been pregnant.

"Just wondering. She was so beautiful, after all."

"Plenty of beaux, of course. Popular girl."

They walked together down the long corridor in silence. "You knew her when she was younger?" Maggie prompted.

"Yes, she lived near us, near Chesterfield in Derbyshire."

Maggie smiled. "It must have been nice to grow up with a playmate."

"It was," he said with a wan smile. "Although I didn't meet her until she was five. She was born in Germany."

"Oh, really?" Maggie said, her head spinning, thinking about the decrypt.

"If you don't mind, I must return to the Equerry's office." He gave a small bow. "Good night, Maggie."

"Good night," she said, resuming her walk down the drafty corridor.

*Could it be that Lily was a spy? A Nazi spy?* she thought.

*But if Lily was a Nazi spy, then who killed her?*
*And why?*

Admiralty Arch was not only a large office building, it was, in fact, an archway, providing road and pedestrian access between The Mall and Trafalgar Square. Nearly undetectable to those who didn't know it was there, carved in marble, was a nose. Just a nose, not a face—embedded in one of the archways. Legend was that it was Lord Nelson's nose, and soldiers passing through on horseback would rub it for good luck.

Just like so many military men before him, Admiral Donald Kirk looked up at the nose and said a short silent prayer to Lord Nelson. Kirk was a trim, smart-looking man with silvery hair and piercing green eyes, wearing a dark blue naval uniform. He leaned heavily on a silver-handled walking stick—a crushed knee in the last war had left him with a stiff, almost mechanical limp. The injury kept him from serving at sea in the current war—which he hated. However, his wife and four daughters, now married and mothers themselves, were grateful he was able to serve his country while staying in London. Sometimes, when they were all together at home and the women were carrying on, he wished for a submarine to command once again.

At the doorway a Royal Marine saluted. Kirk switched the walking stick to his other hand to return the salute, then switched back and proceeded inside. Slowly, for the stairs weren't easy to navigate for anyone, let alone someone with a damaged leg, he made his way down narrow staircases until he reached the windowless Submarine Tracking Room.

Many Londoners were wrapping up work and going home for the evening, but the Submarine Tracking Room buzzed with excitement around the clock. The gray-painted walls were covered with maps studded with different colored pushpins, charts, and photographs of German submarine commanders. Several men in uniform repositioned the colored pins, according to information they received. The centerpiece of the room was a large table, covered with a map of Britain and the Atlantic Ocean and North Sea. Colored pushpins repre-

sented every freighter, warship, and submarine in the
waters, both British and German.

A few officers were repositioning some of those pins,
to reflect the day's movement. Kirk limped over to take a
closer look.

"That U-boat there." He pointed to a red pin just off
the Lincolnshire coast. "What's it been doing?"

The man, young, with a five-o'clock shadow,
shrugged. "It's been there for a while—not doing much
of anything, sir."

Donald Kirk hadn't reached the position he had by
being the strongest or the fastest. His injuries early in
the last war had seen to that. No, what he was known
for was a rigorous intellect, coupled with the ability to
think like the enemy. He squinted at the map on the
table. Something was not right. The submarine's move-
ments had been puzzling him for days. It seemed to be
on a purposeless patrol of the North Sea. The sub hadn't
surfaced, it hadn't attacked, it hadn't seen action of any
kind.

"U-two-forty-six," Kirk said, reaching out to run his
index finger over the tip of the metal pin. It was cold and
hard. "What *are* you doing there?"

# Chapter Twelve

Maggie had another nightmare.

This time, she was out walking the grounds hand in hand with Lilibet, the sky a greenish gray that threatened thunderstorms. A large falcon flew overhead, almost a pterodactyl, huge, with skeletal wings. He swooped down and grabbed the Princess by the back of her coat.

Maggie felt the girl's small hand ripped from hers and began crying as the bird flew higher and higher, taking her away to what Maggie knew was a horrible fate.

Her own screaming woke her up. It was still dark. She was trembling, drenched in cold sweat, heart thumping, limbs cramping. She lay there for a few minutes, gasping for breath, blinking away the images of the dream.

Finally, her heart slowed and she was able to see the shadows in her room for what they were—just shadows, and not terrible birds of prey with sharp talons and beaks. She rubbed her eyes, hard, pinpoints of light breaking through. *Pull yourself together, Hope.*

———

She was able to go back to sleep, but woke up tired and disoriented. At least it was her day off. After completing her daily morning exercise regime, learned at Camp Spook—push-ups, sit-ups, leg lifts, and jumping jacks—preparing her lesson plans for the Princess, and lunch, Maggie put on her wool coat and hat and went to the police station.

It was raining, a cold, damp drizzle that showed no sign of letting up, and a stiff wind blew her large black umbrella inside out, showing its inner spine like a skeleton for a brief moment before she was able to right it. Finally, she reached the red-brick station. "I'd like to speak with Detective Wilson, please," she said to the older sandy-haired man in uniform behind the wooden counter as she began to feel the warmth from the coal heater in the corner. "It's in regard to the Lily Howell case."

"Just a moment, Miss."

Maggie looked around the station. There were the usual posters in primary colors: *National Service Needs You, ARP Auxiliary Firemen Needed,* and *Dig for Victory!*

Detective Wilson appeared. "Ah, hello, there. It's Miss, ah, Hope, isn't it?"

"It is, Detective Wilson."

"Miss Hope, please follow me."

In Detective Wilson's tidy office, Maggie took a seat in front of his desk, noting he had no personal photos there, just a wilting aspidistra. "I've remembered something that Lady Lily mentioned," she began.

"Yes?"

"She was . . . with child." Maggie would have liked to have used the proper medical term—*pregnant*—but it was considered impolite.

Detective Wilson looked up and smiled. "We know."

"How . . . ?"

"Autopsy."

*I'm an idiot—obviously they would know.* "Of course."

"How did you know?"

"She told me, the night I met her."

"She would have had to. Someone only three months along wouldn't be showing. Any idea who the father might be?"

"No, I'm afraid not," Maggie said. "I've asked around—apparently, she was a 'popular girl.' "

"I had an interesting telephone call—from a Mr. Frain. You know him?"

"Yes," Maggie said. *Frain's made contact, of course.* She tried to see where the conversation was heading.

"He mentioned the complications in the case and that MI-Five had a . . . particular interest. And we should help *you* as much as possible." He cleared his throat. "And we, the local police, request the same from you."

"Of course, sir," Maggie said. She realized some toes had been stepped on in establishing the jurisdiction of MI-5 and the local police. "We're all on the same side, after all."


Maggie walked to Windsor and Eton Central Station, to get the train to Slough. It was raining harder, nearly sleeting—but it was Thursday, the day she was supposed to meet her father for dinner. She waited under the eaves of the arched glass roof in the cold for the train.

At Slough, Maggie walked until she found Bell's Tavern. She was early, so she had some tea.

She waited.

The clock ticked on, until the heavy black hands reached six, Maggie and her father's agreed-on meeting time.

She waited. *Of course he might be late. Doesn't mean he forgot our dinner, just that something came up.*

Then she ordered and ate some squash-apple soup and bread and margarine.

She waited. The clock's hands went to seven.

Then a cider. The clock's hands reached eight.

Finally, close to nine, the waitress came over. "Will that be all, love?"

Maggie looked up at the clock, which now read 8:10. "Yes. I'm done." She pulled out her purse to get her wallet to pay the bill, tears threatening to flood her eyes. "I'm really, truly, absolutely done."

On the way to the Slough train station in the dark, Maggie saw three men stagger out of one of the pubs. They walked toward her, pushing one another and laughing, until they blocked her way.

"And what do we have here?" The tall one sniggered.

Maggie clamped her pocketbook under her arm and tried to walk around them.

"Not so fast, love," the one with a beard said. "Fancy a drink?"

"No, thank you," Maggie replied. They circled around her. "Let me pass!"

"Wot? Need to go home to your boyfriend?" the short one said. "I could be your boyfriend. Give us a kiss," he slurred as he staggered toward her.

Maggie looked around. The main street of Slough was deserted. "I said no."

The tall one got up right in front of her, much too close, his breath foul and smelling of gin. "Why don't you pick one of us, love?" He reached out to stroke her cheek. "Or we'll pick for you."

Maggie kneed him between the legs, hearing him howl and his friends laugh, then sidestepped and ran, as fast as she could, to the train station. "Bitch!" they called after her.

Trembling, Maggie called Hugh at his office from a public pay phone on the train platform. "Of course I can meet you," he said.

An hour later, Maggie stepped off the train and exited the Windsor station, taking High Street to Peascod Street. The blackout curtains were drawn at Boswell's Books, but when Maggie rapped at the door, Mr. Higgins answered. "What you're looking for is in the back, Miss."

Maggie went through the stacks to the back room, used for bookkeeping and storage. Hugh was there, sitting at a small round table. He stood up. "Hello." Then, "You look a bit pale. Is everything all right?"

Maggie didn't look at him.

He sat back down.

She took off her coat and her sweater, then rolled up her shirtsleeves.

"Get up," she said.

"Beg pardon?"

"Get up."

He did.

"Help me move the table and the chairs out of the way."

Together, in silence, they cleared the room.

"Are you all right?" Hugh said finally.

"At Camp Spook, my downfall was the physical," she said, ignoring his question. "So, every morning and night, I've been doing exercises. Sit-ups, push-ups, jumping jacks, jackknives . . . you name it. I've started running too, before dawn, so no one can see. I've been practicing shooting with clay pigeons. But one thing I can't do is practice any martial-arts skills."

She walked to the center of the room. "That's what I need you for."

"What?" Hugh was confused.

"Come on, you've had the same training I had, probably more and better."

"Maggie . . ." He looked positively horrified. "I— I can't."

"Afraid a girl's going to beat you up?" Maggie walked up to him and began poking him. They were not gentle pokes.

"Ouch!" Hugh said.

"Come on, you deskbound fop!"

He saw the desperation in her eyes. "All right," he said. "It's been a while for you." He took off his jacket. "Let's go back to the basics."

Maggie took a wide-legged stance and glared.

Hugh loosened his tie. "Your aim is to get your opponent off-balance. Once off-balance, you can use his weight to throw him down." He gestured to Maggie. "Pretend you're just walking along the street."

She walked past him. He reached out to grab her. She threw her arm across him and flipped him to the ground.

"Ouch," Hugh said. He moved his appendages to see if anything was broken.

Maggie paced back and forth in front of him. "Get up."

He did. "Now pretend I'm coming at you again." He came behind her in a choke hold and she bent over and, with a grunt, flipped him over. He hit the floor again with a loud bang.

"Ooof," he said, blinking against the pain.

Archibald Higgins knocked at the door. "Everything all right in there?"

"Just fine, Mr. Higgins," Maggie replied, breathing hard. "Never better."

"All right, then." The door clicked closed.

"Again," Maggie demanded.

Hugh rose to his feet. He rolled up his shirtsleeves. He came at her from the front, going for her neck. She grabbed his arm and twisted it, causing him to bend over and groan in pain.

She let go.

He came at her again, this time trying to kick her. She grabbed his leg and rotated; he fell onto his stomach.

He got up, breathing hard, sweat breaking out on his temples, and came at her again, both hands reaching out to choke her. They wrestled together for what felt like an eternity, before Maggie managed to fall deliberately under him, bringing him down with her. Their lips were almost touching.

Then, with a foot to his midsection, she managed to kick-flip him over.

They both lay on the ground, trying to catch their breath.

Finally, Maggie got up and stood over Hugh. "Are you all right?" she said, extending a hand. He took it and allowed her to help him up.

"I'll live," he said. "You?"

Maggie's eyes were hot and red. She sniffled. "I'm fine."

Hugh led her over to the table. They both sat down on it.

"You're obviously not," he said. "And I don't think it's anything physical."

There was a long silence, then, "I went to Slough today. I was supposed to have dinner with my father. And he forgot. I waited for hours!" She sniffled again. Hugh handed her a handkerchief, which she took and wiped her eyes with. "And then some, some *men* hassled me."

Hugh looked concerned. "Are you all right?"

"Fine," Maggie said. "I made a run for it. And, on top of everything, Lily's *dead*. It could just as easily have been Lilibet! But—my father—and I haven't even seen him since I bumped into him, by accident, at the office. . . . He never even asked me about John! And then—and then, I was stood up by my own father." She blew her nose, making a loud and unladylike snuffling sound.

"Maggie . . ." Hugh made a few awkward pats to her shoulder. "Maggie, listen to me. You have a job to do. You can't let your relationship—or nonrelationship—with your father affect you. You can't let a bunch of buffoons affect you. You can't let what happened to John affect you. And you can't let your fear, and your anger, and your sorrow—" Hugh broke off suddenly.

"I know." Maggie reached out and took Hugh's hand. It was large and warm. "Thank you. I'm all right now."

After a few moments, she let go of his hand. "I have some official business," he said.

Maggie swiped at her eyes again. "Of course."

"We want you to get the King's file on Lily Howell."

"If MI-Five wanted Lily Howell's file, surely Frain could just ask the King for it. Unless you think . . ." Maggie considered. "The King? You think the *King* had something to do with Lily Howell's murder?"

"It's possible," Hugh said. "Or it's possible there are some things in Lily's file the Royals would want to remove, before showing it to us."

"And let's just suppose for a moment I was to get caught by all those Coldstream Guards who protect the king. Would MI-Five stand up for me? Or let me hang?"

"But you won't get caught. We'll make sure of it." His forehead creased. "What's in those files might shed some light on what's been happening at the castle."

"I'll need clay to make imprints of the keys—those files are bound to be locked," she said.

"Your wish is my command." Hugh slipped off the table and went to his jacket, pulling out a wrapped pad of soft brown clay from the inside pocket. He handed it to her. "Get the imprints, and then we'll make you the keys." He bent down to the briefcase again, rummaging.

"And I'll need a—"

Hugh handed her a small camera.

"Ha!" Maggie said, pleased, as she accepted it.

Then he handed her a felted handbag. "Not really my style," she remarked, turning it in her hands and looking at it from all angles.

"There's a false bottom. For hiding the camera."

"Fantastic." Feeling better, she rolled down her sleeves and gathered her things to leave, placing the clay and camera in the purse's false bottom. As she did, she made a mental note to photograph Louisa's files as well.

"By the way," Hugh said. "You're not bad. At fighting, that is."

"Well, I—" Maggie was momentarily flustered.

"For what it's worth, I think you could have held your own in France," Hugh said.

"That means a lot to me, Hugh," she replied. Then she left.


At Maumbrey Cottage, his home at Bletchley, Edmund Hope went to the large wooden desk, picked up the telephone receiver, and dialed. "Margaret wanted to have dinner with me," he said into the telephone receiver.

On the other end of the line, Peter Frain said, "We know."

Static crackled and spluttered over the line.

"I knew she was going to ask me questions about her mother."

"And what did you say?"

"Nothing," Edmund replied. "I didn't meet her." He didn't mention he'd been there, at the pub in Slough, and that he'd stared at her through the plate-glass windows in the dark and cold, before finally leaving. The answers his daughter wanted from him—they just weren't anything he could or would tell her. Even if it meant disappointing her. Even if it meant losing her again.

"Good," Frain said. "Let's keep it that way."

## Chapter Thirteen

Monday morning was Princess Elizabeth's first maths lesson.

It was not going well.

"But Crawfie's *already* taught me how to add, subtract, multiply, and divide," Lilibet said earnestly in the nursery, warmed by orange and indigo flames crackling behind the brass fender. "And we've gone over decimals and fractions. I really don't know what more there is." A few of the corgis were napping in front of the fender on their needlepoint pillows, snoring. Dookie snorted and opened his black eyes for a moment, then went back to sleep.

Maggie smiled. "A *bit* more."

"But it's not as if I'll have to do my own books," Lilibet said, parroting what she must have heard Crawfie say.

"No," Maggie rejoined, "but you may want to keep an eye on those books when you're Queen." She let Lilibet think about it. "Just a suggestion, of course."

"Oh," Lilibet said, considering. "Perhaps you're right."

"Actually," Maggie said, sitting down next to the girl, "I thought we might do something different today. It's maths, but it doesn't really have to do with numbers at all. And it does have to do with a queen. Two queens. And how maths saved Queen Elizabeth's crown."

"Really?" At this, Lilibet perked up.

"Really." And Maggie began to relate the story of how, when Mary, Queen of Scots, was on trial for treason, accused of trying to assassinate the Protestant Queen Elizabeth, and facing a death sentence, she'd used code to communicate with her fellow Catholics. "You see, Mary had actually authorized the plot to murder Queen Elizabeth. But all of her messages were written in cipher. In order to prove her guilt, Queen Elizabeth would have to break the cipher."

Lilibet's eyes were huge. "Yes?"

"Well, luckily, she had on her side a brilliant mathematician, Sir Francis Walsingham, her principal secretary. Walsingham was an expert at breaking codes and ciphers."

"But what does this have to do with maths?"

"We're getting there!" Maggie said, pleased that she now had her young charge's interest. "Mary's letters to her supporters were in cipher—and it would take maths, some pretty sophisticated maths, to break the code." She got up, went to her bookcase, and pulled out a book about Mary, Queen of Scots, in which she'd bookmarked one of Anthony Babington's messages to Mary, written in code. "What do you make of this?" Maggie asked.

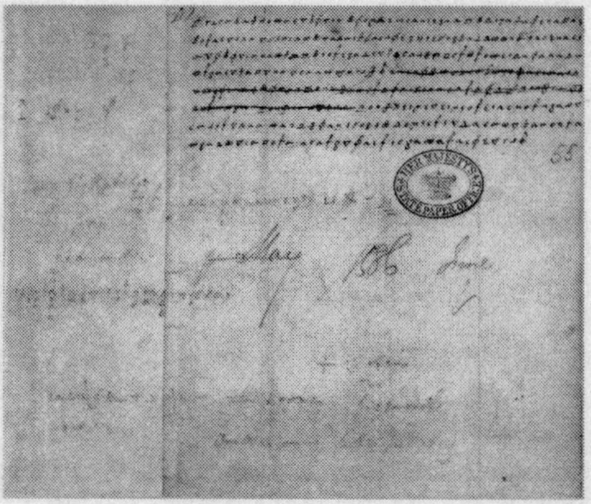

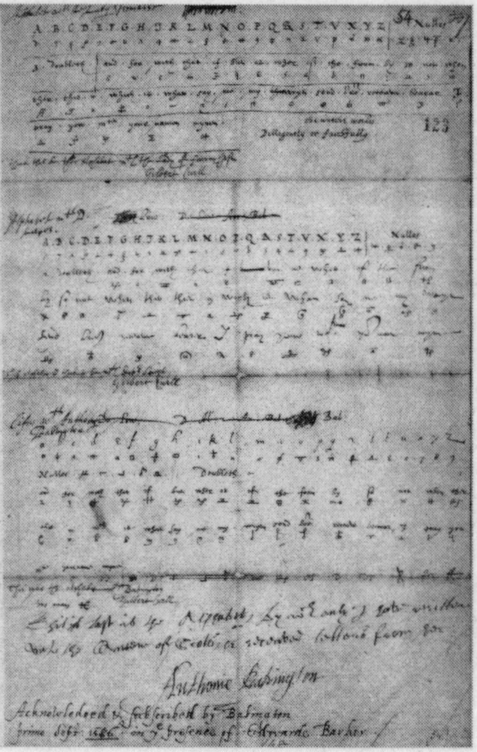

Anthonie Babington

Acknowledged & subscribed by Babington
prime Sept. 1586 in ye presence of Edwarde Barker

"It's . . . gibberish. Those aren't even real numbers or letters." She sighed in exasperation. "It doesn't make sense."

"Ah, but if you know maths, it just might. Not only was it a secret message about the assassination of Queen Elizabeth, written in code, but it, like their other messages, was smuggled in and out of prison through beer barrel stoppers. Queen Mary's servants would retrieve the messages from the beer barrels and place messages back into the hollow of the stopper."

"But how did they figure it out?"

"Sir Francis, Queen Elizabeth's Royal Spy Master, intercepted all of the messages between Queen Mary and Anthony Babington. Each message was copied by the Spy Master and then sent on to its destination intact. Then Sir Francis decoded each message, using the frequency analysis—the frequency of common characters—until a readable text was found. The rest of the message was guessed at by the message context until the entire cipher was understood."

"What's—what did you say? 'Frequency analysis'?"

"Well, think about the alphabet. What are some letters that are used most frequently in words?"

Lilibet considered for a moment. "*E*, of course. And some of the other vowels."

"Yes!" Maggie exclaimed, gratified. "And what are some letters that aren't used very much?"

"Well, Zed, of course. And *X*. And *Q*."

"And *Q* always is followed by a—"

"*U!*" the Princess exclaimed.

"What Queen Elizabeth's code breaker did was figure out which symbols Queen Mary used that appeared with the same frequency as letters of the alphabet. He proposed values for the symbols that appeared most often. By figuring out the symbol used most frequently, he could deduce it was an *e*. And so on. Using math and common sense, he was able to break the code."

"Goodness," Lilibet said. "It probably saved Queen Elizabeth's life."

"It did. And cost Queen Mary hers. Now—I have an idea for something fun to do."

The Princess looked wary. "What is it?"

"Well, how would you and Princess Margaret like to have your own ultra-secret code to communicate in? That no one, not even Crawfie or Alah, could read?"

"Oh, yes, yes, *please*, Maggie."

"Then let's get started, shall we?"

It took a while, but Lilibet created a cipher. Maggie had a decoder, a giveaway from a long-ago jar of Ovaltine. It might have been a toy intended for children, but it was a descendant of the cipher disk, developed in the fifteenth century by Leon Battista Alberti. The center wheel had a circle of numbers, which turned to match a stationary outer circle of letters.

Maggie gave it to Lilibet, who took it with a sort of awe, twisting the dial this way and that.

"The decoder—really a cipher disk—can be used in one of two ways," Maggie said. "The code can be a consistent monoalphabetic substitution for the entire cipher—or the disks can be moved periodically throughout the cipher, making it polyalphabetic."

"What?" Lilibet said, knitting her brows.

"Hmmmm . . ." Maggie remembered her young charge was only fourteen. "The sender and the person receiving the messages would need to agree on a cipher key setting. The entire message is then encoded according to this key. You also could use a character to mean 'end of word,' although this makes the code less secure. . . ."

Lilibet looked concerned.

"Oh, come on, we'll make one up and then you'll see how fun it is," Maggie said.

After a bit of thinking and moving the rings, Lilibet dipped her pen in a bottle of Parker Quink Black and wrote her first note, in code, to Margaret. The code was set for the 1 to indicate the start of the alphabet, set at *E*, for Elizabeth. "+" was to indicate the end of a word.

| 1 | 2 | 3 | 4 | 5 | 6 | 7 | 8 | 9 | 10 | 11 | 12 | 13 | 14 | 15 | 16 | 17 | 18 | 19 | 20 | 21 | 22 | 23 | 24 | 25 | 16 |
|---|---|---|---|---|---|---|---|---|----|----|----|----|----|----|----|----|----|----|----|----|----|----|----|----|----|
| E | F | G | H | I | J | K | L | M | N | O | P | Q | R | S | T | U | V | W | X | Y | Z | A | B | C | D |

And so, "Meet me in the garden" became "9 1 1 16 + 9 1 + 5 10 + 16 4 1 + 3 23 14 26 1 10"—and by twisting the dial, and remembering the *E* setting, Lilibet could get to the correct letters to spell out the message.

"May I go and show Margaret, Maggie? Please? It will make her laugh, and she loves to laugh so much."

"Of course," Maggie said. "We're done for the day. And be sure to teach her how the code works, so she can write back to you."

"Maybe I could use the code when I write to—" the Princess began. Then she stopped herself.

"Write to . . . ?" Maggie prodded.

"Well," Lilibet said, blush staining her cheeks, "there's this boy we all know. His name is Philip."

"Oh?" Maggie said. Her lips twitched as she realized Lilibet had a crush.

"He's a bit older than I am, and in the Royal Navy. But we've been writing to each other. Mummy and

Daddy know, of course." Her face creased with concern. "It's all very proper."

"I'm sure it is. And this Philip—he writes back?"

"He does!" Lilibet exclaimed. "Funny, witty letters with little sketches and doodles. He's about to be made midshipman!" she said proudly.

"Well, he must be quite a good sailor, then."

Lilibet's blue eyes were large. "Oh, he is—he's the best sailor the Royal Navy has," she said. Maggie could see how deep the Princess's feelings were for this young man. Then she started. "Do you have someone special, Maggie?"

Maggie was momentarily flustered. The Princess sensed her discomfort instantly. "It's all right if you don't want to talk about it. I shouldn't have asked. Oh, now you'll think I'm terribly rude."

Maggie laughed. "Of course not. It's just hard to talk about. But I do have someone special." *I did,* Maggie thought. *No, still do.*

Lilibet leaned in. "What's his name?"

"John. John Sterling. He used to be head private secretary to Mr. Churchill—we worked with each other at Number Ten Downing Street last summer."

"And you fell in love?"

"Well, at first we didn't. I didn't even like him much—or so I thought. And I thought he couldn't stand me. We used to bicker all the time."

"Ah . . ." Lilibet sighed.

"But, you know—" Now it was Maggie's turn to blush. "Eventually, we came to admit our, er, high regard for each other."

" 'High regard'?"

"We, you know, we were in love."

"Were?"

*Freudian slip, Maggie?* "He joined the Royal Air Force. I didn't support him—I wanted him to stay at Number Ten. . . ." Tears filled her eyes, and Lilibet searched in her pocket and pulled out a handkerchief, which she handed to Maggie.

"It's clean," the younger girl said. She waited until Maggie wiped at her eyes and nose and could go on.

"He asked me to marry him."

"What did you say?"

"I said no."

"What? I thought you said you were in love with him?"

"I was—I am—I was just so angry he was joining the air force. It was stupid," Maggie said, wiping her face and then blowing her nose. "I was stupid. I *am* stupid. And then his plane was shot down over Germany. And there's been no news of him. So he could be dead. Maybe. But I refuse to give up hope that he's still alive."

Lilibet took in this piece of information and digested the enormity of it. "You're not stupid," she said, patting Maggie's arm. "You just wanted him to be safe. Just like I want Philip to be safe."

Maggie gave a wan smile. "Yes."

"And they'll both come back to us, you'll see."

"Is that a royal command, Your Highness?"

"It is."

"Yes, ma'am."

# Chapter Fourteen

In the conference room at Bletchley, which used to be the manor house's formal dining room, cryptographer Benjamin Batey was sweating, his face pale.

Peter Frain was sitting across the wooden table from him. "Exactly when did your relationship with Miss Victoria Keeley begin?" he asked.

"A—a month ago. I mean, I've known her for more than a year—that is, I knew who she was. But I didn't start to get to know her well until about, maybe, six months ago. We started walking out about a month ago."

"Who approached whom?"

"She, well, she approached me," Benjamin said, fingers of one hand picking at the cuticles of the other. "In the canteen. She asked if she could sit with me. Asked for my help with a crossword puzzle."

"Did she ever mention a woman named Lily Howell?"

Benjamin looked puzzled. "No," he said. "No, she didn't."

Frain made a mental note. "When did you first be-come intimate?"

"Well, we went to one of the Bletchley concerts to-gether for the first time last month. . . ."

Frain cut to the chase. "When did you sleep with her?"

"I'm afraid—"

"Yes, Mr. Batey, you should be afraid. You should be *very* afraid. When did you sleep with her?"

"That—that night," Benjamin said, his face redden-ing.

"Did you ever take work out of the office with you?"

Benjamin looked shocked. "No! Of course not!"

Frain narrowed his gray eyes. "Then how do you ex-plain that Victoria Keeley passed one of the decrypts that you were working on to a third party?"

Benjamin gasped. "It's impossible!"

"I'm afraid not," Frain replied, lighting up a ciga-rette with his heavy monogrammed silver lighter. As he inhaled, the tip glowed orange and red. "Very few things are truly impossible, Mr. Batey. Two women are dead and a top-secret decrypt made its way from your office to London. Let's go over your story again, shall we?"

Hugh Thompson was leaving his office at MI-5. "Please tell Mr. Standish I'm on my way to a meeting," he called out to his secretary, when he heard the urgent ring of the telephone. "And if Caroline calls, just—"

"It's Mr. Frain, sir," she said. "He wants to speak with you."

Hugh went back to his desk. Over the hiss of the line, he could hear Frain light a cigarette and inhale.

"You're being pulled off the Windsor assignment," Frain said without preamble.

Hugh was gobsmacked. "What?" Then, "Why?"

"I want someone older, with more experience. As it turns out, this is an important case. Even more important than I'd originally thought."

"Yes sir, I know—"

"I'd like you on something different. Mr. Standish will fill you in on the details. In the meantime, I'd like you to see Mr. Nevins today, to brief him on Miss Hope."

"Nevins?" Hugh couldn't conceal his shock. "Archer *Nevins*?"

"He'll be her new handler. He's a senior member of our staff, and I trust you'll treat him with the respect he deserves. That is all." And then the phone went dead.

"Nevins," Hugh muttered, as he replaced the heavy green Bakelite receiver. "Just perfect!"


A message alerted her that the book she'd ordered from Foyle's in London was in, the signal she and Hugh had agreed on to meet in Queen Mary's Rose Garden in Regent's Park. Around noon, Maggie left the castle. It was a relief to leave those oppressive stone walls, six feet thick in some places, and to be out in the open air, even if it was chilly and overhead there were swollen gray clouds.

She took the train from the red-brick Victorian Windsor and Eton Central Station over Brunel's bowstring bridge to Slough, then walked over the pedestrian crossing and waited in the cool clammy air until the next train arrived. This one took her from Slough to

London's cavernous and loud Paddington Station, with its high arched glass-and-iron ceiling and grubby pigeons pecking for crumbs on the damp cement floors. From Paddington, she took the Bakerloo line on the Tube to Baker Street. From Baker, she walked a few blocks to Regent's Park.

She and Hugh met in Queen Mary's Rose Garden, a lush, carefully tended section of the park. The skies were leaden, the grass brown, the bark of the bare trees the color of bruises. The last of the rambling, winding, climbing, and clustered red, pink, and golden roses were dying. The cold air smelled of earth and frost and impending winter. A few plump pigeons strutted and cooed, waiting for someone, anyone, to leave crumbs.

Besides the occasional pedestrian and twittering sparrow, they had a wooden bench in the garden with a fine view of William McMillan's Triton fountain to themselves, knowing there was no way their conversation could be overheard. Still, Hugh was on one end, buried in *The Times*, and Maggie was at the other, pretending to read Turing.

"Frain's in Bletchley right now, questioning a cryptographer named Benjamin Batey. He had access to the decrypt. He was also seeing Victoria Keeley." Hugh's breath made white clouds in the air.

Maggie took a sharp breath but kept her eyes on her page. "Is there any evidence that he murdered her?"

Hugh shrugged. "Not so far. Frain's been questioning him. And Frain can be very . . . persuasive. So far, though, Benjamin Batey seems like a sort of hapless victim. They allegedly had their . . . tryst . . . at her flat and then she went to London alone."

"So, we know somehow, perhaps through Mr. Batey,

Victoria Keeley got her hands on a decrypt. We know that she passed it to Lady Lily Howell at Claridge's. We know Victoria Keeley was murdered. And we know Lily had hidden the decrypt and was then murdered also."

"Yes."

"What we need to focus on," Maggie said, "is how Lily Howell was going to send, or take, that information to Germany. No one found a radio, a way for her to communicate?"

"No, she must have been working with someone else."

"Possibly someone at the castle."

Maggie nodded. "Of course, if there's someone else at Bletchley who's stealing decrypts . . ."

"I know, I know." Hugh folded his paper.

"At any rate, we should get the names of everyone at Claridge's the night Victoria Keeley was murdered and run them against everyone at Windsor Castle and Bletchley Park. Of course, people might have used aliases, but—"

"I'm sorry," Hugh said, "but I'll have to pass along your request—to your new handler."

"*New* handler?" The book nearly fell out of Maggie's hands.

Hugh ran his hands through his hair. "I'm afraid so. This is getting more serious than Frain anticipated, so he's pairing you up with someone more senior."

"That's unacceptable. You're an excellent agent. We work well together." She was filled with an overwhelming sense of disappointment and rage, like a child whose favorite playmate was moving away.

"It's fine, really. I mean, of course my pride is bruised.

But mostly I'll miss . . ." He stared at her, searching for the right things to say.

"Yes?" Maggie prompted.

"I'll miss . . . the case. It's been quite the roller coaster already. And I think we've just scratched the surface." He continued to look at her. "But I'm afraid it can't be helped." He rose and tipped his hat. "Good luck, Maggie Hope." And then he walked away, swallowed up by the park.

"And good luck to you, too," she replied to herself, feeling lost and alone once again.

Maggie wasn't the only resident of Windsor Castle spending the day in London. Audrey Moreau was there as well. It was her one day off a month from her maid's duties, and she had told Cook that she was taking the train to London to do some sightseeing.

London was a city of smoking ruins, but many of the shops were open, and what architecture remained was still magnificent. Cold rain was falling, and water gushed in the gutters, filled with fallen yellow leaves.

Audrey had left off her black-and-white maid's uniform and was wearing a woolen dress with her winter coat, which she'd tailored to accentuate her slim figure. A hat with a silk orchid one of the castle's guests had left behind topped off her ensemble. She was rewarded by men smiling and tipping their hats.

She made her way to a bus stop near Piccadilly Circus. The statue of Eros was gone, but the circle was still a popular place for people to meet—sailors in uniform on leave shouting to one another and smoking, WAAFs and FANYs in bright red lipstick, men in dark suits and bowler hats under black umbrellas.

The Circus was surrounded by huge billboards from the Ministry of Propaganda: *Join the Wrens!, It Is Far Better to Face the Bullets Than to Be Killed at Home by a Bomb,* and *God Save the King.*

The rain stopped, and Audrey folded up her umbrella. She waited for the red double-decker bus, and when it arrived she took the narrow stairs to the top deck. As the vehicle made its slow way up Regent Street, she was joined by a man wearing a dark gray coat, a gray bowler hat, and a Trinity College scarf in navy, red, and yellow stripes. He sat next to her, despite the fact that the deck was nearly empty.

She looked up and smiled, beginning what was to be a long conversation in whispered French.

It was sunset at Windsor Castle—red, rose, and tangerine bled out into the western sky, leaving long violet shadows.

Behind battlements on top of the castle stood a large structure, the Royal Mews, a wooden construction with mesh screened doors and windows. Inside were perches with goshawks and peregrine falcons in hoods, tethered with heavy leather jesses.

"There, now, Merlin," Sam Berners crooned, as he slipped the tooled leather hood over the falcon's head. He took a moment to look out over the grounds of the castle, with the Thames and Eton in the shadowy distance.

Alistair Tooke entered the Mews and stood for a moment at the entranceway, repulsed by the smell. "Berners!" Tooke said, his boots crunching on the fresh straw laid down on the floor.

"Got nothin' to say to you," Berners replied, transferring Merlin to his arm.

"Just as long as you don't say anything to the police," Tooke warned. "If you won't, I won't."

Berners looked at his falcon, Merlin, blind in his tooled and painted leather hood. "We're all hunters, then, aren't we?"

"We are, indeed. And I'll keep your secret, if you keep mine."

# Chapter Fifteen

Hugh grabbed the hilt of his épée as he began to advance on the piste that covered a long strip of the highly polished floor of the Reform Club. "Nevins. *Nevins!*" Behind his metal mesh mask, his eyes narrowed. "Fantastic. Absolutely fantastic."

Mark was dressed, as was Hugh, in the traditional white fencers' uniform. He advanced and lunged as Hugh continued to rant, his voice echoing in the high-ceilinged wood-paneled room, decorated with suits of armor and historical swords, its large windows overlooking Pall Mall.

Hugh deftly parried, the clicks and scrapes of metal on metal echoing under the brass and ormolu chandeliers. His breathing was heavy with the intense effort. "Nevins is an *idiot*! And so is Frain, for that matter, for replacing me—with *him*, of all people!"

Mark counterattacked with a passata-sotto, his épée whistling through the air. "Look," he said and grunted. "May I say something?"

Hugh put down his épée and took off his mask. "What?" Perspiration glistened on his face.

Mark took off his mask as well, and wiped drops of sweat out of his eyes with his sleeve. "Nevins is a good agent. He has more experience than you do. And he may be a pompous ass at times, and get a little too friendly with the female staff, but he does his job and does it well. I believe you're letting this get personal."

"Oh, not this again—"

"It's true! You obviously think about Miss Hope more than any handler should—"

They both put their masks back on. "I'm a consummate professional, and you know it," Hugh said as he went back to en garde. "And I'm a better fencer than you too."

"Possibly," Mark said as they parried and their blades clicked. "Well, then take it from the chap who's worked in a small closet with you for over three years— I think you miss her. Not the job. *Her.*"

"Ha!" Hugh exploded, their blades meeting again. "She's a good agent is all. A bit green, but good—smart, intuitive. We had a . . . rapport."

Mark feinted, then thrust, moving in against Hugh now, driving him back. "And now Nevins is going to have that . . . 'rapport' . . . with her. And it's driving you bonkers."

Hugh countered the best he could. "That's rubbish!"

Mark pushed forward for the victory, the tip of his sword against Hugh's heart, winning the point. "No, no it's not."

Hugh was absolutely still. Then, "Prat."

"Ass."

They each lowered their swords and took off their masks.

"So, what do I do?" Hugh said, when he'd caught his breath.

They returned to the garde line, saluted, then stepped forward and shook hands, as tradition dictated.

"I don't think there's all that much you can do, really, if Frain's set on using Nevins," Mark said, as they walked together to the door. "But you might want to start thinking about breaking things off with Caroline. Because if you feel this strongly about another girl, it's not fair to string Caroline along."

Hugh raised his hands in mock surrender. "You're right, damn you."

"Back to the *real* fight, then?" Mark said, clapping his friend on the back.

"Indeed."


A few hours later, Hugh stood in Archer Nevins's office, a thick manila file in hand. He handed it over to Nevins, a charismatic man with glossed-back hair, just a decade older than Hugh. He had a winning toothy grin, like a politician's, and the confidence that came from successfully running a number of spy-finding operations. While he was married and had two sons, he was infamous, among the female staff at least, for his wandering hands and for seducing any number of receptionists, telephone operators, and typists. Nevins opened the file and flipped through the pages. "The infamous Maggie Hope," he said.

"As you can see, her current assignment—"

"I do," Nevins said.

"She already has the clay and the camera, so—"

"And that's why I'm on this case now, Thompson. Anything else I need to know about her? One man to another?"

"No."

"What about Frain?"

"What *about* Frain?"

Nevins looked at Hugh. "Is he still sleeping with her? Or has he moved on?"

Hugh took a deep breath and overcame the urge to punch Nevins in the jaw. "There's nothing unprofessional between Miss Hope and Mr. Frain."

"Oh, come, now, Thompson," Nevins said. "Surely you're not that naïve. How do you think she got this job?"

"Her intelligence and skills."

Nevins laughed. "I think you're just jealous."

Nevins came to the photograph of Maggie, clipped to the back page of the folder. "Well, well, well!" He whistled through his teeth. "Now I know why Frain hired her. Wouldn't kick that out of bed for eating biscuits."

Hugh bit the inside of his cheek. "Try anything funny, and she just might kick *you*."

"Oh, feisty, is she?"

Hugh silently counted to ten. "Will that be all—sir?"

"What? Oh, yes." Nevins was still staring at the picture. He waved one hand without looking up. "That will be all, Thompson. Dismissed."

After the Princess's maths lesson and lunch, Maggie received a message saying the book she'd ordered from

Boswell's had arrived. She left the castle grounds through the King Henry VIII Gate, heels clicking on the cobblestones, walked past the statue of Queen Victoria, then turned right down Peascod Street under the low silvery clouds. But she wasn't alone.

"Miss Hope!" a man called, catching up to her. She didn't recognize him from the castle, and she felt a moment of alarm.

"Miss Hope!" he called again, panting and falling into step alongside her. "I'm Archer Nevins." His breath made clouds in the cold air. "I want to let you know that we're going to make a fantastic duo."

Maggie stopped, her eyes narrowing. So *this* was her new handler. She felt . . . cheated.

"Mr. Frain's assigned Mr. Thompson to a less important case." He wiped at his nose with a linen handkerchief, his monogram embroidered in large ornate letters. "I have more seniority—more experience—and Frain thought you'd be better suited to working with me."

Maggie started walking again. Since arriving at Windsor, she'd gotten into the habit of taking either an early-morning run or a long afternoon walk on the grounds. She'd begun her regime to build up her strength and endurance, but really she just liked to get away from the confines of the castle for at least a few hours a day. In the time she'd been there, she was already getting stronger and faster, and she put her speed to her advantage as they walked down the cobblestoned street.

As Nevins followed, struggling to keep up in his slippery-soled shoes, Maggie felt a wave of anger wash through her. She stopped and faced him, bringing him up short. "Mr. Nevins, I have a question."

"Yes?"

"Have you run the list of names of Windsor Castle and Bletchley Park employees against the list of guests at Claridge's for the night Victoria Keeley was murdered? I asked Hugh, and he said he'd pass the request to you."

Nevins laughed. "So, that was your idea, was it? A regular Mata Hari you are. Well, darling, you'll find I'm not like Hugh Thompson. I, for one, don't take orders from a woman. In fact, let's set this straight—I'm the boss. *You'll* be taking orders from *me*."

"Are you insane?" Maggie hissed. "What are you doing here? And out in the open? Stopping by for tea? Already one woman's been shot in London and one's been decapitated here. Since I'm new, there are any number of people at the castle suspicious of me. You're abusing the privilege of the handler position."

"This is why I don't like to work with women," Nevins said softly, "no matter how attractive the package. You women may be clever—and you're reputed to be quite clever—but you're not intelligent. You may be able to obtain information in a given situation, but you can't put it all together." He smiled. "It's why you have me, of course."

Maggie felt her face grow hot, and started walking again. "That's not how I see things. Or Mr. Frain."

Nevins laughed, a pinched, mean laugh. "Frain's a pragmatist. He saw that he could get you into Windsor, and because of your sex, you'd be less obvious—especially when dealing with a child. A good role for a woman, I suppose. But honestly, I'd rather see Thompson or Standish in the field on this one, not you. Although I wouldn't mind your sitting just outside my office. You'd dress the place up nicely."

"Are you *joking*?" Maggie managed. "Look, Mr. Nevins, I'm a professional. And I expect to be treated as such. Understood?"

Nevins looked as though Cupid's arrow had just pierced his heart. "You have pluck, Maggie," he managed, finally. "So very *American*. And you like the chase, it seems. I just hope you haven't picked up any of your father's habits."

"My father? What's he got to do with anything?"

"You don't know?" Nevins whistled. "He was investigated for being a double agent for Germany in the last war. Now, in this one, he's supposed to be ferreting out a spy at Bletchley. Been on the case for years and still no spy. . . . Do you think dear old Dad might be working for Abwehr? That's what the boys in the back room whisper, at any rate."

"Stop it, Mr. Nevins. Stop it right now." Maggie's head was spinning. *Her father was a spy during the last war? He'd never told her that. And he'd been suspected of being a double agent back then? And now, once again, he was suspected of spying for Germany?*

From a nearby black rooftop, a falcon began his mad laughing caw, then flew off. Maggie turned and watched him sail through the air until he reached the top of one of the castle's high walls. It was a fair distance away, but Maggie squinted to see him land on the shoulder of a man. *Probably Sam Berners, the Royal Falconer.* She gave a grim smile. *If only I could get the falcon to go for Nevins.* "Unless you have some actual information to impart, we're finished, Mr. Nevins."

"It was good to meet you, Miss Hope. I look forward

to using the information you bring me to crack the case."

Maggie turned and started tramping back to the castle, blood boiling, leaving Nevins to stare after her. "Yes," she muttered to herself. "Yes, Nevins, you're finished. *Quite* finished."

Later, in the Octagon Room, still seething at Nevins and wondering about her father, Maggie picked at her dinner, letting the conversation of the others flow and swirl around her.

She heard her name being called. It was Crawfie. "Miss Hope!" she was saying.

She cleared her thoughts of Nevins. "Yes, Miss Crawford."

"I want to include the Princesses somehow in this year's Red, White, and Blue Christmas celebration," she began. "And I was thinking a performance might be in order. They're going to be making public appearances soon enough, and some practice on a stage, in front of family and friends, might help them make the transition."

Maggie nodded, listening.

"I was thinking of a pantomime. *Sleeping Beauty,* in fact. Princess Margaret can play Briar Rose and Princess Elizabeth can be the Prince. I spoke with Mr. Tanner, who's a teacher at the Royal School, in the Great Park, where the other children of Windsor Castle attend school—and it turns out he was a Gilbert and Sullivan player back in the day, and would be delighted to direct. We can charge admission and the ticket money can go to the Queen's Wool Fund." She sighed. "It's been so dull for the Princesses here, and I think it would do them a world of good. . . . May I count on your help, Miss Hope?" Crawfie asked. "For scenery, especially?"

"Of course!" Maggie exclaimed. It was, after all, just the thing to keep an eye on the Princesses and their circle during the time she wasn't tutoring. "Crawfie, I'd be happy—in fact, *thrilled*—to help. Thank you."

Maggie attended the first read-through that night in the nursery. The sheer scope of work the production would entail was staggering. There were sets to be built and painted, costumes to sew, props to make, lights to be hung, and only a few weeks in which to do it. Maggie sat, listening to the Princesses read through the script, taking notes on what would be needed. Mr. Tanner clapped his hands after they'd finished Act I, saying in plummy Welsh tones, "All right, Your Highnesses, that's enough for the night."

Maggie was amused there were no auditions for the roles; it was simply assumed the two Princesses would play the leads—Margaret as the Sleeping Princess and Elizabeth as the Prince.

A resounding bell stood in for the wailing air-raid siren Maggie was used to. Lilibet and Margaret rushed to the windows. "Theirs," they said matter-of-factly, as German planes roared overhead, on their way to London or beyond. The corgis all crowded around the windows but were too well trained to bark. Still, a few of them growled softly.

Margaret went over to Maggie and took her hand. "We can tell the difference, you know," she said, quite seriously, "even in the dark—by the sound of the engines."

Mrs. Tuffts, another tiny and wizened ARP Warden, fluttered in. "Come!" she said, her bony wrists waving and wisps of white hair escaping from under her metal helmet, "to the dungeons! Crawfie, would you please hurry them along?"

"Come, girls," Crawfie urged. "Take your suitcases and gas masks, and we'll be on our way." And true enough, two small suitcases stood by the nursery door, as though the Princesses were off to Paddington Station instead of to a makeshift air-raid shelter in the castle's dungeon.

"Can you believe those suitcases are real Vuitton?" Crawfie confided to Maggie. "They belong to France and Marianne."

"France and Marianne?" Maggie didn't think she'd met them yet.

"Oh, they're dolls. Literal dolls. They were given to the Princesses to mark the King and Queen's state visit to France."

"Aha," said Maggie.

"Come, pups!" Lilibet said to the corgis in motherly tones. Dutifully, they all got up and filed after her. Together, they all traveled through the corridors of the castle, until they reached the kitchen. There, down a flight of stairs, was the Royal wine cellar. In the back rooms of the wine cellar, Mrs. Tuffts rolled a carpet out of the way, revealing a trapdoor in the floor. Crawfie took hold of the iron ring and pulled. The door came up easily, revealing a steep staircase. "I'll go first," said Mrs. Tuffts, turning on a flashlight. "Watch your step, now."

Down, down they went, into the bowels of the castle.

The cold air was damp and stale. The walls were rough stone, and the path underneath their feet was crumbling. In the beam of Mrs. Tuffts's light, Maggie could see shiny black beetles and spiders scuttling away. She thought she saw a fat gray rat out of the corner of her eye but decided it was only her imagination.

Finally, they reached their destination. Maggie saw that the walls had been reinforced and beds had been brought down. Others were there as well: Sir Owen, Lord Clive, Mr. Tooke. Sir Owen was making tea on a brazier. His fussing with the tea tin, pot, and cups seemed incongruous with the sinister gloom of the dungeon and at the same time so very natural for him. Maggie looked around at the walls, wondering about the fates of those who'd been imprisoned here.

"It's a red warning, Miss Hope," Mrs. Tuffts whispered in her ear. Yellow warnings were for when the bombers flew over on their way somewhere else. A red warning meant bombing was going on directly above them. "It's unusual for us. They say Windsor Castle's been spared so far, because Hitler rather fancies it for his own someday."

"I see," Maggie said, a shiver running through her, looking toward the Princesses. However, they were the picture of calm, already settling in with books and toys that Crawfie had brought, accepting cups of steaming tea from Sir Owen. Suddenly, he was at her elbow. "Would you care for a cup of tea, Miss Hope?" he asked.

"Yes, please." He handed her a cup and saucer, the gold bands around the edges of the saucer and cup's rim twinkling in the dim light. Maggie took a sip. It was weak, but it was hot, and she was grateful. "Thank you, Sir Owen," she said, "for bringing civilization with us."

"Of course!" he said, shocked that, even in a Royal dungeon, with Nazi planes dropping bombs overhead, life would be anything less than civilized. "Did you know, Miss Hope, that the soldiers manning the anti-aircraft guns on the roof of the castle shot down a Nazi plane a few months ago? A Messerschmitt one-oh-nine— it landed upside down on the Long Walk. We turned it right-side up and put it on public display. Would you believe people paid a sixpence to see it? The money went to the Hurricane Fighter Fund."

"How fascinating, Sir Owen." Through the gloom, Maggie could see groups of people settling in on metal folding chairs, dimly lit by candles or flashlights. She saw Louisa and Polly with a few of the other Ladies-in-Waiting. Making sure Crawfie and the Princesses were all right, Maggie picked her way over on the uneven stones to Louisa and Polly.

"Quite a nuisance," Louisa was saying in her raspy voice. "I was supposed to have a date tonight."

Maggie looked around, checking who was there. "Where's Gregory?" she said, taking one of the hard metal seats.

"Oh, goodness knows where he's gotten to," Polly said. "He and Lily used to sneak out and go to the roof to drink bottled beer and watch the planes go by."

"He must be terribly affected by her death," Polly said, taking a sip of tea. *Was Lily's baby his?* she wondered. *Do the girls know she was pregnant?*

"Oh, yes," Louisa said. "They knew each other since they were in the cradle. But I'd say he's been more affected by his injuries. He's not been the same since he came home."

"Well, what do you expect?" said Polly. "He was

practically burned to a crisp in Norway. I've heard him say he wishes it had ended there. But only when he's ridiculously drunk."

"Gregory and Lily—they, ah . . ." *Could Gregory be the baby's father? Could he be the killer? Oh, no, no. Not Gregory.*

"We always suspected it," Louisa said, "but they'd never admit to anything."

"Tell me about Lily," Maggie said. "What was she like?"

Polly sighed. "Everyone loved Lily. She had such charm about her, an ease—"

"And that laugh," Louisa interrupted. "Like a raccoon in heat."

"Louisa!" Polly exclaimed, and they both giggled.

"Well, it's true! And if Lily were here, she'd be the first to agree."

"Was she," Maggie said, delicately, "seeing anyone else? Besides, perhaps, Gregory?"

Louisa shrugged. "Hard to tell. She was always secretive about her beaux. But she did like to go to London on the weekends. Couldn't possibly keep her here, you know. Sometimes we'd go with her, on the train, and sometimes Gregory would give her a lift. And always at Claridge's. Never the Savoy or the Ritz or any of the other big hotels—no, those were for tourists. She always stayed at Claridge's."

"My, my," Maggie said, taking another sip of her tea. *And Victoria Keeley was at Claridge's at the same time. Who had access to the decrypts, could have somehow stolen one, and then given it to Lily. And was murdered in the bath.* Maggie had a sudden inspiration. *A trip to London, to Claridge's, to question the staff is in order.*

Maggie looked around. "It seems like there are a lot of tunnels." *And a security nightmare,* she thought.

Lilibet, approaching with a knitted wool lap blanket, overheard her. "There are—it's a veritable labyrinth," she said, handing Maggie the blanket. "Suspected you might be cold."

"Thank you," Maggie said, spreading it over her legs. "Have you and Margaret done much exploring of the tunnels?"

The corners of Lilibet's mouth turned up. "We're not supposed to play down here, of course."

Maggie raised one eyebrow. "Of course."

"But," said the Princess, leaning in to Maggie's ear, "let's just say that we know if you follow the main tunnel, you'll come out near the Norman Gate. And if you follow them further, you'll get to the Henry the Eighth Gate. It's a handy way to cut through a lot of the castle."

"Good to know," whispered Maggie. "Thanks for the tip."

Lilibet looked to Princess Margaret across the chamber and their eyes met, some secret message being exchanged.

Then Lilibet whispered to Maggie, "We'll give you our special tour."

# Chapter Sixteen

Although Maggie wanted to get to Claridge's to carry out her own line of questioning, she still had her original mission. The King's files were kept under lock and key in the King's Equerry's office—Gregory's office. And Gregory, in his position as Equerry, was also Keeper of the Keys. The next evening, with the small bar of clay secreted away in her trouser pocket, Maggie made her way through the maze of the castle to find him. She knocked at the heavy wooden door.

"Come in," Gregory called.

Maggie did, taking in the Persian carpets and heavy carved furniture. The blackout curtains were in place, and Gregory was reading *The Times* by the jewel-like glow of a Tiffany lamp, the light catching on the tray of various cut-glass bottles. He looked up and smiled, his scars less noticeable in the dim light.

"Ah, Maggie," he said, raising his cocktail glass. "To what do I owe the honor of this visit?" He looked pale, and the skin around his scar tissue looked angry and red. He reeked of gin.

*Oh, if only I could tell you,* Maggie thought. *But, given what I suspect about you, I really can't.* "Are you all right?" she asked. "I don't want to disturb your work."

"No," Gregory said, slurring slightly. "Please sit down. You're a ray of sunshine in this gloom. The King's at a very important, very formal, and very long dinner—and while he's there, there's no chance of my being summoned." He indicated a bell near the door. "That's my cue. When it rings, I'm off and running—like one of Pavlov's dogs." He put down the paper and smiled. "I have to admit, though, the work's pretty light. It's more or less six months of paid vacation for us soldiers."

"Well, you certainly deserve it," Maggie said. She looked at the bank of wooden files that lined the wall behind him. They all had locks on them.

"How much of that have you had?" she asked, indicating the glass and a crystal pitcher.

"Not nearly enough," he replied, taking another swig. "Would you like some?"

"Yes, please."

"By the way, who was the man?"

"What man?" Maggie asked. But she was stalling. Gregory must have seen her with Nevins from the castle. *Bloody Nevins,* she thought. *Stupid Nevins.*

He shook gin and a splash of vermouth with some ice in a shaker, then poured the frosty clear liquid into a cocktail glass and handed it to her. "I saw you on Peascod Street today," he said. "Who was that man you were speaking with?"

"Why, Gregory," Maggie dissembled. "Are you jealous?" Heart beating fast, she thought quickly. "He was pretending to be lost, but do you know who I think it was?"

"Who?"

"A journalist!" Maggie said, improvising. "Can you imagine? I can't think that any respectable paper would print a story about where the Princesses were, but there are some unsavory tabloids. . . ."

"Oh," Gregory said. "Right."

"I think I scared him off, though. Gave him quite a stern lecture."

He nodded. *Close call,* Maggie thought. "Long rehearsal tonight," she said, covering a yawn.

Gregory stared off into the middle distance, eyes unseeing.

"Are you all right?" Maggie asked.

He blinked, then shook his head and smiled. "Sorry, just a little distracted. How's *Sleeping Beauty* coming?"

"Oh, it's coming. I could use some help painting the flats, though, if you're so inclined. Somehow, the amount of scenery we need has increased exponentially."

"I know my way around a paintbrush." Gregory grinned. "I'd be honored to help."

Maggie raised her glass, and they clinked. She sipped at her martini and watched him gulp his. "Shall we?"

Crawfie and the Princesses were running lines in the cozy warmth of the nursery. "I've brought reinforcements!" Maggie announced.

"Oh, Lord Gregory," Alah said, looking up.

"Mrs. Knight, I heard I might be of service?" he said.

"Lord Gregory!" Margaret said, standing abruptly and dropping her script. "You've come to rescue us!"

"Your humble servant, Your Highnesses," he replied with a low courtly bow.

Maggie was proud the Princesses had no reaction to his scars. "I'm putting him to work on the flats," she said, indicating the half-painted scenery on a tarp in the corner of the room. "Let's get him a smock and a brush and get started, shall we?"

Maggie noticed Gregory had a key ring attached to his belt. *The key to the files must be in that ring,* she realized. "Perhaps you'd like to change?"

He looked up as he buttoned an already paint-splattered smock. "Oh, I think I'm fine. But thanks for your concern."

"Of course!" But she bit her lip in frustration. This was a situation not covered by exercises at Camp Spook.

"As you can see," she said, "I've finished the flats for the castle's Christening scene, and now I'm trying to do a decent wall of thorns. . . ."

Almost an hour later, they'd made great progress.

"I'm bored," Margaret announced to the room.

"You still need to practice," Lilibet admonished.

"I know my lines," she retorted, sticking out her tongue. "I'm asleep for most of the play, after all."

"But now you need to sleep in character," the older Princess said. "You need to practice with feeling."

*"Feeling?"* Margaret said. "I suppose you'd know all about that. You, with your romance novels—"

"Stop it!" Lilibet said, her cheeks turning pink.

"Oh, yes," Margaret announced to everyone, "Lilibet reads romance novels now. And wears silk stockings. And writes looooong letters to Philip . . ."

"Stop!" Lilibet cried. "Philip and I are friends," she said to the others. "He asked me to write to him while

he's at sea. He's in the Royal Navy, after all. It's my"—
she pulled herself up with the dignity of a fourteen-year-
old—"patriotic *duty,* after all."

Maggie knew the Philip in question was Prince Philip
of Greece, a more and more frequent topic of Lilibet's
conversation before and after maths lessons.

"Duty, yes," Margaret cooed.

Alah clapped her hands. *"Girls!"*

"I know!" Margaret said. "Let's play sardines! It'll be
ever so much more fun with Maggie and Lord Gregory
here!"

Ever the hostess, Lilibet said, "Does everyone know
how to play?" Meaning Maggie.

"If you wouldn't mind going over the ground
rules . . ." Maggie said.

"We turn off all the lights," Margaret explained.
"One person hides, while the others wait here. We all
count to a hundred and then we all go off in search of
the hider."

"And when you find the hider," Lilibet interjected,
"you don't say anything. You just—"

"—sneak in and hide alongside until everyone's hidden together, like sardines in a can. And the last one—"

"—is the rotten egg!" they chimed together.

"The one rule," said Alah, "is that we must stay in
this wing."

"Oh—and there's one room we can't go in," Lilibet
said.

"Really?" asked Maggie, suddenly curious.

"It's the room where Uncle David—that is, King Edward the Eighth, now the Duke of Windsor," Lilibet
said formally, "made the wireless address where he abdicated the throne, to marry 'that woman.' That's what

Mummy always calls her. And the room's been closed up ever since."

"It's as if someone *died* there," Margaret said dramatically.

Lilibet shrugged. "Well, in a way, King Edward the Eighth did. And the Duke of Windsor was born. And then Daddy became King George the Sixth."

The mood of the room had dropped and had become suddenly somber.

"Well, I'm in!" Maggie said, looking at Alah with a question in her eye. Were the Princesses safe traipsing about in the dark? Alah gave her an almost imperceptible nod, meaning of course she'd keep an eye on them.

Gregory threw up his hands. "How can I resist?"

"Maggie will be the first sardine," Margaret announced.

"And, Margaret," Lilibet admonished, "you turn off all the lights."

Margaret did as she was told and the girls' tower was in a state of utter darkness, relieved only by the glow of the fireplace. "Oh, it's so spoooooooky," she said as she came back. In the gloom, the occasional pop and crackle of the log in the fireplace sounded even louder.

"Stop it!" said Lilibet. "Now, we're going to start counting to a hundred. And, Maggie, you go hide. One, two, three . . ."

Heart beating hard, Maggie made her way through the darkness. *It's just a game, don't be silly,* she thought. *But getting the keys isn't a game. . . .*

Her eyes adjusted, and she made her way through the velvety black, looking for a good place to hide. She went into Lilibet's sitting room. Where to take cover?

After bumping a shin on one of Lilibet's chairs and

trying not to swear, she made her way over the thick carpet to the window. Under the heavy brocade drapes, the blackout curtains were drawn, but behind them was Lilibet's window seat. Maggie parted the curtains, then stepped up on the seat, drawing them back as if she'd never been there.

She waited.

It was cold—freezing, really—pressed up against the icy square panes of glass. After the almost total darkness, the bright sliver of a crescent moon glowed and galaxies of stars glittered. The keening wind rattled the windowpanes in their frames. High above, in the box of the valance, were lacy spiderwebs. Maggie shivered and wrapped her arms around herself.

"Ready or not—here we come!" she heard Margaret cry and then the sound of laughter.

She waited in the dark and the cold, waited for the first to find her.

It was Gregory.

"Maggie?" he whispered, drawing back the curtains.

"Shhhh . . ." she said, moving over so that he could step up on the window seat beside her. He did so, and Maggie was aware of him, very close to her, his breath smelling of martinis.

"I must be part bloodhound," he whispered.

"What?"

"I followed my nose—you always wear something that smells like violets."

Maggie was suddenly confused. *Keep your mind on the keys,* she admonished herself.

"It's Après l'Ondée," she whispered back. "My friend Sarah gave it to me."

"Violets after the rain, then," he said. "Gods, it's

cold!" He rubbed his hands together, then reached out to Maggie and began to rub her arms.

"It's the wind, the wind blowing against the glass. Simple thermodynamics, really. You can calculate it if you have both the indoor and outdoor conditions, such as convective coefficients, optical properties, and outdoor velocity—"

Without further ado, he pulled her toward him and kissed her. His lips were warm and dry and tasted of gin. Maggie thought of Lily. Had he kissed Lily like that? Was he the father of Lily's baby? Her murderer? She pulled away.

Gregory pulled her close and held her. "I'm sorry," he murmured. "I've just wanted to do that since I met you, roaming the corridors. . . ."

Maggie slipped her arms around his waist. Her fingers brushed the keys, still attached to his belt. "It's all right," she said. *Now, if I could just get the keys. . . .* "I do really like you, Gregory. Just—not in that way."

He let out a dramatic sigh. "Story of my life."

The curtain rustled, and Margaret pressed her way inside. "I knew I heard you two," she whispered, climbing up on the window seat with them. "Now hush, or they'll find us!"

As they moved to let Margaret in beside them, Maggie pushed in the metal tab of the ring and slipped the keys off Gregory's belt. The iron was cold and heavy, and she trapped them in her sweaty hand to silence them. *Yes!* she thought, making sure he hadn't noticed, slipping them into her skirt pocket. And then, *I'm sorry, Gregory. I'm only borrowing them, I promise.*

Which she did. During the next rounds of sardines, when she was alone, she quickly pressed the keys into the clay, making a clear imprint. When the game was over, she placed the keys near the flats they'd been painting.

"Goodness," he said as he put on his bespoke tweed jacket and saw them glint in the firelight. "I can't be dropping these!" He picked up the keys and smiled at the Princesses, a winning grin. "Don't tell the King. He might send me to the dungeons, for good."

The next morning, Maggie wrapped the key imprint in clay in brown paper and made the prearranged drop-off into the trash barrel near Boswell's Books, which another agent nonchalantly picked up. The next day, in town, another undercover agent pretended to stumble and surreptitiously slipped a set of keys into her open handbag as she had lunch at a small café.

After midnight, flashlight tucked under her arm, Maggie unlocked the heavy oak door to the King's Equerry's office, opened it, went inside, and then closed it behind her with a heavy click. Her heart was pounding. She went to the desk and switched on the stained-glass lamp, the light fighting against the pressing shadows. She turned off the flashlight and put it under the desk and laid down her bag, removing the small camera Hugh had given her.

She went to the files and pulled. Locked, of course. Taking out another, smaller key, she put it in the lock and turned. It popped open with a satisfying click.

Her heart began to pound even faster. She could feel her armpits begin to dampen.

She went through the files to *H*. There it was, neatly labeled with *Howell, Lady Lily* typed in black ink.

Maggie took the file to the desk and opened it in the tiny bright circle of lamplight. The edges of the room were veiled in heavy and almost palpable darkness. For a moment, Maggie had a feeling of vertigo, as if the circle of light were the only stable place, and in the dim light the walls had receded, leaving her on a high and perilous platform suspended in the dark. Then she swallowed, took the camera and began shooting, turning pages, then shooting again.

*My goodness,* Maggie thought, goose bumps prickling on her arms. *I'm actually doing this!*

As she photographed, she skimmed the file's contents. Lady Lily Howell had been born in Germany in 1915, moved to London at age five, and was educated at St. Hilda's at Oxford University, studying history. She made her debut before the King and Queen, with Gregory as her escort. Other than that, and a few letters of recommendation, the file was bereft of anything incriminating. *Bugger,* Maggie thought. *Bugger, bugger, bugger.*

Then Maggie found another file within the main one. This one was different. It had records of Lily's meetings with Sir Oswald Mosley, the leader of Britain's Fascist party, and her trips to Nazi Germany. There were photos of her with Unity and Diana Mitford, at a British Fascist party rally, giving a Nazi salute; one of her at the 1937 Nuremberg Rally, at Hitler's side; one of her with Julius Streicher, publisher of *Der Stürmer* newspaper.

*Oh, Lily, Lily,* Maggie thought. *Who were you? How did you get caught up in all this?*

The items in the folder were letters. There was a handwritten note from Home Secretary Sir John Anderson, calling for her "youthful indiscretion" not to be held against her and her MI-5 file destroyed. There were also notes from him, Neville Chamberlain, and Lord Halifax to the King, asking his Majesty to give Lily a place at court—and keep her past a secret.

*No wonder MI-5 wanted me to get these files. Still, what about Louisa?* So she went back to the cabinet and pulled Louisa's file as well. She brought it back to the desk. Louisa had attended the Institut Alpin Videmanette, a Swiss finishing school, and made her debut. Her file resembled Lily's in its aristocratic banality. However, there was no additional folder, nothing to implicate her in any way.

Maggie heard a noise in the hall. *Damn. What was that?* Maggie checked her small watch. It was 3:15 a.m.—surely no one was up.

She flipped another page and snapped a photo.

The noise was footsteps.

Flipped another page. *Snap.*

They were coming closer.

*Snap.*

If someone found her, what would she say? Maggie considered as she kept working, her hands trembling.

*Keep working,* she thought. *Just a few more pages.*

And then, *Done!*

Quickly, she put the files back in place, locked the drawer, put the keys and camera back in her bag, turned off the desk light, and then dove underneath the desk, curling herself up into a small ball in the kneespace.

She heard the lock pop and the door creak open. *Someone's here!*

Maggie willed her pulse to slow and her breathing to be silent.

There were footsteps approaching. A light came on,

and Maggie blinked her eyes against the sudden bright-
ness. From her vantage point under the desk, she could
see Gregory's polished wingtip shoes. He approached
the desk and stopped.

She thought her heart would burst from the strain.
Surely he could hear her breathing?

In sounds that seemed amplified, Maggie heard him
unstop one of the bottles on his desk and pour himself
a drink, the liquid splashing into the glass. She realized
that if she wanted to, she could reach out and untie his
shoelace.

Not that she would, of course.

The moment felt like hours, but finally the door
swung shut and Maggie heard the lock slide into place.

Maggie stayed underneath the desk, unmoving. *I'll
stay here as long as I need to.* In the inky black darkness,
her heartbeat resumed a normal tempo.

A feeling of triumph suffused her, warm and glowing. *I did it,* she thought.

*I did it!*

# Chapter Seventeen

The next morning, at a tiny newsstand not too far from Boswell's Books, Maggie saw Nevins, paging through *Men Only* magazine. She approached.

Maggie looked through the titles and busied herself flipping through a copy of *National Geographic*. The newsstand's proprietor was overseeing a delivery in the back.

"The mission was a success," she said quietly.

"Terrific. Hand over the film, darling," Nevins said.

"No," Maggie said, not looking up from the pages.

Nevins spun around to face her. "No? Do I need to remind you this is *my* operation? Now give me the damn film."

She looked up. Slowly. "Nevins," she said, appraising him, "this isn't going to work."

"Darling, I'm your superior officer. I give the orders. You follow them."

"I'm the one with the film, Nevins. I'm the one with access to the castle. I'm the one who almost got caught taking these photos. And *I'm* the one questioned because I was spotted talking to *you*—you, who felt the need to just stop by and say hello to your 'darling' out in the open and without a pretext. Yes—we were seen, and I was questioned about it."

Maggie squared her shoulders and looked him in the eyes, deadly serious. "I've realized something recently, Nevins. *I'm* the one with the power. You need *me*. Frain needs *me*. My days of blindly following orders are over. Especially orders from someone like you, who's all ego and no integrity."

Nevins's jaw dropped. "Bitch!"

Maggie's nostrils flared with contempt. "Tell Mr. Frain that if Agent Thompson isn't on the other end of the pickup, he's not getting this film."

"But, but—" Nevins spluttered. "Thompson's a nothing, a nobody!"

"He's an infinitely better agent than you." Maggie put down her magazine and smiled. "As far as I'm concerned—you're fired."

When maths lessons with Lilibet were over, there was a knock at the nursery door. It was Margaret, eyes wide and hand in front of her mouth, trying to stifle a laugh. "It's in the oven," she whispered to Lilibet.

Maggie was packing up her books and notebooks. "What's in the oven, Margaret?"

Lilibet's eyes sparkled with mischief. "Come with us," she said. "You'll see."

Smiling with amusement, Maggie let the girls lead her through the castle's maze of corridors, finally reaching the kitchen with its high ceilings and skylights.

"There you are," said Cook, looking up from a mountain of chopped parsnips.

"Is it done?" asked Margaret.

"Almost." Cook wiped her hands on her apron. "Sit down and I'll get it for you for your elevenses."

"A mystery!" said Maggie as they sat down at a long wooden table. "And sounds like one you can eat too!"

The girls looked at each other and giggled.

From an enormous oven, Cook pulled out a pie. She set it in front of the trio. Maggie looked. The top of the pie was dark orange. She inhaled the fragrance of cinnamon and nutmeg. It smelled familiar, but she couldn't quite place it.

Margaret couldn't hold it in any longer. "Pumpkin pie!" she exclaimed.

"Pumpkin pie?" echoed Maggie, confused.

"Well, we learned about America and the Pilgrims and the Indians," Lilibet told her. "We thought you might miss celebrating Thanksgiving."

*Oh, the dears.* Maggie felt a lump in her throat, part homesickness, part happiness. "Thank you, both," she said. "I'm touched beyond words." As a tutor, she just had to add, "You do know that Thanksgiving was more than two weeks ago, though, yes?"

"We had to save our sugar rations," Lilibet confided.

"Can we eat it now?" Margaret asked.

"Of course," said Maggie, as she sliced the pie and handed out plates.

"And we cooked the pumpkin and mixed the filling ourselves!" Margaret chimed. "It was baking during our lesson!"

"It smells wonderful," Maggie told them.

"Very American?" Margaret asked.

"*Extremely* American," Maggie replied.

Truth be told, the pie was not as sweet as it should have been and was missing, in Maggie's opinion, the all-important allspice. But she blinked away stinging tears as they ate, thinking of her Thanksgivings at Wellesley with Aunt Edith and her friend and lover, Olive, who always managed to produce feasts from their tiny kitchen.

When they were finished, and dishes washed and put away, Margaret had another glint in her eye. "We want to take you exploring," she said, sotto voce, out of earshot of Cook.

"Follow us," Lilibet admonished.

Maggie did as she was told. "Yes, ma'am."

The girls seemed to know every nook and cranny of the castle. Maggie was surprised when they took her down the stairs near the servants' entrance and through narrow damp tunnels and down into the dungeon. Lilibet pulled out a flashlight they'd hidden for these purposes and turned it on, the beam a magic wand in the darkness.

"Where are we going?" Maggie whispered as they walked the low-ceilinged corridors in the dark. "And does Alah know you two do this? I can't help but think she wouldn't like it."

Margaret sighed dramatically. "Alah doesn't like us to do anything except sit and knit," she said. "If I have to sit and knit every day, I shall surely go mad."

"Stop exaggerating, Margaret," Lilibet snapped. "We're at war. People are making enormous sacrifices. Surely if *I* can knit, *you* can knit."

"Yes, your Majesty," Margaret said with mock deference and a low curtsy.

Maggie was counting the twists and turns as they went. "You're sure you know where you're going?"

"And, here we are!" announced Lilibet.

They had reached a small room, part of the old dungeons. Maggie shivered, thinking of those who'd been imprisoned there over the centuries.

"Over here!" Margaret said, running over to a pile of large hatboxes. "Open it, Maggie!"

Maggie walked over with trepidation. What did the boxes contain? Skulls? Bones? Ashes?

Determined not to show fear, she opened the largest. Inside were newspapers. Taking a deep breath, Maggie reached inside. Behind her, the girls giggled. "She stuck in her thumb . . ." Margaret began.

Maggie pulled out something large and heavy, wrapped in tissue paper. ". . . and pulled out . . ." *Is that what I think it is? Could it be?* "The Crown Jewels?"

The crown she held was the Imperial State Crown, gold and encrusted with diamonds, rubies, emeralds, sapphires, and pearls in crosses pattées and fleurs-de-lis, topped with purple velvet and trimmed in white ermine. The large diamonds glittered in the dim light. "'Uneasy lies the head that wears a crown,'" she whispered, thinking of all the heads who'd worn it over the ages.

"Look!" said Margaret, pulling out from another hatbox the long Sovereign's Scepter, topped with a diamond as large as her fist.

"Goodness," Maggie breathed.

"Look at this," Lilibet said, pulling out the Sovereign's Orb, a golden ball set with bands of gems and pearls, topped with an amethyst and then a diamond cross. "Charles the Second once held it—can you imagine?" She held it out to Maggie. "Go on, give it a try."

Maggie accepted the object; it was cool to the touch. "It's heavy," she whispered. Then, trying to remember her role as teacher, "Shouldn't these be in the Tower of London?"

"Here for safekeeping. They *will* be mine one day, after all," Lilibet said. "I wanted you to see them."

"Thank you—both of you," Maggie said. "This was, well, quite an unexpected treat."

"We can give you a tour of more of the dungeons, if you'd like," Margaret said, wrapping the jewels back in the papers and putting them in the trunk.

"Thank you," Maggie said. "A tour would be more valuable than jewels, really."

The next day, after lessons with Lilibet, Maggie took the Windsor and Eton Central train back to London. After arriving at Paddington, Maggie took the Tube's Central Line to the Circle Line, exiting from the Bond Street stop in Mayfair. Above ground, she walked until she saw the imposing, tall red-brick building that was Claridge's. She walked past the doorman, who tipped his hat, over the gleaming black and white tiles, through the perfumed air, to the concierge desk.

The concierge on duty was a tall man, thin, with a long face and droopy eyes and jowls, like a bloodhound. "Good morning, Miss," he said. "May I help you?"

"Good morning," Maggie answered. She pulled out her picture of Lily. "I was wondering if you could help me—have you seen this woman at your hotel?"

"Miss, here at Claridge's, we treat our guests with

the utmost respect, which includes respect for their privacy."

"I understand, sir, but the young lady in the photograph is dead. Any information you could share would be most appreciated."

"Are you with the police?" he asked, voice low, making sure the hotel's guests checking in couldn't hear.

"N-no," Maggie stammered. "I'm—a friend." She pulled out a few pound notes, as she had seen done in the movies.

"Oh, no, no, no, no, no," he said, wagging his finger. "We don't do that here. I'm afraid I can't help you. Good day."

*Ugh, I'm such an amateur,* she thought, annoyed. *If Nevins were doing his job properly . . .* Maggie walked back to the door, and when she got outside, out of sight of the front desk, she showed Lily's photograph to the doorman, slipping him the pound notes. It went a bit smoother this time. "Have you seen this woman?"

He studied the photo. "Yes, Miss," he said, pocketing the pound notes. "She used to come here regular, about once a month, I'd say."

"Did you ever see her come or go with anyone?"

"Sometimes some lady friends. Young, like 'er."

"Pale, black hair, red lipstick?"

"That'd be them, Miss."

"Anyone else?"

"Sometimes, Miss," he said in lower tones, "people don't come and go with the people they're here with, if you get my meaning. But the chambermaids always know. Go around the corner to the staff entrance, ask around there. You may get someone who knows more than I do." He gave a broad wink.

"Thank you," Maggie said, "very much."

She walked into the staff entrance, a world away from the polished surfaces and high ceilings of the lobby—low and dim.

"Miss, you're not allowed in 'ere," a thin older woman said, her rough hands testament to the cleaning she must do.

"Actually, I was wondering," Maggie said. "Have you ever seen this woman here at the hotel?"

The woman stared at the photograph. "No, love, I ain't seen 'er." Maggie pulled out the pound notes again. This time, they had the intended effect. The woman looked around and caught sight of one of her fellow maids. "She might know. Maude! Maude! Come over 'ere?"

"What?" Maude barked. She was a large, burly woman with surprisingly delicate features.

"Miss 'ere 'as a question," she said, looking pointedly at the pound notes.

"Do you recognize the woman in the photo?" Maggie asked.

The woman stared. "Yeah," she said. "Always asking for more towels, that one. What she does with all them towels, I 'ave no idea, 'cept we've gotta wash 'em."

Maggie's heart leapt. "Did you ever see her with anyone?"

The woman squinted at the photo. "Oh, she got around, all right. I know, 'cause I bring her the extra towels to 'er room, and also some others' rooms. Probably took a bath in every bloody room at the hotel. Sorry, Miss."

"That's all right. Do you happen to remember who she was with?"

The woman sighed. "There was a woman, actually. Pretty, with black 'air." She lowered her voice. "The one 'oo was murdered 'ere." She crossed herself.

*The link to Victoria confirmed!* Maggie thought. "Anyone else?"

"A young man. Tall, thin."

"Can you describe him?"

"Oh, I dunno, Miss. All those young men look alike to me. Tall, pale, nose in the air."

"Was he blond or dark?" Maggie pressed. "Did he have scars on his face?" She waited for the answer, heart in her throat. Because she liked Gregory, she really did. And she didn't want him to have anything to do with Lily's murder or the decrypt.

"No, Miss, no scars—I would 'ave remembered that." She thought a bit. "'E 'ad one a those scarves, you know, the fancy university scarves?"

"What were the colors?"

"Blue. Dark blue with red and yellow. I remember it—ugly as sin."

By the time Maggie returned to the castle, snow was falling in earnest and a light dusting had collected on the ground. As she walked up the gravel path, her feet making crunching noises in the still, cold air and the bells from St. George's Chapel clanging, she saw that a truck had pulled up in front of the castle's entrance. In the back was an enormous evergreen from the Great Park, at least twenty-two feet tall and nearly as wide at the tree's foot—the Royal Christmas tree. *How appropriate,* Maggie thought, *since the first Christmas tree in*

*England was the one Prince Albert brought to Windsor Castle from Germany.*

Mr. Tooke was overseeing the men untying the ropes and wrestling with it. He caught Maggie's eye and lifted his tweed cap. "Hello, Mr. Tooke!" Maggie called. She recognized her winking footman, out of uniform. "Hello," she said to him. "It's silly to keep seeing each other and not be introduced. I'm Maggie Hope."

"George Poulter," he said, tipping his cap. "How d'you do?"

"Have you been at Windsor long, Mr. Poulter?"

"Came with Lord Gregory. Lord Gregory Strathcliffe? I used to be his manservant back in the day, at his family's estate. That was before the injuries, of course. He found me a place at Windsor Castle when he came, he did. Good man, Lord Gregory."

"Yes," Maggie said, thoughtful. "Yes, he is."

Inside, the castle was a buzz of activity. Servants arranged boughs of evergreen on fireplace mantels, releasing their sharp, piney smell. There was holly as well, with glossy leaves and bright red berries. Even though the corridors were as long and cold as ever, the decorations lent a homey touch to the place. Maggie was amused to see that, where grand oil paintings used to hang, large posters for *Sleeping Beauty,* featuring Lilibet and Margaret's artwork, were displayed.

Maggie made her way to the vast Waterloo Chamber, where the stage was set up. The room was magnificent: a soaring clerestory ceiling, paneled walls decorated with lime-wood carvings by Grinling Gibbons, an enormous Indian carpet.

Lilibet and Margaret were rehearsing the final ballroom scene with the other children, the sons and daughters of the castle's staff. "Stop it, Margaret," Maggie heard. It was Lilibet, her high, sweet voice echoing through the vast chamber. "You're stepping on my toes."

"Oooooh, wouldn't want to step on the Royal Toesies, now, would we?" Margaret retorted.

Crawfie clapped her hands. "All right, children," she said in her Scottish lilt. "Let's take a break, shall we? Audrey's setting up tea and biscuits in the nursery—come back in half an hour, please."

Maggie walked forward to Crawfie, standing near the platforms of the makeshift stage. "How goes it?"

"Oh, Maggie." Crawfie sighed. "I'd be better off directing corgis, for as much as the children listen . . . and the performance is in less than two weeks."

"That's quite a bit of time—I'm sure it will be wonderful," Maggie assured the woman.

"The sets look fantastic," Crawfie said.

"Thank you. The girls and Gregory are responsible."

"Oh, but the shading—it really looks like a storybook brought to life!"

"Well, it's a bit intimidating, making a castle set to go into an actual castle—but somehow we managed by making it a bit less literal. Thank Gerda Wegener—I loved her illustrations when I was a child."

"You'll be with us? For the performance? To make sure everything goes the way it should?" Crawfie looked pale.

"Of course I shall. Wouldn't dream of being anywhere else." Maggie looked intently at Crawfie. "Are you all right? Maybe you could do with a cup of tea yourself?"

"Oh, I'm fine." Crawfie shrugged. "It's just that, with the Prime Minister coming and all of his people, and the King and Queen, of course . . . and it's such a big event for the children. The first time most of them have been onstage." She shook her head. "I just don't want anything to go wrong."

"No," Maggie said, looking out into the shadows, realizing how vulnerable Lilibet and Margaret were on-stage. "No, indeed."

# Chapter Eighteen

Letters arrived for Maggie occasionally, care of Windsor Castle. The twins, Annabelle and Clarabelle, sent missives describing their adventures as Land Girls working on a farm in Scotland, writing on the same page in two alternating colored inks, purple for Annabelle and Moroccan red for Clarabelle. Sarah sent cards from various stops on the Vic-Wells Ballet's tour of Britain, deftly drawn cartoons of some of her fellow dancers, including ballerina Margot Fonteyn and choreographer Frederick Ashton.

Aunt Edith sent long letters in small, elegant script, lamenting Maggie's career move from typist to tutor. Of all the people she had to keep her secret from, Maggie would have loved to have told Aunt Edith what she was *really* doing.

And she knew David well enough to realize he'd never even think to write.

From Chuck, she received various hastily written missives, in pencil on scrap paper, detailing wedding plans. Then came the day she received the invitation, engraved on heavy cream stock.

DR. AND MRS. IAN MCCAFFREY

REQUEST THE HONOR OF YOUR PRESENCE

AT THE MARRIAGE OF THEIR DAUGHTER

CHARLOTTE MARY

TO

FLIGHT LIEUTENANT NIGEL ALFRED LUDLOW

ON SATURDAY, JANUARY 2

AT HALF PAST TEN O'CLOCK IN THE MORNING

LEEDS CATHEDRAL

GREAT GEORGE STREET, LEEDS

She wrote back to say she would be attending, especially as Chuck had asked her to be a bridesmaid.

*Dear Chuck,* she wrote, *or should I call you Charlotte Mary? I'll be there with the proverbial bells on. Xoxo—M.*

And her father had sent a package. She cut through the twine and removed the heavy brown paper. Inside was a volume of *Grimm's Fairy Tales,* with Arthur Rackham illustrations. She opened the book and inhaled the musty papery scent.

Turning through the frontmatter, she noticed an inscription: *To my darling Clara, with all my love, Eddie. 20 October 1915.* Clara was Clara Hope, her mother. Eddie was Edmund, her father. And 20 October 1917 was only weeks before her mother's death.

*Dear Margaret,* her father had written on a scrap of graph paper. *So sorry we missed each other. Thought this book might answer some of your questions.*

*Oh, right,* Maggie thought. *My life might resemble a*

*Grimm Brothers tale, but I doubt I'll find any answers in here.* With a deep sigh, she put the book away on the shelf.


"Maggie, may we do maths in your sitting room today?" Lilibet asked as Maggie entered the nursery the next morning, carrying several books and folders of notes.

Maggie was surprised but willing to consider it. "Of course, Lilibet, but why? Your rooms are so much prettier. And *warmer.*"

Lilibet sighed. "It's just . . . I'm so restless here. It's always the same. We always do the same things, in the same order, every day. I just thought a change of scene . . ."

"Indeed!" Maggie said, warming to the idea. "That's something Mr. Churchill always said, when he'd go to Chartwell or Chequers or Ditchley to work." She affected her best Churchillian voice: " 'A change of scene is as good as a rest.' "

Lilibet giggled.

"We'll have tea and lessons up there. Come on!"

After the long trek down the cold corridors, they reached Maggie's rooms. In her green sitting room, a fire crackled cheerfully behind the iron grate. Maggie set down their books and notes as Audrey entered and put down a tea tray with a pot, two cups and saucers, spoons, and a plate of digestive biscuits and linen napkins, and then left.

As the tea steeped, Lilibet was uncharacteristically twitchy. She wandered around Maggie's room, picking things up and putting them down. When she found the wireless, she asked, "Do you listen to *It's That Man Again*? Margaret and Alah and I love it."

"I do enjoy it," Maggie confessed.

Lilibet continued to look at her shelves. "You don't have much here."

"No," Maggie agreed. "Most of my things are still in London."

"We used to live in London, you know." Lilibet pulled out a book of photographs bound in ivory moiré silk. "What's this?" she asked.

Maggie took the book and then motioned for the young girl to sit down next to her. "Well," she said, turning the pages. "This is a family album. Here are my paternal grandparents, my father and Aunt Edith when they were children. Oh! And my father and mother's wedding picture. They were married at Saint Margaret's, near Westminster Abbey."

Lilibet's eyes took in the picture of Clara Hope, draped in lace. "Goodness, your mother was pretty," she said.

"Yes," Maggie agreed, giving the photos one last, wistful look before closing the book. "And now it's time to get to work."

But Lilibet had sprung up yet again and was looking at Maggie's books. "Ugh," she exclaimed, examining the titles. "Boring!" She pulled out the Turing and paged through. "You can actually read this?"

"Yes," Maggie said. "And so could you, if you continue with your study of maths. And now—"

"Oh, *Grimm's Fairy Tales*!" she exclaimed. "I just love them!" She pulled the book out, brought it to the tea table, and sat down. "Look, here's 'Hansel and Gretel,' 'The Frog King,' and 'Cat and Mouse'!"

Maggie went to pour the tea, but Lilibet said, "May I?" Maggie nodded, and the Princess poured the fragrant tea into the two cups. "Margaret calls me puritanical about tea, but I like things to be perfect."

Maggie had noticed this tendency in the Princess. Often she would arrange and rearrange her pens and pencils on her desk and become agitated if her books weren't in the proper order or her papers weren't lined up just so.

"Well, we're not going to be perfect today," Maggie said lightly. "I'm afraid I don't have any sugar."

"That's fine, I'm used to it black now," Lilibet replied, coming back to the sofa with the volume and sitting down. "May I borrow it? I know there's a library here and all, but the books are so very old and serious, and Sir Owen is such a Burns about letting them out of the stacks. . . ." Turning the pages, Lilibet started. "Oh, there's an inscription!" she said, reaching for her tea. "Look! *To my darling Clara, With all my love, Eddie. 20 October 1915.* How romantic. Was Clara your—"

And with that Lilibet sneezed, an enormous, violent sneeze. Quite by accident, she splashed hot tea all over the page.

"Are you all right?" Maggie asked, taking napkins from the tray and blotting first the princess and then the book.

"I'm fine," Lilibet said, her blue eyes threatening to overflow with sudden tears. "But, Maggie—I'm so sorry. So very, very sorry. I've ruined your book."

"It's fine, really," Maggie assured her. "No harm done."

Lilibet blotted the inscription. "I think it will be all right. . . ."

"Of course it will," Maggie responded, putting the book on the windowsill to dry. "And now, let's open our textbook to page one fifty-six and—"

There was a knock. It was George Poulter, the winking footman, his hair powdered white with the same mixture of starch, flour, and soap that had been used at the Castle for centuries. He wore the official footman's uniform: blue velvet coat, knee breeches, stockings, and well-shined buckled shoes. He carried a letter on an ornate silver tray.

"Your Highness," he said to the Princess, who favored him with a smile. And then, "Miss Hope." He bowed as he proffered the envelope.

"Thank you," Maggie said. She took the letter and the footman left. She found her hands were shaking.

The return address was an official Whitehall address, and it was written on official-looking RAF stationery.

"Oooh, what is it?" Lilibet said, running over to Maggie's side. "How glamorous!" Then, seeing Maggie's expression, "Oh, I do hope everything's all right. He *is* all right, isn't he?" she asked earnestly. Lilibet reached out her hand and placed it on Maggie's. Her nails were rough and bitten and decidedly un-princess-like. Even in the midst of her own crisis, Maggie realized what a strain the war must be on the young girls, even if they were Royal.

"I know how you must feel, or at least a little bit. If anything happened to Philip . . ."

Maggie slipped the envelope into her skirt pocket. "It's nothing that can't wait until we've finished our lesson," she said briskly. "Now, let's get down to business."

———

It was only later, after Lilibet had closed the door behind her, that Maggie allowed herself to open the letter.
It was from Nigel; she'd know his handwriting anywhere. It was shaky and less legible than she was used
to, but it was Nigel's.

She sat down, not sure if her legs would hold her.

> Dear Maggie,
>
> As a follow-up to our telephone conversation
> a few months ago, I am writing to confirm that
> we still have received no word from John.
>
> He is an extremely able pilot and a loyal officer
> with a deep sense of duty.
>
> However, he has not been able to contact us
> for over six months, and the odds of him surviving
> that long in enemy territory are, I'm sorry to say,
> quite low.
>
> He is now listed as "Missing, presumed dead."
> I thought you would want to know.
>
> Yours sincerely,
> Nigel

About a half an hour later there was a knock on the
door to Maggie's room. It was Lilibet, to pick up the ink
bottle she'd left.

There was no answer.

Lilibet knocked again.

Nothing.

Just as she was about to turn and climb back down
the cold, narrow steps, she heard a noise. It was a high-
pitched keening sound. She opened the door.

There was Maggie, facedown on the sofa, clutching the missive in her hands and weeping.

"Maggie?" Lilibet said at the doorway. There was no response, but the wailing died down slightly, then stopped. The Princess could hear long ragged breaths and the occasional sniffle. "Maggie? Are you ill?"

Lilibet cautiously made her way in, walking gently toward the prone form on the sofa, as though not to startle a wild animal. "Maggie?"

Maggie sat up in a sudden movement, pulling her hair back and then wiping furiously at her red and swollen eyes.

"Lilibet, do you—do you have a handkerchief?" she asked finally.

"Of course," said the Princess, procuring a clean cambric one. "Here you go. Now, tell me what's wrong."

Maggie gave her nose a good, honking blow, then pushed the letter to Lilibet, who read it. She set it down, then reached over to place her hand on Maggie's.

"'Missing and presumed dead.'" Maggie reached for the envelope and paper and crumpled them in her hands. Then threw them both in the fire. The two watched as the orange flames consumed both papers until they turned black and into lacy ash that flew up the chimney. Maggie felt gutted, as though she'd been kicked, hard, in the stomach. It was a physical sensation so fierce, she momentarily put her arms around herself in self-protection.

"Shhhhh . . ." Lilibet said in motherly tones, stroking Maggie's hair as she might pet a horse or corgi. "It will be all right, Maggie. It will be all right."

_____

Some time later, Lilibet had convinced Maggie to wash her face with cold water and come down to the kitchen for some hot tea.

"Maggie's had some bad news," she said to Cook, who immediately went to brew a pot of tea. Then she returned to her work, making up a new tray for Audrey to take upstairs.

"Here you go, Cousin," Cook said to the Parisienne, who smiled at Maggie and bobbed a curtsy at Lilibet before she picked up her tray and left.

At the long wooden table, Maggie didn't want to discuss what had just happened; the pain was still too raw and she was still too numb. Lilibet seemed to understand, and sat next to her in supportive silence. Better to try to think of other things.

"Audrey Moreau is your cousin?" she asked Cook, taking a sip of the hot tea.

"No, Miss," said Cook. "My husband's cousin. She came from Paris. Got out just in time, poor thing. Parents are gone—got an older brother, but he joined the military. Not sure where he is now."

"Thank goodness she made it in time!" Lilibet exclaimed.

"And so she's been here for, what, about eight months?" asked Maggie. "How does she like it?"

"Doing fine, Miss. Does what she's told, never complains." Cook looked concerned. "She's been all right with you, Miss?"

"Oh, yes," Maggie said. "Of course. Consummate professional, lovely person. I was just curious, is all."

*So, John is dead. Did he die on impact, when his Spitfire went down? Or was he found by the Nazis, then tortured for information, then killed?* she thought, before bursting into tears yet again, the heavy pain in her heart nearly unbearable.

*How can life possibly go on?* And yet it did. People in the castle's kitchen chopped root vegetables and peeled apples and pulled feathers off chickens and geese. The clock ticked and the hands moved. The earth on its axis turned on and on. *And this is what life is,* Maggie thought. *How odd, really. He's dead, we're still alive, and the earth keeps spinning on its axis. How very, very droll.*

# Chapter Nineteen

In an effort to keep her mind off John, Maggie decided to redouble her efforts to solve the mystery of Lady Lily's death. After her tea in the kitchen with the Princess, she slipped on her sturdy shoes and tramped over the castle's grounds in the milky afternoon light until she reached the place where Lily had been killed.

The wire had cut through the bark of the tree. It had been tied high up—high enough that it was meant for an adult, on a full-sized horse. Not for a young girl on a smaller pony. *Surely, though, Inspector Wilson had noticed that.*

In the bare branches of the scarred tree, Maggie heard the raspy, scolding cry of a peregrine falcon. Her eyes went from the falcon back to the castle. Sure enough, there was Sam Berners, backlit against the sun. "What did *you* see that morning?" Maggie said to the hawk.

*"Scree! Scree! Scree!"* it responded before it flew off, its large wings creating a small windstorm. Maggie saw him fly up, up, up into the sky, make a long, gliding cir-

cle, then come to rest on the arm of the ever-present, ever-watching Sam Berners. Maggie remembered his agitation the day he was questioned, the way he nearly had to be restrained.

"And, better yet—what did Mr. Berners see?"


It took Maggie a while to walk back to the castle, and then to find her way all the way up to the Royal Mews. Sam Berners was leaning his bulk against the parapets, looking out over the land, cold wind ruffling his unkempt hair.

"Mr. Berners!" Maggie called.

"What ye want, lassie? This isn't a place for ladies."

"I think they're beautiful, you know," she said, looking at the hooded falcons on their perches.

Berners gave her a sullen glare.

Maggie was undeterred. "The morning of the day Lady Lily was decapitated—"

"I seen nothin'," he growled. "Already told the detective."

Maggie considered. "I'm not asking if you saw the actual murder. I'm asking if you saw the person who put up the wire. See?" She pointed to the riding course. "You have a perfect view. And I know you're always up here, watching your birds."

"I seen nothin'. Told you." He trained his eyes back to the horizon.

"What did you see, Mr. Berners?" she asked gently.

"I canna, I canna say," he said finally.

"So, you *did* see something." Maggie's heart beat faster. "Who? Who was it?"

Berners was silent, an agonized look on his face.

"A woman is dead." She took a breath. "It might easily have been Princess Elizabeth. . . ."

Berners looked at her, shocked. It had been the first time he'd looked her in the eyes, and Maggie noticed they were green and flecked with gold.

"Yes, she was out riding with Lily that morning. If she'd been in front . . ."

"The wee Princess?" Berners looked close to tears. "I didn' know. That's different. He shouldna have put the Princess's life at risk. No, no," he muttered, trying to sort out this new revelation.

"So you *did* see something?"

"The person . . . The person who did it knows somethin' 'bout me," Berners said. "Somethin' bad. Real bad." He looked down at his boots. "I don' wanna lose my place here."

"Whatever it is, it can't be as bad as a murder."

"Hunting, murder—we're all righ' savage when you think abou' it."

"Your birds hunt for food. It's natural. It's the food chain, Darwin's survival of the fittest. But whoever killed Lily was committing murder. There's the difference. In many ways, your falcons are more civilized than people."

Berners considered, looking out over the vast lands of the castle. "Aye, lassie," he said finally. "You're right." He took a breath. "He's been poachin' off the King's land, he has. And since I saw what he did, he's been givin' me food. And I take it. I've jus' been so hungry, Miss. So hungry . . ."

"That's all?" Maggie smiled, a wide smile. When Berners saw, he gave a nervous laugh.

"Yes, Miss, that's all. Canna stan' that carrot mess

no more." He shrugged. "An' that Lady Lily was no lady, that's for sure. She a mean one. Oh, not to the other Lords and Ladies, but horrible to the servants. Didn't think the world was any worse with her gone." He scratched his head. "Didn't think about the Princess being in danger, though."

"Mr. Berners," Maggie pressed, "who set up the wire?"

He looked up, eyes wild. "If I tell you what I know, I'll get in trouble. Can't afford to lose my job, Miss."

"Of course not," Maggie said in soothing tones. "But you didn't do anything." She had an idea. "And he did. What if he decides to kill again? Maybe the Princesses won't be so lucky."

"I don't want to get into any trouble, Miss," Berners said, voice breaking.

"You didn't do anything—you're just a witness."

"I took 'is meat."

"But he was the one who did the poaching." Maggie paused. "I've met Detective Wilson a few times. And he seems like a reasonable man. If you tell me who did it, I can tell him how helpful you were. And he might go easy on you. Mr. Berners, please tell me—who killed Lady Lily?"

There was the loud sound of wings flapping and a rush of air. Berners stretched out his arm, and a falcon landed on his long leather glove, wings beating fast and hard until the bird folded them neatly. "What d'you think, Merlin," Berners said. "You think I should tell the young miss?"

Merlin cocked his head and angled one beady black eye at Maggie. "Scree! Scree!" he cried.

"All right," Berners said, giving a heavy sigh. "The

man who put up the wire that killed Lady Lily was Mr. Tooke, Miss."

*Mr. Tooke! The Head Gardener.* He *was the perpetrator?*

"Thank you, Mr. Berners," Maggie said, trying to contain her shock. "And may I call Detective Wilson and tell him you'll speak with him?"

Another long pause, while Berners stroked the feathers at the back of Merlin's neck.

"I'll talk to 'im, Miss," he agreed finally. "Yea, I'll talk to 'im."

Maggie went to the tidy red-brick police building. The older man with sandy hair recognized her and smiled. "Well, hello there!"

"I'm here to see Detective Wilson," Maggie said. "It's urgent."

"He's in a meeting, Miss."

"It's something he'll want to hear right away."

"Then come to his office, Miss."

Detective Wilson excused himself from his meeting, went to his office and listened to what Maggie had learned. Together, they drove back to the castle, where they went first to find Sam Berners on the roof, who told the detective the same story he'd told Maggie.

Then they went to Mr. Tooke's flat, where he confessed everything. He looked almost relieved when the detective said he was under arrest for the murder of Lily Howell, put handcuffs on him and led him to the car to take him to the station. As they drove away, Maggie felt sad. Sad for Mr. Tooke's wife, sad for Mr. Tooke, sad for Lily. She remembered something she had typed once, for the P.M.: *"Never, never, never believe any war will be smooth and easy, or that anyone who embarks on the strange voyage can measure the tides and hurricanes he will encounter."*

*Hats off, Mr. Churchill,* Maggie thought grimly. *You certainly have that one right.*

Back in her room, Maggie shivered. She used the loo, washed up, then changed into her flannel nightgown, adding socks and a cardigan. The fireplace was lit and she turned on the portable radiator in the bedroom, waiting for it to warm. In the meantime, she cleared the small table where she and Lilibet had been working.

She picked up the book, the Grimm. Maggie sighed. It wasn't Lilibet's fault; it had been an accident. Still, it was one of the few things she owned that had belonged to her mother. . . .

Maggie looked at the inscription. It was still there, the black ink now blurred and watery. However, that wasn't what captured Maggie's attention, as she flipped through the pages of the book. There were tiny, tiny holes in the pages. Holes too small to be seen with the naked eye but highlighted by the tea stains.

*Some sort of bugs? Moths?* Maggie thought. Then she headed for bed, to battle yet another night of tears and insomnia and eventual bad dreams.

The next day, Maggie received a package with her breakfast, a pair of leather skates in her size, sharpened and ready. She could interpret only that Hugh was going to meet her somewhere where they could ice-skate.

"Audrey," Maggie asked, "where do people skate around here?"

"I think there's a pond near Frogmore House, Miss," Audrey replied.

"Thank you," Maggie said. She was happy—not because she would see Hugh, of course, but because she'd have a chance to vary her physical fitness routine.

Stately white Frogmore House, a seventeenth-century royal country home, was a good walk south of the castle in the Home Park. Maggie had made it in plenty of time and was sitting on a rough wooden bench by the side of the pond, lacing up her skates, when she spotted Hugh, dressed in tweed trousers and a Barbour jacket, skating and playing tag with a few children. Their laughter, and the rough, scraping sound of blades on hard ice, floated up to the sky, which was leaden and threatened snow. The surrounding grass was a dull brown, and the trees that outlined the perimeter of the pond were now completely bare.

Maggie stepped onto the ice and pushed off on one blade, her breath visible in the cold air. *So long, Nevins.*

One of the children Hugh was playing with fell and cried out, startling a murder of crows pecking at the ground nearby, causing them to flap their iridescent blue-black wings and scream, *"Caw! Caw!"* into the wind. They settled back down to their pecking, as Hugh picked the child up and dusted her off, sending her on her way.

As Maggie skated by and then turned backward, Hugh whistled. "Not bad, Sonja Henie."

"I learned at Wellesley," Maggie said, circling around him, arms outstretched for balance. "Small town near Boston, where I grew up. Every winter we'd clear off

Paramecium Pond at Wellesley College and skate." She grinned. "However, I'm afraid that skating, plus limited self-defense from Camp Spook, are the only sports I can manage. Although I *have* been doing my exercises daily."

"From what I recall," Hugh said, trying to catch up, "your self-defense skills are spot-on."

They glided together for a while, keeping pace with each other, away from the other skaters. The cold wind rushed past them, stirring the bare branches of the trees in the distance. "It's good to see you again," she said.

"Good to see you too," Hugh said. "Er, good to be back on the case."

"Wish I could have been a fly on the wall," Maggie said, turning backward again.

Hugh laughed as he did forward crossovers. "Nevins was fit to be tied, and Frain was none too pleased. But I'm glad. Really glad. So, thanks." Then, "How did it go?"

"Well, except for having to hide under the desk when Gregory came in unexpectedly, fantastic. He didn't see me, by the way."

"Good. And even if you had been found, I'm sure you could have talked your way out."

Maggie did a few three-turns, her knitted scarf flying behind her. "You were right about Lily, by the way. Fascist involvement from way back, trips to Germany with the Mitford girls, photographs with Hitler . . ."

"And letters pleading with the King to cover it up, right?"

"Exactly."

Hugh shook his head as he turned to go backward. He almost fell but then righted himself. "If you're rich

enough and your family has enough connections, you
can make anything go away."

"By the way, I photographed Louisa's file too, while I
was there. Camera's in my bag."

"Anything?"

"No," Maggie said, slowing down. She bit her lip.
"But I just have a feeling that something's not right
there."

"Why? What *specifically* makes you feel that way?"

"Well . . ." Maggie thought. "She's arrogant. She's
mean. She owns a snake. A *snake*!"

Hugh shrugged. "Doesn't mean she's guilty of anything, including colluding with Lily. If you suspect her
of something, you need evidence."

"Frain told me to be a 'sponge'—and I've absorbed a
very bad feeling about her."

"Well, keep an eye on her."

"I will."

"You have any suspicions of anyone else?"

Maggie thought about Audrey and how she'd just
come from France. Then she shook her head. *That's ridiculous.*

They skated together in silence as the wind picked
up velocity, blowing the large, lacy snowflakes sideways.
Most of the children were cold and had left the pond.
"Thanks for getting me back on the case, by the way,"
Hugh told her.

"Of course," Maggie replied. "We're a team."

"Yes," he said. "Although great work solving Lady
Lily's murder there, solo."

"Sam Berners was the key. Berners was up on the
parapet, watching his birds, when he saw Tooke string
up the wire. Tooke realized that Berners had seen him,

but blackmailed him—Berners had been holding back some of the pheasants and rabbits his falcons killed for himself as well as selling them on the black market—and Tooke threatened to expose him."

"Well, that takes care of that, then—but we still have no idea where Lily got that decrypt or whom she was going to give it to."

He tried another turn, as a falcon dove into the underbrush to ambush its prey, and nearly fell again. "Argh," he said. "My concentration's a little off today."

Maggie glided on one foot and lifted up her free leg in an arabesque, arms outstretched. She looked back at the castle. Sure enough, there on the rooftop was the large and unmistakably broad figure of Sam Berners. *Rabbit stew tonight,* Maggie thought. *Thank you, falcons.*

"You seem agitated," she said. "More than usual."

There was a long silence. "Broke up with the girl-friend. It was . . . awkward," he said finally.

There was another silence. "As it turns out, John—my, well, my almost-fiancé—is dead. 'Missing, presumed dead' as they say. But no one seems to have much hope after all this time."

"Oh," said Hugh. He rubbed his gloved hands together for warmth. "I'm sorry for your loss."

"Yes, thank you," said Maggie. Then, "I need to go now—to prepare tomorrow's maths lesson. We're starting algebra, heaven help us."

They skated over to the benches on the perimeter of the pond and sat down, unlacing their skates. "Nevins mentioned, well, that he'd told you about the suspicions surrounding your father," Hugh said. "I always put it down to idle gossip, personally, but you must have a lot of questions." He gave a deep sigh. "I don't know if you want it, but I 'borrowed' his file. It's in my skate bag."

Maggie was stunned. "Thank you," she managed. She took Hugh's bag and hoisted it over her shoulder. He did the same with hers.

"I hope you feel the same," he said, "after you've read it."

In the bowels of U-246, in the cold waters of the North Sea, Gernot Schneider and Hermann Hoffman lay in their narrow racks, six-foot bunks affixed to the walls, one on top of the other. The air was close and rank, punctuated by snores from the other men.

"I just don't get it," Schneider said on his back, making a steeple of his hands.

"Shut the fuck up!" called another man, in another bunk, trying to sleep while he could.

"Shut the fuck up, yourself!" Schneider snarled back. Then, to Hoffman, in a lower voice, "We're on one of the most elite U-boats in the fleet. Kapitänleutnant Hackl has the Knight's Cross, for God's sake."

"Pinned on by *der Führer* himself," Hoffman said.

"So, why are we here?" Schneider said. "Why aren't we seeing any action?"

The man called out, "You want action? If you don't shut up, *I'll* give you action."

"I wouldn't complain if I were you," Hoffman whispered. "You just might jinx it. Besides, I have a fiancée to return to."

"*Ach,* Greta Kruger, with the big bottom, who makes the world's best *Apfelstrudel*." Schneider rolled his eyes in the dim light. "But I didn't join the Kriegsmarine just to eat cabbage soup and smell my fellow sailors' farts. I want to see battle!"

"Commandant Hess has a plan for us, that I trust," Hoffman said.

"You're right." Schneider turned over and yanked his thin cover with him. "And when we finally learn what it is, I hope it'll be big."

Maggie went to the library at Windsor to read her father's MI-5 file. There, in a leather-tufted chair, under the fading gray light pouring in from the mullioned windows, she read.

And read.

And read.

What she read was disturbing. Her father had been a spy during the Great War, when he was supposed to be just a professor at the London School of Economics. *He lied to me about that,* Maggie thought, hands clenching, still angry at his not asking about John, at being stood up in Slough. *Lied to.*

But what was most disturbing was that some material was blacked out, specifically in regard to a certain agent, Neil Wright. *And who are you, Agent Wright? What kind of relationship did you have with dear old Dad? Why would it be censored?*

Sir Owen clasped his hands behind his back and approached Maggie. "May I help you with anything, Miss Hope?" he asked.

Maggie closed the file and put it away in her bag, so that he couldn't see anything. "No, Sir Owen—thank you. Actually, I believe I have, well, almost everything I need right here."

———

The next day, Hugh was waiting in the back room of Boswell's when Maggie arrived.

"You all right?" Hugh asked, for Maggie was paler than usual and had deep circles under her eyes.

"The King and Queen have planned a sleep-and-dine holiday—they're calling it a Red, White, and Blue Christmas. Very patriotic."

"I know," Hugh said, wrinkling his forehead. "A security nightmare."

"If Louisa—or anyone—is going to try anything, that would be the time to do it."

"We know. Everyone's going to be on sharpest alert. Even I."

"You?"

"I'll be there. With Frain."

"Oh." Maggie wasn't sure how she felt about his being at Windsor Castle. "I see." She shook her head. "I've read my father's file. What do you know about Agent Neil Wright and the blacked-out material?"

"The censored material sparked my curiosity, yes. I tried to get Agent Wright's folder, but it's gone."

"Gone?"

Hugh shrugged. "At least it's not where someone as lowly as I can find it. All there remains are the basics— that he was born in Hampstead Heath in 1885, went to Christ Church at Oxford and graduated with honors in history in 1906, was recruited to MI-Five not long after." Hugh took a breath. "Also, he was MI-Six, not MI-Five."

"MI-Six?" Maggie was confused. Like the CIA and the FBI, MI-6 dealt with foreign threats and MI-5 with domestic. "MI-Six wouldn't be involved with my father unless . . ." Her mind grappled with the answer. "Unless they suspected him of being a double agent."

"That's what I came up with too," Hugh said.

"And at that point in time, we were at war with Germany. . . . He might have been a German spy!"

"But why would MI-Five keep him on, then? He must have been cleared."

*There must be* some *way of finding out more.*

"I need to find out about Agent Wright." Maggie, the scholar, knew where she had to start. "I'm going to the library."

"The library? There's certainly not going to be anything on him there. Too public."

"Well, I have to start somewhere. Do *something.*"

Later that afternoon, Maggie went back to the castle's library. "Hello, Sir Owen. I'm looking for something today, actually," she said.

Sir Owen smiled and rubbed his hands together in glee, and Maggie realized he must be a little lonely among all the volumes sometimes. "Anything, Miss Hope."

"Well, I'm looking for information on a man named Neil Wright. He was born in Hampstead Heath in 1885 and graduated from Christ Church, Oxford, in 1906. I'm not sure what there will be, if anything."

"At least a birth notice," Sir Owen said, "and marriage and death, if applicable. Let me see what I can do."

Maggie settled in to wait with a copy of *Great Expectations.* Sir Owen eventually returned, with two yellowing copies of *The Times* of London. "If you look here, Miss Hope," he said, opening the first on the polished wood table, "you'll find a birth notice—Neil Reginald Wright was born in London, to George Fletcher Wright and Nancy Grace Wright, on March twenty-first, 1885. However," he said, opening the second, "this is the one you'll probably be most interested in. I'm sorry, I wasn't trying to pry, but the names—"

Maggie looked up at him, not comprehending.

"Well, you'll understand when you read it," he said gently. "I'm sorry for your loss, Miss Hope."

Maggie turned her attention to the second paper. The headline read "Two Dead from Accident on Icy Road, Another Injured." Maggie smoothed the brown and crumbling edges and began to read.

London, Sunday, May 1—Two people were killed and one seriously injured shortly after midnight Thursday in an automobile accident at the intersection of Grosvenor Road and Vauxhall Bridge Road.

Clara Hope, age twenty-four, was taken to London Bridge Hospital and died from injuries sustained in the crash. Neil Wright, age thirty-two, died on the scene. Professor Hope, a noted economist at the London School of Economics, was taken to London Bridge Hospital and is in stable condition.

"From the look of the accident scene, it appears that Professor and Mrs. Hope's car swerved on Grovesnor Road and hit a lamppost. Mr. Wright's car, following close behind, crashed into theirs," a spokesman for the Prefecture of Police said.

There, in stark black and white, was a picture of Neil
Wright next to a picture of Maggie's mother and father.

*Neil Wright, the agent who was investigating my fa-
ther, died in the same car accident as my mother,* Maggie
thought, shocked, saddened, sickened. She read the article again.

Then she sat down to think. *Neil Wright was an
MI-6 agent, charged with protecting Britain from foreign threats. If he was pursuing my father, he must have
believed him guilty of some sort of wrongdoing—given
that it was during the Great War, spying for Germany is
the most likely offense. Because of this,* she realized,
feeling nauseated, *Wright was chasing my father in a car.
My mother was a passenger. The cars crashed, and both
Wright and my mother died.*

*My father,* she thought, *killed Neil Wright.*

Then, realizing, she felt like vomiting. *He also killed
my mother.*

Maggie felt a wave of anger, primal and hot, wash
over her. *He's not going to get away with this.*

# Chapter Twenty

Maggie met with Hugh in London, at Highgate Cemetery, under a threatening sky with low-hanging clouds. They met in front of Maggie's mother's gray marble headstone: *Clara Beatrice Hope 1892–1917*. She leaned over and traced the letters with her gloved fingers, then set down her bouquet of bittersweet.

"When I was a little girl," she said, "I thought my Aunt Edith was my mother. But when I was about eight or so, she told me my parents had died in a car accident in London. In the version she told me, my father and mother were at a stoplight. A man in another car must have fallen asleep. His car drifted over the white line. His car crashed into theirs and they both died." Maggie took a ragged breath as the wind whispered through the nearly bare tree branches.

"But then, last summer, I found another version of the story. In this one, there was an accident and my mother died—but my father didn't. But he went insane—which is why my Aunt Edith adopted me and lied to me—told me he was dead.

"Then when I returned to England, I found out my father was not only still alive, but he was also as sane as you or I—he was merely posing as deranged, to try to catch a spy at Bletchley.

"Neil Wright was an MI-Six agent, hunting down a Sektion agent in London—my father. What happened that night was no accident. Wright must have been chasing my father. One of the drivers lost control and the cars crashed. Whatever happened, it circles around to the same conclusion. If my father hadn't been a Sektion agent, on the run from MI-Six, my mother would still be alive today. His treachery ended up getting her killed. And Agent Wright too."

Maggie brushed tears away. "I'm sorry to tell you all this, but I just—well, who am I supposed to talk to?" She laughed, a short, bitter laugh. "My former almost-fiancé who's been shot down over Berlin and is 'missing and presumed dead'? My Aunt Edith, who thinks I'm throwing my life away to be a governess? My friends Chuck and Sarah, who're civilians? I can't even tell David, my best friend, because he's not cleared. This spy business is lonely—no one tells you that. And everyone lies."

"I don't," Hugh said.

Maggie turned to him. "I want to reopen the case."

"What? Why?"

"What if he's a double agent?"

"MI-Five's cleared him."

"What about the file? There were pages missing. Maybe it *didn't* end twenty-five years ago. Maybe he's still working for Germany! That's what Nevins thinks. That's why there's gossip about him—why he's been at Bletchley for so long, and never caught a spy. *He* could have given Victoria Keeley those decrypts! And no one would know—because he's the one supposedly guarding the henhouse."

Hugh put both hands on Maggie's arms. "Maggie, stop. All right? Just stop. What matters, what's important, is our mission—finding out what Lily Howell was doing and who killed her and why. How she got those decrypts and what she was going to do with them. Your father's *helping* us do that. He's on our side."

"My father's working at Bletchley. That's all we know for certain. It's impossible to know what side he's on."

"He works with us, Maggie."

"Nothing's what it appears to be!" Maggie exclaimed, pulling away and biting through each word. "War took our world and what we once thought was normal. And now we're all like, like Alice through the looking glass, in some sort of crazy upside-down world where truth is a lie and lies are truth."

Hugh shifted. "Look, I understand we're talking about your father here, and that if he sold secrets to Germany—or, even worse, *is* selling secrets—that would be hard. Incomprehensible. Untenable."

"I want—no, I *need*—to know the truth."

"Before you do anything, let me find out if he's still under any kind of suspicion. I'll check some more files, ask some of my father's old friends. . . ." He looked at her. "You're shivering. Here," he said, putting his arm around her. Maggie was aware of how close they were, and felt a peculiar jolt when she realized how much she liked it.

"No, I'm sorry," she said to Hugh, shrugging off his arm. "I'm sorry, but I just can't. . . ."

"Maggie—" Hugh reached out and put his hand on her forearm.

She shrugged off his hand. "No. I *will* find out the truth. My days of waiting patiently are over. No. More. Lies."

Maggie knew she had another resource, the head of MI-5 himself, Peter Frain. When she found out from Mrs. Pipps that he was at his club, she decided to see him there. "Oh, Miss," the wizened older man with the thick white hair at the front desk said, gazing up and over his thick eyeglasses. "I'm so sorry, but ladies aren't allowed—"

Maggie ignored him and stalked up the grand staircase. At the top of the stairs was the club's library, with floor-to-ceiling bookcases, oil paintings of huntsmen in red on horses, green leather-covered chairs, and thick Persian rugs. *Do these upper-crust Brits see no other possible way to decorate?* Maggie thought irritably.

Frain looked from a folder of papers he was reading at a polished table. "Why, Maggie, how lovely to see you."

"What's the meaning of this, Frain?" snapped an older man in a tweed suit and a hairpiece.

"It's all right, Your Grace," Frain said, raising a hand. "She won't be here long."

"Women!" the man grumbled as he shoved back his chair and swept up his newspapers. "They're everywhere. And *this* is where we go to try to get away from them!" He left and slammed the door behind him. Maggie and Frain were alone.

"Why don't you have a seat?" Frain said.

"No, no, thank you. I'd rather stand."

"Suit yourself. Well, what brings you to this eminent institution? I'll have you know that the food is nothing special. Just nursery food, like potted duck, ham and pear soup, and Eton mess—we old men seem to crave meals from our childhood."

"I know," Maggie said in a low voice, "about my father. That he was an agent during the Great War. That he was suspected of being a double agent for Sektion. That he was being investigated by Agent Neil Wright of MI-Six. And I know my mother died because Wright went after him."

Frain shook his head. "Maggie . . ."

"Who was this man, Neil Wright? What did he find out?"

Frain sighed. "You can't know everything all at once, Maggie."

"I can and I will!" she exclaimed. Her voice echoed up to the clerestory windows.

Frain remained unruffled. "Need I remind you, Maggie, that Enigma is at stake? People's lives are at stake. *Your* life, for that matter. What you think you know, you don't."

"Then *tell* me!"

"You don't have the proper approval."

Maggie was outraged. "Are you *serious*?" she managed.

"Yes," he said, with the patience of a teacher with a very young child. "You don't have the proper approval. I'm sorry, but there it is."

"And how would I go about getting the 'proper approval,' as you so Britishly put it?"

"You would ask me. And then I would tell you 'no.'"

"To be told how my mother died? My father's role in it?"

"There are rules, Maggie," he said, not unkindly.

"Then break them, goddamn it!"

Frain pulled out a cigarette and lit it with his silver lighter. He inhaled, pale blue smoke drifting toward the frescoed high ceiling. "I sometimes forget that you were raised in America. Here in England, we have more respect for rules. And, in wartime, rules are what keep us alive."

"I don't *care* about your damn rules!" Maggie cried. "I need to know what happened!"

"You *want* to know what happened. But you don't *need* to know." He took a drag on his cigarette, the tip glowing reddish orange. "You're a smart young woman, Maggie. And you've seen a lot. You're going through quite a bit, I know. But I know you're smart enough not to draw simple conclusions and then assume that they're the truth. Remember your maths? The truth is always far more complicated. And I would think if anyone had learned that lesson, it would be *you*."

Maggie bit her lip. *This isn't the end. Oh, no, it's not.*

"What I *have* learned, Peter, is that if I want something done, I'd better do it myself. And, with or without your help, I *will* find out what happened. He's under suspicion for spying again, you know," she said. "The other agents suspect him of being a mole." She turned and headed to the door.

"Although I'm well aware of the office gossip surrounding Edmund, I'm not swayed by it. And I'm quite surprised you'd give it any credence. I prefer you don't pursue this matter."

"Well, it's not up to you, now, is it?" she said, turning

to fix one last glare on him. Then she left, running down the immense staircase, causing the older men in tattersall and tweed to look after her askance.

If Maggie had turned back, though, she would have seen the tiniest hint of a smile curling one side of Peter Frain's mouth.


It was late by the time Maggie returned to Windsor. She'd missed dinner, and the sun had long set. Still agitated from her meeting with Frain, not to mention thoughts of Hugh, she paced around her rooms, chilly despite the fire dancing in the grate, finally throwing herself on the sofa. She picked up the *Grimm's Fairy Tales*. *Maybe reading will help me calm down,* she thought.

She kicked off her oxfords and tucked her feet under her, then picked up the book. *What gorgeous illustrations,* she thought, looking at the four-color Rackham pen-and-ink drawings, softened by watercolors. She began to read the first story, "Hansel and Gretel."

Again, she noticed the tiny holes that the spilled tea had spotlighted. *Damn bugs.* But on closer examination, the holes were too regular in their appearance, too specifically spaced.

What they were, Maggie suddenly realized, was a series of tiny pinpricks in the pages of the book, each over a letter, in seemingly random order. It was code of some sort. Maggie's heart beat faster.

Hard by a great forest dwelt a poor wood-cutter with his wife and his two children. The boy was

called Hansel and the girl Gretel. He had little to
bite and to break, and once when great dearth fell
on the land, he could no longer procure even
daily bread. Now when he thought over this by
night in his bed, and tossed about in his anxiety,
he groaned and said to his wife: "What is to become of us? How are we to feed our poor children,
when we no longer have anything even for ourselves?" "I'll tell you what, husband," answered
the woman, "early tomorrow morning we will
take the children out into the forest to where it is
the thickest; there we will light a fire for them,
and give each of them one more piece of bread,
and then we will go to our work and leave them
alone. They will not find the way home again,
and we shall be rid of them." "No, wife," said the
man, "I will not do that; how can I bear to leave
my children alone in the forest?"

That was all of the pinpricks. There were no more.

*Pinprick encryption,* Maggie thought, her mind
whirling wildly. *First used by Aeneas the Tactician, an
ancient Greek historian, who conveyed secret messages
by making tiny, almost imperceptible pinpricks under
letters in chunks of text. Imperceptible—that is, unless
someone spills tea on them.*

Getting a pad of paper and a pen, she copied down
each letter, in order, that had a pinprick over it. There
weren't that many, really. When she was finished, she
had:

tandersensfaulkeshthompson

From there, shivers dancing up and down her spine, it was easy enough to get to:

T. Andersen, S. Faulkes, H. Thompson

A list of British-sounding names, sent in secret code to her father. Names. But of whom? And why? *To get information from them? To try to turn them? To assassinate them?*

Maggie went back over the list of names. *H. Thompson?* Hugh had mentioned his father had worked for MI-5, as well.

That he had died in the line of—

*Oh, no,* Maggie thought, suddenly realizing. *Oh, no, no, no, no, no . . .*

The next morning after Lilibet's maths lesson, Maggie climbed the pitted and crumbling stairs of the parish church of St. John the Baptist, on High Street in Windsor, and walked inside, her steps echoing on the cracked tiles. It was between services and the cavernous arched church was empty, except for an organist to the left of the altar, behind a glowing bank of candles, practicing Bach's "Wachet auf, ruft uns die Stimme," the majestic reedy tones echoing through the open space. Maggie saw Hugh and took a seat in the row in front of him. Hugh knelt behind her, on a wooden pew worn from centuries of use, hands folded as if in prayer.

In a rush, dread in her heart, Maggie whispered, "Thanks for meeting with me." She wished with all her heart that she could go back to that moment when he'd put his arm around her. Back before she knew.

"I knew if you contacted me, it had to be important."

There was a pause, and the organist began the left hand's countermelody. Then Maggie began. "My mother—my mother loved to read, and my father would buy her books, fairy tales mostly, German. He sent one to me, after he stood me up in Slough. Last night, I discovered code hidden inside those books. Code! It must have been how Sektion was sending him messages."

"What kind of code?"

"Pinprick encryption."

Hugh raised one eyebrow. "Classic Sektion."

"Exactly."

There was another long pause, before Maggie got up the nerve to speak. She knew she had to. And she knew that things would never be the same between her and Hugh, ever again. "The code—it spelled out a list."

"A list?"

"A list of names," Maggie said, hating what she was about to tell him.

"All right," Hugh said, "a list of names. I can check them out."

*There was still a chance, though. Still a chance that it was just a horrible coincidence. A cosmic joke of the worst sort.* "Hugh," she said gently, "I need to ask you, what was your father's name?"

Hugh's eyebrows knit together. "Why do you ask?"

"Was it also Hugh?" Maggie asked, dreading his response.

"Why, yes, yes it was," he said. "But—?"

"Hugh Thompson? H. Thompson? And did he die in 1915?"

"What—?"

Maggie passed him a Bible, in which she'd hidden the Grimm text and her notes.

"Oh, Hugh," she said, as he began to read. "I'm so, so terribly sorry."

## Chapter Twenty-one

In a fog of shock, Hugh returned to the MI-5 offices in London. Without apparent emotion, he dropped the book and Maggie's decryption of the pinprick code on Frain's desk, leaving Frain, for once, looking shocked. Then he went to his office and sat down at his desk. He didn't even pretend to work, just stared at the wall.

A while later, Mark entered the small windowless office and looked at Hugh. Then he sat down at his own desk, pretending to work.

Finally, Hugh spoke. "Maggie broke the code found in her mother's book. The names of three MI-Five agents. All of whom were assassinated. Including my father."

"Jesus." Mark reached into his desk drawer and pulled out a bottle of gin. "Drink?"

"Do you need to ask?"

Mark took out two tea mugs and poured gin into each. He got up and handed one to Hugh.

"Thanks," Hugh said, accepting the mug. He downed the gin in one gulp.

Silently, Mark poured Hugh another, then went back to his desk and pulled out some paperwork. He pretended to be engrossed in it, crossing things out, scribbling in the margins.

Finally, still staring at the same spot off in the distance, Hugh spoke. "It's a strange thing, you know. When you're a child, you learn that your father's dead. You don't really know what that means besides your mother always crying and everyone wearing black. At some point you put it all together—that he's not away on a trip, that he's never coming back. He's gone. Forever.

"Then, when you're older you learn more—that he was 'killed in the line of duty.' But even that's vague. It doesn't tell you where, or when, or how." He downed the gin. "Or by whom."

Mark was thinking ahead. "Should we go to the Red Lion? Because given what's just happened, I doubt that Frain would mind." He closed his folder and stood up. "And, if he does, he can bugger off."

Hugh went on, as if he hadn't heard. "And then, then you find out the details. The particulars. That the Germans knew about your father. That they wanted him dead. That his name was written in code. In a line of tiny pinpricks. In a book. Then you learn that the book belonged to your friend's father. Who carried out the assassination."

There was a sharp rap at the door, then Nevins opened it and walked in. He had a sheet of paper in his hands, which he handed to Hugh.

"Quite the day, I gather," he said. "Frain told me. Maggie Hope just called him."

Hugh took the paper, like an automaton, and put it down without reading it.

Mark shook his head. "Jesus, Nevins. Perhaps you'd like to look up the word *diplomacy* in the dictionary?"

Nevins shrugged. "This is *huge*. Maggie Hope's father—your father . . . Well, I can't imagine how you must be feeling."

"Obviously," Mark said.

Nevins wouldn't take the hint. "And, you know? I think Saul Levy's going to be good for you. Just the thing to straighten you out."

Hugh looked down at the memo and read it. Then he crumpled it and threw it in the metal wastebasket. "I'm not seeing Levy."

Nevins leaned up against the doorframe. "I'm afraid Frain's insisting. Levy may be a Jew, but he's supposed to be a damned good psychiatrist—studied with Freud and all. He must live for this sort of thing. Positively Oedipal."

"Just get out," Mark said. "Now."

"Well, it's not up to you two," Nevins said, turning to go. "It's mandatory."

Hugh stood up. "You serious about that pub?" he said to Mark. "Because I need to get very, very drunk."


The same winter rain that had drenched Windsor had moved out to the coast, flooding Norfolk and its coast as well. It was raining hard in Mossley by Sea, a small village on the coast of the North Sea, not far from Grimsby. Mossley was tiny—there were only a few blocks of what was considered the main street, with the chemist, hardware store, grocer, the Royal Oak and Six

Bells pubs, and the gray-steepled church with its neighboring graveyard, the stones crumbling, covered in velvety moss and damp lichen.

Christopher Boothby had taken the train from Bletchley, reaching Mossley as the cold driving rains became their heaviest. It had taken the residents a while to get used to him—they weren't used to strangers—but his story of being a veteran of the Battle of Norway, now doing clerical work in Bletchley, needing a weekend place, stirred their maternal instincts, despite their official classification as a restricted military zone. Adding to the tale were rumors of his being a widower—wife and baby buried in the Blitz, don't you know—which had the village's matrons clucking. Why shouldn't he buy that little cottage on the shore and fix it up? Didn't he deserve a little peace after all he'd done for his country, after all he'd lost?

From the train, Boothby walked through the downpour, protected by his oilskin coat, heavy boots and nor'easter, striped Trinity scarf at his throat. He unchained his bicycle, waiting where he'd left it at the fence, and started off, struggling to keep upright in the punishing wind on the pitted and potholed roads.

He was an ordinary-looking man of about thirty—light hair, light eyes, average height and weight, clean-shaven. His nose was ordinary as well; it had once been patrician, but he'd broken it in a fight with the communist Reds when he'd been a follower of Oswald Mosley and a Fascist at Cambridge, and now the bridge was just slightly flattened and off-center. He was a chameleon, adept at blending into any environment, including as wounded veteran and grieving husband and father.

The brackish cold air assaulted his face as he rode,

turning it mottled and red, his breath coming in short bursts.

As he pedaled, chain clanking, the rains abated. Cresting the top of the low-rising hill, Boothby could see the brown fields, the mudflats, the salt marshes with their tall feathery dying reeds, adapted to live in either fresh or salt water. Beyond the salt marshes was the gray-green ocean, waves roaring faintly upon the rocky shore in the distance.

From his vista he could see the cottage. It was small and dilapidated, but it was his, along with the battered van alongside it. He turned off the main road, onto a side one, and then into the gravel drive, getting off the bicycle and walking it to a protected space under the eaves. Stamping his boots on the mat, he reached into his oilskin's coat pocket and drew out a heavy brass key. Then he let himself in. "Audrey?" he called into the shadows with his clipped accent. "Audrey, are you there?"

It hadn't been hard for the Nazis to convince Audrey Moreau to work for them. After they'd invaded Paris, she'd been harassed by groups of German soldiers as she went to and from her job at a local café. There, German officers would order pastries and coffee, talking and laughing. Audrey would clear the dishes of half-eaten *palmiers, chausson aux pommes,* and iced *mille-feuille* and take them back to the kitchen, where she and the rest of the staff would fall on them, famished, not caring that there were bite marks or that cigarettes had been crushed out in the custard.

When one of the officers, a young man with shocking

white-blond hair and a cleft chin, had begun to harass her, she kept her eyes down and stayed silent. Day after day she endured his assaults, patting her derrière, pinching her cheek, asking her if she liked it on her back or on all fours, while his fellow officers egged him on and laughed.

The next week, his commanding officer, Otto Graf, appeared. He was closer to fifty than forty, with black hair and green eyes. When the cleft-chinned boy began his antics with Audrey, Graf strode across the room and slapped him across the face, hard, with his black leather glove.

"I'm sorry, Commandant," the boy said.

"Don't apologize to me," Graf said, in a soft voice, "apologize to *her*. We are guests in her country."

He did, turning red and stammering.

"Now leave," Graf said. As the boy made his way out the door, Graf said, "And you have my apologies as well, Fräulein. Why don't you sit down with us and have some coffee?"

Audrey looked over to the owner, her boss, a bald middle-aged man with a shiny pate. He nodded. Whatever the Germans wanted, the Germans got.

Graf patted the empty chair, and she sat down. "Now, tell me about yourself, *Liebchen*."

Of course they became lovers. One night, in bed at his suite at the Ritz, when he learned she had relatives in England, he was thrilled. "It would be so easy," he said, rubbing her cold hands with his, to warm them. "Your cousin married an English woman—who's a cook for the British King and Queen, no less—let me see what I can do."

A few weeks later, Audrey arrived in Windsor, feign-

ing gratitude that her cousin was able to get her out. She
knew who was already in place, and she awaited further
instructions. Commandant Graf had no worries about
Audrey's cooperation—he knew very well where her
parents and brother and sister lived. And he'd made it
clear what would happen to them if she didn't oblige.


In the cottage, Boothby called out again, "Audrey?" He
fumbled for a lantern.

"I'm here," she responded from the shadows.

"Good. Let's go over the plan again."

# Chapter Twenty-two

During preparations for the three-day Red, White, and Blue Christmas weekend, excitement buzzed through the castle like a shot of adrenaline, which was a good thing, as the days were getting shorter and darker. Marquetry floors were waxed, silver polished, carpets taken out of storage and beaten, chandeliers washed and rehung, guest rooms aired. The enormous kitchen was filled with aromas of bread and cakes and roasts, and servants picked bouquets of flowers from the greenhouse to arrange and display throughout the State Apartments.

After everything she had learned about her father and what she'd had to share with Hugh, Maggie was grateful for the distraction of seeing David and Mrs. Tinsley from the Prime Minister's office, in addition to Mr. Churchill himself, of course. Frain was coming as well. Maggie felt as though her worlds—No. 10, MI-5, and Windsor Castle—were all about to collide.

———

The morning's long procession of black cars from London—Daimlers and Bentleys and Rolls-Royces—rolled slowly up the Long Walk, through an avenue of elm trees planted by Charles II. Maggie watched from one of the high lancet windows in the York Tower as, finally, they reached the Sovereign's Entrance. Drivers in livery came around to the passenger side of the cars, opening the doors, and helping their occupants out. When she saw Mr. Churchill and David walk up the stone stairs to the entrance and the doors swing open, she gave a small gasp, then ran to the entrance.

Footmen in white-powdered wigs and dress uniforms flanked the Grand Staircase, dominated by an enormous white marble statue of King George IV. At the very top, under the glazed Gothic lantern ceiling, were the royal couple, the King in dress uniform, the Queen in a becoming wisteria wool dress and a bib of glistening graduated pearls. Next to them were the two Princesses, dressed alike in matching plaid skirts, white blouses, and red wool cardigans.

Maggie peeked from around a corner as Mr. Churchill made his way up the stairs. The P.M.'s face looked thinner than she remembered; the strain of war had aged him. He bowed to the King and then the two shook hands with great vigor. Maggie could see the twinkling blue eyes she remembered. He bowed low to the Queen, kissing her bejeweled hand with great reverence. And then he bowed gravely to the two Princesses, making them giggle and blush.

While more of the War Cabinet continued to march in—Lord Hastings Ismay, Clement Attlee, Arthur Greenwood—those already greeted milled about in the Grand Vestibule under the watchful eye of the marble

Queen Victoria, before moving on to the Crimson Drawing Room.

There, in red silk and golden gilded splendor, guests congregated in front of the enormous black marble fireplace with its bronze satyrs, the dancing carroty flames trying to cheer the room and provide heat, although there was still a damp creeping chill in the air. The room was decorated with great boughs of fragrant evergreens, white roses, and holly with bright red berries.

As the hall rapidly filled with guests—men in uniforms or dark suits and a few women here and there in dark day dresses—Maggie found David. "You came!" she cried above the growing din of upper-class accents and the chords of a harpsichordist playing a Handel gigue in the background.

"Maggie!" he exclaimed, kissing her on both cheeks.

"Welcome to Windsor Castle."

"Love what they've done to the place," David said, looking around.

"It's not as glamorous as it might seem today. Mostly it's like living in a very cold museum in the off-season." Maggie noticed that David was carrying a briefcase. And that it was chained to his wrist. "I've heard of being chained to your desk—but, really. . . ."

"Just until I can get it to the safe," he assured her. "I won't be attending the ball with a briefcase as my escort, I can assure you."

"Well, good. Because I'd like a dance."

"Don't suppose there's anything to drink?" David said. "Long ride from London, you know." He spied a long table at the other end of the room, covered in white linen and piled high with porcelain tea settings and silver urns, etched trays piled high with pastries. "Suffering Sukra, I suppose tea will have to do. Come on!"

Lilibet and Margaret appeared at Maggie's side. "We're making the butter pats for the dinners," Margaret announced proudly.

"They have little crowns on them," Lilibet added. "We're making ever so many—and we're not allowed to eat any of them."

"You don't say, Your Highnesses," David said, bowing. "I don't know how I shall eat any butter pats at all during my stay, knowing that your Royal hands have touched them."

The girls giggled.

David asked Lilibet, "And how is Miss Hope doing as your maths teacher? Is she any good?"

"She's terrible!" Margaret exclaimed, pulling on Maggie's skirt and laughing. "We need to send her to the dungeons, where she'll be eaten alive by a horrible dragon!"

"She's quite wonderful." Lilibet glared down at her sister. "I've learned ever so much. Not just maths but codes and things."

"Codes?" David raised an eyebrow. "Really, now."

"Lilibet's an excellent student," Maggie said.

The Princesses giggled and wandered off, arm in arm.

Maggie spotted Mrs. Tinsley in the crowd. Mrs. Tinsley was still Mr. Churchill's head typist and the woman Maggie had once reported to; once upon a time, she had found the older woman intimidating. But now it was a joy to see her, with her customary rope of creamy pearls around her neck. "Mrs. Tinsley!" she exclaimed.

"Why, hello, Miss Hope," Mrs. Tinsley said, taking the younger girl's measure over the frames of her glasses.

*Just like old times,* Maggie thought.

Mrs. Tinsley tucked back a strand of black hair threaded with gray. "You look well. The country air agrees with you."

"And you look as lovely as always. How is Miss Stewart?"

"She's well. Back at Number Ten, holding down the proverbial fort. She sends her well wishes to you—and I'll tell her you asked after her."

"May I offer you a cup of tea, Mrs. Tinsley?"

"Thank you, that would be delightful," she said, making a beeline to one of the gilt and red-silk chairs.

Maggie went to the large table and poured a cup of tea, black just the way Mrs. Tinsley had taken it at No. 10. When she returned with it, handing it to the older woman, she heard, "Well, Hope's at Windsor Castle now!" in a loud, gruff voice. "And all's right with the world."

It was the Prime Minister, wearing a navy blue suit with a burgundy polka-dotted bow tie and a sprig of holly in the buttonhole—*probably placed there this morning by Mrs. Churchill,* Maggie thought.

"Mr. Churchill!" she exclaimed.

"Miss Hope," he replied, bowing slightly.

"Is Mrs. Churchill with you, sir?"

"She's joining us this evening."

Suddenly Gregory was at her elbow. "Maggie, you never told me you traveled in such impressive circles."

And then the male staff, under the watchful eye of Lord Clive, began to escort the guests to their rooms.

"Toodle pip for now, love," said David to Maggie, as his escort appeared.

"Maybe we can all get a drink before dinner tonight, yes?" Gregory suggested.

"Suits me," David replied. "Maggie?"

"Of course," Maggie answered. But she had already spied Frain and Hugh in the crowd. She knew they were coming, of course, but it was still a shock to see them at Windsor. She stood perfectly still, uncertain of how to proceed, her heart beating fast as a hummingbird's.

David sized up the predicament and called Frain over. "Mr. Frain," he said, "you remember Maggie Hope, don't you? One of Mr. Churchill's typists?"

"Of course," said Frain. "Miss Hope, a pleasure to see you again."

"And you, Mr. Frain."

"This is my associate, Hugh Thompson," Frain said.

"How do you do, Mr. Thompson," Maggie said, offering her hand, which he took.

He winked at her. "How do you do, Miss Hope?" As Frain made his way over to the Prime Minister and David and Gregory drifted off, Maggie and Hugh stood, face-to-face, in the crowd. "You have a little something—" He reached for her hair.

"What?" Maggie said. "What is it?"

"Fairy dust—or so it seems." She stood very still as he pulled something from her hair, then handed it to her. It was white and sparkling, like an opal. "Oh," she said, cheeks turning pink, as she took it from him. "It's the artificial snow they've put on the Christmas tree and some of the garlands. Gets onto everything if you're not careful . . ." Maggie said, flustered.

"I hope you'll save me a dance, Miss Hope," he said,

giving an almost imperceptible bow as one of the servants came to lead him to his room.

"Of—of course, Mr. Thompson."

In the Submarine Tracking Room in the Admiralty Arch, a young man moved a red pushpin on a map-covered table, one of thousands of different colored pins on the turquoise blue areas of the map representing the Atlantic. Donald Kirk was reading a memo, but he caught the movement out of the corner of his eye.

He limped over, leaning heavily on his walking stick, to take a closer look. "That U-boat there," he said, pointing to the red pin the young man had just moved, "U-two-forty-six. What's it doing?"

The man, olive-skinned with a shiny nose and forehead, shrugged. "Seems to be on the move now, sir," he said. "Heading closer to shore than we've seen before."

Kirk looked at the map, to the Norfolk coast. *What's the Captain doing?* Kirk thought. He looked up the submarine's captain, a Captain Jörg Vogt. Vogt might not even know himself, yet, what they were doing there.

"Keep an eye on it."

"Yes, sir."

Dinner that evening was a formal affair and Maggie got dressed with Polly and Louisa. In Louisa's rooms in Victoria Tower, with Irving presiding from his glass container, Maggie pulled out her blue dress with the black velvet-tipped flowers.

"Oh, you're not wearing *that,* are you?" Louisa asked.

"Why not?" Maggie asked.

"Well, not only have we all seen it ad nauseam, but the Queen most likely will be in light blue. She almost *always* wears light blue. It's an unwritten rule of sorts that no other woman in the castle may wear light blue around Her Majesty."

"It *is* a lovely gown, though," Polly piped in.

"Thank you," Maggie said to her. "And it's the only one I have with me. As Louisa pointed out."

Louisa began to rummage through her closet. "I might have something from a few years ago that might fit—it was Lily's. You don't mind, do you? You're about her size." She pulled out a green silk dress and threw it to Maggie. "Not the best color for a redhead, but beggars can't be choosers, yes?"

"Lovely," Maggie said, gritting her teeth. "Thank you."

Polly pulled out a bottle of gin and Angostura Bitters. "And while we get ready, who'd like some Pinks?"

The bagpipers, dressed in traditional doublets with gold buttons and a drape of plaid held by a golden brooch on the shoulder, pleated kilts, and horsehair sporrans, were sounding the fifteen-minute call to dinner as the three young women made their way down to the Waterloo Chamber for cocktails.

"Ladies, may I say, you look magnificent," Gregory declared, catching sight of them. He did a double-take when he saw Maggie and blanched and seemed to sway a bit.

"Are you all right?" Maggie asked.

"Are you mad?" Gregory cried, voice rising. People

turned to look. "That belongs—belonged—to Lily! How dare you?"

"I'm—I'm sorry," Maggie stammered, taken aback. "I didn't realize it would cause any upset." She looked at Gregory, who was pale and shaking, then at Louisa and Polly, who were smirking. Obviously they'd known the sight of her in the dress would cause upset. "I can change into something else—it's all right," she said. Slowly, the guests turned back to their own conversations.

"Steady, there, old man," David said, pressing a hand against Gregory's back. "It's just a dress."

"Of—of course," Gregory said, recovering. "Just haven't seen it in a while is all," he said, struggling to smile. "You look ravishing in it, Maggie. Lily would be so pleased. I'm sorry for my reaction. Completely out of proportion."

"Not at all," Maggie replied, glad to see him pull himself together. "And you two look wonderful, as well." And indeed, the men were resplendent in their full evening dress: white ties, starched wing collar shirts and waistcoats, black trousers, and tailcoats with grosgrain facings.

The bagpipers played Robert Burns's "Brose and Butter," the interplay of the guests' chatter juxtaposed against the steady reedy sound of the drones.

"I see you've found the martinis," Louisa said, looking at the nearly empty glasses in the men's white gloved hands, "but is there champagne?" She and Polly set out in search of a servant with a silver tray of glasses.

"Dinner is served," announced the King, in his RAF dress uniform.

As the pipers began to play again, the glittering guests proceeded into St. George's Hall, its arched ceiling studded with hundreds of shields, glowing with the light of the fire in the fireplace and the light of long tapered beeswax candles in six-foot-tall candelabras, showing multiple St. Georges battling countless incarnations of the infamous dragon.

The hundred and fifty guests were to be seated at one lengthy Cuban mahogany table, polished to a high sheen, reflecting the glow of the candles. Huge bouquets of velvety red roses, spiky orchids, crimson amaryllis, and creamy white Casablanca lilies in golden bowls dotted the table. Yeomen of the Guard, in their red ruffed-collar Elizabethan costumes, red stockings, and red, white, and blue rosette-decorated shoes, stood at attention against the walls, alternating with wig-wearing footmen, in state livery of scarlet with gold braid.

Maggie found her gold chair near the bottom of the table, her name on a small engraved card held in a gilded holder, which glinted in the candlelight. She was to be seated next to a retired Admiral. Between them was a menu, written in calligraphy, on heavy white stock embossed with the golden initials GR at the top.

But before she could sit down, David deftly took the place card next to her on the other side and switched it with his own.

"David!" Maggie exclaimed. "Really, now."

"Oh, don't take that older-sister tone with me," he said. "War rations on priceless Royal china, how droll." He picked up the charger in front of him, with panels of cobalt blue, a gold-stippled border, and painted birds and insects. He flipped it over to look at the maker. "Tournai, 1787. Excellent."

"*David!*" Maggie whispered. The plate had been set with military precision between a full set of gleaming vermeil flatware and multiple crystal wineglasses, engraved with the Order of the Garter star and the royal emblem.

As per tradition, everyone remained standing behind his or her chair as the head table was led in by the King, in his military uniform with the Order of the Garter sash and star, and the Queen, in a powder blue gown and ruby and diamond Oriental Circlet tiara. They were followed by Prime Minister Churchill and Clementine Churchill. When the four reached the head table, the pipers stopped playing and stood at attention. An empty place next to them was set in memory of those killed during the war. After the King said a prayer, the pipers played "Flowers of the Forest." And after the Irish and Scots Guards played "God Save the King," the King made a champagne toast to the Prime Minister.

Everyone sat down, settling in, pulling the elaborately folded white damask napkins to their laps, and the staff began to serve. Gregory began, "I'm amazed you two got any work at all done at Number Ten."

"Well," Maggie allowed, tasting the consommé with sherry, "we did have a few laughs. But it really was hard work. Or, as Mr. Churchill would prefer us to say, 'challenging.'"

Seated next to Gregory was a dowager, her sagging neck swathed in emeralds and diamonds. "And. Who. Are. You?" she asked Maggie over her pince-nez as the fish course was served, sounding like the Caterpillar from *Alice's Adventures in Wonderland*.

"Maggie Hope, ma'am. I tutor Princess Elizabeth in maths."

"Really," she said, turning her attention to the

poached salmon in sauce mousseline, clearly not pleased to be sitting near a glorified governess.

"And Mr. David Greene works with the Prime Minister. Don't you, David?" Maggie asked, giving him a poke.

"True, true," he admitted, then led the conversation to the antics of the Churchills' menagerie of pets, all of whom roamed No. 10 freely. Once he had everyone, including the dowager, laughing, Maggie relaxed. Across the table, Gregory winked at her with his good eye, and she smiled back as the meat course was served: filet mignon with mushroom sauce, with beans, broccoli, and potatoes Anna.

"Maggie," David said with a sigh, watching her put down her knife and pass her fork from her left hand to her right, "why must you continue to eat in that revolting American style?"

"Because it's what I do, David, and I'm not going to change because I'm in Saint George's Hall."

"Young man!" called an old Admiral from a few places down, fixing his gaze on David.

"Yes, sir."

"Say, you work for Churchill, do you?"

"Yes, sir."

"Any idea when the damn Yanks are going to get here?"

"No, sir," David said. "I'm afraid they haven't sent in their R.S.V.P. yet."

Maggie shot him a look.

"Yanks," the Admiral muttered. "Late to every war!"

"The Prime Minister is in constant contact with President Roosevelt, of course—"

"As much good as that's done. But as we all know too

well from the last war, you can always count on the Americans to do the right thing—after they've tried everything else."

After the meat course came the salad. Maggie noticed Gregory didn't eat much throughout the dinner but called the footman over to refill his glass more than a few times.

"So, Maggie tells me you rowed for Cambridge?" David asked Gregory over the torte au chocolat blanc.

"Yes," he replied, taking a sip of champagne. "Eton and then Cambridge. Thirty-four was the dead heat. In thirty-five, we won the Boat Race."

"That's the annual race between Cambridge and Oxford," David explained to Maggie. Then, to Gregory, "I was on the Oxford team a few years later than you. Coxswain."

"Brothers in blue," Gregory said, smiling. "I was at Trinity."

"Magdalen? Excellent," David said, dunking his fingertips into the proffered glass finger bowl and wiping them on the provided linen napkin, then tucking into the fruit course—red Windsor apples served with elderflower-wine-marbled Windsor red cheese, fig jam, and walnuts, served on Queen Victoria's Royal Minton china, bordered in turquoise with panels of flowers and gilding. The conversation had given Maggie pause, for although she was happy to see David and Gregory discover they'd both rowed, John had gone to Magdalen with David. Even hearing the name of John's college brought back a rush of memories and a stab of pain to her heart. Still, it wasn't quite as bad as before.

The dinner and the conversation went on, the long tapers burning down and voices getting louder and more relaxed with bottle upon bottle being brought from the castle's vast wine cellar. The dinner ended with petits fours and black coffee. When the guests had eaten and drunk their fill, the King and Queen put their knives and forks down—and, as per royal etiquette, everyone else did the same. Then the King rose to his feet, offered his arm to the Queen, and they left St. George's Hall for the Grand Reception Room.

The P.M. and Mrs. Churchill followed behind, along with the rest of the high-ranking officers and War Cabinet Ministers. Maggie stood up with the others, waiting for the head of the table to file out first.

"I'd love that dance later, David," Maggie said.

"Oh, darling, and I'd love to oblige, but I have some work to do, I'm afraid."

"Maggie," Gregory said. "Let's show your friend to my office and set him up there. If you *must* do work on a holiday weekend, at least do it in comfort. I have a fantastic bottle of twenty-two-year-old Scotch, by the way."

David smiled. "I like the way you think. Lead on, Macduff."

# Chapter Twenty-three

Maggie, David, and Gregory strolled the chilly corridors of the castle, en route to the Equerry's office. When Maggie saw Hugh in one of the hallways, staring intently at one of the *Sleeping Beauty* posters, she stopped.

"You boys go ahead," she told David and Gregory. "I think someone might be lost."

After the conversation of the two men had receded into the distance, Maggie spoke. "How—how are you?"

Hugh took a casual tone. "Oh, fine. Trying to explain to my mother why I'll be away for the holidays again. It's bad enough I'm not in the armed services, as far as she's concerned, but to miss Christmas. . . ."

Maggie heard voices in the distance. "In here," she said, leading him into a dark room with high ceilings and sheeted furniture. They were alone. She closed the door. They both leaned against the wall, their eyes adjusting to the darkness.

Hugh was silent for a long moment. "Because of the secret nature of their work, there aren't any memorials or tombs for MI-Five veterans. But there's a wall at MI-

Five, a marble wall with poppies carved in it, on the left-hand side as you enter. And on that wall are names. Names of agents lost in action. No clues as to how or where—or even when. All we know is that they died in service to Britain."

He took a deep breath. "I was five when my father's name was chiseled into that wall. And now I pass it every day."

"Hugh, I'm so sorry."

For a moment, Hugh looked as though he was going to say something. Then he changed his mind.

"It's fine, Maggie. I mean—well, it's not fine. But it's done, it's over, and you certainly had nothing to do with any of it. I want you to know that. That it's nothing you had anything to do with. I don't blame you."

He reached into his black dinner jacket pocket and pulled out a small package, wrapped in silver paper and bound with a red satin ribbon. He handed it to Maggie.

"What?" she said, surprised. "Oh, really—you shouldn't have."

"I know. It's highly irregular. But I was thinking of you . . . and it *is* Christmas, after all." He shifted his weight. "Anyway, I hope you like it."

"I'm sure I will," Maggie promised.

Slowly, she raised herself up on her tiptoes and kissed him on the lips.

He put his hands on her waist and drew her close. Then he leaned down and they kissed again, longer, this time. *It's different from the way it was with John*, Maggie realized, and then she stopped thinking.

Finally, they broke apart. "We can't do this," Maggie said.

"I think we just did." Hugh reached out to stroke her cheek.

She put her arms around his neck and leaned against him, smelling his bay rum cologne. "We do work together, after all."

"I haven't forgotten," he whispered. "But I do think you're wonderful."

Maggie pulled away. "We can't . . ."

"Of course," Hugh said. "You're right."

Maggie stepped past him and opened the door.

"Happy Christmas, then," Hugh said, and turned to walk away.

"Happy Christmas, Hugh," Maggie called after him.


Back up in her sitting room in Victoria Tower, fire already lit, Maggie sat down, gift in her hands. She pressed her fingers to her lips, smiled, and shook her head. She undid the red ribbon and took off the paper.

In a small silver frame, there was a watercolor portrait of her. While the colors were delicate, her features were defined and strong, vibrant and alive.

*Oh, Hugh,* she thought. *It's beautiful. Really beautiful. And you really shouldn't have.* She felt pardoned for all of the sins of the past, although whether she felt she deserved Hugh's forgiveness was another matter.

She put the painting on the mantel, smiling.

There was a knock at the door. It was Polly. "Oh, *here* you are!" she said. Her fair, round face was flushed with excitement and drink. "You just disappeared. We were wondering where you'd gone." Polly gave a sly smile. "And with whom." She plopped down on Maggie's sofa. "David—it's David, isn't it?—is quite the dish."

*Oh, if only Polly knew.* "Not my type," Maggie said. "So, what are you doing up here?" she asked. "Although of course I'm delighted to see you."

"One of the old Admirals keeps trying to pinch my cheek. Can you imagine? And then he suggested we 'take a walk.' Please—he's old enough to be my father. I'd rather be with someone like David. Or even Gregory, for that matter." Polly looked up at the painting on the mantel.

"My goodness," she said, getting up and going over to the fireplace and picking up the picture in the frame. "Is that you? Very nice."

Maggie nodded. "Yes," she said. "It was a Christmas gift."

"It's beautiful," Polly said. Then, "I've got my chocolate ration from the last few weeks hidden away in my room—want to share? I'm in the mood for a bit of a binge."

Maggie smiled. "No. Thanks, though. I should probably get back to David, anyway."

"Suit yourself," Polly said. "More chocolate for greedy me."

Back in Gregory's office, David had been set up to work at the desk, and Gregory had mixed and poured him the promised martini. When Maggie arrived, Gregory raised his glass. "I haven't had the chance to say it before, but you do look beautiful tonight. And, again, sorry about before."

"Oh, Maggie always cleans up well," David interjected from the desk chair.

"You did, actually," she said, "but thank you." She hesitated a moment, then said, "Haven't you had enough to drink tonight?"

"Hardly," Gregory said. "I'm British—it's what we do."

David smiled. "Cheers to that, old man," he said, clinking his glass with Gregory's.

Maggie noticed something in the air, an electric connection between the two men. *Perhaps Gregory's interested in boys as well as girls? He certainly does seem drawn to David.* "Then why don't I leave you two rowers to your martinis?" she said.

"Well, we'll miss you terribly, of course. But I'm happy to show David where everything is," Gregory said.

*I bet you are.* "Of course," Maggie said. "Good night, you two."


Maggie decided to swing by the nursery, to see how the girls were getting on with their rehearsals. She was pleased to see the corgis look up from their pillows and thump their tails in greeting.

"Oh, Maggie," Margaret cried, "we keep forgetting our lines! And then Lilibet forgot her sword—the sword!—can you imagine?" She giggled. "How can you cut through the briars if you don't have a sword?"

"A bad dress rehearsal means a good performance—at least that's what I've heard," Maggie said. "And how are you holding up, Crawfie?"

"It's all very exciting, but I admit I'll be relieved when

it's over," she said, as the girls went on with their rehearsal. "To perform in front of the King and Queen—
not to mention the Prime Minister . . ."

"It will be fantastic, Crawfie," Maggie said. "Don't
forget that the King and Queen, and Mr. Churchill, for
that matter, are parents. The children can do no wrong
in their eyes."

"I do hope you're right, Maggie."

"Have you—" Maggie began, "Have you noticed
anything *unusual* these past days?"

"Only that I've found a few new gray hairs."

"Well, I'll be backstage with you all during the performance," Maggie said. "Just to make sure the scenery
changes go smoothly."

"At least *something* will go smoothly, then."

In their spacious office at Abwehr, Torsten Ritter threw
a paper airplane at Franz Krause. It hit him on the left
temple.

"*Allmächtiger!* What's your problem?" Ritter said.

"No problem—good news, actually—radio message
from Wōdanaz. He's got something for us—important
documents—and wants extraction. We can combine his
pickup with Operation Edelweiss," Krause replied.

Ritter knit his brows. "We're going to need to coordinate, then. Logistical nightmare really."

Krause gave him a wide, white-toothed smile. "We
can do it. After all, we're Germans—we're nothing if
not efficient."

"I'll radio Captain Vogt and tell him to ready U-two-
forty-six for guests," Ritter said.

Krause smiled even wider. "Are you thinking what I'm thinking?"

"That if we can pull this off we'll get promoted?"

"Exactly."

Ritter turned serious. "Just pray that Operation Edelweiss goes as well, or else. . . ."

"Becker will be pissed."

"Not just Becker. I'm worried about Hess."

# Chapter Twenty-four

Day two of the Red, White, and Blue Christmas.

After Maggie had woken, dressed, and begun the long trek to the nursery, she heard the sound of a radio coming from the breakfast room and stood by the door to listen to the BBC report on the wireless, detailing the previous night's Luftwaffe raid on London. There were also highlights of the Prime Minister's radio address, which he'd made from his makeshift office at Windsor, the previous evening, to the people of Italy, blaming Benito Mussolini for leading his nation to war against the British, in the face of Italy's historic friendship with them: "*One man has arrayed the trustees and inheritors of ancient Rome upon the side of the ferocious pagan barbarians.*"

Maggie looked in to see guests from the previous evening's banquet now helping themselves to breakfast from silver chafing dishes set up on large sideboards. Most were dressed in hunting attire: red coats, pale breeches, and glossy black boots. Louisa was there as well, in the requisite uniform accented with a yellow vest and a strand of gray pearls. She called to Maggie, "Coming along?"

"Back to work for me, I'm afraid," Maggie replied.

Louisa frowned as she contemplated the idea of "work." She looked up as Polly arrived and beckoned her over.

Like an obedient puppy, Polly obeyed. "Have you ever chased the wily red creatures, Maggie?" Polly asked, plump cheeks aglow in anticipation of the hunt.

"No," Maggie said. For she hadn't—and had no wish ever to do so.

"Oh, it's great fun," she enthused. "So exhilarating."

"Probably not for the wily red creatures."

Louisa was nonplussed. "Well, these days we're hunting more for meat than for sport. Deer season, don't you know. Survival of the fittest."

Gregory, helping himself to a Bloody Mary, caught sight of Maggie, and meandered over to meet the ladies. "Good morning!"

"We British are a bloodthirsty lot beneath our formality," Louisa added.

"Are you hunting too?" Maggie asked.

"No, no," he said. "I find the sounds of shots being fired a bit disturbing after Norway."

"Of course," Maggie said, realizing that for Gregory being around guns might bring back bad memories. "And how was the rest of your evening?"

"Fantastic," he said. "Your friend David's quite a wit."

"He is, isn't he?" Maggie felt a sisterly pride in David. *I wonder what* really *happened last night*.

"Actually," Gregory said, "I thought I could perhaps

be of service to you and Crawfie, as I know the big performance is tomorrow."

"You're an angel," Maggie said.

Audrey, in her black dress and starched white apron, came in with another silver platter of scrambled eggs, which she set down on the loaded buffet table.

"It's a big weekend for everyone," he said.

David had some time while the Prime Minister was in meetings and, briefcase safely ensconced in his room's safe, decided to take a walk around the Great Park, even though the air was cold and the sky overhead a sullen gray.

There were footsteps behind him, crackling on the dead grass. It was Gregory, in his tweeds, cap set at a jaunty angle, striped school scarf around his neck. "Taking some air?" David said.

"Coming to warn you," he replied. "Most of the castle's guests are hunting today. They're both armed to the teeth and still drunk from last night—or the hair of the dog. I'm concerned it's not safe out here, under the circumstances."

"By Jove, I think you're right," David said. Behind the high stone walls of the castle, he could hear the clomping of horses' hooves, men's shouts, dogs barking, and the occasional high whinny. Then, "I'll need to get back to work soon anyway."

They walked along together, their breath visible in the cold air. "And does work always come first for you?" Gregory asked.

"Only during wartime." David noticed that Gregory was pale beneath his scars, and not quite steady in his steps. "Shall we sit down for a bit? I'm not used to all this country air."

Gregory smiled, seeing through David's ruse, but sitting down with him anyway on a low stone bench. "Over that way," he said, "is the Thames and the Eton boathouse. One of my favorite places in the world."

"Can you—" David knew he should tread carefully. "Are you still able to—row?"

"Yes, I can still *row*," Gregory said with significance. "Thank God. I go over every once in a while and take out a shell. Good to get the blood flowing. I can really think out there, on the water. Really feel free."

"That's fantastic," David said. "Feeling free doesn't come often these days."

"I'm looking for freedom now, David," he said. "I don't want to go back to the Air Force in the new year— I only have a week or so left at Windsor, as the King's Equerry, before I'm supposed to report back for active duty. But I'm still finding it quite difficult to be one of the walking wounded."

"You're hardly the walking wounded." David tried to keep his tone light.

"Thank you for saying that, but I'm nothing like the man I used to be. Outside or in."

"I think you're selling yourself short," David said.

"Perhaps," Gregory said. "Perhaps." Then he stood up. "We'd best outrun the hunters."

Late that afternoon, the guests in their scarlet jackets returned, then hastened to their rooms to clean up and dress for dinner. In the Green Drawing Room, the enormous fireplace was blazing. As more and more guests came in, champagne flowed freely, and laughter echoed off the damask-covered walls.

That evening, the ladies were in red, white, or blue silk and satin, taffeta, and tulle, as per the Queen's order. Maggie felt, under the circumstances, it was absolutely appropriate to wear her blue chiffon dress. In the Waterloo Chamber this time, alongside men in dress uniforms and full evening regalia, they made their way through multiple courses. Once again, Maggie noticed that Gregory didn't eat much but drank a great deal. As the long candles dripped wax and dessert was being served, Winston Churchill rose to his feet and the gentle murmurs of the dinner guests quieted.

"First, let me thank the gracious hospitality of our King and Queen, for having us here this weekend. And showing us such wonderful patriotic spirit," he began in the tones and cadences Maggie had grown to know so well when she'd worked as his typist. She felt her fingers twitching instinctively, mock typing on her Irish linen napkin.

"This is a strange Christmas Eve. Almost the whole world is locked in deadly struggle, and, with the most terrible weapons which science can devise, the nations advance upon each other. Here, in the midst of war, raging and roaring over all the lands and seas, creeping nearer to our hearts and homes, here, amid all the tumult, we have tonight the peace of the spirit in each and every generous heart.

"This Christmas, let the children have their night of fun and laughter. Let the gifts of Father Christmas delight their play. Let us grown-ups share to the full in their unstinted pleasures before we turn again to the stern task and the formidable years that lie before us, resolved that, by our sacrifice and daring, these same children shall not be robbed of their inheritance or denied their right to live in a free and decent world.

"And so, in God's mercy, a happy Christmas to you all."

"Hear, hear!" called a silver-haired Navy Admiral weighed down by medals, raising his glass.

"Hear, hear!" the crowd echoed.

Somewhere down the long table, a strong tenor voice began, "For He's a Jolly Good Fellow," and everyone joined in.

*Everyone, that is, except Gregory,* Maggie noticed. She realized that once again he was in white tie and tailcoat, instead of his dress RAF uniform. *How strange,* Maggie thought. *Maybe he doesn't want to be reminded of the Air Force when he has only a few days left before he has to go back.*

After dinner, Maggie saw Gregory and David in the Grand Reception Hall, standing by the fireplace, each holding coupes of champagne, their images reflected back in the long mirror above. For the occasion, the Gobelins tapestries had been taken out of storage and rehung, and the delicate gilded needlepoint chairs uncovered. Two huge chandeliers dripping with French crystals, each bead and prism carefully washed, had been rehung from the high gild-laced ceiling. With Gregory and David was a young man Maggie didn't recognize. "Hello there," she said, approaching the group.

"Maggie, please meet Christopher Boothby, a friend from Cambridge." Gregory's voice was tired and sounded as though it were coming from far away.

Maggie offered her hand. "Quite the reunion, isn't it?" she said.

"A pleasure to meet you, Miss Hope." He had a touch of an accent—or was it an inflection?—she couldn't quite place.

The Grand Reception Room was crowded with guests, and as Maggie and David walked into the room, the orchestra swelled into "You Stepped Out of a Dream." Maggie scanned the crowd and saw Hugh, standing with Frain at the room's edge. They exchanged a secret smile before studiously ignoring each other.

As the swirling melody of the violins mingled with the sounds of conversation and laughter, David swung Maggie into his arms and they began to dance, her cheek fitting comfortably against his neck. "You smell very nice," she said.

"Blenheim Bouquet," he replied, giving her a spin. "There may be a war on, but that's no excuse not to stay fresh."

Maggie laughed. She remembered how, even in the midst of the worst air raids, David always looked impeccably pulled together. She looked around at the other guests. There were high-ranking officials in dress uniform with gold braid and ribbons and medals, of course, and ladies in patriotic hues—cardinal feather red, the blue of a sailor's collar, the white of freshly fallen snow—their hair done up in diamond tiaras or pearl combs, wearing long twenty-button gloves. The room itself was decorated with velvety crimson hothouse roses and a huge Christmas tree in the corner, lit with colored wax candles in gilded holders, and covered in artificial snow, wrapped gifts, toys, and sweets. The effect was magical.

"This way," David said, deftly spinning her through the crowd, away from a statuesque Countess, her curves straining at ruby satin, sagging neck wrapped in yellow diamonds. "It's a shame that once women are in a position to own jewels like that, they no longer have the necks for it," he mused.

Maggie saw Gregory with his champagne, sitting alone at one of the tables near the perimeter of the dance floor, in a world of his own.

"Gregory looks lonely," she said, indicating with her chin.

"Already looking for a new partner, Maggie?" David teased. "I'm crushed."

She gave his arm a gentle smack. "I thought maybe there was some . . . frisson last night. I was wondering if anything happened."

"Nothing yet," David replied. "Work, you know. But maybe tonight . . ."

"Do you think—do you think he's all right? I noticed he's drinking quite a lot, even more than he usually does."

"He's a veteran. He's been through hell. And he'll be back with the Air Force soon enough. Let the man relax and have some fun."

"All right," Maggie said, allowing herself to be convinced. "Then perhaps we should join him?"

"I like the way you think, my dear." David spun her to the table.

They sat down in delicate gold chairs as the orchestra segued into Noël Coward's "If Love Were All." Gregory sprang to his feet. "Maggie, you look lovely," he said, kissing her gloved hand.

"Perfect evening," David enthused, taking a seat and

motioning to a waiter with a silver tray of champagne coupes.

As the castle's clocks all chimed midnight, the orchestra segued into "Auld Lang Syne." Around her, the guests stopped to sing the Robert Burns words: *"Should auld acquaintance be forgot, and never brought to mind? Should auld acquaintance be forgot, and auld lang syne?"*

Her thoughts went out to John. Wherever he was.

Gregory got up and stalked away, heading for the French doors leading to the gardens.

He looked upset.

"I've got it," David whispered in Maggie's ear and then followed after. *"For auld lang syne, my jo, for auld lang syne, we'll take a cup o' kindness yet, for auld lang syne."* Maggie had always found the song sad, and around her she heard voices crack and men wipe at their eyes. The war wasn't even that old, and yet so many weren't coming home.

David followed Gregory through carpeted hallways and then outside, to the North Terrace, overlooking playing fields and Eton. It was freezing outside. As his eyes adjusted to the night, David shivered in his dinner jacket. The only sound was the faint music from the party and the creak of bare tree branches blown by the wind. The stars in the dazzling darkness seemed close enough to touch.

Near a low stone wall punctuated with crenellations, David caught up with Gregory. "Need a bit of fresh air?"

"It's just that song. Lots of old acquaintance not coming back. By next year or the year after, they'll be forgotten."

"Or coming back strangers. A friend of mine was shot down in the Battle of Britain. He's back at work now, but—I don't know who he is anymore. He's a completely different person."

"He is," Gregory agreed. "Something I know far too well."

The two men stood at the low stone wall that lined the terrace and looked over the grounds in the light of the waning moon.

"David," Gregory said, not looking at the other man, "I think you're very special."

David moved his hand on the smooth flagstone so that his pinky touched Gregory's. "And I feel the same about you."

"If that's the case, why don't you come away with me?"

David laughed, a hearty laugh that rang out across the empty grounds. "Very romantic, but where could we possibly go? An island in the South Seas, with white sand and palm trees? Live on bananas and coconuts?"

"No, the Japanese have taken those islands," Gregory said seriously. "I'm thinking more of Argentina. Buenos Aires."

"Well, I'm afraid the British government might frown on that."

"I'm not joking."

David looked at Gregory's scarred, serious face. He was not.

"The world's at war, Gregory," he said, shrugging. "There's nowhere to run."

"You have no idea what it's like. You see the scars on my face—you have no idea how scarred I am inside."

David nodded.

"Millions of Germans are dead now. Millions of Poles, Czechs, Dutch, French, Norwegians. . . . Do you know how many Chinese have died since Japan invaded in thirty-seven? And what for?" he asked bitterly.

"The Nazis are evil, Gregory," David said. "You know that. Hitler's not just out to conquer the world, he's set out to destroy anyone he's declared to be 'sub-human'—Jews, Czechs, Russians, Poles. The mentally ill. I'm Jewish and 'like that,' so I'd have been thrown up against a wall and shot years ago if I lived in Germany under Hitler. At least here I'm, well, relatively free."

"With that fair hair of yours, you could pass for Aryan. And besides, it all depends on who's defining evil. Churchill's just as racist as Hitler when it comes down to it—and to win the war he'll have to cozy up to Stalin—as if he's any better than Hitler?"

"Churchill would cozy up to Satan himself if it would defeat Hitler. And I would too."

Gregory snorted. "At some point the Americans will join, and they'll die, trying to save us. The Chinese and the Japanese will always be at each other's throats. The Raj will rise up and slaughter the British in India, not to mention the Hindus and the Muslims. . . . I'm just . . . done. Finished. I did my bit—and now I want out."

After making sure they were alone, David reached up and touched Gregory's scarred face gently. "I can't imagine all you've been through."

"They're sending me back, you know," Gregory said. "Back to the Royal Air Force. I can still fly, so they want me up there," he gestured to the sky. "Just the thought of getting into a plane makes me ill. I can't. I just can't do it," Gregory said, grabbing David's hand. "I mean it.

I'm done. I'm leaving. And I'd like you to come with me. To Switzerland."

"No," David said, pulling his hand back. "I can't."

"You can," Gregory insisted. "Look, invasion is certain. Churchill will be one of the first lined up and shot—and you and the rest of his staff with him. They'll take out the present King and put the Duke of Windsor back on the throne."

"That's a future I'd hate to see, of course," David said. "But that's one of the reasons I'm staying—to make sure it *doesn't* happen."

David looked up at the starry sky, Gregory's former battleground. "Gregory, you're a hero. You did your part in Norway. You paid—you're still paying—for it. It's hard. I can't imagine how hard it must be for you. But you can't give up."

The other man gave a short, bitter laugh. "Of course. I'm being ridiculous. Christmas is hard for me. You must forget I ever said anything."

"Of course," David said. But he knew he wouldn't. Maggie was right. Something was wrong with Gregory.

---

In his small, drab room in the castle's servants' quarters, George Poulter was getting ready for bed. The door opened. "Audrey!" he hissed. "You shouldn't be here."

"It's our last night," she said. "Then we'll be out of here." He was silent as she sat next to him, pressing herself against him. "It will be fine. That's why I came. Tomorrow will be busy, and we won't see that much of each other. I just wanted to talk with you."

"I know," he said, as she kissed his neck. "Just a bit nervous is all."

"We've been over it so many times," she said, pushing him back on the bed. "You do your part and I'll do mine."

"And then?" He groaned as she massaged him, and then unbuttoned his fly.

"And then," she said, climbing on top of him, "Commandant Hess has everything set up for our escape from this godforsaken island."

Captain Vogt finally received his orders. "Type, 'Danke, Commandant Hess,'" Vogt said to his first mate, who tapped out Morse code to reply. "Then, 'I'll move her into position.'"

In the deep, dark waters of the North Sea, U-246's engines started up and the submarine began to move ever closer to the eastern British shore.

# Chapter Twenty-five

All of the furniture had been taken out of the Waterloo Chamber and a stage had been erected, with platforms and backdrops, looking just as it had in Queen Victoria's time, when she'd regularly had theatrical productions in the castle. Footlights and follow spots had been procured from London. The delicate gold chiavari chairs were now arranged in rows, with a long center aisle. It had been transformed into a theater.

In the nursery, the children were getting ready. Margaret was thrilled at the opportunity to wear stage makeup, not to mention her crinoline dress, white Marie Antoinette–style wig, and small black patch for a beauty mark. "Not too much lipstick!" Crawfie warned, as Margaret applied pink to her lips.

"But Crawfie," Margaret protested, her eyes shining with excitement, "I *need* it, otherwise I'll wash out under the lights. That's what Maggie said. Didn't you, Maggie?"

Maggie had, remembering her former flatmate Sarah's elaborate makeup for her ballet performances. She looked over at Lilibet, who was sitting a little apart from everyone, her lips moving, going over her lines. The rest of the children in the cast were putting the finishing touches on their costumes, erupting in fits of giggles before shushing themselves.

"Girls," Alah said, clapping her hands, "we have five more minutes to get ready. Then we'll walk quietly to the Waterloo Chamber, where you will quietly get into your positions for the beginning of Act One. *Quietly,* let me add."

Audrey knocked at the door and Alah let her in. "For the Princess Elizabeth, ma'am," she said, holding out a bouquet of golden roses.

"For me?" Lilibet said, running over to claim them and reading the card. She clasped it tightly to her. Even dressed as Prince Charming, with sword and shield, she exuded a womanly glow.

"Are they from Daddy?" Margaret asked, her rouged face breaking into a pout.

"None of your business," Lilibet replied, tucking the small card into her tunic.

"Probably from Philip, then," Margaret announced to the room as Lilibet ignored her.

*I have a bad feeling about this,* Maggie thought, as they all walked from the nursery to the Waterloo Chamber. The Red, White, and Blue Christmas, with all of the guests, opened the castle up to more dangers. Maggie knew there was extra security, but still, she couldn't shake the feeling that something was in the air, an off-tune vibration that was making her anxious. She peeked from behind the curtain, looking out into the audience, searching for . . . something. She shook her head. *Keep your eyes open but don't borrow trouble,* she reminded herself, as the children got into their positions for Act I.

From backstage, Maggie watched as Lords and Ladies, Dukes and Duchesses, Earls and Countesses filed in, the murmurs of conversation filling the room. Mr. Churchill was there, in the front row, of course, and then everyone stood as the King and Queen entered. When everyone was seated, the lights dimmed and the performance began.

Maggie needn't have worried about the children's acting abilities. Margaret shone as Briar Rose, first in her village girl dress, and then in a splendid satin Marie Antoinette–style gown and powdered wig for the finger-pricking scene. The other children were delightful in their roles. Lilibet was both heroic and dignified as the Prince in her velvet britches and lace jabot.

"It's so much more fun with an audience!" Margaret exclaimed as they came offstage for her curtain call. "I wish I could really be an actress someday!"

"You all did a wonderful job, children," Lilibet said to the assembled cast, still using the low tones of the prince. "Thank—"

There was a sudden bang.

Then a very loud pop.

Then a moment or two of horrific silence.

Backstage, everyone froze, listening. Then, from out front, the screaming began. Then the sound of people running, men shouting, "The King! The King!"

Maggie turned to Crawfie and Alah. "Watch the children!" She peeked around the flat of scenery. There were people milling about, shouting. The King was doubled over in pain, clutching at his shoulder. He and the Queen and Mr. Churchill were surrounded by Coldstream

Guards, who began hustling them out. More Cold-stream Guards were running through the ballroom, guns in hand.

"Who did it?" Maggie asked one of the guests, the woman she'd seen at the hunting breakfast.

"One of the footmen," she answered breathlessly. "I didn't see him shoot, but there was that horrible sound, and then the King bent over. Then we all saw him run. . . ."

Maggie realized the shooter was still at large in the huge castle. *The Princesses.* Maggie whirled and ran backstage.

"We have to get the children to the nursery!" she said to Crawfie and Alah. "Hurry!" Without another word, they surrounded all their charges and made their way out, back to the Lancaster Tower.

The King was taken to his study, where the royal physician was summoned to look after his wounds. "Put the castle into lockdown," the King said, blue eyes blazing. "Find Lord Clive—he knows the protocol. No one goes in or out until we catch whoever did this." Shock and anger seemed to have overpowered his stutter.

The Queen looked to the doctor. "He's going to be fine, Your Majesty," he assured her. "I know there's a lot of blood, but the bullet just nicked the shoulder. He's going to be fine."

"Oh, thank goodness," she said. Then she put a hand to her heart. "The girls!" she said, running to the door.

"Stop!" ordered the King. Then, in a softer tone, he

said, "They're fine, dear. Alah and Crawfie will take care of them."

"I must go to them!" his wife wailed.

"No," the King said. "There's a shooter at large. We can't risk it."

The Queen went to the King's desk and picked up the telephone. "The nursery," she said into the receiver. "Hurry." There was a long pause. Then, "Alah? The girls?" The Queen's face lost some of its tension. "Oh, thank goodness. And the other children?" Another pause. "And you and Crawfie?" She nodded to the King. "And Miss Hope?" After reassuring Alah that the King would be fine, the Queen spoke to both her daughters and told them that she loved them. Then she hung up the receiver.

"They're all right," the King said in soothing tones as the Queen began to cry. "You'll see—everything is going to be all right."

David had skipped the performance and was working in the Equerry's office when Gregory arrived, out of breath. "Someone shot the King!" he cried, eyes wild.

"Merciful Zeus!" The blood drained from David's face. "When? Where?"

"Just now in the Waterloo Chamber. The castle's on lockdown. Nobody in or out." Gregory's eyes darted back and forth, as if following invisible ghosts.

"The P.M.—he's . . . ?"

"Fine," Gregory answered, still out of breath. "The shooter hit the King, not sure how serious it is." He pushed through the blackout curtains and let himself out through French doors, to a flagstone-paved terrace.

"Gregory?" David called. He put the contents of what he was working on in the briefcase and handcuffed it to his left wrist, then followed him, briefcase in hand. It was freezing outside. As his eyes adjusted to the darkness, David shivered in his dinner jacket and thin-soled opera pumps. It seemed he was alone. The only sound was the creak of the bare tree branches blown by the wind.

"Gregory!" David called.

He heard a low moan and followed the sound to a stone staircase that led to a garden. Gregory was sitting on the top step, head in hands. "She's here," he whispered.

"Who?" David said, glancing around before sitting down next to him on the cold stone step, setting the briefcase down beside him. "Who's here?"

"Lily," he replied, eyes wide. "She's here, waiting for me."

"Gregory, Lily's dead," David said, laying a hand on his arm. "Maggie told me what happened."

He shook his head wildly. "No! 'She walks in beauty, like the night.' She haunts me. She laughs at me." He looked around the darkness, indicating the Great Park. "She's still here, along with the rest of the ghosts."

David smelled the alcohol on Gregory's breath and rose to his feet and extended his hand. "Come on, Gregory," he said firmly. "Let's get you back inside. Have some coffee. We'll call and find out how the King's doing."

Gregory grasped his hand and staggered to his feet. "Oh, Lily, Lily . . ." he moaned.

As David moved to help him, he heard a footstep— and just as he registered that they weren't alone, he heard an explosive noise and felt a blinding sting in the back of his head.

As he blinked and fell to his knees, undone by the pain, he felt darkness begin to close in around him. Just before he lost consciousness, he heard Gregory say, to his unknown assailant, "You really shouldn't have done that."

Back in the nursery, the corgis were restless, whining their anxiety. Alah and Crawfie bustled about, helping all the children feel at home by removing their makeup with cold cream and having them take turns in the bathroom getting back into their regular clothes. Lilibet and Margaret helped the other children. "Remember, children," Lilibet said, "we're British."

"Stiff upper lip!" Margaret added.

Maggie thought about Hugh, then shook her head. *He's a trained professional—he's fine. This is why they don't want agents to get involved with each other.*

When the Coldstream Guard knocked, Maggie, Alah, and Crawfie looked at each other. "Open in the name of the King!" he shouted.

Maggie went to open the door. It was with palpable relief that she saw it was a guard. He called to the Princesses. "His Majesty wants you to know that he's all fine," he said. "Nick to the shoulder is all."

Lilibet and Margaret hugged each other, and Margaret tried very hard not to cry. "It's all right, it's all right," Lilibet said, stroking Margaret's hair.

"And are you—well?" the guard said. "Your Highnesses?"

"We're fine," Lilibet answered.

"Good, Miss. That's what I'll report back to the King and Queen, then. Her Majesty just wanted someone to actually check. . . ." He began to back out.

"No!" Margaret cried, her eyes overflowing. "We're going with you!"

Lilibet stood up. "Yes, we're going with you."

Maggie walked over to them and knelt down. "I know you want to be with your parents, but you're safe here and they're safe there. The entire castle is on lockdown, and they're going through, room by room, until the man who did this is found. Everyone must stay where she is until we do."

Lilibet saw the wisdom of this argument, but Margaret didn't. "Noooooo!" she shrieked. "I want Mummy! I want Daddy!" Lilibet wrapped her arm around her sister and held her tightly.

The guard left, the corridor echoing with Margaret's cries, even after he shut the door behind him.


After the shot was fired, the Prime Minister was surrounded by his private detective and a squadron of Coldstream Guards, who shielded his body from any potential shots and got him to safety, ensconced in his suite. Frain was with him.

"Give me your gun!" the P.M. was saying to his private detective.

"No, sir," the man replied.

"I order you! Now!"

"Winston—" Frain tried to interrupt.

"Goddamn it, man!" Churchill exploded. "Someone tried to assassinate the King of England—within the sacred walls of Windsor Castle, no less! I was considered a crack shot in the last war. I'm going to hunt the blaggard down myself—and let him have it!"

Frain poured a glass of Scotch and handed it to the P.M. "Please sit down, sir," he said. "The castle is on lockdown and the guards will find the shooter. In the meantime, we need to keep you safe as well. You're worth a lot more to Britain alive than dead."

Churchill accepted the heavy crystal tumbler. "Very well, then," he growled, waving a hand. "But if the bugger bounds in here, you'd better take him out on your first shot."

In the nursery, all the children, including the Princesses, were still on edge. Alah had found a tin of biscuits she'd saved for an emergency and distributed them among the children, who accepted them and ate them greedily.

There was a nervous rap. Maggie jumped up and went to the door. "Who is it?" she asked.

"*C'est moi*, Mademoiselle. It's Audrey."

Maggie opened the door a crack. There was the young French woman, carrying a tray of sandwiches and pots of tea. "Come in, Audrey," she said. "Look, children," she said to the room. "Audrey's brought you something to eat!"

The young people nearly fell over themselves to get to the sandwiches, while Alah set to work pouring the tea. Maggie noticed that the two Princesses held back, waiting to make sure there were enough sandwiches for everyone, before helping themselves.

"Thank you so much, Audrey," Maggie said. "The children were getting hungry, although they didn't complain."

"Poor little things," she said. "I couldn't help but think of them here, especially the little Princesses."

"They're doing fine," Maggie said. "I'm sure this drama will all be over soon."

"I'll be on my way then, Mademoiselle," Audrey said.

"No," Maggie said. "You couldn't possibly go back. It's bad enough you risked yourself by coming here. Stay until it's over."

"Of course, Mademoiselle," Audrey said. "Of *course* I'll stay with the Princesses."


"We hadn't planned on a lockdown, for Christ's sake!" Boothby said to Gregory, looking down at David's body lying on the cold stone terrace.

"No," Gregory said. "But if we don't act tonight, we'll miss our chance. I've already contacted Hess. If we don't do it tonight, we're stuck here until God knows when. And," he said, poking a toe into David's body and jostling him, "he's our ticket out of Britain."


"Sir, you can't enter this area," the Coldstream Guard said. He was standing in front of one of the entrance-ways to the kitchen. Then he took a closer look at the man. It was George Poulter, out of his usual footman's uniform, as he had been for the pantomime. The guard narrowed his eyes. "Wait—aren't you—?"

Poulter pulled out his gun from the waistband of his trousers and shot the guard through the heart. As the man's eyes glazed over, he dropped to the floor.

"Sorry, mate," Poulter said as he shoved the gun back

into his trousers, then took the narrow stairs down to
the wine cellar and began rolling up the carpet. Hidden
underneath the carpet was the trap door in the floor,
leading into the castle's dungeons.

It was getting late. In the nursery, Maggie was next to
Margaret on the sofa, while Lilibet had settled near one
of the windows, peeking out behind the blackout curtains. Audrey sat down on a needlepoint footstool, close
to the Princesses. One of the corgis growled low in his
throat and bared his small, sharp teeth. "Dookie!" Lilibet snapped. "Stop that!"

"Thank you, Your Highness," Audrey said. "I must
confess, I don't like dogs very much."

"Oh, Audrey, thank you so much for bringing the
sandwiches and tea," Lilibet said earnestly. "It was extremely brave of you."

"It was nothing, Miss," Audrey said. She looked
around. Everyone, including Alah and Crawfie, was either engaged in low conversation or sleeping where they
could.

She lowered her voice. "There was a phone call for
you, Miss. From—Lieutenant Mountbatten."

"Philip?" Elizabeth said, hand going to her heart.

"Yes, Miss. I told him about the shooting, then that
you were being kept in the nursery. He sounded beside
himself with worry."

"Oh, no," Lilibet said. "Poor Philip. And we're fine.
I *must* let him know."

Audrey leaned in. "He asked if you would call him
back," she said. "He practically begged me. He'll be

waiting by the phone in, let's see," she looked up at the clock on the mantel. "In ten minutes."

"Ten minutes!" Lilibet said. "Why, if I don't call, he'll think something is terribly wrong!"

Audrey whispered in Lilibet's ear, "Pretend to get something from Margaret's room. I'll follow you a few minutes behind, and then we can go down to the kitchen so you can call Philip."

Lilibet's face clouded as she looked over at Alah, dozing peacefully in the tufted chair in front of the fire.

"He's waiting for your call, Miss."

Emboldened by her feelings, Lilibet made up her mind.

Slowly, slowly, David began to regain consciousness.

"You gave us all quite a scare," he heard Gregory say over the loud noise of an engine.

David tried to open his eyes. The pain was excruciating.

"What the—?" he managed, voice cracking. He tried to sit up, causing explosions in his head. He tried to put a hand to his wound, but they were tied together in front of him. His briefcase was still handcuffed to him, and was leaning against his side.

"Where are we?" he asked, squinting at Gregory, who was sitting beside him, silver flask in hand.

"We're on our way to the coast. There's a U-boat waiting for us not far offshore."

"Who's driving?"

"My old friend, Christopher Boothby."

As David closed his eyes again, his mind raced. *Why?* Why would Gregory betray England? What could his ties to Nazi Germany possibly be? He was an RAF pilot, a war hero—one of Churchill's "few." He'd nearly died in Norway.

David could smell petrol and the brackish Thames. It was cold in the back of the car, and he shivered. Gingerly, he tried once again to move.

Trickles of blood from his head wound had run down his face and were now congealing.

"David," Gregory said, wiping at the man's face with his handkerchief, "I wanted you to come with us," he said, his breath reeking of alcohol. "But not this way."

David squinted up in the darkness. "Why?" Overhead, Messerschmitts and Heinkels whined, on their way to drop their deadly cargo on London.

Gregory checked his watch. "Almost one," he called up to Boothby, in the driver's seat. "The window for our pickup opens in half an hour. We need to hurry."

*"Jawohl, mein Herr"* was Boothby's response.

"I suppose you've figured out what I've done," he said to David.

"You've kidnapped me—and my briefcase. And we're going to Germany. But I still don't understand why."

Gregory took another long draw on the bottle. "Oh, where are my manners? Would you like some?"

"No," David said. "I never drink while kidnapped."

Sarcasm was lost on Gregory. "More for me, then," he said, taking a sip and spilling a little as the car hit a bump in the road. He wiped his mouth with the back of his hand. "It wasn't you so much as your tantalizing briefcase. It was a present, from Father Christmas himself. You, with that." He looked at David. "Now, you mustn't think I'm a monster, I did try to get you to come with me." He grinned and placed his hand on David's leg. "And I was very persuasive."

David was silent, repulsed by Gregory's touch.

"Still, you, the Jew patriot, were unmoved. And so, Boothby and I took more—definitive action. He wanted to cut your hand off, by the way, and leave you at Windsor. I was the one who said we should bring you with us."

"But why?"

"I like you, David. And I'd hate to see you go down with the losing side. To be honest, I just don't give a damn who wins this bloody war anymore. Quite frankly, despite all of Churchill's brave talk, it looks pretty certain Germany will win—sooner or later." He shrugged. "And, you see, in Germany, my contact will pay me—us," he said, looking to Boothby in the driver's seat, "dearly for the information you have. Whatever you have in your briefcase must be worth a small fortune. It's enough to let me disappear quietly to Switzerland."

"Or Buenos Aires," David said, remembering.

"Somewhere like that." Gregory looked at David. "The offer's still good, you know."

"Go to hell."

Gregory smiled. "Germany first."

"This is it," Boothby said in his perfectly enunciated English. He slowed and took a hard left, pulling up and cutting the motor.

"And now," Gregory said, pulling out his gold pocket watch, "we wait."

# Chapter Twenty-six

Pretending she was going to the bathroom, Lilibet had successfully pulled off her escape from the nursery. "Thank you so much," she whispered to Audrey as they tiptoed down long drafty corridors.

"Of course, Miss," Audrey said, letting Lilibet go on ahead. "I know I would do anything for *l'amour*."

"Ah, *l'amour*," Lilibet sighed, pressing her hand to the note hidden in her skirt pocket.

When they reached the castle's vast kitchen, Lilibet headed for the telephone. She picked up the heavy receiver lying on the counter. "Hello? Philip? Hello?" Lilibet said as Audrey looked around to make sure they were alone, then pulled out a handkerchief and a small bottle of clear liquid from her apron pocket. She wet the cloth with the liquid, then reached from behind and held it over Lilibet's nose and mouth. It had a sickly sweet smell. Lilibet struggled, then went limp in Audrey's arms.

———

When Lilibet didn't return, Dookie went to the bathroom door and got up on his hind legs to growl and paw at it, agitated, his claws clicking on the wood for the door. "Dookie! Stop it!" Maggie whispered. But the dog continued to whine and paw. Maggie got up and knocked. "Your Highness?" she called. "Lilibet?" There was no answer. She and Dookie locked eyes and he gave a series of low whines that sounded like sobs. She pounded on the door. "Lilibet? Open the door!" She reached for the knob and the door opened easily. The bathroom led into Margaret's rooms. The door to the hallway was still open.

"Bloody hell," Maggie muttered, as she ran through Margaret's open door and then down the long corridor, calling "Lilibet! Lilibet!" Dookie followed her, barking loudly. She ran down the corridor to the kitchen, where she spied the two. "Lilibet!" she screamed, seeing the unconscious Princess. She looked at Audrey in shock. "What the *hell* do you think you're doing?"

"Nothing that concerns you," Audrey said, dropping Lilibet to the floor, then going to the door to the wine cellar. She knocked and Poulter opened the door. "There you are," he said.

"We have company," Audrey said, indicating Maggie, who ran to Lilibet and tried to rouse her. Dookie followed behind, ears pinned back and giving a low growl.

Audrey came at Maggie, who stood up, ready for the attack. When Audrey tried to grab her, she reached for her right arm and twisted, bringing the Frenchwoman down to the floor. But Poulter had come behind Maggie, and before she could react, he picked up the handkerchief with chloroform and pressed it over her mouth and nose with one hand, while his other arm held her in a choke hold. Dookie tried to bite his ankle, but Poulter kicked the little dog so hard he was thrown against the wall, too stunned to stand.

After a moment or two, Maggie slumped to the floor.

"Leave her and the *chien*," Poulter ordered Audrey, shoving her to the side with her boot.

Audrey went back to the Princess. "Help me," she grunted. "She's not as light as you might think."

Poulter picked up Lilibet's limp body. "We must hurry," he warned, as he descended the stairs to the wine cellar and the tunnels through the dungeons. "We only have a very short window of time to get to the U-boat."

Maggie began to regain consciousness.

"Are you all right, Miss Hope?" she heard Mr. Churchill say. "Damn it, girl—wake up!" he said, patting at her cheeks.

Maggie tried to open her eyes, which were heavy and uncooperative.

"Where?" she managed, trying to sit up.

"The P.M.'s rooms. One of the guards carried you," Hugh said, voice tight.

She suddenly remembered. "Lilibet!"

"What about her?" Frain asked.

Maggie sat up, shaking her head to get rid of the fog from the drugs. "They took her."

"The Princess? Who took her?" Churchill barked.

"Moreau. The maid, Audrey Moreau. She somehow lured Lilibet from the nursery, then chloroformed her. I followed them, and Moreau did the same to me. She was working with George Poulter, a footman." *The winking footman,* Maggie thought.

"I tried to stop them," she said, the enormity of what had happened breaking over her. *Why did I spend so much time being suspicious of Louisa? Why, when all the while it had been Audrey planning to abduct the Princess? And I had been suspicious when Cook told me about Audrey's recent exodus from France. I just never pursued it. . . .*

"Is there anything else that you remember?" Frain said. "Quick!"

"There was a trapdoor in the floor." She rose, swaying, then steadying herself. "They must be using the tunnels to get out of the castle. Come on! I know the tunnels—the Princesses showed me. If we hurry, there's still a chance we can catch them!"

Lilibet, unconscious, had been carried over Poulter's back, like a sack of potatoes, through the dark and winding tunnels and then up the stairs before being unceremoniously dumped on the cold flagstones outside the Henry VIII Gate.

"Hurry!" Audrey hissed to Poulter. "We need to make it to Mossley while the U-boat's still there."

While he was gone, Lilibet's eyelids fluttered. She came to, then lay quietly, appraising her situation. She realized she was being kidnapped. She was gathering her strength to make a run for it, back into the castle, when she felt Moreau's foot in her back. "Don't even think about it," she said, springing a switchblade.

Normally, Lilibet could have outrun her, but not in her still-drugged condition. Then she saw a small stone and picked it up, considering. She began scratching on the stones.

"Hey," Audrey said, looking over, suspicious. "What are you doing?"

"Nothing," Lilibet said in her clear voice. "Maths homework."

Audrey, with the help of light from the moon, partially obscured by dusty spiderwebs of clouds, looked at what the Princess was doing and saw:

```
23172614121+
121117816114+
16+
91115158121+
1724112316+
1252571712+
```

She gave a Gallic shrug. "People always wondered if you girls were right in the head, you know," she said. "Especially with so much inbreeding."

Lilibet didn't reply but kept at her message, impervious to everything, even the cold seeping through her wool dress and cardigan. Poulter returned, pushing the car, but even with the extra precaution, he drew the attention of one of the Coldstream Guards patrolling.

"Stop!" the young man said.

Poulter fired. The wound spurted a gush of blood between his eyes that looked black in the darkness, and then the man crumpled.

As Lilibet closed her eyes in horror, Poulter came with a length of rope, swiftly tying the girl's hands and feet, and dumping her into the back of the van without ceremony. He didn't notice the markings she made with the stone. She didn't know who would find them, or when, but she did know that Margaret and Maggie would be able to read them. And then they would know where she was being taken.

She quietly prayed that they would find her in time.

With Mr. Churchill manning the situation from Windsor, Maggie, Frain, and Hugh ran down the corridors to find the trapdoor in the wine cellar floor.

"Here it is!" Maggie said. She grabbed the iron ring, opened the trapdoor and started down the stairs, grabbing Lilibet and Margaret's hidden flashlight and switching it on. "Follow me," she said. "I know the way. If we continue through, we'll end up at the Henry the Eighth Gate."

After running through the tunnels, through twists and turns and past dungeons, they found the stairway up and opened the trapdoor. They climbed, then ran on outside, in the cold, wet air, to the Gate. *Have they already gone?* Maggie wondered, heart pounding. *Did we miss them?* The dread of the unknown made her feet fly. At the gate, they all stopped.

Frain sniffed the air. "A car's been here," he said.

"Look," Hugh said, pointing to the still body of the Coldstream Guard. He ran over and put his hand to the guard's throat. "Dead."

"Yes, I'd say they came this way," Frain said.

*Oh, no,* thought Maggie. *Too late, too late.* She wanted to stamp her feet, throw rocks, swear at the top of her lungs. But she had a job to do. "They could be taking her anywhere," she said, pacing. "They could have a plane tucked away somewhere, they could be going anywhere on the coast for a ship. . . ." Maggie looked down. Then she used the flashlight to take a better look. "Wait—Lilibet left us a message!"

Frain and Hugh came over and looked at the markings, then looked at each other.

But Maggie was already kneeling, her heart bursting with hope. "Oh, smart girl," she said. "Brilliant, *brilliant* girl."

"We can't read that," Hugh said.

"But *I* can." She quickly decrypted the message, using the alphabet code Lilibet had created. "Audrey and Poulter are taking her to Mossley. For a U-boat pickup." *Finally, a lead! At least this way we have a shot at intercepting them before they get to the water.*

She got back to her feet and wiped her hands on her skirt. "Peter, call the cavalry and tell them we're going to need them in Mossley."

"Yes, ma'am," Frain said, his face twisting in a grim smile.

Maggie began running to the castle's car park. "Come on, Hugh," Maggie said over her shoulder, "let's get going!"


From the P.M.'s rooms in the castle, Peter Frain ran the search. Every police station from Windsor to Mossley was alerted. Descriptions of Audrey Moreau and George Poulter were circulated. Frain used motorcycle couriers to dispatch photographs of the two to cities, towns, and villages en route. Most were only told that there had been a kidnapping.

Frain contacted the Admiralty and advised them to be on the lookout for U-boats approaching the coastline in the Norfolk area. He contacted the Coast Guard and asked them to keep a watch for any small craft heading out to sea. He telephoned the Y-service radio monitors and asked them to be on the lookout for suspicious wireless transmissions.

When Frain had done all he could think of, he rose from the desk, rubbing the back of his neck. Things were grim, he knew, and every second that passed made things worse.

The Prime Minister looked at him from across the room. They exchanged the glance of battle survivors—dazed and weary. The King had joined them on hearing the news. He now sat alone, head bowed, hands twisting around each other. His arm was bandaged and in a white sling. The P.M. rose and walked to him. The room was silent.

"We've covered every possible escape route," Frain said. "Now we just have to wait."

"How's your shoulder, sir?" Churchill asked the King.

"I can't even th-th-think about the shoulder," the King replied, his eyes still unfocused.

The P.M. lit yet another cigar. "How's Her Majesty?"

"She's with Margaret now," he said, almost inaudibly.

"Good, good," Churchill boomed. "Best place for her."

"Would you like to lie down and rest, sir?" Frain asked.

"I want to be here," the King replied. "In case there's any news."

"Gutsy move of theirs," Churchill said, pacing back and forth in front of the fireplace. "An assassination attempt and a kidnapping right under our very noses! They've got stones, I'll give them that," he said, punctuating his words with jabs of his cigar. "*Stones!* But they won't leave this island. I swear to you."

The King blanched.

"We've covered every possibility," Frain said. "Now we just have to wait for something to break."

"There's a map in the glove compartment," Hugh said as he drove. The blue-black sky was encrusted with stars. A waning moon hung in the sky.

Maggie opened the box. In it were the map, a flashlight, and a gun. She held the lit flashlight in her teeth, pulled out the map, and squinted at it. "Yes, we're on track," she said through the flashlight.

They drove together in silence for a time. Finally, Maggie spoke: "What happened between us—"

"Yes?"

"Well, it can't ever happen again. There's a reason why agents can't be involved with each other. We're working together."

"Of course," Hugh agreed. "I'd never do anything to compromise your safety."

"That's just the point. It's not my safety you need to worry about—it's the Princess's safety."

"I know, Maggie. I know this may be hard to understand, but I've been doing this longer than you have."

Maggie felt a flash of anger—then realized he was right. "Sorry."

"Don't worry about it."

She took a brief moment to think of how it might work for them. Then dismissed the thought. "Thank you for the painting. It's beautiful."

"Glad you like it." Hugh cleared his throat. "So, what's the plan, once we get there? Sounded like you had one."

Maggie's smile was crooked. "As we say in America, Hugh—we're going to wing it."

Frain's call to Scotland Yard had caused local police precincts to scramble to put up roadblocks, but the van with the Princess was already racing along the AI, on its way to Mossley. Poulter and Audrey were in the front seats, while Lilibet, tied up, was lying in the very back. The van, one used by the castle staff for transporting large game animals from the grounds where they'd been shot to the slaughterhouse, had the metallic smell of old blood. Poulter drove past cities, villages, and hamlets: Hatfield, Welwyn, and Stevenage; Letchworth, Foster, and Baderton.

The winds had picked up. Between the motion of the van as it sped over the darkened roads and the gusting of the wind, the insides shuddered and shook. The passengers were silent as Poulter turned off the main road onto a narrower one, less likely to be blocked by the police. It was rough going, and he had to reduce speed, but he was convinced it was better to be safe than sorry.

"Shit," he said, seeing lights and a roadblock ahead. He could see at least four men in police uniforms, gesturing for him to slow down and stop.

Audrey's eyes were wide as she reached into the glove compartment. There she found two guns. She passed the first to Poulter, then picked up the second, wrapped her hands around the pistol, hiding it in the folds of her skirt. "*Merde,*" she whispered.

Then she turned back to Lilibet. "Lie down and keep silent!"

Poulter slowed the van, braking to a stop in front of the barricade. He rolled down his window. "Good evening, officers," he said, smiling.

"Please step out of the van, sir," the fresh-faced officer said.

"Look, it's late," Poulter said, "and my wife and I are tired. Would you mind just letting us pass?"

"Where are you and your 'wife' going, sir?" the bobby asked.

Poulter could see the other officers conferring in the background, probably matching their faces to an issued description.

"Grimsby—visiting family there," Poulter answered, even as one of the officers came up to Audrey's door and the two others around to the back of the van.

The young officer pulled out his gun and then opened Poulter's door. "All right, sir, we'll need you to get out of the vehicle. Slowly, please. Mind the step."

In the back of the van, Lilibet lay with her hands and feet bound. She'd seen the lights from the front window and felt the van slow and then stop. She'd seen Audrey pass Poulter his gun. She heard Poulter's side of the conversation with the officer, for they had to be police officers. She'd also heard the door open and saw them both getting out of the van. She'd been afraid, too afraid to think, but now that was passing. She was still afraid, of course, but she was starting to get angry, too. How dare they! And Audrey! Cook's husband's cousin! They thought they were helping a poor French girl get out of occupied France, when the whole time she was plotting against them. Lilibet felt not only angry but betrayed.

After seeing them shoot the Coldstream Guard, Lilibet had no doubts about what they were capable of. She had to warn the officers. But how?

"Help!" she wanted to call, but no one would hear her.

In the dim light, she rolled over on her back and started yelling "Help!" with all of her might.

Before the officers could react to the banging from the back of the van, they were dead.

While Poulter grabbed the men and dragged them, one by one, to the side of the road, Audrey went to the back of the van and opened up the rear doors.

"You little bitch," she hissed at Lilibet, then slapped her hard across the face. "Thanks to you, they're dead."

Lilibet recoiled at the pain but wouldn't allow herself to cry. She'd bitten her lip and tasted blood. They were dead? She was responsible for their deaths? Poulter had pulled the trigger, but if she'd only kept still . . .

"Don't even think of pulling a stunt like that again! Unless you'd like to change this little scenario from kidnapping to murder. I, for one, would be more than happy to oblige." Then she slammed the doors shut.

In the darkness, the Princess realized she had to behave, that she couldn't risk any more deaths of innocent civilians. She would have to see this through, on her own. She blinked away tears and set her mouth. She would wait for an opportunity and then use it. Yes, that was what she would do. They wouldn't get away with this.

As Audrey climbed back into the front passenger seat of the van, shaking out her hand, still burning from the slap, Poulter consulted the map. "We're not far now."

Finally, Audrey, Poulter, and Lilibet reached Mossley by Sea. The tiny white cottage appeared in light from the dim headlamps. And Audrey was relieved to see a man standing in the drive with a kerosene lantern, directing them in.

The man was Gregory Strathcliffe.

Gregory, holding the lantern as well as his nearly empty flask, led them inside the cottage. The interior was cold, with just a few plain furnishings. He took off his hat and unbuttoned his mackintosh. David was lying, passed out again, on the stained sofa. Audrey was behind the Princess Elizabeth, whose feet had been untied to walk, although her wrists were bound. Every few moments, she prodded the Princess in the small of her back.

"Christopher Boothby, you already know Mademoiselle Audrey Moreau and Mr. George Poulter." Gregory gestured grandly, as though they were at sherry hour. "And, of course, Her Royal Highness, the Princess Elizabeth." He gave a sardonic bow. He pointed to David's still form. "David Greene." He walked to the window and peeked out. "The BBC's been airing reports about a shoot-out at Windsor Castle. I don't suppose that has anything to do with you two?"

"What're the reports saying?" Poulter asked.

"Nothing about the attempt on the King. Just that you killed one guard and wounded another. Oh, yes, gave your names, your descriptions—everything. Mounted a nationwide search. By dawn, the entire country will be out in force to look for you."

"Well, then it's a good thing we'll be in France," Audrey said.

Gregory, swaying slightly under the influence of all the alcohol, took down a radio from the cupboard. He placed it on the wooden kitchen table and switched it on. Static hissed from it. He took out his pocket watch and checked it again.

"It's almost two," he said. "The U-boat should be waiting just off the coast. We'll let them know we're here and then set out. They're going to be ten miles due east of Mossley and wait for us until six a.m. If we don't make it, they'll head back out to sea and try again in three days."

"We'll make it," Poulter said, as Gregory sat down and began keying Morse code into the radio, alerting the U-boat that they were on their way.

"How are we going to meet the sub?" Audrey asked. "All the ships and boats have been confiscated since Dunkirk."

"We have a small fishing skiff hidden in the barn," Boothby answered. "We'll use that to meet the submarine."

"In this weather?" Poulter said. "Don't you think that's a bit dangerous?"

Gregory narrowed his eyes. His escape from the RAF, from Britain, from all of his problems, was in his reach— he wasn't about to let the chance slip away. "Do we have another option?"

———

Beeston Regis was a village just in Norfolk, near the coast of the North Sea. Roman in origin, it was mentioned in the *Domesday Book* of 1086 as Besetune. Now, it was just a small village like so many others. The ruins of St. Mary's Priory drew a few tourists before the war, but other than that, it was quiet, with one main street, boasting one bank, one grocery, one pharmacy, one barber shop, and one beauty parlor.

Mary Manley, a young slim girl of just eighteen, was making her way from the house she shared with her mother, father, and five sisters just outside of town, up the hill to Beeston Bump. She was going to work, as a radio operator at the Y-station. Beeston Bump was one of the many Y-stations in a network of Signals Intelligence collection sites. These stations collected material to be passed to the War Office's Government Code and Cipher School at Bletchley.

It was a damp, dark evening and the higher she climbed, the stronger the icy wind blew. It smelled of salt water and seaweed. Cold and wet, Mary was grateful to reach the concrete bunker and go inside. Once past the entrance, she took off her coat, hat, and heavy wool mittens and put them in her cubby. She flashed her badge to the guard on duty, Lenny Doyle, even though they had known each other since they had been toddlers and he'd stuck chewing gum in her long, honey-colored hair and she'd had to get it cut out. She hated him from then on and got in the habit of avoiding him. But now they worked together. He scrutinized her photograph on her card.

"Come on, Lenny," she said, "it's the same as yesterday and the same as the day before that. And it'll be the same tomorrow."

"Just doing my job, Mary. Just doing my job." He handed it back to her.

"Yes, I feel *so* much safer with you here."

She marched into the radio room, the rubber soles of her shoes squeaking on the concrete, and slid into her seat between two other women before Mr. Leaper could notice she was late.

It was dim in the room, and damp, the smell of wet concrete pronounced. In front of her, the dials of her RCA AR-77 communications receiver glowed. She slipped on her heavy black headphones and listened.

Her job was to eavesdrop on Morse code that German senders were tapping out throughout Europe. She turned her receiver to "her" band of frequencies and listened in.

The German Morse code senders were fast, especially the professionals at BdU, the Kriegsmarine headquarters. However, they each had their own fist. They could recognize them as easily as seeing a familiar face across a room.

This evening, however, Mary heard an unfamiliar fist.

Instead of the typical burst of fast-paced typing, this transmission was slow, with awkward pauses, indicating uncertainty and unfamiliarity with the transmitter.

Still, she recorded the transmission on an oscillograph, creating a radio "fingerprint," called a Tina, and then transcribed the Morse code that had been sent.

After the tentative sender had finished, there was a rapid-fire burst of code as response from whoever received it. He was a radio operator on one of the Nazi U-boats, one that was very close to the coast.

They went back and forth a few times, the amateur and the Nazi, and then the channel went ominously silent.

Mary felt the hairs on the back of her neck raise. She went to the oscillograph and collected the printout. Usually she just put it in a metal basket to be collected at the end of her shift, bundled up with the rest of the communiqués, and sent on by motorcycle courier to Bletchley Park.

Still . . .

She got down a Morse code book from a shelf and began to decode.

"Miss Manley!" called Martin Leaper from across the room. He was a narrow middle-aged man with a narrow pencil mustache, and the station's overseer. The memo Frain had dispatched to all the Y-stations by motorcycle courier was lying on his desk, unread.

Mary didn't look up from her translating. "Sir," she said, "you're going to want to look at this."

"Yes, Miss Manley?" he said, pursing his lips and walking over.

"Sir, someone here, in England, just signaled to a U-boat."

"What?"

"It could be a spy!" she ventured. "A spy signaling a U-boat for a pickup!"

"Control yourself, Miss Manley," Mr. Leaper admonished, shaking his head as he took the papers away from her. "I'm afraid you've seen far too many movies."

———

In the cottage, Audrey finished tying Princess Elizabeth to a ladder-back chair. She took some moldy hard bread from the cupboard and stuffed it in the Princess's mouth, securing it tightly with a tea towel around her head. If it were up to her, she would have killed the Princess—for keeping her alive was a bigger risk. Still, she was following the orders of Commandant Hess. And from what Commandant Graf had told her, one didn't question Hess's orders.

Lilibet kept very still, but her blue eyes glittered with defiance as Audrey went about her work. "I want you to be a good little girl," Audrey said as she gave the knot at the back of Elizabeth's head a final tightening. "Or I'll kill you myself." She smiled and came over to face Lilibet, her breath smelling sweet, like violet chewing gum. "And I know how to make it look like an accident."

*You just wait,* Lilibet thought. *This isn't over yet, you know.*

In the control room of U-246, First Officer Horst Riesch approached Captain Vogt. "Sir, our friends in Britain have given us word. They're ready," Horst said.

"Good, good," said Vogt. "What's the weather?"

"Clear now, sir, but the wind's picking up, seventy kilometers per hour."

"Christ," Vogt said, rubbing his stubble-covered chin—water was too precious in a submarine to waste on shaving. "They're probably coming in a dinghy, for all we know. Still, can't be helped. I'll set a course for the rendezvous point and have the men prepare to surface. You organize a reception party. Also, Horst told me they'll have two prisoners with them."

"Yes, Herr Vogt," Riesch said, saluting. Then he issued a long string of commands to the crew. Moments later, U-246, like the mythical kraken, was making its way through the black waters of the North Sea, up to the rendezvous point, ten miles off the coast of Mossley.

## Chapter Twenty-seven

A fierce wind was blowing as Gregory, Poulter, and Boothby went to the barn to uncover the small boat they'd hidden away, a twenty-foot gasoline engine–powered fish tug, with a V bottom. The three men strained and grunted as they pushed it over the rocks and grasses until they reached the stone-strewn beach.

Gregory looked out over the rough sea. "Not the best night for a sail, eh, lads?"

"It's that or hide out for another three days, for another pickup," Boothby said. "I'd rather take my chances on the water."

"No, it's now or never," Gregory said, staggering slightly in the wind. "I'll stay here with the boat. You two go back and help Audrey with the prisoners."

Maggie and Hugh pulled up to Mossley by Sea's two piers, with only a few fishing boats rocking wildly in the black water. The local police were there. Maggie got out of the car, heading into the stiff wind. Hugh grabbed the flashlight and gun from the glove compartment, slipping the gun in the back of his waistband under his coat, then followed her.

"These look like locals," Hugh shouted into the wind. "So, where's the cavalry?"

"I'm sure they're coming," Maggie shouted back. But she was worried. She thought that by now the Army would have soldiers assembled, Navy ships offshore, RAF planes overhead. Where were they?

As a police officer in a sou'wester waved them over, Hugh took out his MI-5 identification card. "Agents Thompson and Hope here," he shouted, his words nearly blown away by the wind. "What have you got?"

"We're on it, sir. If they're here, we'll find 'em." He looked at them, still in their light clothing. "Why don't you go back to the station, have a nice cup o' tea? Me and my boys'll take care of things here." He walked off to confer with his men.

Hugh and Maggie looked at each other in the darkness. They were not reassured. "There are police all over—they won't get these boats," Hugh said, scanning the dock.

Maggie was thinking. Gregory and his crew were too smart to try to use a boat from the dock. "But what if they're not using a boat from here? It's possible they have their own, hidden away. They could carry it down to the shore and then launch from there."

"In this weather?" Hugh asked. "Couldn't be a very large boat, then."

"They might not have any other option. And they just might be desperate enough to try it. I wouldn't put it past them."

"So we have two choices. Wait at the station, or—"

Maggie was already off, leaning into the wind as she made her way to the beach.

"—or we look for them ourselves," Hugh finished. "Right, then. Off we go."

They picked their way over stones and pebbles on the shore in the semidarkness. The white-tipped waves were crashing in, creating a low roar. The light from Hugh's flashlight was ineffective against the crushing darkness. Only a waning moon overhead provided any useful light.

"There!" Maggie shouted, over the din of the waves. She pointed to a small shack on the beach.

The shack was made of planks and covered in tar paper. The edges of the door were illuminated. Maggie and Hugh approached cautiously. He held the gun as Maggie rapped at the door. There was no answer. She pushed at the door. It swung open easily.

The stench hit them first—the overwhelming odor of stale smoke, sweat, and alcohol. The room was bare, except for a bulb and an old, stained mattress in the corner. On the mattress, a man was lying on his back, snoring loudly, a ratty wool blanket pulled over his legs and a half-empty bottle of gin clutched to his chest.

Trying not to inhale through her nose, Maggie went over to him. "Excuse me, sir," she said, kneeling down and giving him a firm shake. "Sir?"

"Wha—?" he said, opening his eyes. He was unshaven and unkempt, with thinning gray hair and a weather-beaten face. His plaid flannel shirt had yellow stains under the arms.

"We're looking for some people, sir," Hugh began. "Not from around here. They might be in a cottage or shack close to the beach? Have you seen anyone?"

"Go 'way. Wanna sleep."

"Sir!" Maggie said. Which was not at all the word she wanted to use.

No response.

*No, no, no—we've come too far to be stymied by a drunk.* She wanted to slap him, but instead grabbed the gin bottle from his lax hands. "I will take this gin and pour it all over the floor if you don't answer our questions."

"Bitch!" he slurred, trying to reach for the bottle with dirty hands with broken fingernails.

Maggie tipped the bottle and let a few drops of liquid trickle out. She had to admit that while it was technically illegal to dispose of his property, it was probably the fastest way to get him to talk. It was also grimly satisfying.

"Al' righ'," he said, propping himself up on his elbows. "Give i' back!"

"Not until you tell us what you know." Maggie held on to the bottle and kept it out of reach.

"There's a girl. Pretty," he slurred. "Pretty. French. Pretty French girl."

Maggie started. "Audrey?" she said to Hugh, who nodded.

"Where?" Hugh said. "Where have you seen her?"

"Pretty girl," he repeated. He tried to sit up and then dropped back down. "Comes to the cottage sometimes."

"What cottage?" Maggie asked. "Where is it?"

"Downna beach," he said, pointing, then turning back over. "Givver a kiss for me. . . ." he managed before beginning to snore again.

Maggie set the bottle down as she and Hugh looked at each other. It could be any French girl. Or it could be Audrey. "Come on," she said at the door, bracing to run through cold wind again. "Let's go 'downna beach'!"


A new shift had just started at the Submarine Tracking Room. "Sir," a young officer said to Donald Kirk, sitting behind his desk in his office. Kirk was looking over various memos. One was an alert, issued from the War Office, saying a man and a woman, plus a kidnapped girl, were on the run and might be trying to leave the country by boat. The next was a memo from Beeston Regis Y-station, saying that they had intercepted a radio communiqué between a location somewhere near shore and a Nazi U-boat. Martin Leaper, head of the Y-station, said that the transmission on the British side came from somewhere near Grimsby. The man had no idea what he'd stumbled on.

The two memos in hand, he rose, and with the help of his silver-tipped cane, made his way to the main room and the North Atlantic map table. The junior officers were repositioning various pushpins to reflect recent movement.

Kirk stared down at U-246. It hadn't seemed to have moved much. He jabbed the point of his cane at it. "U-two-forty-six!" he called to the heavyset middle-aged man moving the pins.

The man snapped to attention. "Yes, sir."

"Is that her current position?"

The man, beginning to sweat, checked his list of co-ordinates. "No, sir."

"Where is she now, then?"

The man looked to his clipboard and noted the position, then moved the red pin symbolizing U-246 toward land.

"Looks like she's moving in closer to shore, sir."

Two people on the run with a kidnapped girl, a radio transmission from the coast, a U-boat moving into position. It could mean only one thing—a pickup and rescue of two spies. And whoever the girl was. But there was only one girl, in all of Great Britain, who would be that important. . . .

"Get me Peter Frain, MI-Five on the line," Kirk barked. "And hurry!"

Maggie and Hugh, breathing heavily, knocked at the door of the cottage. Maggie's lungs were burning, but she couldn't even think about her body, she was so focused on Lilibet's safety.

There was no answer.

Inside, Audrey froze. Lilibet tried to scream through her gag.

Maggie and Hugh tried the door. It was locked.

Hugh pulled out his gun and handed it to Maggie. As she covered him, he kicked open the door. Even in the throes of the chase, Maggie was surprised and not a little impressed—she'd never seen Hugh in action before. But there was no time for that.

As the rickety door flew open, Hugh and Maggie entered the cottage, taking in the gagged and bound Princess, with Audrey standing beside her. An unconscious David, hands tied, was lying on the sofa.

"David?" Maggie gasped before she pointed the gun at Audrey. *What's he doing here?* "Hands up," she managed to get out. "On your knees." *Oh, what I wouldn't give to pull the trigger,* Maggie thought, surveying the petite Frenchwoman. *What I wouldn't give . . .*

As Audrey obeyed, Hugh went to the Princess. "We'll get you out of here in no time, Your Highness," he said, working at the knots.

"Ahem." Maggie and the others turned to see Gregory and Poulter standing in the doorway, dripping water.

Gregory was just as shocked to see Maggie, holding a gun no less, as she was to see him. It was with a mix of admiration and shame that he ordered, "Put your gun down on the floor. No one's going anywhere. At least, not until I say so."

"Gregory?" *It has to be some sort of hallucination,* Maggie thought. *It can't be Gregory. He can't be wrapped up in this mess too—can he?*

At the Y-station in Beeston Regis, Leaper went to his office and sat down at his desk, still shaking his head. "Spies!" he muttered, going through his inbox. "Indeed! That's what comes of having these young girls about, with their movie-star daydreams and their—"

He suddenly remembered the courier delivery and picked up the MI-5 memo about the alert. He read it, feeling the blood drain from his head. As he put his head between his legs in order not to faint, he called out his door, "Miss Manley!" Then, louder, "Mary Manley! Get in here with that U-boat transmission right away!"

———

As Poulter tied up Maggie and Hugh, she wondered, *How did I get so much so wrong? Why did I waste so much time worrying about the wrong people? When it was Gregory,* she realized, feeling sick. As much as she thought, she found no easy answers—except that she'd let her own prejudices blind her and lead her astray. Then she started to add up what she'd observed: Gregory's increased drinking, his erratic behavior, a few of his more cryptic sayings, that he didn't wear his RAF uniform to dinner. . . .

She looked over at Lilibet, who was pale, with shadows under her eyes and the beginning of a mottled bruise on her cheek where she'd been slapped. "It's all right," she said to the girl. "Everything's going to be all right." Her heart nearly broke when she was able to get a better look at David, his hands and feet tied with heavy rope, a gag in his mouth. Trickles of blood from a head wound had run down his face and were now scabbing over. Never had she felt more powerless. *Think, Maggie. Keep your head and you'll get them out of this.*

"What time is it?" Audrey asked.

Poulter checked his watch. "Almost three-thirty. We need to hurry." He jerked his chin at Maggie and Hugh. "What are we going to do about them?"

"Actually," Gregory said, "the question is, what are we going to do about you?" He and Boothby exchanged a look. Without preamble, Boothby shot Poulter through the heart, and then, before Audrey could scream, he shot her through the forehead. They each slumped to the floor. Then he took aim at Hugh.

"Nooooo!" Maggie screamed.

"Give me the gun," Gregory said.

"What are you doing?" Boothby snapped.

"Give me the goddamned gun!"

Boothby handed it over and Gregory shot Hugh in the thigh, wounding but not killing him.

Hugh doubled over, moaning. "Sweet Jesus!"

"Hugh!" Maggie fought against the ropes binding her. "Are you all right?" she cried.

"I'll live," Hugh managed to gasp, trying to keep pressure on the wound. Nonetheless, crimson was staining his pant leg.

"Don't want you following us," Gregory said. "Sorry, mate. And I also need someone to tell the muckety-mucks that their precious Princess is still alive. And on her way to Germany."

"Us?" Maggie said. She and Hugh locked eyes. *It's going to be fine,* she tried to tell him mentally. *I'll take care of Lilibet. And I'll be all right, too. I promise.*

Gregory nodded. "You're coming with us. Take care of him," he said to Boothby, indicating the body. "I'll bring the ladies."

As Boothby lifted David's inert body while still keeping a gun on the girls, Gregory untied the Princess from the chair, leaving her hands bound and gag in place. "I suppose you've figured out what I've done," he said, grabbing Maggie and the Princess by an arm and hustling them to the door. Maggie gave Hugh one last look and then they were outside, in the cold and dark. He sounded just the slightest bit guilty.

"A lot of it," Maggie said, trying not to trip on the stones. "But I still don't understand Lily's part."

"Lily and I grew up together, remember?" he said,

his voice rising against the wind. "We spent every summer together. We were soul mates."

"So you and Lily had planned this operation?" Maggie tried to appeal to his vanity. "That's quite the coup. How did you manage to pull it off?"

Gregory smiled, a grim smile. "Lily and I grew up with any number of other privileged young people. Another was Victoria Keeley."

Realization dawned. "The woman from Bletchley who was murdered at Claridge's," Maggie said. "So, how does Benjamin Batey fit in?"

"Benjamin Batey was walking out with Victoria, and she exploited it. She stole the decrypt from him."

"But why?"

Gregory snorted. "Why do you need to know?" The little party was trying to keep their balance on the slippery rocks strewn with seaweed, nearing the boat.

Maggie thought desperately. "Well, it's been quite the victory for you, after all. I was sent by MI-Five to figure everything out and I didn't—not in time, at least. So you might do me the professional courtesy of telling me how you did it."

Lilibet's eyes widened as she heard Maggie reveal that she wasn't really a maths tutor but an agent.

And then she realized—the decrypt hidden in Lily's copy of *Le Fantôme de l'Opéra* was meant for Gregory. *It was right in front of you the whole time!* Still, there was no time for self-flagellation. "Tell me your part— and I'll tell you what happened to the decrypt."

"The decrypt?" Gregory staggered a little and looked stunned. "How the hell do *you* know about that?"

"Tell me what I want to know—and I'll tell you what happened to it."

Gregory looked shocked, then smiled. "Victoria stole the decrypt because Lily *asked* her to. But Victoria, unfortunately, had fallen obsessively in love with Lily. And when Lily made it clear she wouldn't be with her exclusively, Victoria threatened to expose Lily as a traitor."

"So Lily killed her," Maggie said, understanding. "And then Lily herself was killed, not long after, by Mr. Tooke."

"Actually," Gregory said, "Boothby killed Victoria. He was concerned Victoria might make good on her threats and jeopardize our little operation. He took the decrypt from Victoria's hotel room at Claridge's and gave it to Lily. She said she'd hidden it—where *did* she hide it? And how did *you* find it?" They were approaching the boat.

"Tell me the rest first," Maggie said with a tight smile, picking her way over rocks that gave way to coarse wet sand. She stumbled, then righted herself.

Gregory was breathing hard. "Clever girl."

"If you knew about Enigma," Maggie continued, "then why did you even need the decrypt? Surely your connections in Germany would have believed you?"

They'd reached the boat, and Boothby overheard this. He began to chuckle, and Gregory joined in. "Oh, Maggie. You may know many things, but you don't know Germans—their pride, their arrogance. They believe they've written the ultimate, the unbreakable code. Quite simply, they would not believe anyone could possibly break it without proof. Absolute proof." Boothby dumped David's body into the boat.

"So without the decrypt, you had no proof," Maggie said. "And then David, with his briefcase of top-secret documents, came to Windsor. And you kidnapped him, along with his briefcase."

"He had it handcuffed to him. And I didn't have the heart to cut off his hand." He smiled. "I think he'll thank me for it, someday. You see, in Germany, my contact will pay me—us, that is—dearly for the information you have. Whatever David has in his briefcase must be worth a small fortune."

"And Boothby?"

"Boothby—do you want to tell her?"

Boothby gave a barking laugh. "My name isn't really Christopher Boothby," he said in his too-perfect English, "it's Krzysztof Borkowsky. I'm Polish. I was one of the Poles that Chamberlain and Britain betrayed when he traded us for 'peace in our time.' " He spat. "A peace paid for with the blood of Poles."

"How did you get to England?"

"I was born and spent my childhood in Poland, but I moved to Britain when I was ten. I was up at Cambridge, with Gregory, when Poland handed over her Enigma machine to the British. And then I was recruited to work at Bletchley, to help translate for some of the Poles that came over with it."

"Ah." Christopher was the spy at Bletchley that her father had been trying to find! *Two misses!* Maggie thought. *Thanks a lot, Dad.*

She turned back to Gregory. "And what's your relation to Audrey and Poulter?"

"Poulter was my manservant for years and another of our little group. You see, we are quite democratic. He began sleeping with Audrey, who was working for someone named Commandant Hess. Poulter shot the King, while he and Audrey arranged the kidnapping of the

Princess with Commandant Hess in Berlin. The plan is to put the Duke and Duchess of Windsor on the throne when Germany invades. How *is* the King, by the way?"

"He's fine," Maggie said grimly.

"Pity."

Boothby snapped, "Less talking, Gregory."

"She knows what happened to Lily's decrypt!"

Boothby whistled. "The lost one?"

"My dear girl," Gregory said, ignoring Boothby. "You can come with us, or I'll have to kill you." In a jovial tone he said, "Set sail with us—what do you say?" He looked at her and she realized that he didn't actually want to kill her. And yet he would if he had to.

Maggie knew the risks of getting into a boat with these two, but she had no intention of letting them take the Princess or David anywhere without her.

"Fine," she said, feigning more bravado than she felt. "I'll go." Lilibet and Maggie stepped into the craft and took their seats, Maggie's heart beating wildly. *The goddamned Royal Navy's supposed to be here,* she thought. *The Coast Guard. The police, even. Where the hell is everyone?*

Boothby and Gregory pushed the boat into a few feet of water, then jumped in themselves. The boat rocked violently, then steadied.

"And off we go," Gregory said. "Just like old times." He took a seat opposite Maggie as Boothby started the motor. "Keep an eye on her, would you?" he said to Boothby.

The tiny craft set out through the wind and roiling white-tipped waves, out to sea. As they pulled away from the shore Maggie could see the headlights of cars on the shore and tiny black figures running toward them.

*Here! We're here!* She wanted to scream into the wind. But they were still too far away to catch up.

"What about Lily's baby?" she asked. She hadn't forgotten that a baby had been murdered as well. "Was it yours?"

"I knew about the baby," he said. "She told me, right before she was murdered. But it wasn't mine. I, alas, can't have children."

"Whose was it, then?" Maggie called.

"Christopher's."

Maggie wasn't expecting this. "Christopher's?"

Boothby nodded his assent. His face was unreadable.

"You wouldn't understand," Gregory said. "Lily, Victoria, Christopher, and I—we—we shared many things."

"I see," Maggie said. She managed a quick glance at Lilibet. Maggie hoped the girl didn't know what he meant.

"Would you take off her gag, at least?" Maggie asked. "It's not as if anyone can hear us out here."

Gregory pulled out his flask from his inside jacket pocket. He took a long pull, emptied it, then tossed it over the side. "Go ahead," he said to Boothby, who went over to the Princess and undid the knots that tied the gag. As it loosened, she spit the moldy bread out of her mouth.

"Thanks, Maggie," she managed, cold spray dousing her.

"'*Elizabeth and Leicester/Beating oars.*'" Gregory winked at Lilibet. "I suppose that would make me Leicester."

"I hardly think Eliot was thinking of us all '*Supine on the floor of a narrow canoe,*'" Maggie said. The wind was stronger now and she wrapped her arms around herself to keep warm. The waves were making her nauseous. She looked at David. In the darkness, she could see his eyes were still closed.

"So now it's your turn," Gregory said. "Where was the decrypt?"

Maggie gave a grim smile. "In the frontispiece of Lily's *Le Fantôme de l'Opéra*."

"How the hell do *you* know?"

"Because *I* was the one who found it," Maggie shot back.

"It was Lily's nickname for me—after I was burned so badly on one side of my face. It was our little joke, her calling me *Le Fantôme*." Then, "This is it," he said to Boothby, who cut the engine and turned on a kerosene lantern.

"Ship?" Maggie asked.

"Submarine," he corrected. *Oh, fantastic,* Maggie thought.

Boothby used a flashlight to check his watch. "The pickup window is open for one more hour."

# Chapter Twenty-eight

The Prime Minister's rooms at Windsor Castle had been transformed into makeshift War Rooms, with maps and pushpins and memos. The roar of the fire behind the andirons nearly overcame the soft and relentless tick of the mantel clock. The P.M. and King sat in large leather chairs while Frain paced.

"We have the Princess's code, telling us they're going to Mossley, which is near Grimsby. We have an intercept from a Y-station, saying that someone near Grimsby radioed a German U-boat. We have a German U-boat moving into position off the coast of Mossley. It's obvious they're trying to get the Princess out of Britain. However, the U-boat can't get too close to shore—she'll need at least five miles. Which means that either a few men from the U-boat will form a landing party and try to get to shore in one of the U-boat's rubber dinghies. Or they have a boat hidden away on shore and will use that to meet the U-boat."

The King sat very still. "What are the weather reports?"

"High winds, Your Majesty," Frain answered. "They need to do it at night, under the cover of darkness. If they decide the conditions are too dangerous, they may try to establish another rendezvous, in a few days. But they must know that putting it off would increase their chances of being found."

"After Dunkirk, the Royal Navy seized everything that could float!" Churchill barked.

"Yes, sir," Frain replied. "But it's possible that someone hid away a fishing skiff or other small craft, for just this very occasion."

The telephone rang, a shrill sound. Frain dove for it. "Yes?" he said, then listened intently. "Thank you, Admiral Kirk."

He put a hand over the receiver. "Kirk, from the Admiralty," he told them. "They've pinpointed the U-boat. The U-two-forty-six is moving closer into shore, near Mossley."

"Wonderful!" the King said, his face not as pale as it had been.

"Not exactly," Frain said. "They could be anywhere near Mossley. And the weather isn't helping."

"Put every man on it," Churchill growled. "Have them sift through every grain of sand and drop of water—until we find the Princess!"

Frain spoke into the receiver again. "Move two of our submarines into the area and see if you can get an exact location on U-two-forty-six. Move two of the Royal Navy's corvettes in, as well. If we can't get a lock on them by dawn, I'll have the air force do a patrol."

"I'm assuming, sir," Kirk said on the other end of the line, "that the hostage is valuable?"

"Yes," Frain replied. "Extremely valuable. Tell all your boys to keep that in mind."

Maggie was gripped with fear and pain, but adrenaline kept her sharp. Jaw clenched against the cold and wind, she scanned the sky and sea in the moonlight, looking for anything—British ship or plane, Nazi U-boat. Who would reach them first? Mathematics were true and cruel. *You have a fifty-fifty chance, Hope. Probability equals the number of desirable outcomes divided by the number of possible outcomes. A coin flip. And that's only theoretical—a big wave might take you out first— better make that one of the possible outcomes. Probability of survival dips even lower, then. . . .*

She realized that at this point, even if she and David were disposable to the British, the P.M. might not shoot the U-boat, in order to save the Princess's life. She remembered the cyanide pill David had in his pocket and how matter-of-fact he'd been about needing to take it if it came to it.

*But it hasn't come to that,* Maggie thought. *Yet.* Was she ready, if it did? *Best to worry about that if and when the time comes.*

"David needs a doctor," Maggie said, shouting to make herself heard over the wind.

"Don't worry," Gregory said. "He'll be fine. Believe me, it was a love tap. Wouldn't want anything to happen to my ticket out of this mess."

"Do you mind if I see to his wounds?" Maggie asked, looking at Gregory with what she hoped was an imploring look. She did her best, considering the high wind and saltwater spray. "I have a handkerchief—I can at least clean his face."

Gregory and Boothby locked eyes. "No," Boothby said. "Stay where you are."

"Oh, Boothby," Gregory said. "What's the harm? We're not barbarians, after all." He motioned to Maggie.

Gingerly, Maggie made her way to the back of the boat and sat down near David, pulling his head into her lap. She pulled a handkerchief from her pocket and gently pressed it to David's face. The sensation seemed to revive him, and his eyelids fluttered open.

"Maggie," he said weakly, gazing up at her, words getting lost in the wind. "You—you look awful."

"You don't look so great yourself," she countered. He tried to sit up, but the ropes and the pain were too much for him. "May I untie his hands and feet?" she asked Gregory. "The ropes are too tight."

Boothby scowled. "No!"

"Please," Lilibet implored, eyes filling with tears.

"Oh, Christopher," Gregory said. "Do you really think a Princess, a slip of a girl, and a poof can do much of anything?"

"Poof?" David muttered, stirring. "And here I thought you liked me."

"I do," Gregory said, having the grace to look chagrined. "And I'm terribly sorry about all this. When we get to Germany, I'll make sure you're treated well."

David wasn't buying it. "You do still remember I'm Jewish, yes?"

"You might want to keep that detail to yourself."

"Gregory and Boothby plan to turn you over to Abwehr," Maggie explained. "You and your briefcase."

Maggie undid the ropes tying David's hands and feet. Carefully, he rose to sit. "Bloody hell!" he said, clutching his head with his free hand.

At that moment, without warning, a long, thin, dark shape, like a sea monster, broke through the water, causing the small shell to rock back and forth in the waves. The protruding sail was black and painted with a red and white swastika and *U-246*. Maggie held on to David, and they both tried to keep their balance before sitting down, hard.

"Finally!" Gregory shouted into the wind. Boothby grinned.

Two German officers emerged from the hatch. "*Ihr habt's geschafft!*" one called.

"*Noch ein bisschen! Werfe uns doch das Seil runter, es ist verdammt kalt!*" Gregory shouted.

Maggie could understand what they were saying but found the German words and accent chilling.

They threw a rope out. Boothby maneuvered the small boat around until he could grasp it, then used it to pull them closer to the sub.

Maggie took a last look at the horizon, now beginning to turn a pearly gray, hoping against last hope for a rescue. With blinding disappointment, she turned her gaze from the horizon to her captors. She, Lilibet, and David were helped from the craft into the U-boat.


Inside, it was dim and humid and tight, with low ceilings and the stench of too many men in close quarters. The submarine's engines made a dull roar, along with the hissing pipes. Every surface was covered with buttons, dials, pipes, handles, and gauges.

They were taken by the Nazi crewmen through narrow passageways lit by fluorescent overhead lights to the ship's brig, a small, low-ceilinged room, with two thin bunks built into the wall. The men left them and locked the door from the outside. The bolt slid into the lock with a resounding clang. Maggie's nerves were stretched to breaking. She never thought they'd get to this point. *Where's your goddamn cavalry, Peter? Taking tea?*

Lilibet went to one of the bunks and sat down, hard. She had dark circles under her eyes and she was biting her lower lip, in an obvious attempt not to cry. Maggie sat down beside her. "Are you all right?" she asked, putting a hand on the Princess's thin shoulder.

The girl wiped her eyes on her sleeve and drew herself up. "Quite all right, thank you," she said.

"Good girl!" Maggie exclaimed, impressed by the girl's bravery. She couldn't afford a hysterical child now; they all had to keep their heads. "Now, look here—we're alive. We're together. And we *will* get out of this."

"Not exactly the Saint Crispin speech, but it'll do," David managed. "You have a brilliant plan to get us out of this, I assume?"

"Ha!" she retorted, the strain of the day finally getting to her. Her mind swam, contemplating escape scenarios, none of which would work. She took deep breaths, trying not to panic, willing thoughts of Aunt Edith, of Hugh, of Sarah, of Chuck, of Nigel, of everyone she loved, out of her head—focusing on what needed to be done.

"Where are we, by the way?" David asked. "Do you know?"

"We're off the coast of Mossley, near Grimsby," Maggie said, grateful to focus on facts. "Gregory plans to take us both to Germany with him. Use us for information."

"And, let's be honest here—between us, we have quite a bit of information."

Maggie nodded. "They—well, Audrey and Poulter, actually—had a plot to assassinate the King and kidnap Lilibet. They want to put Edward and Mrs. Simpson on the throne when the Nazis invade. The King survived with a flesh wound, but . . ."

"It's my fault," Lilibet said. "I knew better than to leave the nursery. But then Audrey said there was a phone call." She cast her eyes down. "From Philip." Her face turned red with shame at the memory.

"It's *not* your fault," Maggie said, thinking, *No, it's mine, I was the one who knew Audrey. I'm the one who was so blinded by Louisa that I didn't see what was right in front of me.* "I don't want to hear you say that."

"Without being overdramatic here, Mags, I'll kill myself before I'd let them hand me over to the Nazis," David said.

*I know,* Maggie thought, remembering his cyanide pill. *And I would too.* "Well, let's not get ahead of ourselves." She tried to keep her tone light. "They couldn't get your briefcase without you."

"Gregory's an arsehole. Er, sorry," he said to Lilibet.

"No," the Princess said. "I agree."

Maggie bit her lip to keep from laughing hysterically at the prim Princess. Hysterical laughter was just as useless as tears. "We need to do anything it takes to stop this sub from reaching France."

The submarine suddenly seemed to dip and then turn. The three of them put their hands up to their ears as the pressure changed.

"Who else knows we're here?" David asked.

"Hugh's back at the cottage, shot, but alive, I think. Not sure how long it will take him to get back, or even if he can." Maggie's heart lurched as she thought of Hugh in pain. "Frain knows we're near to Mossley. And Mr. Churchill. They've alerted the navy and air force." *And a fat lot of good they've been to us.* "But out here, we can't depend on them to save us. How much do you know about U-boats?"

"A fair amount. I know that there are any number of security measures in place that will keep us from reaching the cockpit," he said, trying the door, which refused to budge, "even if we could get out of here." He gestured with his briefcase-handcuffed hand. "I wish I could get rid of this."

"We're probably about twenty minutes from France, if that," Maggie said, considering. It was hot in the room, and steamy. She was covered in sweat and a few beads started to trickle from her hairline down her face. She struggled to think of something—anything—that could save them. *Think, Maggie, think. You have to get this tin can up to the surface. Nothing's going to do that unless there's some sort of emergency. . . .*

She looked heavenward, the only sound the steady, rhythmic pulse of the engines.

"We don't have time to pray, Mags."

"No," Maggie said. "Look up. At the ceiling."

David and Lilibet both did. Next to the fluorescent light was a sprinkler, attached to a long, thin pipe. *"Feueralarm—"* Maggie read in German.

"—fire alarm," David finished, knowing what she had in mind. With his free hand, he fished through his trouser pockets, as Lilibet watched with wide eyes.

They were trapped now, they really were. If this didn't work, it would be time to plan what they would do when they reached France. Maggie saw terror in David's and Lilibet's faces. She hoped that they didn't see the fear in hers.

"I know, it's a filthy habit." David tried to smile, coming up with a box of matches, from the Langham Hotel in London.

"A *wonderful* habit!" Maggie cried. " 'How about a little fire, Scarecrow?' " She winked at Lilibet, forcing gaiety for the girl's sake.

David took the thin gray sheets from the beds and placed them in the corner. "Well, ladies," he said as he tried to light the wooden match. It was too hard with the briefcase.

"I'll do it," Maggie said, and she took the match and the box from him, lit the match, and threw it into the bedding, "I really hope this sets off a boat-wide sprinkler system and forces this sub to surface. Otherwise . . ."

The match smoldered, but then the flame caught. The fire burned brightly and the small cell was filled with smoke and heat.

If the sprinklers didn't extinguish the flames, they'd be burned to a crisp within minutes—that is, if they didn't suffocate from smoke inhalation. "Come on, come on," Maggie muttered. *I don't want to die like this. Not on a sub, in a fire. I want to die at age a hundred and one, in my own bed, surrounded by grown children and fat grandbabies. . . .* The lights went out and dim red emergency lighting came on. An alarm sounded a series of low wails.

It was a long, long moment, but eventually the ceil-

ing sprinkler began to trickle, then splutter, then finally
spray water. The fire belched smoke, then sizzled out.

Maggie, Lilibet, and David waited, in silence broken
only by the keen of the alarm. Finally, after what felt like
several lifetimes, they felt the U-boat move. They held
hands and swallowed hard as the sub seemed to rise up,
up, up—their ears popping—to what they could only
hope was the surface of the water.

Without warning, a crewmember in gray coveralls
opened the door to the cell. His face was mottled with
rage. *"Was ist—"*

David swung his briefcase, which hit the sailor
square in the jaw. He crumpled to the floor, unable to
finish his sentence. David stumbled as he recovered his
balance. "Oh, that felt good."

"Come on, Lilibet," Maggie urged, taking the girl's
hand, all senses straining. They made their way down
the dark, narrow corridor. Red lights blinked at them
and steam hissed through pipes.

Lilibet tripped and fell, letting out a small yelp.

"Come on!" David said.

Lilibet looked up at Maggie, her face white. "My
foot. I think it's broken."

*Oh, Gods, what now? What more can we endure?*
But there was no time to lose. Just as she did at Camp
Spook, Maggie hoisted Lilibet up and into a fireman's
carry. "You weigh less than Molly Stickler," she panted,
taking off in a trot as fast as she could.

"Who?" Lilibet asked.

"A girl from long ago and far away." Maggie was
grateful for her morning regime of sit-ups and push-ups
and all the early-morning runs she'd taken since those
muddy days at Camp Spook.

The submarine's emergency sirens continued to wail. Maggie, carrying Lilibet, and David retraced their steps back to the ladder that led back up to the hatch. Over the intercom, they heard, *"Die Gefangenen sind geflohen! Die Gefangenen sind geflohen!"*

"They're saying 'The prisoners have escaped!'" Maggie gasped.

"Oh, hell," David said. "So much for stealth."

He climbed the narrow gray-painted ladder to the hatch and wrestled with it until it opened. They had predicted correctly. The fire safety system had caused the captain to take the boat to the surface.

Then Maggie, breathing heavily, but not slowing down, went up the ladder first, helping Lilibet. With his free hand, David helped the young Princess when she emerged. Outside, on the hull, they all drew great breaths of cold fresh air, watching the frothy whitecaps crest on the gray waves, illuminated by the rising sun. The channel was rough and the U-boat bobbed in the choppy water like a child's bath toy.

"Do we have a plan?" Lilibet asked.

*Oh, Your Highness, if only we did.* "Let's climb to the top of the sail," Maggie said, sounding surprisingly reasonable as she felt the sweat in her hair start to freeze. At least they'd be farther from the hatch that way.

Maggie, helping a limping Lilibet, and David all scrambled over the top of the hull until they reached the sail. They climbed up yet another long, thin ladder to reach the highest peak of the sub.

Cold, damp winds gusted around them. They held on to the railing of the sail for dear life—David muttering curse words, Lilibet with her mouth set in a grim line, and Maggie, fighting panic, trying desperately to think of a next step. While she was overwhelmingly grateful for an escape from inside the submarine that had seemed impossible, being up on the sail of a Nazi sub in the middle of the gray-green North Sea didn't seem all that much better.

The submarine could continue sailing this way, on the surface, all the way to France. Unless they wanted to swim in the freezing waters, they were as trapped on the sail as they were in the bowels of the submarine. Her eyes scanned the horizon for any sign of a British ship. *Come on, Mr. Churchill, I'm running out of tricks.*

She looked at David and Lilibet. David had a nasty head wound; his blood still caked in his hair and on his face. Lilibet's face had scratches and bruising and was stained with tears. Around them, on all sides, was nothing but sky and the ocean.

Gregory emerged from the hatch. He had a desperate expression on his face. He was followed by Boothby and two armed crewmen.

"No!" Gregory cried, his voice getting lost in the freezing wind, as he approached their perch on top of the sail. He climbed toward them as Boothby and the two sailors came behind him.

"Come back inside! You're safe with me! I never meant to hurt anyone!"

The group stared at him, as though he were an apparition. He certainly looked like one, his face gaunt, his eyes haunted.

"You don't understand!" Gregory called. "I can't go back to England!" His eyes leaked tears, as his voice grew frenzied. "I can't do it!" He kept climbing. "It's freezing cold up there in those planes, it's dark—they shoot at you, you shoot at them. People die, but before they do, they scream—horrible high-pitched screams. Men cry. I've seen people with limbs burned off, with melted skin and bone."

He reached them and raised his hands in supplication; his eyes had a cold, dead look to them. "I just want it all to stop. The nightmares and the memories and the horror—I can't go back. Can't even seem to drink myself to death! That's why I made this deal with the Devil. This way I *don't have to go back*!"

Gregory's pain was palpable. Was he a villain, or just a casualty of war? Maggie felt a mixture of both horror and sympathy wash through her. She knew him—or thought she did.

"Then no more killing," she said. "End it. You're not your father—you don't have to be." *Just as I don't have to be mine,* she thought, almost absently. "Don't sell us all out to the Nazis just to save yourself. You might live, but what about your conscience?"

But he couldn't meet her eyes, and turned away. "Let me worry about my conscience, Maggie," he said, calmer now.

The wind began to die down and the waves weren't quite as violent. And she could also hear the rumbling engine of a ship. They all looked toward the direction of the sound.

Whose ship was it? German or British?

"It's German," Gregory said, as if reading their minds. "You quite cleverly disarmed the sub, but they've radioed to France for a pickup from a German patrol boat. There's nowhere for you to run. Even if I wanted to help you now, I couldn't. Things are in motion and have taken on a momentum of their own."

"That's pathetic, Gregory," Maggie called. "Don't be a coward. Be the hero I know you can be."

The sound of the engine seemed closer, and Maggie felt a tingle of horror. She knew what she had to do, if the worst happened. David would have to use his cyanide tablet, and she'd have to jump overboard. The Nazis weren't going to take them alive. And she had to believe that Lilibet would be treated well in Germany and that Frain and Churchill would somehow rescue her.

The sun was rising in the sky. Maggie could see the Nazi patrol boat coming toward them, and she put her arm around Lilibet. *Red sky in the morning, sailors take warning,* Maggie thought absently. She looked around her. *So, this is how it ends,* she thought. *Well,* she thought, looking over at David, *at least we're fighting the good fight together.*

And then, without warning, the world seemed to explode. There was a wall of noise. Bright flashes and flares of light. The stench of smoke. Time itself was pierced by a thunderous detonation. The waves roiled and crested and the sub lurched to one side and back again. Boothby and the crewmen struggled to keep their balance.

Lilibet fell against Maggie, whose back hit the guardrail, hard.

David took advantage of the swaying to grab Gregory by his coat and sideswipe him with the briefcase, which hit his face with a loud *crack*. Gregory staggered back, stunned. He put his hand to his cheek, and his face lit with rage. He lunged for David, grabbing him by the throat and squeezing, eyes wild.

Maggie saw David struggling to get free from Gregory. She ran to Gregory and tried to pry his hands off David's neck. Lilibet, seeing what was happening, crawled over to Gregory, brave as the Prince in *Sleeping Beauty*. Just as Maggie kneed him in the groin, Lilibet bit down on his ankle as hard as she could. "Good girl!" Maggie managed.

Gregory cried out in anguish and released his grip on David, who fell to the deck, gasping for air. Gregory stumbled backward and fell as well, curling into a fetal position.

"*That's* for calling him a poof!" Lilibet yelled into the wind. Maggie was filled with both amazement and sisterly pride.

Before anyone had a chance to recover, there was another enormous blast—the approaching German ship exploded in smoke and lacy white froth. One final detonation, and the ship burst into a ball of orange and red flames, reflected in the gray water. Boothby and the two crewmen watched helplessly.

Gregory managed to turn himself over and whistled through his bleeding teeth and lip. "Goddamned British navy."

"You want to know a British military secret?" David shouted, propping himself up on his elbows. "We're equipped with *really big guns,* you . . . jerk!" he said, realizing the Princess was present.

Maggie went to Lilibet and cradled her in her arms, keeping her eyes west. "The British are coming."

"About time, Paul Revere," said David, before turning back to Gregory. "You'll have quite the story to tell before they hang you for treason."

But Gregory was already unlacing his heavy boots and stripping off his mackintosh. "But it seems like such a lovely morning for a swim," he said, a man with nothing to lose, nothing to live for.

"No!" Maggie screamed. "Don't do it!" She didn't know how she felt about Gregory—disgust, hate, pity? But she did know she didn't want him to die. "You'll never make it!" Even if he could swim to France, the water was too cold. It would kill him before he could reach the shore.

"But I might," he said, winking at her with his good eye. "And it's better than the alternative," he called back to them before he dove into the sea.

Maggie watched Gregory's head bobbing amidst the waves. Then he vanished beneath the surface, rising again, choking on seawater. His eyes locked with Maggie's as he slowly, slowly slipped beneath the surface of the water. She watched him sink into the darkness until she couldn't see his face any longer.

*Oh, Gregory, what a waste,* was all she could think, feeling her eyes well up with hot tears. *What a tragic, tragic waste of a life.*

She, David, and Lilibet, exhausted, huddled together for warmth, until the rubber dinghy reached them.

# Chapter Twenty-nine

That day, after being debriefed and arriving back at Windsor Castle, Maggie and David were taken to the Royal Family's private apartments. They'd been given hot baths, glasses of cognac, fresh, dry clothes, and a chance to sleep. Now up and dressed and looked over by the Royal Physician, they entered the Royal Family's private sitting room. David's head was bandaged, as was the wrist that had had the handcuff on it. Maggie looked tired and pale, but otherwise none the worse for wear.

It was a large chamber, but cozy, with buttercup-yellow silk walls, a soft red Persian carpet, and a plethora of needlepoint pillows. The King and Queen were there, sitting on an overstuffed sofa, surrounded by their corgis. Winston Churchill and Peter Frain sat in chairs opposite. Hugh was present as well, sitting next to Frain, a pair of crutches at his side. He and Maggie locked eyes. She smiled and his face relaxed. He tried to stand.

"Please don't," Maggie said. She tried to remember her Royal etiquette, making a shaky curtsy. David did the same, with a bow.

"Please, sit down, both of you. You poor dears," Queen Elizabeth said. Maggie smiled. She sounded just like a mother—which, of course, she was.

"Quite an adventure you two had, heh?" Churchill said, getting up. He gave David a bear-like embrace, slapping the younger man's back repeatedly, while David winced. Then he kissed Maggie's hand. "Can't seem to keep you out of trouble, Miss Hope."

The King had risen as well. "Jolly good show, both of you. If anything had happened to Lilibet . . . Well, I just can't bear to think of it."

"Well, it didn't," said Frain. "And they didn't get Mr. Greene and Miss Hope with the knowledge they each possess, either. The U-boat's been captured and the surviving men all taken into custody. I have just one question. What happened to Gregory Strathcliffe?"

"He decided to swim for France, Your Majesty," Maggie said.

"And?"

"He—he drowned."

"Good." Frain nodded. "More paperwork, of course, but that's that, then."

The Queen indicated an ornate silver tray with a porcelain teapot, with enamels and gilding, as well as matching translucent bone cups and saucers on the low table in front of one of the sofas. "Please sit down, everyone. Who would like a cup of tea?"

"Thank you, Your Majesty," Maggie said, taking a seat as the Queen poured cups for both her and David.

"How is the Princess, ma'am?" Maggie asked, accepting the cup and saucer. "Her foot?"

"She's, well, she's had quite the time of it. The doctor's seen to her and it's just a sprained ankle, thank goodness. She's resting with Alah now. But she has her grandmother's strong constitution—and she's going to be fine."

"She was very brave," Maggie told the King and Queen. "She helped save us."

"Of course she did," said the King, taking the Queen's hand and beaming with pride. "She's our daughter."

"Mr. Thompson," Maggie said, "how is your leg?"

"Fine," replied Hugh. "I'll be on crutches for a while but expect to make a full recovery."

"Good," Maggie said, wishing she could say so much more.

"I must apologize for my role in all this," the King said. "I knew about Lily's background and I allowed her to stay at Windsor anyway. If I'd sent her away, as I should have . . . Instead, I sent away Marta Kunst Tooke, who was completely innocent."

"And I let my prejudice against Louisa blind me to the fact that it was actually Audrey and George Poulter who were setting up the kidnapping plot," Maggie interjected.

"All's well that ends well, then?" the Prime Minister said.

"Indeed," added Frain. Then, to Maggie and Hugh, "I'll see you two at my office on Monday morning, after the New Year," he said. Then his tone softened. "In the meantime, happy Christmas."

"Thank you," David chimed in. "Still Jewish, of course. But I do love a cup of mulled wine and those little almond cookies at this time of the year. And the trees are always pretty."

As Churchill, Frain, David, and the King and Queen

began a long political discussion, Maggie leaned over to Hugh. "So, how's the leg?" she asked. "Really."

"I'll live," he told her. "Just needed a few stitches."

"That's good."

They listened to the discussion for a while, then Hugh said, "So, you're off to Leeds for a wedding, then?"

"How did you—?" Maggie began, then realized that she'd had to clear her schedule with MI-5 months ago and of course he'd know. "Yes, off to my friends' wedding. I'm a bridesmaid."

"Are you, um, bringing anyone? As a date, I mean?"

"No," Maggie said. She wished she could ask him, but they both knew it wasn't in the cards.

"Well," he said, not hiding his pleasure. "Good."

The next day, after breakfast, Maggie and David packed up their things. From Windsor, they would drive straight to Leeds, for Nigel and Chuck's New Year's wedding.

"Merciful Minerva," David exclaimed, "in all the excitement, I'd nearly forgotten about good old Nigel's getting hitched."

"Well, as a bridesmaid," Maggie said, "I've been getting regular updates all fall. You wouldn't think Chuck would be so girly about her wedding, but she really did get into the spirit. We might need to start calling her Charlotte Mary."

They walked past the doors to the nursery. "Do you mind?" she said to David. "I'd like to check in on Lilibet."

"Of course," he replied.

Maggie gave a soft knock at the door. Alah opened it. "Oh, Miss Hope!" she cried, falling into Maggie's arms. "We're ever so grateful to you, for bringing our Lilibet back!"

Maggie was stunned, and held the woman, patting her back. "She was truly brave," she said. "A credit to you and Crawfie."

Alah sniffled. "If anything had happened . . ."

"But it didn't."

Alah wiped at her eyes. "It didn't. You're right. Stiff upper lip, Miss Hope. Stiff upper lip."

"May I see Her Highness?" Maggie asked. "I'm off to a wedding and then, well, I'm not really sure what's next."

"Of course," Alah said. She went to Lilibet's bedroom door and knocked. "Miss Hope is here to see you!"

The door popped open and Lilibet and Margaret both burst out. "Oh, Maggie," Lilibet said, hopping to her on her good leg and wrapping her arms around Maggie's neck. "It all seems like a dream now, doesn't it?"

"A bit," Maggie said, smiling.

"Were you *really* on a German submarine?" Margaret demanded. "Because sometimes Lilibet likes to tease me."

"We really were," Maggie answered. "Cross my heart."

"Maggie," Lilibet said, taking her hand and leading her over to the sofa, "I want to thank you—and Mr. Greene—for everything."

Maggie blinked back tears as she sat next to the young woman. "It was our pleasure, Your Highness. And now you and Margaret have a wonderful Christmas and New Year."

"Will you be back in January?" Lilibet asked. As Maggie searched for an answer, the girl suddenly realized, "You—you weren't here to teach me maths, were you." It was more of a statement than a question.

Maggie smiled. "Well, that's *partly* why I was here," she said. "And you have to admit it came in handy."

"The code—" Lilibet began.

"Yes," Maggie finished. "So, keep working on your maths, all right? And I'm sure we'll see each other again. Someday."

The day of Chuck and Nigel's wedding dawned clear and sunny. Maggie awoke from her trundle bed, set up in Chuck's old room, and spent a moment looking out the window, watching the gray turn to bright white and then, finally, a bright azure.

"Wake up, sleepyhead, it's your wedding day!" she said to her old friend, still fast asleep.

Chuck groaned and pulled the pillow over her head. "Five more minutes . . ."

"Up!" Maggie pulled the duvet off.

Chuck sighed and turned over, a dreamy smile on her face. "It really is today, isn't it?" She looked over at her wedding ensemble, on a hanger over the door. It wasn't a white dress—not enough rations—but it was a lovely portrait-neck burgundy silk suit that Chuck's mother had done over with an ivory lace collar.

"It'd better be," Maggie said, sitting down on the corner of Chuck's bed. "I don't think my back can stand that trundle bed any longer."

Chuck sat up. "Now, just because it's not a featherbed in a *castle*."

"Oh, please. Living at Windsor was like 'camping in a museum,' as Crawfie used to say."

"Well, I hope it wasn't too awful. I'm so glad you came a bit early—dealing with all of the wedding plans, plus the family and the future in-laws—or, as I like to call them, 'the outlaws.'" Chuck rolled her eyes. "Well, let's just say I'll be glad to finally be married."

"And you're going to be a beautiful bride."

"Nigel thinks so, at least, and that's all I care about." Chuck rubbed the sleep out of her eyes. She wasn't a conventional beauty, but she was handsome and her intelligence and wit gave her a sparkle that drew people to her.

"Well, we might as well start by getting you some tea and breakfast," Maggie told her. "Don't want the bride fainting away, now do we?"

"Is it going to be strange for you, Maggie? I mean, without John?"

It was, but Maggie didn't want Chuck to spend even a moment of her day worrying about it. "It's hard. Every day is hard. But life goes on. And I know he'd be so happy to see you and Nigel finally tie the knot. So, I'm fine, darling. Really."


Maggie was dressed and putting on Chuck's lipstick when Sarah arrived.

"Kittens!" she squealed, putting down her valise. "You both look ravishing!"

"Sarah!" Chuck and Maggie chorused, running to the slender, glamorous woman in the smart cherry-colored suit and matching turban. "You're here!"

"Without a moment to spare," she said. "The Ballet's in Liverpool this week. The damn train kept break-ing down. I've been up all night—never thought I'd get here."

"Well, you're here now," Maggie said, "and that's all that counts."

"Plenty of time," Chuck said.

"My, aren't you calm for a bride-to-be!" Sarah ex-claimed.

Chuck motioned to the glass of Buck's Fizz Maggie had made for her. "That certainly doesn't hurt."

Sarah's eyes lit up. "Oh, may I have one?"

"Of course," Maggie said, mixing orange juice and champagne. "Let's have a toast."

The three women raised their glasses. "To Chuck," Maggie began. "A beautiful bride and a beautiful woman, inside and out. We wish you a lifetime of hap-piness."

They clinked glasses.

"To the honeymoon!" Sarah said, with a sly smile.

They clinked again.

Then, "To friends," Chuck said. "War, bombs, rationing—my engagement—I couldn't have done it without you."

"And you're going to need us." Maggie smiled. To Sarah, "I don't know if you've met her in-laws yet, but they make the Germans seem like Beatrix Potter's bun-nies."


Holy Trinity Church was small and stone, with a sharp Gothic bell tower pointing heavenward. The young women and Chuck's parents parked in the lot, then walked in the cold, crisp air, past the graveyard with its gray lichen-covered headstones, to the entrance. They passed over the threshold and waited in the vestibule for the organ music Chuck and Nigel had chosen, Purcell's "Welcome, Glorious Morn." The sunlight streamed through the stained-glass windows, making them glow and casting reflections of sapphire, ruby, amethyst, and emerald on the hard wooden pews.

Chuck's mother proceeded down the worn stone aisle, followed by Maggie and Sarah. There was a pause and the small group in the first few rows of the church rose as Chuck took her father's arm and began the walk down.

Nigel waited for her at the altar, smart in his RAF dress uniform, still a bit barrel-shaped, but thinner now, his face showing more angles and planes. As Maggie took her position at Chuck's side, she managed a glance at the congregation in the pews. David was there, looking handsome.

Maggie looked away, back to Chuck and Nigel, as her heartbeat quickened. She was overwhelmed with conflicting feelings—happiness, relief, longing, anger, and anguish, all at once.

The ceremony was short, solemn, and sweet. And after it was over, the bride, groom, and wedding guests walked over to the wedding luncheon, held in the back room of Anthony's, the town's finest restaurant. In the small room, tables were pushed together. The guests sat down as waiters brought in trays of champagne coupes, for the toast. As soon as the speeches were made, waiters brought bowls of steaming parsnip soup and trays of dainty-looking sandwiches—cucumber, ham, and mustard, mock crab salad. The drinks began in earnest—

pints of beer, shandies, and gin-and-tonics pink with Angostura Bitters and glistening ice cubes.

Maggie found herself caught up in the swirling joy of the day, raising her glass to Nigel and Chuck's health and happiness for at least the fifth time. It was infectious and there was no way she could resist.

"You doing all right, love?" Sarah asked.

Warmed by a glass and a half of shandy, Maggie answered, "I'm fine. Really. It's Chuck and Nigel's big day and I couldn't be happier."

## Chapter Thirty

Back at David's flat in London that evening, Maggie telephoned Hugh at the office. "So, we don't work together anymore, do we?"

"Well, technically, we both work for MI-Five, yes. But, to the best of my knowledge, since the Windsor case is closed, I'm not your handler anymore. So, yes— and no."

"Well, David's going to be out and I'm going to try and cook something tonight. If you happen to be passing by—"

"I'll be there," Hugh interrupted.

From across the room, Mark laughed.

Hugh grinned and mouthed, "Shut up."

Over dinner, Maggie's attempt at Potato Jane, a bake of potatoes, leeks, cheese, and bread crumbs, and vinegary red wine, the two had their first somewhat normal conversation. "You have the advantage, though," Maggie said, "because you know more about me than I know about you. You have my file."

"You're more than your file."

"Well, I know you're a Chelsea Blues fan."

"How did you know that?"

She smiled. "You wear blue socks on game days. Also, you play the guitar."

"No." This time he smiled, and reached for his wine.

"No?" Maggie was surprised. "You have calluses on the tips of your left fingers, but not your right."

"Cello," Hugh admitted.

"Ah. A lovely instrument. Very soulful." Then, "So, what did I miss?"

"You know most of the other details. My mother raised me. I ended up at Selwyn College, at Cambridge, for a degree in theology. And, for a while I thought I wanted to be a priest."

"Catholic?"

"Anglican."

"Well, well, well." Maggie had no idea of Hugh's religious proclivities.

"Do you go to church?"

"Er, no," Maggie said. "I was raised Episcopalian—what you'd call Anglican—but more because my Aunt Edith said it was a cultural necessity. That the Episcopalians use the King James Bible, which, according to her, is the best—meaning most literary—translation. And it would be impossible to understand history and literature without reading it. But I consider myself a scientist, first and foremost."

"Are science and religion mutually exclusive, then?"

"Not necessarily. My position concerning God is that of an agnostic, in the Jeffersonian tradition." Her smile widened. "So, how are the Chelsea Blues shaping up for the spring season?" They talked easily and freely, laughing loudly and often, and ate with gusto.

When they were through with dinner and wine, Maggie rose and began to clear the dishes from the dining room to the kitchen. Hugh began to clear as well.

"Oh, it's all right," she said, running the water in the sink and adding some homemade dishwashing soap, made from baking soda and Borax.

"How about if I wash and you dry?"

"Excellent."

Dishes put away, they went into the parlor, where Maggie put on one of David's records. Hugh picked up the Vera Lynn album that Maggie had listened to, thinking of John, before she'd left for Windsor. "Oh, not that," she said without thinking.

"Too many memories?" he asked. "How about Noël Coward's 'Bitter Sweet'?"

"Perfect."

On Monday morning, Maggie rose from her bed in her room at David's flat and stretched.

"Must you go?" Hugh murmured, eyes still closed, reaching for her.

"Yes," she said, leaning back to kiss him, "and you must too."

In the weekend they'd spent together, Maggie had experienced such joy in his company, his wry grin, his pointed way of looking at the world, the simple pleasure of—behind closed doors, at least—being a normal couple. Despite the gray morning outside their window, she was still surrounded by a feeling of surprising happi-

ness, a feeling that had only grown during their time together. As she watched him stand naked in the dim light,
she delighted in how very beautiful he was. Despite, perhaps because of, his injury.

"Poor leg," she said, taking in the bandages.

"Much better now," Hugh said.

Maggie threw a pillow at him. "Stop smirking!"

"That wasn't a smirk. It was more of a leer, I believe."

She put her arms around his neck and he put his
around her waist. They kissed, a long kiss. "I'll see you
at the office," she said, voice serious. Her meeting with
Frain was today.

"I know," he answered. "I'm there for you—no matter what happens."

Maggie and Hugh sat next to each other in a large conference room in the MI-5 offices, at a long, polished
wood table, dotted by a few heavy glass ashtrays. It was
impersonal, except for a framed photograph of the King
and a large black clock. Maggie had her book in front of
her. Outside the windows the day was chill and gray.

"You sure you're all right?" Hugh asked, as men in
dark suits began to filter in, taking seats around the
table. A few of them lit cigarettes.

"I didn't realize this was going to be such a big meeting," Maggie whispered, wishing she could take his
hand.

"Neither did I."

As the clock on the wall ticked, they all waited. Then
Frain walked in. He was followed by Edmund Hope.
Maggie took a sharp intake of breath.

"Good morning, gentlemen, Miss Hope," Frain said, as he took the seat at the head of the table. Edmund sat down next to him.

Maggie looked at Hugh, confused. He raised an eyebrow, surprised as she was.

Frain cleared his throat. "Our first order of business is the review of the attempt to smuggle critical information from Bletchley Park to the Germans, and the assassination attempt on the King and the attempt to kidnap the Princess Elizabeth. In addition, there was a last-minute attempt to smuggle out an important aide to the Prime Minister, one who knows nearly everything Churchill himself knows, with a briefcase full of classified documents. Thanks to courage, bravery, and quick thinking by our team, disaster was averted. The stolen decrypts never left England. The King is recovering nicely, the Princess is safe at home, and Mr. Churchill's private secretary is back at work at Number Ten this morning."

"Hear, hear!" Maggie heard. She and Hugh exchanged small smiles.

"Yes, and we owe special thanks to the two young agents here—Margaret Hope and Hugh Thompson."

There was warm applause.

Suddenly Winston Churchill opened the door, lit cigar clenched between his teeth. Everyone rose.

"Please come in and take a seat, Prime Minister," Frain said, offering up his own. Churchill did.

*What's he doing here?* Maggie wondered as they all sat down again.

Frain held up his hand. "However, we can't ever rest on our laurels. We're still at war—there are still any number of threats to the Royal Family, the Prime Minister, the carefully kept secrets that give us an advantage in this war. And Commandant Hess is still in Berlin, a most formidable foe."

"Commandant Hess?" Maggie asked.

Frain and Edmund exchanged a look. "The mastermind behind the King's assassination and the Princess's kidnapping plot," Frain explained.

Edmund Hope shifted in his seat.

"Ah, yes," Frain said. "There's one additional matter we need to discuss." He gestured to Edmund. The room was silent. Mr. Churchill puffed impassively on his cigar.

"Good morning, everyone," Edmund said, rising. "As most of you know, I've been working as an undercover agent for years, most recently at Bletchley, and was part of the team investigating the stolen decrypt. Thanks to the work of my daughter, Margaret Hope, and Hugh Thompson—Christopher Boothby, an engineer at Bletchley, has come to light as the spy we were searching for—and he has been arrested, along with the rest of the crew of U-two-forty-six. However, there's another matter I would like to address at this time—a more personal one."

All eyes were fixed on him. Edmund continued. "I knew weeks ago that my file had been removed." He looked at Hugh, who looked uncomfortable. "And that certain people were suspicious of my actions during the Great War, regarding the German group Sektion, the precursor to today's Abwehr. Actions which cast doubts on my integrity as an agent, and as a father, today."

Maggie and Hugh exchanged glances.

Edmund looked directly at Maggie. "The pinprick encryptions you found in those books—yes, they were orders from the Sektion. Yes, they were orders to kill British intelligence officers."

"Including Hugh Thompson, Senior," Maggie stated.

Hugh swallowed. Maggie put her hand on his arm, aware that he was in the same room as his father's murderer. Her father.

"Yes," Edmund said.

Maggie was in shock. *We're right? And yet here he is at MI-5? Admitting to all of it? Why isn't he in handcuffs? In jail . . .*

"But, Maggie—" His tone softened. "*I* wasn't that agent."

Across the long table, Maggie met his eyes.

"Then who was it?" she asked, softly.

"It was—" Edmund faltered, unable to continue.

"Oh, good Lord, man, just rip the bandage off!" the P.M. interrupted. "I'm sorry to have to tell you this, Miss Hope—I truly am—but the double agent in question wasn't your father.

"It—*she*—was your mother."

Unblinking, Maggie pushed back her chair and rose to her feet. Then she slowly walked to the door. Once through it, she began running down the long hall, her footfalls echoing on the marble floor.

"Maggie!" Edmund called. "Wait! Please!"

Maggie stopped in the middle of the empty corridor but didn't turn around.

"You can't . . ." Edmund chose his words carefully. "You can't let this affect you."

She spun to face him. "You know what—*Dad*? You

have no right—no right to lecture me. Or to tell me how I should deal with this!"

"I know how horrible this feels. I'll never forget how I felt when I learned the truth."

"And having a child? Was that part of the plan too? Did Sektion dictate *that* as part of the cover story?"

Edmund was silent in the face of her accusation.

Maggie turned on her heel and left.


Meeting adjourned, Hugh caught up with Maggie outside of the MI-5 building on St. James's Street.

"Quite the piece of news," he said, falling into step beside her.

"I adore British understatement."

"Let's find somewhere to sit down, all right?"

She shrugged.

"Or, we can just keep walking."

"Let's go to Saint James's Park."


Eventually, they reached a bench by the bottle-green lake, which was wrinkling in the wind. Hugh put his arm around her and Maggie started talking, words pouring out of her. "When we were on the U-boat, I watched a man die. Someone I cared about." Despite the bucolic picture in front of them, they could still hear the sounds of traffic and the bells of Big Ben.

"Gregory Strathcliffe was a traitor. If he hadn't drowned, he would have been taken into custody and hanged. Do you really think once you reached Germany, you'd just be sent back to England? Or that you and he would go quietly to Switzerland? Gregory was a bad man. The worst kind, actually—a turncoat."

"A weak man, perhaps," Maggie admitted, watching the swans circle warily around the geese on the water. "I'm not exonerating him, but the way he grew up, and then the stress of battle, and his injuries . . ." She sighed. "I suppose it doesn't matter. He did what he did. But the truth is, he's one in a long line of people I've known who've betrayed me, who've lied to me. And where does that leave me? Never knowing whom to trust. Since I've come here, since I've gotten involved with these people, it's becoming a part of me. And I'm afraid of becoming what I despise."

The cold wind rustled what leaves were left on the enormous ancient maple trees. "Maggie, you're a brave, loyal, strong Briton, despite that accent of yours. What you've done—are incredible accomplishments. You should feel proud."

"I got distracted," Maggie said, admitting her secret guilt. "I didn't like Louisa and I let that color my perception of her. You were right all along—she wasn't an exemplary human being, but she never did anything wrong. And I was so convinced she had, that I let my feelings trump logic." She gave a sharp laugh. "I did that with my father too. I was so mad at him for abandoning me, that I let it cloud my judgment—and lead me to suspect him of being a double agent."

"The file was incriminating."

"No," Maggie snapped. "It was *inconclusive*. I let my emotions cloud my judgment." Then, in gentler tones, "I miss maths—two plus two always equals four." Maggie thought for a moment. "Although, as Kurt

Gödel theorized, there's a vast difference between the truth and the part of the truth that can be proved."

"Er, what?"

"Gödel's Incompleteness Theorem tells us that it's impossible to fulfill Hilbert's wish to find a complete and consistent set of axioms for all of mathematics. In other words, we'll never be able to prove everything. We might know something to be true, or we might want something to be true, *need* it to be true—but we may not ever be able to prove it."

"Let's take this back to the practical—you had theories and you followed them."

"I wasted valuable time on Louisa, when I could have been looking for the real threats: Gregory and Audrey. And I missed the connection between Lily and Gregory. She called him Le Fantôme. Then she hid the decrypt in *Le Fantôme de l'Opéra*. It was plain as a nose on a face! How on earth did I miss that?"

"It's easy to see these things after the fact."

Maggie snorted.

"Personally, when I think of intelligence, I like to think of Sherlock Holmes. Not the hot-on-the-trail-of-the-killer Holmes, but the man sitting quietly at his desk, putting two and two together. It's not glamorous in the least—it's hard, boring, often exasperating work. You need to organize the facts, assess them, dismiss the irrelevant. Then, using induction and deduction, you come to a conclusion."

"I know—"

"But you've got to do this without emotion, or prejudice or even hope clouding your judgment."

"It was so much easier when it was just maths. You throw all these people into the mix—"

"It's hard, yes. But now you know. You have experience. And I know you—you won't make the same mistake again."

"*That's* for certain." Maggie looked off across the lake. After a few moments of silence, "Thank you."

"We're partners, Maggie. And friends. And . . . more. I'd do anything to help you."

"I know."

Prime Minister Winston Churchill was in his large Victorian bathtub in the Annexe when his butler, Mr. Inces, showed in Peter Frain.

The P.M., plump, rosy, and naked as a cherub, was immersed in steaming water, smoking a cigar, glass tumbler of brandy and soda balanced on the edge of the tub.

"Prime Minister," Frain said.

"Sit down," Churchill growled. Then he shouted to Mrs. Tinsley, seated outside the bathroom door with her noiseless typewriter propped on her lap. "We're done, Mrs. T.! Go away!"

"Yes, sir," she said serenely, picking up the typewriter and her papers and making her way downstairs.

Frain sat down on the wooden chair placed in Churchill's bathroom specifically for meetings. He tried not to stare at the large, pink form. "Sir."

The P.M. splashed like a child, then a shadow passed over his face. "Inces!" he bellowed.

The beleaguered butler appeared in the doorway. "Sir?"

"I believe the temperature of my bath has dropped

below one hundred and four degrees, Inces. Check. Now."

The butler entered the bathroom and went to the tub. He knelt, rolled up one sleeve and reached into the water, pulling up a thermometer that was attached by a thin chain to the faucet.

"Well?" the P.M. demanded, chewing on the end of his cigar.

"Ninety-nine degrees, sir. Shall I add more hot water?"

"Damn it, yes! Do I need to tell you everything?"

"No, sir," Inces said mildly as he turned on the hot water tap.

Frain permitted himself a small smile, thinking of the rest of Britons with their five-inch water mark and limited supplies of hot water. Rules just never seemed to apply to Winston Churchill.

As the tub filled, the P.M.'s lip jutted forward in a pout. "Now get out!"

"Yes, sir." Inces took his leave.

Churchill rested his cigar in a cut-glass ashtray, then sank beneath the waterline and blew bubbles. Rising to the surface, he stared up at the ceiling, floating. "I was thinking about our meeting at MI-Five today."

"Yes, sir."

"It occurs to me that, with Miss Hope's connections, we have an in."

"The thought has occurred to me, too, sir. Miss Hope did well at Windsor. She's in much better physical shape now, stronger, with more endurance. I think with some additional training up at Beaulieu, we'll have her ready to go in a few months."

Churchill blew a few blue smoke rings. "War's a nasty business, my friend."

"It is, indeed, sir."

"And when we see an advantage, we must press—no matter what the personal cost."

"If that's your decision, sir."

The P.M. took a swig of brandy and soda. "It is." He waved Frain away. "Tell Mrs. T. to invite Miss Hope to Number Ten this afternoon."

Frain rose. "Yes, sir."


It was strange for Maggie to return to No. 10 Downing Street after so many months and so much that had happened. She remembered how nervous she'd been when she'd first knocked on that dignified front door, so plain and black and unpretentious. She was met by Richard Snodgrass, her former nemesis, now her colleague and friend.

"Good afternoon, Mr. Snodgrass," she said, extending her hand.

He shook it. "It's a pleasure to see you again, Miss Hope. Follow me, please."

She followed Mr. Snodgrass through the dignified hallways of No. 10, past the main entrance with its grand cantilever staircase, and through several carpeted hallways. They reached a small conference room, where a projector and screen were set up. A cut-crystal bowl of apples—green Bramleys, bright red Bismarcks, and mottled Pippins—was set in the middle of the polished wood table.

"Hello, David," Maggie said, surprised, as David rose to greet her.

"I just found out about all of this myself, Maggie."

"All of what?" she asked as Mr. Snodgrass left them.

"You'll see."

The door opened and in came Frain and another man, short and round, where Frain was tall and slim. He was in his late fifties, with a beaky nose and a shiny pate. "Hello, Maggie, David," Frain began. "I'd like to introduce Sir Frank Nelson, head of the so-called Baker Street Irregulars."

"Sir Frank," Maggie said, extending her hand. "How do you do?"

They shook. "A pleasure to meet you, Miss Hope."

Maggie's mind was racing. "Baker Street Irregulars?" She'd heard rumors of a secret spy organization, but had always assumed they were just that—rumors. "How very Holmesian."

"Nickname for the Special Operations Executive, or S.O.E.," David said, pleased, for once, to know something she didn't. "Also known as Churchill's Secret Army, Churchill's Toyshop, or the Ministry of Ungentlemanly Warfare."

"We're a bit off the grid, Miss Hope. Our mission is to coordinate espionage and sabotage. All hush-hush, of course," Sir Frank said.

Maggie shot David a look. "Of course."

They all sat down at the conference table, waiting. Finally, the door burst open. It was the Prime Minister. "You're all here? Good, good," Churchill rumbled, taking a seat. He waved his already-lit cigar. "Let's get on with it, then."

Frain began. "Maggie, what can you tell me about your mother?"

*My mother? Will it never end?* "Not very much,"

Maggie replied. "As you know, I was raised by my Aunt Edith Hope, outside of Boston, Massachusetts. She didn't talk about my parents much, and I never pushed her to." She shrugged. "Until this very morning, I thought that my mother was a typical English house-wife, who'd died far too young in an automobile acci-dent. I knew that she played the piano, loved books. In my mind, in the past that I constructed, she was a loving mother and an adoring wife." She gave a sharp laugh. "Well, that was the fantasy, anyway."

"Your father sent you one of her books."

"Yes, he sent it to me at Windsor. The Princess Eliza-beth spilled tea on some of the pages, and—well, you know the rest."

"You found code contained in that book, code to a Sektion agent. The code contained the names of three MI-Five agents who were to be assassinated."

"Yes," Maggie said, her heart pierced with sadness as she thought of Hugh's father and the other agents killed.

"You believed your father was the double agent. But today, you found out it was your mother who was the Sektion agent."

"Yes." Then, "Look, what's this all about? Why, with a war going on, are we talking about something that happened over twenty years ago?"

"Because, Miss Hope," Sir Frank said, "your mother is, indeed, still quite relevant to us in this war, right now." He motioned to David. "Mr. Greene, would you turn on the projector?"

David turned off the overhead lights and then flipped the switch, the incandescent lightbulb glowing and the fan whining. Mr. Stevens turned off the overhead lights.

Maggie was bewildered. First she was told it was her mother, not her father, who was a double agent responsible for murdering five British officers. Now she was back at No. 10, asked to watch—a slide show?

David dropped a slide in the projector. The black-and-white slide was old; still, the lovely woman photographed was obviously Maggie's mother, at approximately Maggie's current age.

Sir Frank took a deep breath. "This is Clara Hess, better known to you as Clara Hope. In 1912, she was recruited to Sektion by Special Agent Albrecht Kortig."

Maggie stiffened.

Sir Frank paused but pressed on. "She was given a mission. She was to pose as a British woman, a student at the London School of Economics. She was to make the acquaintance of a British agent, Edmund Hope. She was to make him fall in love with her, to become his confidante."

"And to murder three MI-Five agents," Maggie managed.

"Yes," Sir Frank replied, evenly. "And then, she faked her own death in a car accident, and made her way back to Germany. Next slide, please." David hit a button. The picture was now of an older woman, with the same thick hair and fine features. Her eyes were inscrutable.

If Maggie hadn't already been sitting down, her legs would have buckled under her. *What more can they throw at me?* "Is that her? But that's a recent picture! Surely that's not possible?"

"Clara Hess, the woman known in Britain as Clara Hope, returned to Germany," Sir Frank said, ignoring Maggie's questions. "Ultimately, she became the agent known as Commandant Hess, along with Walther Schellenberg one of the most dangerous figures in the Abwehr. The figure behind the attempt to assassinate the King and kidnap the Princess."

"*She's* Commandant Hess?" Maggie breathed.

David turned the overhead light back on.

Winston Churchill studied her, with eyes blue and cold. "You've proven yourself to be mentally, emotionally, and physically capable of being an S.O.E. agent. How would you like to go to Berlin?" He glanced at Frain. "We have a few things that need doing over there—including a few that have to do with Clara Hess. We thought, after all your hard work, that you'd like to do the honors."

# Chapter Thirty-one

Maggie, in her room at David's flat, was packing the last of her things in a trunk. She was going for three months of intensive training at an S.O.E. camp called Beaulieu, in Hampshire, and then, when ready, a nighttime parachute drop into Germany.

Edmund Hope stood at the doorway, coat still on, twisting his hat in his hands. "Maggie, I don't want you to go."

"Dad, this is my job now. I must." Finding an armload of socks and stockings, she dropped them into her open trunk. "She's a German spy, one who nearly succeeded in running a mission to kill the King and kidnap the Princess. One who's plotting God knows what else as we speak. That doesn't bother you?"

"Of course it does," he snapped, "but it doesn't need to be *you*!"

"Mr. Churchill asked me." She went to her closet.

"Forget Churchill! It's too dangerous."

"I would disagree," Maggie said, taking a few dresses

off hangers. "And the Prime Minister and Mr. Frain think otherwise, too."

"Look, she's a despicable human being, a sociopath. Do you really think you can just walk up to her and say, 'Hello, Mother'?"

Maggie gave a tight smile as she folded the dresses and placed them in her suitcase. "That's not in the mission plan."

"And even if you do have a moment where you can reconnect, it doesn't change what she did!"

She turned back to the closet, rummaging for sweaters on a high shelf. "Dad, I know. Hugh is—one of my best friends. How could I possibly forget what she did to his father, the pain he still carries? And that she did the same thing to other families?"

"Do you expect her to say, 'Oh, my dear darling daughter, how I've missed you all these years. Let's go shopping and then have tea'?"

"N-no. No! Of course not!" Maggie took down a few sweaters, then turned and looked Edmund in the eye. "There's one thing I've been wondering about, though."

"Yes?"

"When I went to what I thought were your graves at Highgate Cemetery—which turned out to be only her grave—there were fresh white roses by the headstone. I remember the gardener said a man came regularly, to leave them. Is that you? Were you—are you—leaving flowers on her grave?"

Edmund lowered his eyes. "Yes," he said finally.

"But why? She betrayed you—betrayed us. She's not even there, not even dead! Why?"

"I loved her," Edmund answered. "Or at least the person I thought she was."

"I see," Maggie said, not seeing at all. She placed the sweaters in the trunk.

After a few moments passed, Edmund rubbed at his eyes with his fist, then said, "And what, exactly, is your mission?"

"I'm afraid, Dad," she said, closing the trunk and tightening the leather buckle, "that it's classified."

They both heard voices in the flat. "Maggie? Maggie?"

"Coming!" she called. Then, to her father, "They're giving me a little party before I leave." There was an awkward pause. "Would you like to stay?"

Edmund tugged at his collar. "I have to get back to the office, actually. I'm off the Bletchley case now. Getting a new assignment."

"I'll walk you out, then," Maggie told him.

People had already begun to arrive. David put a Fred Astaire record on the phonograph and she could hear him in the kitchen, using a pick to make ice chips for shaking cocktails. As "Let's Face the Music and Dance" began to play, he came in with a tray of glasses full of amber liquid.

"Sure you won't stay?" she asked.

"Afraid not," Edmund said. "Good luck, Maggie."

"Thank you. To you too." She let him kiss her cheek before he left.

After the door closed, the party began in earnest. David was there, as was Hugh, talking to Sarah, perched on the windowsill. And there were a few dancers from the ballet and people from No. 10, including Richard Snodgrass.

"Don't suppose you can tell us what you're up to next, Miss Hope?" Richard asked as Hugh handed her a martini.

"It's terribly boring," Maggie said as she accepted the glass. "Off to the country, to do goodness knows what sort of paperwork."

"That's your official story, then?" Richard asked.

"I'm afraid so." She smiled. "And I'm standing by it."

Hugh raised his glass. "To Maggie," he said. "Wherever her travels may lead. Although, I must say, I hope they ultimately lead her back to me."

"Thank you, Hugh," she said, blushing.

"To Maggie," the rest chorused.

She was momentarily speechless, then pulled herself together. "Thank you," she said. "But I must toast to you, all of you—it's a horrible war we're in, but it's had a strange way of bringing people together—and helping us all achieve much more than what we think we're capable of. To us, then."

"To us! Cheers!"

And they drank and danced long into the night.


The pilot had survived, but barely.

He'd survived first by burying his parachute. He'd survived by limping, then finally crawling, through fields and woods until he found a barn. He'd survived by drinking rainwater from a pig trough and eating the scraps. He'd survived by hiding his identity disks and ripping out any British labels in his clothes. And he'd survived by staying in the barn's hayloft during the day, afraid to move a muscle or make a sound.

Still, with the internal organ damage he sustained, he wouldn't be able to survive much longer, at least without proper medical care. Which was why, finally, he gave himself up to the farmer and his wife, Herr and Frau Schäfer.

They did not turn him in to the local police.

Instead, they put him to bed in a room with fresh white sheets and fed him brown bread soaked in milk. When he had slept for hours and hours, he awoke to see Frau Schäfer sitting at his bedside, knitting a heavy wool sweater with hand-spun yarn.

"It's all right," she said in German, her gnarled fingers moving like lightning. "We know who you are, and you're safe here."

"Thank you," he replied in German. He wished he had studied more in school. Still, he tried his best. "I appreciate everything you and your husband are doing."

"You're very lucky," she said, pointing a knitting needle at him.

"Lucky," he repeated, and gave a sour laugh. In some ways he was—lucky to be alive, lucky to be picked up by sympathetic Germans—and in some ways he wasn't—injured in enemy territory, mostly ignorant of the language. . . .

"You *are* lucky," she insisted. "God was looking out for you."

He was a pro-forma Anglican who attended church services at holidays only, and then mostly for the music. "I'm not sure if God had much to do with it."

Herr Schäfer heard them talking and came in, his bulk blocking most of the doorframe. "God has everything to do with everything. Now make the poor man some breakfast, Maria. I've brought in the eggs."

———

What saved him from despair was the courage of Maria and Hans Schäfer. He had no idea what the price would be for harboring an enemy soldier, but it had to be bad.

The Schäfers knew he had flown over their land, dropping bombs, and yet they fed him white asparagus with butter, golden fried potatoes, coarse sausages, and plum cake. They would not take any of his marks, which all RAF pilots flying over Germany were given in case of an emergency, to help out with the added food ration. "We live on a farm," they said to him. "What is one more mouth to feed?"

In return, he held hanks of coarse, greasy yarn between two upraised hands while he lay in bed, while Frau Schäfer wound it into balls. Often they would sit together in silence. Sometimes she would speak to him, and he would try to keep up as best he could. And sometimes she would pray, her eyes closed, her hands still wrapping strands of yarn around the ball. This was his favorite time. Whatever happened—and he knew that anything could happen, at any moment—this was peace.


They knew they couldn't take him to a hospital, but they called their veterinarian, to take a look at the Briton.

The veterinarian, Dr. Lang, a stooped-over man with scraggly white eyebrows, examined his injuries with cool, gentle hands. His ken was pigs and sheep and chickens—not humans. Certainly not humans this damaged. "Wait here," he said to the young man, as if he were in any condition to get up from the bed, and then went to talk to the Schäfers.

"It's beyond what I can do," Dr. Lang said, sitting down at the table to a cup of coffee and *Brötchen* with sweet butter and gooseberry preserves. "The boy needs a hospital."

The Schäfers looked at each other. They had been married for more than thirty years, raised three daughters who lived nearby with their own families, and could read each other's minds with a glance. It was clear they both thought it was unsafe to take their British refugee to a hospital.

"I have an idea," Dr. Lang said. "My son—I still have my son's Luftwaffe uniforms." Dr. Lang's son, Helmut, had died in one of the early air raids over Britain. "There is a comradeship among pilots, even pilots of warring nations. I know he'd want . . ." He swallowed. "I mean, if Helmut had been shot down, over England—"

Frau Schäfer put her hard, callused hand over his. "—you'd want an English family to take care of him. Of course."

Dr. Lang shook his head, focusing on the present. "So, we put him in the Luftwaffe uniform and I drop him off at a hospital in Berlin. I say that he must have been shot down. He's been gravely injured—and that, because of trauma, he can't speak."

"Do you think they'll believe it?"

He shrugged. "What choice do we have?"

And so, after profuse thanks that only seemed to embarrass the Schäfers, and promising to return after the war was over, the British pilot was carried into the truck Dr.

Lang usually used for transporting large animals. Dr. Lang drove from the rural countryside of Rietz to Charité Mitte in Berlin.

The young nurse at the admissions desk wanted his papers, but Dr. Lang feigned insult. "Look at him!" he cried. "Look! A German pilot, a war hero, shot down while defending his country. Defending *you*!" The more he said, the easier the lies poured from his lips. "His entire plane went down in flames—you really think he had time to reach for his *papers*?"

"Of course not," the nurse said, backtracking. "I'm very sorry, sir. We will admit him immediately, and have our very best doctors examine him."

"Thank you, Nurse," Dr. Lang said, giving the pilot a wink. He placed a hand on the younger man's shoulder, then whispered in his ear, "You'll see, they'll take good care of you here."

Looking around at all the doctors in long white coats with swastika armbands speaking rapid-fire German, RAF Flight Lieutenant John Sterling felt a wave of fear. Then he thought of Maggie. And so he smiled at Dr. Lang, and then at the young nurse in gray who came around from behind the nurses' station.

"I am Nurse Hess," the young nurse said by way of introduction. "Elise Hess. I'll be taking care of you while you stay with us."

# Historical Notes

As with *Mr. Churchill's Secretary*, *Princess Elizabeth's Spy* is not a history, nor is it meant to be—it's a work of fiction.

However, as with *Mr. Churchill's Secretary*, I've relied on historic sources for *Princess Elizabeth's Spy*. In particular, *The Little Princesses: The Story of the Queen's Childhood by Her Nanny, Marion Crawford*, ostensibly the first Royal tell-all (although certainly innocuous by present-day standards), was the source I relied on most for specific details. It describes the everyday life of Princess Elizabeth and Princess Margaret at Windsor Castle during World War II, including the daily schedule of the young Princesses, their nursery, and going down to the makeshift bomb shelter in the Castle's dungeons, in great detail.

Like the fictional Maggie, real-life Marian "Crawfie" Crawford lived on the top floor of Victoria Tower (now renamed Queen's Tower). Head butler, Ainslie, Royal Librarian Sir Owen Morshead, and Governor of the Castle, Lord Clive Wigram, are all real people who lived at Windsor Castle during the winter of 1940 and are mentioned in Crawford's book. "Dukie" (formal name Rozavel Golden Eagle) really was one of Princess Elizabeth's favorite corgis. In addition, the Princesses did put on a number of pantomimes at Windsor Castle during the war years, including a Christmas pageant, *Cinderella,* and *Arabian Nights.*

Of course there were other sources as well, including *Royal Sisters: Queen Elizabeth II and Princess Margaret* by Anne Edwards; *Lilibet: An Intimate Portrait of Elizabeth II* by Carollyn Erikson; and *Elizabeth the Queen* by Sally Bedell Smith.

*Windsor Castle: An Illustrated History* by Royal Librarian Sir Owen Morshead, who ultimately became Royal Librarian Emeritus, was also a significant resource, with a detailed history of the castle's occupants and its architecture.

*The Private Life of the Queen: By a Member of the Royal Household* by C. Arthur Pearson is about Queen Victoria, not Queen Elizabeth II—but was nonetheless helpful in its descriptions of Windsor Castle, especially the layout of the servants' quarters.

*For the Royal Table: Dining at the Palace* by Kathryn Jones was a great help in writing about Windsor Castle's china, cutlery, and table settings. *Roberts' Guide for Butlers and Other Household Staff* by Robert Roberts was excellent for specifics on Royal servants' tasks and cleaning methods.

To research Bletchley Park, I'm indebted to *Bletchley Park People: Churchill's Geese That Never Cackled* by Marion Hill, and *Code Breakers: The Inside Story of Bletchley Park* by F. H. Hinsley and Alan Stripp.

For insight into code breaking in general, especially

Mary Queen of Scots and Anthony Babington's code, as well as pinprick encryption, I relied on *The Code Book: The Science of Secrecy from Ancient Egypt to Quantum Cryptography* by Simon Singh. Singh's book, which itself reads like a thriller, also had invaluable sections on Alan Turing, Bletchley Park, and how Enigma machines work. I read extensively about post-traumatic stress disorder; the best, and most heartrending book I found is *Soft Spots: A Marine's Memoir of Combat and Post-Traumatic Stress Disorder* by Clint Van Winkle.

Many documentaries were also helpful with research, including *Hitler's British Girl* (about British Nazi sympathizer Unity Mitford), *Windsor Castle: A Royal Year,* and *The Windsors: A Royal Family.*

I've incorporated excerpts from Princess Elizabeth's and Winston Churchill's actual radio addresses, as well.

In addition, I would like to thank the Imperial War Museum's Principal Historian, Nigel Steel, and Uniforms Curator, Martin Boswell, for help with the "dog tag" versus "identity disk" question.

A special thank you to Paul Johnson, at the National Archives in London, for working with me to secure permission to reprint the Babington code illustration.

# Acknowledgments

As always, thank you, Noel MacNeal—your kindness, generosity, and support leave me speechless.

Thank you to Idria Barone Knecht, one of the sharpest minds I've ever encountered—and one of the loveliest people, as well—for her time and editing insights.

I am grateful to Victoria Skurnick at the Levine Greenberg Agency, the best agent imaginable at the best agency ever, who makes everything possible.

Thanks to the always-patient-with-me editor Kate Miciak, who believed Maggie's story could continue, and actually asked for a second book (as well as a third and fourth!). And, of course, associate editor Randall Klein, who is never, ever "kerfluffled."

Thank you to "wicked smart" M.I.T. friends: Monica Byrne, Wes Carroll, Stephen Peters, Mary Linton Peters, Erik Schwartz, and Larry Taylor for advice and help with various math and code questions. Thanks to Laura Redding Koeppen, and her son, Zach Harris, for various boat- and ship-related questions.

I owe a huge debt of gratitude to Dr. Leslie Jette, Dr.

Meredith Norris, and Dr. Mary Linton Peters for answering medical questions. (How long can someone actually talk in the freezing cold water of the North Sea in December? was one.) Thanks to friend and Londoner Claire Weldin, for answering architecture questions and good-naturedly traipsing around Westminster, Mayfair, and Bletchley with me. Thanks to Jeffrey Kaiserman, for sharing his fencing expertise. Thank you to Dr. Ronald Granieri, for his patience and help in translating German.

Thank you Jennifer Stock and Fran Feeley, for generously answering 1940s library-related research questions. And special thanks to early readers Tricia Burns, Scott Cameron, Fidelma Fitzpatrick, Emily Klein, Christine McCann, Ji Hyang Padma, Kathryn Plank, and Jennifer Stock.

I am grateful for friends Christina CB Bauer, Jennifer Boyer, Danielle Bruno, Tricia Burns, Fidelma Fitzpatrick, Aymee Garcia, Ron Granieri, Shannon Halprin, Emily Klein, Melissa Leeper, Joyce Luck, Lauren Marchisotto, Jane Beuth Mayer, Christine McCann, Jennifer Valvo McCann, Terry Mumma, Kathryn Plank, Amy Putnam, Audra Branum Rickman, Rebecca Carey Rohan, Caitlin Sims, Sally Smith, Jon Stucky, and Lilly Tao, for daily laughs.

A special thanks to Robert Lopez and Kristin Anderson Lopez, Jodi Kantor and Ron Lieber, and Kathryn Fletcher and John Hodgman, for graciously letting me house-sit their apartments for a "room of my own," while they were off visiting glamorous places. And thanks to the New York Writers Space.

If you enjoyed
*Princess Elizabeth's Spy,*
you won't want to miss the next ingenious
mystery in the Maggie Hope series.
Read on for an exciting look at

# His Majesty's Hope

## BY SUSAN ELIA MacNEAL

Published by Bantam

# Chapter One

Maggie Hope was feeling her way through thick darkness. She was panting after shimmying up a rickety drainpipe, knocking out a screen in an upper-story window, avoiding several trip wires, and then sliding silently onto the floor of a dark hallway. She took a deep breath and rose to her feet, every nerve alert.

Beneath her foot, a parquet floorboard creaked. *Oh, come now,* she thought. She waited for a moment, slowing her breathing, feeling her heart thunder in her chest. All around her was impenetrable black. The only sounds were the creaks of an ancient manor house.

Nothing.

All clear.

Maggie could feel dampness under her arms and hot drops of sweat trickling down the small of her back. Aware of each and every sound, she continued down the hall until she reached the home's library. The door was locked. *Well, of course it is,* Maggie thought. She picked the lock in seconds with one of her hairpins.

Once she'd ascertained no one was there, she turned

on her tiny flashlight and made her way to the desk. The safe was supposed to be under it. And it was, just as her handler had described.

*Good,* she thought, sitting down on the carpet next to it. *All right, let's talk.* That was how she pictured safecracking: a nice little chat with the safe. It was how the Glaswegian safecracker Johnny Ramensky— released from prison to do his part for the war effort— had taught her. She spun the dial and listened. When she could hear the tumblers dropping into place—not hear, but *feel* the vibrations with her fingertips—she knew she had the first number correct. *Now, for the second.*

Biting her lower lip in concentration, immersed in safe-cracking, Maggie didn't hear the room's closet door open.

Out from the shadows emerged a man. He was tall and lean, and wearing an SS uniform. "You're never going to get away with this, you know," he lisped, like Paul Lukas in *Confessions of a Nazi Spy.*

Maggie didn't bother to answer, saving her energy for the last twist of the dial, the safe's thick metal door clicking open.

In a single move, she gathered the files from the safe under her arm and sprang to her feet. She turned the flashlight on the intruder. He squinted at the light in his eyes.

Maggie ran at him, kneeing him in the groin, hard. While he was doubled over, she elbowed him in the back of the head. Satisfied he was unconscious, she ran to the door, folders still in hand.

Except that he *wasn't* unconscious. An arm shot out and a hand grabbed Maggie's ankle. She fell, files sliding across the floor. She kicked his hand off and scrambled for the door.

He struggled to his feet and ran after her, catching and

holding her easily with his left arm while he wrapped his right hand around her throat. She gasped for breath, trying to throw him off, but she couldn't get the proper leverage. He threw her up against the wall, pinning her—

"*Stop! Stop!*"

Then, again—the voice amplified by a megaphone, louder this time: "OH, FOR HEAVEN'S SAKE, STOP!"

The man's arms around Maggie relaxed and released her.

"What on earth . . . ?" she muttered in exasperation.

The hall's lights blinked on, bare bulbs in elaborate molded ceilings. It wasn't actually the home of a high-ranking Nazi in Berlin but the Beaulieu Estate in Hampshire, England. Beaulieu was considered the "finishing school" of SOE—Special Operations Executive—Winston Churchill's black ops division. Some of the recruits joked that SOE didn't stand for Special Operations Executive as much as "Stately 'omes of England," where all the training seemed to take place.

"What now?" Maggie grumbled and started to pace the hallway.

A severe-looking man in his late forties with a full head of gray hair walked out into the hall with a clipboard. "All right, Miss Hope—would you like to tell us what you did wrong?"

Maggie stopped, hands on hips. "Lieutenant Colonel Ronald Thornley." Maggie had to remember *not* to call him Thorny, which was his unfortunate nickname among the trainees. "I picked the lock, cracked the safe, took the folders, disarmed the enemy—"

"Disarmed. Didn't kill."

Maggie stopped herself from rolling her eyes. "I was just about to do the honors, sir."

"You were about to be killed yourself, young lady," Thornley barked.

The tall man in the SS uniform walked up behind Maggie, rubbing the back of his head. "Not bad technique there, Maggie. But they told me that if you only knocked me out and didn't fake-kill me I'd have to come after you again."

She gave him her most winning smile. "Sorry about the knee, Phil."

"Not at all."

Thornley was not amused. "Not killing the enemy is the worst mistake *because* . . ."

Maggie and Phil looked at each other.

From behind Thornley came a loud, high-pitched nasal voice: "*Because the only safe enemy is a dead enemy.*"

"Oh, Colonel Gubbins—we didn't know you were there," Thornley said, as Gubbins stepped out of the shadows.

"There is nothing more deadly than an angry Nazi—remember that—you're not killing a person, you're killing a Nazi. A Kraut. A Jerry."

Colonel Colin McVean Gubbins was Head of Training and Operations at Beaulieu—a haunted-looking man with dark, recessed eyes, thick eyebrows, and wispy mustache. "Only sixty percent of agents dropped behind enemy lines survive, Miss Hope. You're the first woman to be dropped into Germany—the *first woman* to be dropped behind enemy lines in this war, period. Lord only knows what your odds are. We're taking an ungodly risk. And we want you to be prepared."

Maggie's frustration cooled. This wasn't about her—it was about the mission succeeding. "Yes, sir."

"You're going in to deliver a radio part to a resistance group in Berlin, and also to plant a bug at a high-ranking Abwehr officer's home. For whatever reason, the Prime Minister has asked for you for this mission specifically. And if you take out a Nazi or two in the process, so be it. This is no time to be squeamish or sentimental. Do you understand?"

*The P.M. asked for me specifically for this mission!* Maggie glowed with pride but tried to damp it down so Gubbins wouldn't notice. "I do, sir."

"With your fluency in German, and the skills you've been working on, you just *might* pull it off," he said. "But it's dangerous work and that's why you can leave nothing—and no one—to chance."

"Yes, sir." Maggie had dreamed about becoming a spy sent on a foreign mission. She'd dreamed of it working as a typist to Prime Minister Winston Churchill and she dreamed about it while she was acting as a maths tutor to the Princess Elizabeth. Now, finally, was her chance.

"Let's try it again," Gubbins said. "And this time, Miss Hope, I want you to finish the Nazi off. Kill the damned Kraut."

It was ungodly hot and humid, even though it was still early morning. The skies were dark and swollen with bloated clouds. Above the buildings soared the baroque verdigris roof of the Berliner Dom, its golden cross pointing heavenward like an accusing finger.

Elise Hess navigated the narrow cobblestone side streets of Berlin-Mitte in order to avoid the parade on Unter den Linden, fast approaching the Brandenburg Gate.

The Nazis had reason to celebrate. Not only had they already seized Holland, Belgium, and France, but now German troops had invaded Russia, destroying Russia's 16th and 20th Armies in the "Smolensk pocket" and triumphing at Roslavl, near Smolensk. The German military seemed invincible. Despite the Atlantic Charter with the United States, Britain's defeat was clearly only a matter of time.

Elise could hear the steady beating drums of the Hitler Youth and the coarse clamor of the crowd in the distance, singing the Horst Wessel Song. She could see the scarlet banners with their white circles and black *hakenkreuz*—broken crosses—which the *Volk* had hung from their windows. Papering the limestone walls were tattered posters of Adolf Hitler in medieval armor, on horseback like a Teutonic knight, captioned *Dem Führer die Treue:* Be True to the Führer. Trash, cigarette butts, and broken glass from the rally the night before lined the gutters, and the air stank of stale beer and urine.

The ground was marked with chalk squares for the children's hopping game Heaven and Hell. Boys and girls were playing, throwing a small stone, then hopping on the chalked squares, trying to make it from one end to the other and back again. The boys were well scrubbed, the girls had intricate braids. All had round, rosy cheeks.

As one, they spied a small boy with a clubfoot, walking with a crutch, twisted ankle dragging behind him. He hobbled as close to the wall as he could, trying not to be noticed. But like a pack, the group set on him, herding him away from the wall. They formed a circle around him, holding hands, as the boy's eyes darted, trying to find a way to escape. One of the older boys started singing a familiar nursery rhyme:

> *Fox, you've stolen the goose*
> *Give it back!*
> *Give it back!*
> *Or the hunter will get you*
> *With his gun,*
> *Or the hunter will get you*
> *With his gun.*

The other children joined in:

> *His big, long gun,*
> *Takes a little shot at you,*
> *Takes a little shot at you,*
> *So, you're tinged with red*
> *And then you're dead.*
> *So, you're tinged with red*
> *And then you're dead.*

In the distance, church bells tolled the hour.

"Children!" Elise said, clapping her hands together. "Stop! That's enough!" They looked over at her, angry.

The boy with the clubfoot took their momentary distraction as an opportunity to burst through the circle and make a hard right into an alley, staggering as fast as he could with his crutch. The children picked up rocks and flung them after him but didn't bother to give chase. "Are you going to the parade, *Fräulein?*" one girl called to Elise.

"*Nein,*" she replied. "I have to work."

"Too bad!" the girl called back, skipping and laughing, as the boys slapped one another's backs.

Walking away, Elise shook her head. "*Gott im Himmel* help us."

Elise took one of the many bridges over the Spree and arrived at Charité Mitte Hospital damp with sweat.

She went to the nurses' changing room. It was small, with walls of gray lockers and a low wooden bench. There was a poster on the wall, of a handsome doctor and a mentally disabled man in a wheelchair, with the caption *This hereditarily sick person costs the Volksgemeinschaft 60,000 R.M. for life. Comrade, it's your money, too.*

Elise slipped out of her skirt and blouse. She kept on her necklace with the tiny gold cross, a diamond chip in its center. The door opened. It was Frieda Klein, another nurse. "*Hallo!*" Elise said, smiling. Shifts were always better when Frieda was working.

"*Hallo,*" Frieda replied. She put down her things and began to change. "*Gott,* I wish I had breasts like yours, Elise," she said, looking down at her own flat chest. "You're the perfect Rhine maiden."

"I'm too fat," Elise moaned. "As my mother *loves* to remind me. Often. I wish I had collarbones like yours—so elegant."

Whereas Elise was curvaceous, Frieda was thin and all angles. Whereas Elise had dark blue eyes and chestnut-brown curls, Frieda was blond and pale. And whereas Frieda was phlegmatic, Elise had a habit of speaking too quickly and bouncing up and down on her toes when she became excited about a finer point of medicine, swing music, or anything at all to do with American movie stars. The two young women, friends since school, had both wanted to be nurses since they were young girls.

They put on their gray uniforms, with starched white aprons and linen winged caps. "Do you mind?" Elise asked, indicating the back strings on her apron.

"Not at all," Frieda said and tied them into a bow. She turned around. "Now do mine?"

Elise did, then slapped Frieda on the bottom. They laughed as they walked out together to the nurses' station to begin their shift.

In an examination room that smelled of rubbing alcohol and lye soap, a tiny blond girl in a hospital gown asked, "Will there be blood?"

The only picture on the wall was Heinrich Knirr's official portrait of Adolf Hitler—the Führer's figure stiff, his hard eyes gazing impassively over the proceedings.

Elise smiled and shook her head. *"Nein,"* she answered. "No blood work today. The doctor just wants to take a look at your ears. To make sure the infection's gone."

The girl, Gretel Paulus, was sitting on a hospital bed. She held a small brown, well-loved teddy bear and spoke with a slight speech impediment. Her thick lower lip protruded and glistened with saliva, her tongue overlarge. She had a round face, pointy chin, and almond-shaped eyes behind thick, distorting eyeglasses.

Elise smiled. "What goes ninety-nine *thump,* ninety-nine *thump,* ninety-nine *thump*?"

Gretel shrugged.

"A centipede with a wooden leg, of course!"

That won a weak smile out of the young girl. Elise

took an otoscope from the cabinet, cleaned the earpiece with alcohol, and then put it to the girl's right ear. Then the left.

"Nurse Hess?"

"When it's just you and I, you may call me Elise."

"Elise—why do my ears always hurt?" Gretel wanted to know.

Elise knew all too well that ear infections were common with Down syndrome patients. "It's just something that happens sometimes," she said, putting the otoscope away and returning to rub the girl's back. "And you feel better now, yes? The medicine worked?"

"If I feel better, why do I still have to see the doctor? The new doctor?"

Gretel didn't miss a thing, Elise realized. "His name is Doktor Brandt. And he wants to make sure you don't have any more ear infections."

The door to the examination room opened, and in walked Dr. Karl Brandt. He was relatively new to Charité, one of the SS doctors who came in the late winter of 1941, with their red armbands with black swastikas, and their new rules and regulations. Young, handsome, with thick, dark hair and impeccable posture, Brandt radiated authority.

Elise handed Gretel's chart to him. Without preamble, he marked the black box in the lower left-hand corner of the medical history chart with a bold red X, the last of three. He looked out the door and beckoned. Two orderlies arrived, strong and broad-shouldered in white coats with swastika armbands.

"Am I going home?" Gretel asked the doctor.

"Not yet, *Mäuschen*," Brandt replied, smiling. "We're going to make sure this never happens to you again."

Gretel beamed. "Oh, thank you, *Herr Doktor*!" she lisped as the two orderlies escorted her back to her room to get dressed. She hugged her teddy bear to her small body.

"Take this to the nurses' station," Dr. Brandt said to Elise, handing her the file. He headed toward the door.

"What should I tell her father and mother?" During the course of Gretel's multiple ear infections, Elise had come to know the child's parents.

He eyed the cross she wore around her neck. "Just deliver the paperwork to the nurses' station. They will take care of everything."

Elise was stung by his brusque tone. "*Jawohl, Herr Doktor,*" she replied, following behind him.

Dr. Brandt turned and frowned in response but did not discipline her. "Go," he said. "There are forms to fill out."


Elise made her way down the hallways to the nurses' station. She handed the file to the nurse on duty. "*Another one?*" the gray-haired woman grumbled, looking at the three red Xs on the chart.

"What does that mean?" Elise asked.

"It means a lot of paperwork."

"What kind of paperwork?"

The gray-haired woman, Nurse Flint, gave Elise a sharp look. "The kind that keeps me here, instead of at home with my husband and children, that's what kind," she snapped, stacking Gretel's file on top of similar folders.

Elise caught sight of Frieda, rounding the corner; her friend pointed up with one finger. Elise caught her meaning and nodded. She held up one hand, palm out—their code for meeting on the roof in five minutes.

Before she met up with Frieda, Elise wanted to check on someone. She walked down the corridor and into a ward filled with wounded soldiers in narrow white beds. Some moaned in their sleep, some stared listlessly out the windows at the leaden sky, others sat up in their wheelchairs and played cards.

Elise wanted to check on the temperature of a young man all the nurses called *Herr Geheimnis*—Herr Mystery. He'd been running an intermittent fever over the past few days. The patient had curly brown hair, an angular face, shoulders full of tension, and eyes wild with fear. Who was he? Where was he from? Did he have a girlfriend? Was he married? Why couldn't—or wouldn't—he speak?

"Is he all right?" Flight Lieutenant Emil Eggers asked, indicating with his chin the bandaged body asleep in the narrow bed next to him. Eggers, a beefy, blond man with the face of a cherub, was a Luftwaffe commander. He'd had a close call in France but survived his crash landing and had been brought back to Berlin to convalesce.

"Is that any business of yours, Lieutenant Eggers?" Elise admonished as she shook a thermometer and slipped it into Herr Mystery's mouth. She might be young, but she was strict with the men, who often seemed grateful to be ordered about as they convalesced.

"Well, there's not much to do in here . . ." Eggers said, trying his best to look winsome and failing.

"True," Elise agreed in gentler tones, picking up the chart hanging at the end of the bed frame. "He's one of yours—a pilot. Had quite a bad crash landing. A veterinarian from somewhere outside Berlin found him and patched him up as best he could and brought him in, but he had a lot of internal injuries."

"Is he going to make it?" Eggers asked. He didn't recognize the man, but there was a code of solidarity among pilots.

Elise may have been young, but she was also a realist. "I hope so." She removed the thermometer from his mouth and looked. A hundred and one. "His temperature's still a bit elevated." She made a note in the pilot's chart, then walked over to Eggers. "And how's your leg today, Lieutenant?"

Eggers pulled back the rough sheet and gray wool blanket to reveal a bandaged stump. "Still gone, I'm afraid."

After, Elise met up with Frieda on the hospital's roof. The tar paper was littered with cigarette butts. A crumpled packet of Milde Sorte was stuck under a drainpipe. The sun was blisteringly hot—1941 was turning into Berlin's warmest summer on record. Frieda lit a cigarette and took a puff, then handed it to Elise. "I hate this place."

Elise accepted the cigarette and took a long inhale. "Charité? Berlin? All of Germany?" she asked, blowing out rings of pale blue smoke.

"Everything. All of it."

They leaned over the railing. The city of Berlin spread out before them: the river Spree glittering in the harsh sunlight, long red Nazi banners snapping in the breeze, the black, burned-out dome of the Reichstag.